The Warhammer world is one of brave heroes in the face of powerful enemies. Now for the first time the tales of these mythical events has been brought to life in a new series of books. Divided into a series of trilogies, each brings you hitherto untold details of the lives and times of the most legendary of all Warhammer heroes and villains. Combined together, they will reveal some of the hidden connections that underpin the history of the Warhammer world.

◄ THE BLACK PLAGUE ►

The tale of an Empire divided, its heroic defenders and the enemies who endeavour to destroy it with the deadliest plague ever loosed upon the world of man. This series begins with *Dead Winter*.

◄ THE WAR OF VENGEANCE ►

The ancient races of elf and dwarf clash in a devastating war that will decide not only their fates, but that of the entire Old World. The first novel in this series is *The Great Betrayal*.

◄ THE BLOOD OF NAGASH ►

The first vampires, tainted children of Nagash, spread across the world and plot to gain power over the kingdoms of men. This series begins with *Neferata*.

Keep up to date with the latest information from the **Time of Legends** at *www.blacklibrary.com*

The War of Vengeance

THE GREAT BETRAYAL

Nick Kyme

BLACK LIBRARY

To my writing partner in crime, Chris 'Pointy Ears' Wraight.

A BLACK LIBRARY PUBLICATION

First published in Great Britain in 2012 by
Black Library,
Games Workshop Ltd.,
Willow Road, Nottingham,
NG7 2WS, UK

10 9 8 7 6 5 4 3 2 1

Cover illustration by Jon Sullivan.
Map by Nuala Kinrade.

A CIP record for this book is available from the British Library.

UK ISBN: 978 1 84970 191 4
US ISBN: 978 1 84970 192 1

See Black Library on the internet at
www.blacklibrary.com

Find out more about Games Workshop
and the world of Warhammer at
www.games-workshop.com

Printed and bound by CPI Group (UK) Ltd, Croydon, CR0 4YY

In the elder ages when the world was young, elves and dwarfs lived in peace and prosperity. Dwarfs are great craftsmen, lords of the under deeps, artificers beyond compare. Elves are peerless mages, masters of the dragons, creatures of the sky and air. During the time of High King Snorri Whitebeard and Prince Malekith, these two great races were at the pinnacle of their strength. But such power and dominion could not last. Fell forces now gather against elves and dwarfs. Malekith, embittered by his maiming in the Flame of Asuryan, seeks to destroy them both but still darker powers are also at work. Already strained, disharmony sours relations between them until only enmity remains. Treachery is inevitable, a terrible act that can only result in one outcome... War.

The dwarf High King Gotrek Starbreaker marshals his throngs of warriors from all the holds of the Karaz Ankor, whilst the elves, under the vainglorious and arrogant Caledor II, gather their glittering hosts and fill the skies with dragons.

Mastery of the Old World is at stake, a grudge in the making that will last for millennia. Neither side will give up until the other is destroyed utterly. For in the War of Vengeance, victory will be measured only in blood.

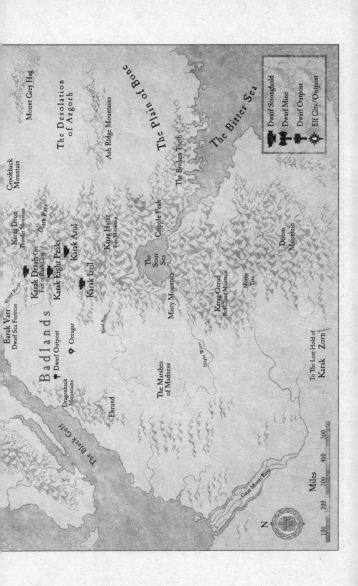

⫷ SINS OF THE ANCESTORS ⫸

I

THUNDER ROLLED ACROSS the slopes of Karag Vlak, shaking the earth for miles. Fire wreathed the sky, warring with the furnace at the mountain peak that glowed hot and angry through swathes of pyroclastic cloud. Shadows lurked within that grey smog, drifting against the wind on membranous wings…

Eclipsed by the mountain, two great hosts had gathered on a blasted plain of scorched rock studded with the corpses of petrified trees. Death had changed this place. Pastureland had become a sprawling battlefield of skulls, flattened by war engines and thousands of booted feet. Air tasted like ash and the rivers were veins of smoking acid. Mordant horns and harrowing death cries supplanted the shrill of birds, the bray of elk.

In the middle of this carnage, a soaring monument of stone reached into the fiery sky. It was called the Fist of Gron, so named for its ugly, knuckled shape and reputedly after the dwarf king who had supposedly shaped it with his bare hands. Once it might have been a magnificent mountain pinnacle but some past cataclysm during the shaping of the world had reduced it to a flattened edifice. Other than the lesions of dead forest puckering the landscape, it was the only feature for miles.

And like the swell circling the eye of a maelstrom, a great battle raged around it. Thurgin Ironheart eyed the enemy charging at his throng across the hellish plain and scowled.

The dwarf was part of the second vanguard, summoned from his place at the foot of Karag Vlak where the rest of the host was encamped. He and his warriors were to fill the gap left by the throng of Karak Drazh. Thurgin had already lost sight of their shields, the sigils of the Black Hold trodden underfoot in the eagerness of the enemy to shed more blood.

'They are swift,' he said, drawing a nod from his nearby kinsmen. Thurgin felt the tremor of hoofbeats through his heavy black boots and iron-wrought armour. Runes of warding fashioned into the breastplate began to ignite in a chain of forge-bright flares that emblazoned the metal as the enemy neared. The fierce effigy of his dragon-faced war helm caught the flicker of fire. His short emerald cloak stirred in a foul wind rolling off the mountain. Muttering an oath to Grungni, he gripped the haft of his rune axe.

They would need an ancestor's blessing this day.

Never before had dwarfs waged war against such a foe. All of the orcs and goblins festering beneath the world could not come close in number to the horde riding down upon them now. The cavalry were but a small part of it.

Two hundred feet away from bloodying his axe and Thurgin growled an order. Despite distance and the clamour of the battle, his words carried to every warrior in the throng.

'Sons of Grungni, lock your shields!'

It was a resounding shout, made louder by the rune magic of his war helm, and a call to arms from which there could be no turning back.

Dwarfs do not turn back. In Khazalid, the language of the *dawi*, there is no word for retreat.

Across the slopes of Karag Vlak, ten thousand dwarfs of Karak Izril obeyed.

They were but the first rank.

Drums beat, horns blared. Eight more armies marched slowly into the fray. Here was where the fighting grew fiercest. Several massive regiments of infantry had already engaged farther down a long, rippling line. Thurgin's throng were coming forwards like the end of a gate with their hinge a half-mile to their left, about to close on the cavalry charging at them.

Amidst the clash of arms, Thurgin saw the banners of Kadrin, Vlag and Eight Peaks amongst those of his own hold. Thousands of dwarfs fought hammer and axe against the enemy hordes. His heart swelled with pride at the sight, even though he knew it might be his last. Other holds joined in as the dwarfs came together as one, but it was to the standard of the High King that Thurgin's eye was finally drawn.

Almost a mile away, standing upon the Fist of Gron, Thurgin saw him.

It was said the High King could break the stars. To witness the rune blade he wielded in a two-handed grip, splitting heads as if they were rotten barrels, Thurgin could believe it.

There was no time left to worry about the fate of the High King. Thurgin's march had brought his warriors into the fray. The horns lessened and the drums stopped beating as the dwarfs of Karak Izril waited silently for what they knew would happen next.

Less than a hundred feet away, the enemy came fast and hard on hooves of silver flame.

Thurgin felt the solidity of his clan brothers at either shoulder and smiled.

This would be a good day for the dwarfs.

Vengeance would be theirs.

He shouted, voice louder than a hundred war horns, '*Khazuk!*'

The throng of Karak Izril answered, its many ranks adding to the fury of their reply: '*Khazuk!*'

Axes and hammers began to beat shields, rising in tempo as the riders closed.

'*Khazuk!*'

Thurgin slid the ornate faceplate over his eyes and nose until it clanked into place, and the world became a slit of honed anger.

His brothers' chorus resonated through his helm, chiming with the clash of arms.

'KHAZUK!'

It meant *war*.

War had come to the enemies of the dwarfs.

GLARONDRIL THE SILVERN spurred his riders to greater effort. Standing up in his stirrups, he let the fire of the angry mountain reflect in his gleaming armour. Without a helmet, his long white hair cascaded down the back of his neck like a mane of frost. His eyes were diamond-hard, his jaw set like marble.

The enemy was close; a thick wedge of mailed warriors that seemed to stretch the length of the horizon, clutching blades and shields.

Twenty thousand noble lords at his command, armour glittering with the falling sun, lowered their lances.

They had raced hard and far to reach this hellish plain. Glarondril would not be found wanting on the slopes of the mountain. He would see the battle through to its end, even if that meant his death. Whispering words of command to his mount, he drew the riders into a spear tip of glittering silver.

'In the name of the Phoenix King,' he roared, unable to keep his battle-lust sheathed any longer. A sword of blue flame slid soundlessly from his scabbard. 'For the glory of Ulthuan!'

The enemy were so close… Glarondril saw their hooded eyes, shimmering like moist gemstones, and smelled the reek of their foul breath, all metal and earth.

'None shall live!'

The blue-fire sword was held aloft as a thicket of lance heads drew down before the charge.

THURGIN FELT HIS body tense just before the moment of impact.

'Hold them, break them!' he roared, 'No mercy! Kill them all!'

Here before them was a foe worthy of dwarf enmity.

The shield wall dug in, backs and shoulders braced. All fifty thousand in this single throng came together. The muster from Karak Izril was large, but far from the largest of the holds. Deeper into the plain, Thurgin knew there were others similarly embattled. He prayed to Valaya for their souls as well his own and that of his men.

Behind the thick infantry formations, he heard the slow tread of the *gronti-duraz*. Through the dense earth he could feel the tremor of their footfalls as the low, sombre chanting of their masters animated them. Thurgin was glad to have the stone-clad behemoths at his back.

Above, lightning cracked the sky as magical anvils were made ready.

On the far mountain flank to Thurgin's left, the bolt tips of ballistae twinkled in the dying light through a rolling fog. They looked like stars.

Dwarfs did not need the stars, or the sun. They were dwellers of the earth, solid and determined. They would need those traits today, as they would need all the craft of the runesmiths and the engines of the guilds to overcome the horde upon the plain.

They were foul and wretched creatures that the dwarfs would drive from the Old World forever.

At last the enemy reached them, a collision of barbed lances and mewling steeds against dwarf shields and tenacity.

As he raised his axe to strike, Thurgin knew no quarter would be given.

He would ask for none.

GLARONDRIL AND HIS knights swept into the armoured horde, piercing flesh and shattering bone. Severed heads fell from the necks of his foes as he swept around his blazing blue sword in a killing arc. A jab disembowelled another, as hundreds of lances struck flesh, impaling dozens with every vengeful thrust.

'I am the Master of Dragons,' he roared. 'Behold your doom!'

Incandescent fire spewed from the jaws of the elven mounts. It rose in a tide that burned their enemies to ash. No defence was proof against the Dragon Princes of Caledor. No foe, however determined, could resist their charge. The few who did survive found their attacks repelled harmlessly by dragonscale harder than plate. The beasts snarled in contempt, crimsons, ambers, emeralds and azures, a myriad of colour and fury, tearing at limbs with fang and claw.

Hundreds of the enemy died in the first seconds, spitted by lances, devoured by the dragons or burned alive, their corpses left to ruin in the sun. What began as a contest swiftly became a slaughter.

A leader, his armour thicker than the rest, bellowed a challenge at Glarondril who accepted without hesitation.

'For the king!' he shouted above the eager roar of his mount, as he took the enemy leader's head.

'FOR THE KING!' urged Thurgin, chopping into the riders blunted on the dwarfs' wall of shields. A spurt of ichor splashed across the dark lacquer of his vambraces but he ignored it, thumping with his shield and hacking with his axe. The runes on the blade flared like star-fires as it hewed through iron-hard skin like it was parchment.

Though the foe pushed and pressed, using every ounce of their depraved strength, the dwarfs held back the tide. Utterly implacable, the shield wall didn't budge and the enemy cavalry buckled as they rolled against it. Riders in the rear ranks, unable to arrest their momentum, barrelled into those in front. The enemy's formation rippled, mounts and riders sent sprawling only to be crushed by those that followed in their wake, or butchered by dwarf axes.

Thurgin knew they had weathered the worst of it, and now what they had to do next.

'Forward!'

Fifty thousand booted feet stomped in unerring unison. The enemy resisted at first, but once the dwarfs had overcome the inertia caused by the broken bodies underfoot they were unstoppable. The throng of Karak Izril moved slowly but inexorably. Like a landslide, and with the same momentum, they cascaded over the cavalry and destroyed it. Already smashed against the dwarfs' resilience, the riders scattered. Harried without mercy by the triumphant dwarfs, the enemy cavalry had lost two-thirds of its warriors before the charge was ended. Thurgin himself had accounted for no fewer than fifteen of the creatures.

Seeing no gain in pursuit, he called the throng to a halt. His chest was heaving and there was a burning sensation in his shoulder from the violent axe-work, but it was a good pain.

Taking a moment to look around, he realised the battle was perched on a dagger's edge. A heavy toll had been taken of the enemy, but they were numerous and their will bordered on fanatical.

Lifting up the faceplate of his dragon helm, Thurgin's eye was drawn upwards to a vast shadow approaching him and his warriors from out of the sun. Not one of the throng of Karak Izril so much as flinched.

'We have the east flank,' he called out. An elven dragon rider, leading his scaled host, answered with a clenched fist and a broad, warlike smile.

Glarondril landed gracefully and bowed in the saddle to the thane-lord of Karak Izril. So too did his beast.

'Well met, Thurgin son of Brak.' He wiped the ichor from his sword before sheathing it. Behind him, almost twenty thousand dragons lowered their heads in respect to their allies. Each of their riders, every one of them a prince, nodded.

The dwarfs slammed their fists against their breastplates, raising a mighty clamour.

'High prince,' answered Thurgin, thumping his own chestplate and the angular rune engraved upon it. 'I am always glad to see the Master of *Drakk* and his host.' He gestured to the mound of sundered daemon corpses strewn around them. They were ugly creatures with hell-red skin, hooves and coiling horns that jutted from canine skulls. Foul steam rose off their broken bodies as the slow dissolution of their natures rendered them down to nothing but essence.

'I am especially glad,' Thurgin went on, 'when his intervention crushes my enemies so gloriously and hands us a piece of the field to hold on to.' He gestured to the slain host littering the ground for a hundred feet or more in front of them.

Glarondril regarded the daemon corpses with disdain.

'We had best make the most of our good fortune then,' remarked the elf, already spurring his mount.

'Indeed…' Thurgin turned his eye northwards where the bulk of the daemons festered and gibbered. 'Those two fiends won't kill themselves, now, will they?'

Even in the distance the leaders of the horde were easy to discern as they towered above their vassals: the feathered sorcerer and the bloated lord. Each was a prince of daemons with the innumerable hosts of Chaos at their command.

As the daemons retreated on one corner of the battlefield, they swelled in another. Thurgin saw them, the bulk of the cavalry he had butchered, the remnants left by Glarondril and his dragons, gathering around the Fist of Gron. And on that flat spur of rock was High King Snorri Whitebeard and the Elf Prince Malekith, alone and besieged by hell.

II

A SEA OF red-skinned death surrounded the king of the dwarfs and the prince of the elves. Though the Fist of Gron was over a hundred feet across, they could see the creatures capering and undulating below them because the horde stretched so far back onto the plain. Had they both stood in the middle of the flat, featureless rock that capped the Fist, Snorri and Malekith would still have seen them.

As it was they stood at either end, close to the edge, as determined warriors would defend a wall during a siege. But it was the braying, the animalistic moans and lascivious promises emanating from beneath them, that told the nobles their enemies were climbing up to fight them.

'They are eager,' shouted the High King, clashing his hammer and axe together in a challenge.

'Try not to be as keen, old friend,' the elf prince replied. 'They are coming.'

Snorri and Malekith faced away from each other, but each knew that their counterpart was smiling.

This was the war to end all wars, the final battle against the daemons and the power of Ruin. Here, history was being made. Malekith and Snorri were its architects. But although legendary, this was not the first time that Chaos had challenged for mastery of the Old World.

Long ago the hosts of Chaos had come from the north. An icebound, unforgiving land, the north was thronged with feral tribes and great primordial beasts. These creatures were the first amongst the servants of Ruin, the denizens of the glacier caves and frost-bitten valleys quick to bend their knees in worship. Succour was granted without mercy, their bodies reshaped into horrific forms, just as their souls were cast to damnation. Through a great gate, from a hellish netherworld where all the laws and fabric of nature were mutable and perverted, Chaos spilled into the mortal realm.

Its essence had bled into the lands beyond, turning trees into claws, rivers into arteries of blood and natural beasts into abominations. Like shadows, wisps of half-seen smoke or nightmares witnessed in periphery, the daemons marched alongside these beasts. On leathery pinion, on hoof or claw, slithering on their bellies the monstrous horde had swept across the Old World devouring all before it. Bloated on corruption, swollen with mutation, it could not be allowed to endure.

Grimnir was the most warlike of the dwarf ancestor gods. Legend told that he had closed the Chaos Gate himself and been doomed by the very deed. Left behind by Grimnir's sacrifice, his fellow deities Grungni and Valaya passed from the mortal realm and went back into the earth, never to be seen again. But even the might of the ancestors could not prevent the canker of Ruin escaping. Disaster was averted, destruction of all life forestalled for a time, but Chaos lived. It bred and permeated the very cloth stitching reality together. It became pervasive, an invisible stain that would only spread with the passing of millennia.

Statues and memories were all that remained of the ancestor gods now. Even their lesser children were dust, with only scant temples to remember them. Such numinous beings could not exist forever and so it fell to their scions to try and rid the world of Chaos...

Snorri Whitebeard unleashed a bolt of lightning through the haft of his hammer. It sparked and cracked with all the fury of the ancestors, luminous and burning. A tide of hell-spawn that had come crawling over the lip of the flat rock where he made his stand was sent reeling. Blackened and smouldering, the creatures pitched over the edge and did not return. Sulphur-stink tainted the air as they were banished, the unreality of this place the only thing keeping them from dissipating immediately.

It had been a verdant valley once, the rich volcanic soil of the mountain giving life to acres of forest. All that had changed with the coming of Chaos. A blasted landscape, scorched black and seized in the grip of a half-frozen waste, was all that remained.

A mire of corpses piled up around the foot of the rock, putrefying with the taint of Ruin. From the steaming carcasses that were dried to husks and broken open by the baleful sun further abominations arose. Dewy eyelids blinked and nictitated in the light. Tentacles, claws and fleshy protuberances burst from skin-taut bodies eager for transformation. Carapace, chitin and malformed bone swaddled beasts already overrun with corruption that advanced against the elves and dwarfs.

These were the spawns of Chaos, hell-ravaged abominations birthed by fell sorcery of the darkest kind.

Uttering a cry to Khaine, the elven war god, Malekith speared a basilisk through its gullet. Viscous ichor spewed arterially from the wound. Mercury-swift, the elf prince leapt forwards and decapitated the beast without pause with his blade, Avanuir. Its dead, collapsing mass crushed several lesser beasts and swept many others to their doom as it fell.

Hundreds more of the wretched creatures now littered the rock where the lords of the dwarfs and elves made their stand. Daemons of every malformed persuasion and aspect had fallen beneath their weapons.

With a grunt, Snorri kicked a corpse over the edge. If they allowed the bodies to accumulate both elf and dwarf would soon be slipping on tainted entrails. Malekith's dragon had not borne them here just to die ignominiously for no purpose.

''Tis thirsty work,' remarked the dwarf in a moment of rare respite. Snorri licked his lips, smiling at the elf prince who hurled his spear into the belly of a bloated troll. Fire ignited along the haft, immolating the beast.

'We'll toast our victory later,' Malekith replied, pointing to the southern edge of the rock where a horde of glaive-wielding beasts had just appeared. It was like an ever-lapping tide, with Snorri and Malekith acting as breakwaters. Horned and cloven-hoofed, heat bled off the daemons' muscled bodies in a gory steam. Malign intelligence flickered in their pit-black pupils. It warred with a terrible, consumptive rage.

Attracted by the scent of power emanating from the dwarf and elf, the daemons came on in droves. Eight became sixteen then over twenty as more and more of the daemons wanted to taste the flesh of true heroes. Like sharks drawn to blood, an insatiable hunger motivated them.

'*We are the devourers…*' they said as one in a horrible collision of voices patched together from a thousand different shouts of anger and wrath.

Grinning wickedly they began to circle the lords, beckoning them towards death and damnation with the tips of their hell-blades. Loping between the bloody daemons were brass-collared hounds, bigger and more brutish than any normal canine and with a vaguely reptilian aspect.

In seconds, the edges of the flat rock were festooned with daemons and the lords were surrounded.

Snorri backed up, snarling with wrath palpable enough to make the abominations pause.

'*We shall feast upon your mortal soul…*' promised the daemons. A hound leapt at the dwarf with an echoing roar.

But it would take more than a daemonic dog to fell the

High King. 'Then chew on this,' he said. Silver fire flared, too fast to truly see, and the hell-beast was cut in half.

'Tasty?' asked Snorri, brandishing the head of his gore-stained axe at the other monsters.

Three more hounds sprang after the first, but were swiftly struck by a flight of pearlescent arrows. Every shaft was a heart shot.

Snorri only half turned, giving Malekith a sidelong glance.

The elf nodded to the dwarf, lowering his bow and stowing it to draw Avanuir.

'That's a debt I'll have to repay now,' said the High King. Snorri grinned at the elf, showing two rows of crag-like teeth within the forest of his long beard. 'We stand before the world's ending, elfling.'

Malekith gave the dwarf a wry glance, but his attention was partly on the daemons advancing across the Fist of Gron. He lost count after fifty, and was acutely aware he had retreated several paces. Elf and dwarf were almost back to back.

'You sound almost pleased.'

'Aye, think of the saga it will make. Immortality awaits!'

Malekith didn't sound convinced, 'Not if there is no one left alive to write it, and all existence has come to an end.'

'Good point,' the dwarf conceded. 'Let us hope not then.'

Snorri eyed the daemons as he would dung upon his hobnailed boot, swallowing back a bitter taste in his throat at their stench. A cage of iron-hard, blood-red monsters surrounded them and its bars were tightening.

'We need room to fight,' he muttered, then hefted both his rune weapons and beckoned to the daemons. 'Come on then!'

In one gnarled fist the dwarf had a gromril axe, its face etched with three angular runes. In the other he had a hammer, a lightning bolt embossed upon the head in gold. Thick links of gilded mail swathed his broad, muscular body. His arms, dark from the forge and the earth, were bonded with torcs and vambraces. A red, fur-trimmed cloak fell from slab-like shoulders armoured with pauldrons fashioned into the faces of ancestor gods. He wore no helm, for he wanted his enemies to see his fury, but carried a crown upon his brow instead. Runes inscribing every inch of his armour shimmered. Flawless rubies, verdant emeralds and pellucid sapphires studded every ring and bracelet.

I am the High King, they said. *I am Lord of the Dwarfs and my vengeance is terrible. Behold! For your doom has come.*

Snorri beat his chest with a clenched fist.

'Khazuk!'

It was not meant as a challenge, but a death sentence.

The daemons heard neither but attacked as one, hounds and masters both. They were a crimson tide, of rage, hate and a desire to end all things.

Snorri cried out to Malekith as the daemons rushed them, 'Hold on, elfling!' and brought his rune hammer crashing down on the rock with all the potency of a lightning bolt.

Tremors rippled from the point where the dwarf had struck, cracks jagging outwards in an ever-expanding crater of sundered earth. Stone split, sending teeth of razor-edged rock into the daemons, scything into hellish flesh and spilling their tainted ichor.

Malekith was fast as quicksilver, darting between the spears of rock thundering out of the ground, running ahead of the quake. He weaved around the lazy blow of one daemon, severed the head from another. A third he impaled, before swinging the twitching corpse around to bludgeon three more. Destruction from the dwarf's hammer rained around him, but did not touch the elf. Not one scratch.

Avanuir took a heavy toll, almost acting as an extension of the elf's will and fury. Not to be outdone, the dwarf king weighed in with his axe, smashing into anything that had survived his first titanic blow.

Howling, bleating, furious, the daemons were slaughtered.

A heavy pall of dust engulfed the survivors, their balefire eyes the only thing visible at first. The storm presaged a seismic crescendo, an aftershock of power that cast the rest of the bloody daemons back over the edge of the rock. They fell screaming, raging before being dashed to paste or impaled on the upraised blades of the monsters below.

Malekith was crouched down, his head bowed. He held

on to his spear haft, using it to anchor him to the rock until the storm had passed. With the tremors fading, he rose to his full height again.

The elf prince was as impressive as the dwarf.

A long coat of ithilmar mail draped his lithe but honed body. Nearly twice as tall as the High King, his face was thin and pale but noble. There was wisdom in his eyes, born of the esteemed bloodline of the greatest *asur*, but coldness too that the dwarf did not fully understand. At times, it bordered on cruelty. Angular, almost almond-shaped, the elf prince's eyes were concealed behind a tall, conical helm that left only his mouth visible. A mane of griffon hair cascaded from the peak and ran the length of Malekith's back.

Snorri was tired. Breathing hard, the dwarf leant his forehead against his hammer's pommel and bent one knee to rest. It was almost genuflection. The oath on his lips had been spoken to Grungni, so it was as if he were praying at the altar of his own rune-crafted hammer.

The hand on his shoulder lifted him, and brought strength back to his weary limbs.

The dust was receding, spiralling away on the hot breeze. But through the slow dispersion of the cloud, claws could be seen and heard reaching for the summit of the rock.

'Relentless bastards, aren't they?' the dwarf remarked, raising his chin.

Malekith pulled his gore-streaked spear from the ground. In his other hand was Avanuir. Although it had reaped many monstrous heads during the battle, the silver sword's blade remained untarnished. Just a part of its magic – along with its brutal killing edge.

'Old friend,' said the elf, 'I think it is almost time for us to depart.' With the spear's tip, he pointed to the battlefield below where their armies warred against the Chaos hosts. Judging by the fury of the unfolding melee, the clash had reached a tipping point.

'Aye, lad, you may be right,' Snorri admitted, deciding to slake his lust for grudgement on the beasts below. Weary, he got to his feet.

Malekith laughed. It was a hollow sound, but had genuine mirth.

'*Lad*, am I? You ever manage to amuse me.'

'*Old*, am I?' Snorri replied, his grin as broad and wide as an axe blade.

Though he was far the younger of the two, an age of living beneath the earth, of sweating in the forges and furnaces of the underdeep, had left the dwarf with skin like baked leather. Unlike the elf, he was not immortal, although relatively long-lived.

'See there?' The elf hastened to the edge of the flat rock, thrusting again with his spear. He kicked at a daemon that had come close to the lip, giving it little thought as it plummeted hundreds of feet to its doom.

Snorri joined him, hacking into the face of another beast that had reached the edge of the Fist. The dwarf followed the elf's pointing spear tip. Crow's feet at the corners of his eyes deepened as he squinted into the fading sun.

'A breach in their lines.'

Through the mad swell, the pitch and yaw of the battle, it was difficult to see at first, but the ranks of the Chaos host had thinned. Where before a seemingly impenetrable tide of monsters had barred the way for the elves and dwarfs to reach the feathered sorcerer and the bloated lord, now there was a gap. A slim gap. A slim hope, but hope it still was.

The dwarf's plan was straightforward. Use them both as bait.

His thane-kings and the other lordlings of the elves too had argued against it but Snorri would not be swayed, nor Malekith who saw its virtues at once. The elf's dragon had brought them high above the battlefield to the Fist of Gron where all the foul daemons of Ruin could see and taste them. Eager to kill the elf prince and the dwarf king, the horde would flock to them, but in their eagerness would leave their daemonic masters less well protected.

'Your ruse has worked, old friend.'

'Of course it worked, I am a dawi!'

Malekith laughed again, but this time it was deep and hearty.

'Fighting at your side, I do not think I have ever been more at peace,' he said, flashing the dwarf a warm smile.

Snorri frowned at him.

'You find your solace in the oddest of places,' he shrugged, 'but then you are an *elgi* and as strange to me as the sky.'

Snorri grew stern. Despite this relative victory, the plan would only succeed if their armies held and could maintain the breach until he and Malekith arrived to lead them. The High King gazed out from the Fist of Gron, trying to gauge how the dwarfs were faring. They were fighting hard, thane-kings leading their warriors from the slopes of the distant mountain into the heart of the daemonic hosts and their beasts. On the vast left flank, lightning speared from runic anvils in their dozens and turned the monsters into ash. Immense pillars of flame rolled out from other runic war engines. Daemons and beasts caught up in the conflagration were swiftly rendered to charred hunks of tainted meat. Earth trembled as runesmiths in their hundreds called forth powerful quakes that opened up great chasms in the ground, swallowing scores of monsters before closing ominously.

Behind the stout phalanxes of dwarf warriors leading the attack, Snorri saw giants. Creations of stone and metal, these ancient golems were slow to rise and quick to slumber. Only the most powerful runelords could rouse them. Like the anvils, they were magical machineries fashioned by the supreme artifice of rune masters. The craft to forge them anew was lost, but the gronti-duraz lived still. It meant 'enduring giant' in the dwarf tongue.

On this great day when elf and dwarf stood together united in purpose, they had woken in their hundreds. The sight brought a tear to the old dwarf king's eye. It was to be their final battle, for the magic to animate them was getting harder and harder to craft, seeping away like a draught through a slowly widening crack.

From the craggy flanks of Karag Vlak a horn blast resounded, seizing the High King's attention. Ballistae gathered in serried ranks turned the air dark with flights of bolts the size of lances. Farther up the mountainside, mangonels and onagers hurled stones. Chunks of rock etched with runes of banishment and daemon-killing crashed and rolled amongst the horde. Beasts and daemons alike were crushed and skewered by the deadly rain pouring from the ranks of war machines.

Though monsters of every stripe had been unleashed against the armies of Snorri and Malekith, it was a plague-ridden tide that faced the dwarfs. Even high above the battlefield, Snorri could see hundreds of horned and hunch-backed daemons. Tallymen, he had heard them named. One-eyed, bloated bellied, the stench of their decaying flesh assailed his nostrils all the way up on the Fist of Gron.

Lesser, maggot-ridden beasts loped alongside them in their thousands. Some had once been men. Slug-like beasts with gaping maws like cages of acidic slime slith-ered behind them. Daemonic tallymen rode on the backs of the beasts, rusted bells ringing at their shrivelled necks. Diminutive, wide-mouthed daemons, covered in boils and pustules, swarmed like a rancid sea. They gathered at the edges of the horde, giggling like manic children.

'Such horror…' breathed the High King of the dwarfs, knowing even this was not the worst of it. Snorri followed the diseased ranks of the enemy until he saw the bloated lord.

Behind its pestilent legions there loomed a malevolent creature, cankerous and rotten as its vassals. Clad in rags and strips of flesh, a cloud of flies buzzed around it like a miasma. Tattered wings hung from its emaciated arms and a flock of rotting crows perched on its hulking shoulders, cawing malevolently.

Alkhor, it had named itself. Defiler, it boasted. Tide of Pestilence and Harbinger of Nurgle, it claimed. None of which were its true names, for daemons would never relin-quish those.

Disgusted, Snorri saw a throng of warriors attack the beast and his heart swelled with pride. The banner of Thurgin Ironheart fluttered on the breeze. Snorri clenched a fist as a flash of fire tore down the daemon prince's flank. For a moment it burned, and the dwarf dared to hope…

But then the rent flesh began to re-knit, hideous slime filling the wound and resealing it.

Alkhor's foul laughter gurgled on the breeze. Its crow host cawed and chattered as a stream of utter foulness retched from the daemon's ugly mouth.

Thurgin and his clansmen were overwhelmed, drowned in a stinking mire of vomit. Dwarf skeletons, half clad in rotting plate and scraps of burned leather, bobbed to the surface of the miasma. Hundreds died in seconds, their gromril armour no defence against Alkhor's disgusting gifts.

'That creature needs sending back to the abyss, as do all its debased kind,' said Malekith.

Deep as an abyssal trench, a roar split the heavens. It brought an answering cry from the elf prince before he declared to the dwarf, 'The war hinges on the next few moments.'

Snorri's jaw clenched. The elf was right.

On the other side of the vast plain, the elves fought a very different foe. Lurid, gibbering creatures cavorted in unruly mobs. Bizarre, floating daemons dressed in skirts of transmuting flesh spat streamers of incandescent fire from their limbs. Feathered beasts, bull-headed monstrosities and hell-spawn wracked with continuous physical change roved next to the daemons.

'They were all once men,' said Snorri, 'the barbarian tribes of the north.'

Malekith looked grim. 'Now they are monsters.'

Overhead, the sun was eclipsed as a massive shadow smothered the light.

Lifting his gaze, the prince of the elves saw a massive host of dragons coursing through the red skies. He longed to join them, his fist clenched as he watched the princes of Caledor and their mounts clash with flights of lesser daemonic creatures.

Amidst the swathe of dragonscale, he saw the smaller forms of eagles circling with the dragons. They picked apart the hellish flocks so the larger beasts could bring their fury to bear on the Chaos infantry. No less proud, the belligerent cries of the eagle riders carried through the battle din to the glittering elven warriors below.

He recognised one of them, noble Prince Aestar. He was keen-eyed and raised a quick salute to his lord, which Malekith returned before turning his gaze on the elven warriors below.

A large phalanx of knights, riding hard alongside scores of chariots, hit a thick wedge of pink, gnarled daemons that blurred and split apart as they were killed. Malekith gaped in disbelief as smaller blue imp-like abominations sprang from the ashes of their larger dead hosts and swarmed over the mounted elves. Victory looked far from certain for the knights, who were on the verge of slowing down and being overwhelmed when a conclave of Sapherian mages riding pillars of storm-cloud rained enchanted death down on the daemons. The creatures squealed in pain and delight, before the knights ended them and the mages flew off to confront a coven of sorcerers riding screaming discs of flame.

It was madness, a desperate struggle where the fates of not just lives but souls were at stake.

'There…' Malekith gestured to the second daemon lord, the feathered sorcerer. 'The creature is drawn into the open at last.'

'Like poison from a wound,' snarled Snorri. 'We must act swiftly,' he said, with half an eye on the edges of the rock where more beasts had begun to appear.

The feathered sorcerer was a creature of mischief and convoluted machination. Though they had never seen its true form, for it wore many, it had chosen an imperious aspect and was swathed in varicoloured flesh-cloth. Beneath its cowl, there was the suggestion of a beak. In one claw the daemon prince clutched a staff of obsidian carved with the faces of the damned. Souls were enslaved within its haft, ever screaming, ever changing as the Architect of Fate moulded them to its will. Unlike Alkhor, it did not attack but merely watched. But as the elves pulled open the threads of its legions, the daemon would soon have to act.

A massive shadow loomed above Malekith, and he

averted his gaze from his enemy to crane his neck and search the skies. Something was approaching through the choking cloud, the thump of its wingbeats like peals of thunder.

From below the rock shook, the earth underfoot trembling as if in fear as something massive neared the summit.

'Time to leave,' said the elf.

'I crave a moment longer...' Snorri stared straight ahead at the massive claw that had just reached up over the edge.

After a long climb, a cyclopean brute had gained the Fist of Gron's flat summit.

A second claw joined the first and slowly a massive, tusked head came into view. It snorted, releasing a drool of snot from its blunt, scarred snout. Tiny eyes, hooded by a sloping brow, glinted like rubies shot through with dark veins of anger. Its hide-wrapped chest was brawny and swathed in a thick fur. Scales colonised its abdomen, swallowing muscular forelegs and then back legs as the shaggoth heaved itself up.

'I saw it earlier,' Snorri confessed, 'when we were at the edge together, lingering behind the lesser beasts.'

Malekith had put some distance between them both, so the dwarf had room to fight. He shook his head.

'You were waiting for it, weren't you?'

As if bored with the exchange, the shaggoth bellowed and thumped its chest. It hefted a cleaver as large as a tree in one meaty fist. Plates of armour, shields and pieces of cuirass taken from dead heroes, wrapped its torso. A shoulder guard fashioned from battered war helms hung from strips of sinew lashed around its neck, back and chest.

'Not exactly,' the High King lied.

Snorri swung his rune axe in a practice arc, eyeing with dangerous belligerence the massive brute that had just crested the rock. He had fought one of these creatures before with Malekith at his side. It was many years ago. He had been a younger dwarf then, and his friendship with the elf was in its infancy.

'No, you wanted to kill it,' Malekith protested, circling around to try and reach the monster's blindside.

'Well… it has climbed such a long way to taste the bite of my axe.'

'There'll be plenty for you to kill below. More than enough to satisfy any battle-lust,' the elf reminded him.

'Aye, but I want this one,' said the dwarf, catching the monster's reflection in the blade of his axe.

Scenting blood, the shaggoth threw up its head and roared at the lightning wracking the sky. Its ululating challenge was eclipsed by another as an even larger beast armoured in carmine scales descended on the shaggoth like an owl upon a rat. Hide and metal plate tore open like parchment. Fire spewed from the dragon's jaws in a red conflagration that set hair aflame and sizzled flesh. The shaggoth recoiled in agony, realising the larger monster's dominance, but Malekith's dragon raked it with sword-long claws and clung on. Strips of meat and sinew ripped away from the shaggoth's body as it fought desperately to free itself. A cleaver blow went wild and the dragon chewed off the other monster's arm, releasing a font of spewing gore from the point of dismemberment. Then it bit down on the shaggoth's neck, tore out its throat and the brief one-sided brawl was over.

The slain monster staggered back, not quite realising it was already dead, and fell off the rock to the earth below.

Spreading its wings, the dragon unleashed a deep-throated bellow that prickled the High King's beard.

'No need to shout.'

'Hope there are no hard feelings, old friend,' said the prince with a wicked smile.

Snorri glowered at the beast, but his wolfish grin returned quickly. 'Consider that one I owe,' he said. 'Our friendship is worth more than the stolen scalp of some shaggoth.'

The dragon growled in empathy and Snorri laughed despite the beast's formidable size and presence.

Malekith muttered a heartfelt greeting to his mount that Snorri didn't catch. As he approached where it was perched on the edge of the rock, the dragon lowered its serpentine neck so the prince could stroke it.

Snorri frowned, then sighed. 'Another of your customs I cannot fathom, elfling.'

Ignoring him, Malekith swung up onto the saddle and looked down. 'We've lingered long enough,' he said, nodding towards the smoke-choked battlefield. 'Our warriors have need of us, old friend.'

Through the murk and the carnage, the elves and dwarfs were fighting hard but their strength was finally waning. A last effort, a determined push that looked chaotic from above, widened the fissure in the daemons' ranks a little farther. Beyond it there lurked the lords of the host.

'The sorcerer is mine,' snapped Malekith, before proffering a gauntleted hand to the dwarf.

Snorri declined.

'I can make my own way,' he replied. Sheathing his axe, he began to swing his hammer above his head. The lightning rune engraved upon it started to glow, and the heady aroma of the forge filled the air. 'Step back,' he warned.

Malekith and his beast obliged, watching the hammer's arc grow wider and wider.

The dwarf frowned in consternation.

'Why so grim-faced?' asked the elf prince, as his dragon sent a belt of flame over the north edge of the rock. A cacophony of screeching told them the beasts climbing up it had been destroyed.

'Because I *hate* being storm-borne…'

Snorri smashed the hammer into the earth. A flash of lightning, a dense clap of thunder and the High King was gone, carried off by the power of the hammer's ancient rune magic. Just a patch of scorched earth was left behind, a tiny circle where the dwarf was kneeling.

'Always with another trick beneath your beard, eh, old friend?' Malekith chuckled to himself. 'Ride the lightning,' he whispered, kicking his heels into the dragon's flanks. With a single beat of its huge wings, the elf prince soared skywards. His mount screeched a final curse at the encroaching hordes as they reached the flat summit of the Fist of Gron too late.

Elf and dragon breached cloud and smoke, ascending to the higher heavens. Below, glimpsed through a greying fog, the rock was overrun. Like an anthill swarmed by its denizens, the Fist of Gron was engulfed as a red sea rose up to claim it. The anguished hell-cries of the teeming masses followed him all the way back to the elven battle line.

III

HIGH KING SNORRI Whitebeard emerged at the edge of the battle through a jagged tear of light. Tendrils of lightning still played across his pauldrons and rivulets of power spilled over his breastplate as the magic he had employed was slow to dissipate.

The cohort of five hundred hearthguard who greeted him tried not to appear shocked at his sudden arrival, for the elder rune on the High King's hammer was slaved to his throne, the earthing point for its magic. Only half hiding his smile, enjoying the little piece of theatre, Snorri ascended the stone steps of the immense throne awaiting him.

An artefact from an ancient age, forged when the ancestor gods still roamed the deeps of the world, the Throne of Power was unique. It bore the Rune of Eternity, believed to have been inscribed upon its high back by Grungni. The dwarf name for it was *Azamar*, a rune so potent that nothing in existence could destroy it.

Fifty paces ahead of the High King were the backs of the gronti-duraz lumbering alongside the warrior clans and brotherhoods. Another hundred paces beyond them were the daemons and one of their masters. Snorri eyed the bloated lord with vengeful relish just as the stone-clad giants began to part, letting him through.

'Thronebearers.' The High King's voice was a deep rumble as he spoke to his retainers. 'Bring me to war.'

'Khazuk!' Grunting with effort, four burly dwarfs lifted king and throne aloft. Singing their deathsongs, they began to march.

The hearthguard fell in beside them. Thanes borne on their own war shields ordered their clansdwarfs to gather around the king's throng as he passed them, flanked on either side by the gronti-duraz. Snorri nodded to them, though the creations of metal and stone could not respond.

Vagrumm, his standard bearer, bellowed above the din of tramping boots and clashing shields to announce him.

'For Karaz-a-Karak! In the name of the ancestors and the High King!'

'Khazuk!' the throng replied.

A last bulwark of mail parted before the High King, the vanguard of the dwarf army hearing their liege-lord's return and rejoicing. Their ranks bowed aside only to reform again behind the hearthguard as slowly they reached the front where the fighting raged.

No sooner had he joined the front, than Snorri was immediately embattled.

A daemonic tallyman flung itself at the High King but was cut in half before it could land a blow. Rotten viscera sizzled on the ground but turned into mist where it touched the Throne of Power, the rune of Azamar flaring brightly. Another daemon was smashed asunder by the thronebearers as they pushed against the horde, trying to throw them back.

Hearthguard were hacking great inroads into the daemonic ranks, whilst the other thane-kings wrought similar carnage on either side of the king's throng.

It was wide, a two-hundred-foot hammer-head driven deep into the heart of the enemy. With Snorri leading them, the dwarf advance was inexorable and devastating. His sheer presence, and the innate resistance of the dwarfs, seemed to drain the creatures of Chaos, and as the fell magic drenching the plain waned, so too did the corporeal bonds binding the lesser daemons to it. Plague-infested corpses began to dissipate, cast back into the Realm of Chaos. Sloughing away, burning down to bone and ash, dissipating into smoke, hundreds of daemons surrendered to instability and were banished.

The tide turned.

Like an armoured plough scything a field of pestilential wheat, the dwarfs slew every Chaos beast that came before them until the High King was face-to-face with the bloated lord himself.

Alkhor chuckled at this reckoning. The bloated lord was many times larger than Snorri and towered over the dwarf until its shadow eclipsed the entire Throne of Power. It seemed to relish the fight to come.

Snorri was only too happy to oblige. Feet braced either side of his ancestral seat, he stood up to level his axe at the daemonic prince.

'Now you are mine.'

IV

MALEKITH FLEW LOW across the daemon ranks, his dragon spitting fire. Since leaving the Fist of Gron, he had made straight for his war host and the feathered sorcerer they fought against.

A hideous clutch of hell-spawned creatures spat tongues of iridescent fire at the elf prince but their aim was poor and he evaded the barrage. Issuing a mewling challenge, half plea, half roar, the beasts snapped their malformed jaws in frustration.

The dragon snarled back, despising the foul stench of the hell-spawn.

'Burn them,' Malekith whispered.

Liquid sulphur drooling from the dragon's snout burst into flame and streaked across the battlefield to engulf the Chaos beasts. They recoiled, reduced to little more than a dark silhouette amidst all the haze and smoke. Against such fury, the spawns' charred remains capitulated into ash. What remained of their mutated bodies sank into a heap.

One of Malekith's lieutenants, Klarond, saluted. They had been struggling against the monstrous spawn until the prince of Nagarythe's timely intervention.

'For Anlec and King Bel Shanaar!' roared Klarond, stabbing his sword into the air. The cheer from his warriors drew a sneer to Malekith's lips which he hid well before soaring back into the sky.

As he ascended he was met by Glarondril of Caledor. A host of dragons circled with the prince, the other nobles of the mountainous realm.

'I see no daemon lord, Malekith,' said Glarondril, an edge to his voice.

Malekith ignored the thinly veiled slight and instead surveyed the battlefield.

'It is here somewhere.'

His eyes narrowed, alighting on the dwarf throng where the king fought his own daemon lord. Many of the hearthguard lay dead around his feet, and one of the king's thronebearers could no longer fight.

Turning his gaze back to the dragon host, Malekith gestured to a trio of eagle riders that had just joined the flight.

'My lords,' he said, recognising again Prince Aestar as he addressed them, and glancing darkly at Glarondril, 'come with me.'

Malekith arrowed out of sight a moment later, piercing the cloud layer in seconds. Avian shrieks behind him told the elf prince that Aestar's eagle lords had followed.

The dwarf king looked beleaguered.

'I am coming,' he said, and urged his dragon to fly faster.

V

ROPES OF MUCUS drooled from the bloated lord's mouth. Its teeth were blackened nubs, rotting in the gum. Its breath was beyond foul, and rose from its maw in a noisome gas the dwarfs fought hard to ignore. Worst of all was the daemon's laughter. A hideous chuckle burbled from its lips, echoed mockingly by the crows perched upon its shoulders and fluttering around its corpse-like body. Alkhor was laughing when its jaw distended to impossibly wide proportions and it unleashed a stream of filth.

Snorri brandished his hammer and a shield of lightning sprang up to protect the king and his charges. The deluge seemed unending, a veritable torrent of puke and acidic bile from the very pit of the daemon's stomach. It spat and crackled like cooking fat against the runic shield, burning to smoke and sulphurous vapour that clung to armour, skin and hair. Merciful Valaya was by Snorri's side, as the foul slop ceased at last and the High King was left alive and miraculously unharmed.

The hearthguard fighting either side of the throne were

not so fortunate. Dwarfs died in their droves, their armour melted, skin and bone rendered down to nothing, sloughed away by the disgusting miasma. Above the fading screams the stentorian tones of Haglarr Grudgekeeper, he who had served the High King for centuries, could be heard recording each and every name and the reckoning that would follow.

'Heed that, beast,' snarled the High King, 'your infamy shall be remembered. I shall reckon it here and now. You'll burn for this.'

Lashing out savagely, Snorri carved a notch into Alkhor's plague sword. The daemon's bulk belied its swiftness as it parried the High King's axe and the runes upon it flared in anger at this denial of their power. A blow like that should have snapped the daemon sword in two, but the wretched weapon was ensorcelled. Rusted and pitted with serrated teeth, the glaive looked ancient and broken but was far from it. Encrusted with aeons of filth, Snorri knew just by looking at it that the slightest cut from the weapon's blade would fill its victim with a cornucopia of disease. Flesh would blacken, bones would crumble and organs liquefy until all that remained was a soup of corruption.

Seven brave dwarfs had already succumbed to that fate. Many more had been devoured by the daemon, swallowed into its belly. With every morsel, the bloated lord swelled until it had become a behemoth of utter foulness.

Shouting his defiance, Snorri was determined it would grow no further.

A chip of tainted blade came loose like a rotten tooth as the dwarf yanked out his axe. He swung the rune weapon around, circling the plague sword. Snorri went to attack again when an unholy swarm spilled from Alkhor's widening mouth and engulfed him.

Bloated flies, the daemon's host of tiny familiars, crawled over his eyes and armour, scurried into his beard. They bit his skin, buzzed in his ears. Suffocated, blind, Snorri spat out a wad of insects trying to burrow into his mouth and uttered an invocation.

'*Zharrum!*'

Lightning arced from the haft of his hammer, drawn into

a thunderhead that wreathed the king in a furious storm.

A shriek of agony, louder than the storm, split the air. It took a moment for the High King to realise it had come from the fly swarm, speaking with one voice as they burned and died. The enchanted fire had lifted the malaise, and Snorri shook the insects from his beard, brushed them hurriedly from his armour and breathed again.

Alkhor loomed, mocking the dwarf with its gurgling laughter. Its plague sword was raised for a cleaving blow. Blinking away the filth crusting his eyes, Snorri thrust upwards with his rune hammer and crafted a lightning bolt from the storm that speared the daemon's bloated chest.

Mirth became pain, the face of the daemon contorting as rune fire devoured and purified its flesh. It staggered then slumped, legs giving way to agony and bringing it within striking distance of the High King.

'I said you would burn!' Snorri roared, and slashed Alkhor open like a boil.

A slew of foulness erupted from the wound in the daemon's stomach. Half-digested corpses, chunks of armour and cloth, scraps of corroded leather and the remnants of skeletons eroded by the daemon's intestinal acids spilled out.

'Don't touch it,' warned the High King, and his retainers stayed back.

Alkhor staggered again. Unable to regenerate, the daemon clutched its wound, spitting bile and curses at the dwarf who had hurt it. Pathetically, it began to sob.

Unfurled from its back, a pair of tattered fly-like wings started to beat.

But Snorri wasn't finished with it yet.

'Closer, filth,' he growled, stepping down from his throne, 'so I can take your ugly head.'

As Snorri's booted feet hit the ground, Alkhor's sobbing turned into derisive laughter.

'*Foolish little creature,*' it burbled and tugged at the edges of the wound the dwarf had made. From within the rotten ropes of intestine, the sacs of pus and putrefying organs, a welter of tentacles burst forth. One wrapped around the High King's arm, the other pinned his leg. A third quested for his neck but he swatted it with his rune hammer before it could strangle him.

Each of the tentacles was swathed in sharp teeth that champed and gnawed at Snorri's armour. Slowly, they began to drag the dwarf into Alkhor's gaping maw.

RISING IN THE saddle, Malekith put the bloated lord firmly in his sights – along with Snorri entangled in the daemon's intestines, losing his fight for survival. Malekith was about to even the odds.

Digging his feet into the stirrups arrested the elf's descent and the dragon pulled up sharply, its long neck angling downwards and nostrils flaring. Trails of smoke extruded from the corners of its mouth, carried away on the breeze.

'I hope that armour of yours is impervious as you claim…'

Inhaling a deep, sulphurous breath, the dragon unleashed fire.

FLAMES ROARED HUNGRILY across the daemon's wretched body, burning away pestilence and purging rot. Clods of fat, festering slabs of skin sizzled and spat. Alkhor squealed as the tentacles rippling from its stomach were reduced to charred meat, writhing like headless vipers.

'*Htarken…*' it pleaded, but the feathered sorcerer did not appear.

'So that is your name,' the elf prince muttered.

The daemon pulled away, its tattered wings beating furiously and spewing gouts of filth in its desperate attempt to escape. Slowly, Alkhor began to rise. Its body was still smouldering, shrinking as the dragon fire consumed it.

Snorri swung and missed. He cursed the daemon's cowardice, hurling vengeful insults as it fled.

Malekith flew his dragon low and into the dwarf's eye line.

'Are you hurt, old friend?'

Snorri looked rueful, but otherwise uninjured.

'Only my pride. Killing that thing will salve it.'

A feral smile turned the corners of Malekith's mouth as he set his gaze on the fleeing daemon. Spurring his mount, he was about to pursue when he had to pull up sharply to avoid a burst of incandescent light exploding in front of him. Blinking back the after-flare, the elf saw a figure emerge from the sudden luminance. Clad in varicoloured robes, held aloft on feathered wings, Htarken barred Malekith's path.

The elf reacted as quick as thought but his thrown spear evaporated into mercury before it could impale the daemon. Its outstretched claw and swiftly spoken incantation was enough to destroy the weapon. Htarken returned its talon to the folds of its robes, yet made no motion to attack.

All the while, Alkhor was escaping. Thinking quickly, Malekith turned to the lord of the eagle riders who had just arrived from on high.

'Prince Aestar,' he said, thrusting his sword in the plague daemon's direction, 'slay that thing!'

Nodding grimly, Prince Aestar soared through the clouds after the daemon, his brothers close behind. Malekith was left to face Htarken.

He would not be alone. A conclave of three Sapherian mage lords rose up beside the prince on pillared coruscations of gold.

'You are finished, daemon.' He gestured to the valley below where the hell-hosts were slowly dissipating, their mortal followers fleeing with the dissolution of their immortal allies. 'Chaos has been defeated.'

'*Has it?*' Htarken spoke with a hundred different voices at once. Some were not even voices at all. They were the crackle of fire, the howling of the wind or the breaking of wood. They were cries of slaughter, pleas for mercy and the gibbering laughter of the insane. Birds, beasts, dwarfs and elves all collided in an unsettling union that put the prince's teeth on edge.

Malekith grimaced as the sound of Htarken's 'voice' echoed in his mind. Like a cancer, it sought to take root and destroy him from within.

'*Change,*' said the daemon, with the prince reeling, '*is inevitable. Even with all your many gifts, the heritage of your bloodline, you cannot fight entropy.*'

Malekith wondered why the mages had not yet banished this thing, and then he realised they were transfixed.

Seized by a sudden palsy, they trembled as all the horrors of change were visited upon them. As the minds of the mages died, so too did the pillars of fire holding them up.

Htarken had them now, bound to puppet strings. And they danced, they jerked and spasmed until they exploded into transmuted globs of flesh and flailing limbs. They were loremasters of the White Tower of Hoeth and the feathered sorcerer had vanquished them as if they were nothing more than apprentices.

'Fate is mine to manipulate,' said the daemon. *'I have seen yours, elf. Would you like to know it?'*

Malekith was about to answer when a terrible pain seized his body. He convulsed, clutched at his skin.

His dragon mewled in fear and confusion.

'I am…' Malekith tore off his helm, ripped at his gorget and cuirass, 'on fire! Isha preserve me!'

'All endings are known to me. Every skein of destiny is mine to behold. I see past, present and future. Nothing is occluded. Your doom has c–'

Agony lessened, the fires in the elf's mind faded to embers.

As he opened his eyes, Malekith saw a rune hammer lodged in Htarken's chest. The daemon clutched at it feebly, arrested in its sermonising.

A gruff voice called from below.

'You'll find it hard to speak with dwarf iron in your gut.'

Relief washing over him like a balm with the dissipation of Htarken's sorcery, Malekith nodded to his friend.

Snorri was not done. He outstretched his hand and the hammer's haft began to quiver. As if snared by an invisible anchor the daemon came with it, drawn down by the runecraft of the weapon, unable to remove it from where it had impaled its ribs and chest.

'I am master of fate…' Htarken was weakening, his many voices becoming less multitudinous with every foot he descended. *'I see all ends… I see…'*

'Bet you didn't see this, hell-spawn,' Snorri snarled through gritted teeth. The daemon was almost in front of him. He readied his axe in one hand, drew in the hammer with the other.

Htarken was weeping… no, *laughing*. Its spluttering mirth paused for agonised breaths and to spit ichor from its mouth. The hood fell back in its pain-wrecked convulsions, a savage parody of what it had done to the mages, revealing a grotesque bird-headed fiend. Narrow eyes filled with pit-black sclera glared over a hooked beak.

'*I am oracle, architect and thread keeper…*' it gasped, every second bringing it closer to the bite of the dwarf's axe. Htarken coughed, its laughter grew deeper and its struggles ceased. '*Your doom is certain, you and your pathetic races. Chaos has come and already a change is upon you. Feel it warp your bones, the very course of your bloodlines. It will shape the future and I will be there to witness it. Htarken the Everchanging shall stand upon the ashen corpses of you all and exult. Doomed…*' it cawed, eyes widening in a sudden fervour. '*Doomed, doomed, doomed, doom–*'

'Elfling!' Snorri cleaved the raving daemon with his axe as Malekith plunged Avanuir into its heart.

Htarken screamed a thousand times all at once as it was cast back into the abyss. An inner fire consumed it, possessed of chilling heat that made the elf and dwarf recoil.

In a flare of light, the last gasp of a candle flame before its air has run out, Htarken was gone and left only colourful ash motes in its wake.

MALEKITH FELT HIS heart beating hard in his chest like a drum. His arm was shaking where he held Avanuir and he had to lower it to keep from dropping his sword.

'Isha…' he breathed and turned to the dwarf.

Snorri was on one knee, holding himself up with his axe as his chest and back heaved up and down.

A shaft of sunlight blazed down from the sky, lancing through the bloody cloud that was slowly turning back to white. Snorri looked up into it and let the warmth bathe his face.

Malekith took off his helm to wipe the sweat from his brow. He smiled.

Snorri was nodding.

'Good,' he said, licking the dryness from his lips.

With their leaders banished or fled, the hell-hosts were dying. The lesser daemons were gone, the beasts and thralls were slowly being destroyed by the triumphant armies of the elves and dwarfs.

Snorri sighed as if a heavy burden had been removed from his shoulders and tramped wearily up the stone steps of his throne where he sat down heavily.

'Thus ends the threat of Chaos to the Old World,' he said. 'We have followed in the footsteps of our ancestors, of Grimnir and Grungni and Valaya.'

'Of my father Aenarion and Caledor Dragontamer,' said Malekith as his dragon bowed low to let him leap from the saddle and be at the dwarf's side.

They stood shoulder to shoulder, the lords who had challenged darkness and cast it back to hell.

'You look tired,' said the elf.

Snorri slumped against the throne.

'I am.'

Still clutched in one hand, his rune hammer drooled black smoke from a cleft in its head. Malekith knew the weapon's name was *Angazuf*, which Snorri had told him meant 'sky iron'. In banishing the daemon it had been ruined.

Snorri looked sad to see its runic strength diminish; the hammer was older than some hold halls.

'What else has been lost to this fight, I wonder?' he uttered, suddenly melancholy.

Around them the battle was ending. With the defeat of the Chaos hordes, order was returning. Life would return in time, but this would forever be a tainted place. For the touch of Chaos is a permanent taint that cannot ever be entirely removed.

Above them, Karag Vlak was quiescent, its anger spent like that of the dwarf king.

Around the mountain and before it, elves and dwarfs lay dead in their thousands.

But it was for his friend that Malekith's eyes betrayed the most concern.

There was rheum around Snorri's eyes. Age lines threaded

his face, gnarled skin and lesions showed on his hands. Like his rune hammer, he was broken. The elf wondered just how much this last fight had taken out of the dwarf, how badly Alkhor had really wounded him.

'Don't look so afraid, I am not dead yet,' growled the king.

Silent as statues, his thronebearers and hearthguard were grim-faced.

Malekith smiled, though it was affected with melancholy. He looked around at the battlefield, at the dying and the dead.

'We have paid a great price for this,' said the elf, finally answering the dwarf's question. 'Here we witness the passing of a golden age, I fear.'

He watched the elves and dwarfs as they fought together to cleanse the battlefield of the last remnants of resistance. Some had already begun to celebrate victory together and exchanged tokens and talismans. For many, it would be the last time they would see one another.

So different and yet common purpose had formed a strong bond.

'But perhaps we can usher in a new one. Either way, let us hope this is an end to hell and darkness.' He added, without conviction, 'To war and death.'

'Aye,' Snorri agreed, 'it is the province of more youthful kings, I think.'

Malekith nodded, lost in introspection.

'I had expected more joy, elfling,' said the dwarf. He leaned forwards to clap Malekith's armoured shoulder. 'And you say that we are dour.'

The elf laughed, but his eyes were far away.

'We should feast,' he said at last, returning to the present and leaving his troubles for now, 'and honour this triumph.'

'Back at Karaz-a-Karak, we will do just that, young elfling.' Some colour had returned to the dwarf's cheeks at the prospect of beer and meat. 'And yet you still seem moribund. What is it, Malekith? What ails you?'

'Nothing…' The elf's eyes were fixed again on a dark horizon, his mind on the remembered fire that had ravaged his body. It felt familiar somehow. 'Nothing, Snorri,' he said again, more lucidly. 'It can wait. It can certainly wait.'

ACT ONE

Of Dwarfs and Elves

━━◄ CHAPTER ONE ►━━

Rat Catching

THE TUNNEL WAS dank and reeked of mould. Darkness thicker than pitch was threaded with the sound of hidden, chittering things. Far from the heat of the forges, here in the lost corridors of the underway, monsters roamed. Or so Snorri hoped.

'Bring it closer, cousin. I caught a whiff of their stink up ahead.'

Morgrim held the lantern up higher. Its light threw clawing shadows across the walls, illuminating old waymarker runes that had long since fallen into disrepair.

'Karak Krum,' uttered the older dwarf, his face framed in the light. A ruddy orange glow limned his black beard, making it look as if it were on fire. 'The dwarfs there are long since dead, cousin. No one has ventured this deep into the Ungdrin Ankor for many, many years.'

Snorri squinted as he looked at Morgrim over his shoulder.

'Scared, are you? Thought you Bargrums had spines of iron, cousin.'

Morgrim bristled. 'Aye, we do!' he said, a little too loudly.

Two dwarfs, standing alone in a sea of black with but a

45

small corona of lamplight to enfold them, waited. After what felt like an age, the echo of Morgrim's truculence subsided and he added, 'I am not scared, cousin, merely thinking aloud.'

Snorri snorted.

'And who do you think you are, oh brave and mighty dawi, Snorri Whitebeard reborn?' said Morgrim. 'You have his name but not his deeds, cousin.'

'Not yet,' Snorri retorted with typical stoicism.

Grumbling under his breath, Morgrim traced the runic inscription of the waymarker with a leathern hand. There was dirt under the nails and rough calluses on the palms earned from hours spent in the forge. 'Don't you wonder what happened to them?'

'Who?'

'The dawi of Karak Krum.'

'Either dead or gone. You think far too much, and act far too little,' said Snorri, eyes front and returning to the hunt. 'Here, look, some of their dung.'

He pointed to a piled of noisome droppings a few inches from his booted foot.

Wrinkling his nose, Morgrim scowled. 'The reek of it,' he said. 'Like no rat I have ever smelled.'

Snorri unhitched his axe from the sheath on his back. He also carried a dagger at his waist and kept it close to hand too. Narrow though it was, he didn't want to be caught in the tunnel's bottleneck unarmed.

'Make a point of sniffing rats, do you, cousin?' he laughed.

Morgrim didn't answer. He glanced one last time at the runic marker describing the way to Karak Krum. Passed away or simply moved on when the seams of gold and gems had run dry, dwarfs no longer walked its halls, the forges were silent. Merchants and reckoners from Karaz-a-Karak had brought tales of a glowing rock discovered by the miners of Krum. It had happened centuries ago, the story passed down by his father and his father before him. It was little more than myth now but the stark evidence of the ancient hold's demise was still very real. Morgrim wondered what would happen if the same fate ever befell Karaz-a-Karak.

Snorri snapped him out of his bleak reverie.

'More light! This way, cousin.'

'I hear something…' Morgrim thumbed the buckle loose on his hammer's thong and took its haft. Leather creaked in the dwarf's grip.

From up ahead there emanated a scratching, chittering noise. It sounded almost like speech, except for the fact that both Morgrim and Snorri knew that rats could do no such thing.

Morgrim turned his head, strained his ear. '*Grobi*?'

'This deep?'

In this part of the underway, the tunnel was low and cramped as if it hadn't been hewn by dwarfs at all. Such a thing was impossible, wasn't it? Only dwarfs could dig the roads of the Ungdrin Ankor that connected all the holds of the Worlds Edge Mountains and beyond. And yet…

'A troll, then?'

Snorri looked back briefly. 'One that talks to itself?'

'I once encountered a troll with two heads that talked to itself, cousin.'

Snorri shot Morgrim a dubious look.

'No. Doesn't smell right. Can tell a troll from a mile away. Its breath is like a latrine married to an abattoir.'

'Reminds me of Uncle Fugri's *gruntis*.'

Snorri laughed, and they moved on.

A larger cavern loomed ahead of the dwarfs, unseen but with the shape and angle of the opening suggesting a widening threshold, the scent of air and rat together with the sound-echo hinting at a vaulted ceiling. Dwarfs knew rock. They knew it because it was under their nails, on their tongues, in their blood and ever surrounded them.

It was not merely a cavern ahead of the two dwarfs, where the tunnel met its end. It was large and it was a warren infested with rats.

Snorri could hardly contain his excitement.

'Are you ready, cousin?' He brought up his axe level with his chest and clutched it two-handed. There was a spike on the end of it that could be used for thrusting, a useful weapon in a tight corner. For the last mile the dwarfs had been forced to stoop, and the prospect of standing straight was abruptly appealing. At least, it was to Morgrim.

'As ready as I was when you defied your father's wishes, slipped your retainers and dragged me along on this rat hunt.'

'See,' Snorri explained, inching closer to the cavern entrance, 'that's what I like about you, Morgrim. Always so enthusiastic.'

Snorri touched a finger to the talisman around his neck, muttered, 'Grungni...' and peered around the edge of the tunnel.

Several large rats were gathered in the middle of a vaulted chamber. It might once have been the old entry hall to Karak Krum. Gnawing frantically at something, chattering to one another in high-pitched squeaks and squeals, the creatures seemed oblivious to the presence of the dwarfs.

'Are they wearing rags?' Morgrim was so incredulous he shone the lantern closer.

'*Hsst!*' Snorri hissed, scowling at his cousin. 'Douse the light!'

Too late, Morgrim shuttered the lantern.

One of the rats looked up from its feast, fragments of calcified bone flaking from its maw as it screeched a warning to its brethren.

As one the others turned, snarling and exposing yellowed fangs dripping hungrily with saliva.

Snorri roared, swinging his axe around in a double-handed arc.

'Grungni!'

The first rat fell decapitated as it lunged for the dwarf, its head bouncing off the slabbed floor and rolling into a corner. At the chamber's edges it was dark, so dark the dwarfs could not see much farther than the glow of the lantern.

Snorri cut open a second, splitting it from groin to sternum and spilling its foul innards, before Morgrim crushed a third with his hammer. He battered a fourth with a swing of the lantern, the stink of the rat's burning fur enough to make him gag as it recoiled and died.

'Two apiece!' Snorri was grinning wildly, his perfect white

teeth like a row of locked shields in his mouth, framed by a blond beard. The heritage of his ancestors was evident in the sapphire blue of his eyes, his regal bearing and confidence. He was prince of the dwarf realm in every way.

Morgrim was less enthused. He was looking into the shadows at the edge of the chamber. It was definitely the old entry hall to Karak Krum. Mildewed wood from thrones and tables littered the floor and a pair of statues venerating the lord and lady of the hold sat in cobwebbed alcoves against the east and west walls, facing one another. Sconces, denuded of their torches, sat beneath the statues, intended to illuminate them and the chamber. They were all that stood out at the periphery of the hall, except for the glinting rubies now floating in the darkness.

Morgrim cast the lantern into the middle of the chamber where it broke apart and flooded the area around it with firelight. Scattered embers and the slew of ignited oil illuminated a truth that Morgrim was aware of even before he had unhitched his shield.

'More of them, cousin.' He backed up, casting his gaze around.

Snorri's bright eyes flashed eagerly. 'A lot more.'

The dwarfs were surrounded as a score of rats crawled from the darkness, chittering and squeaking. To Morgrim's ears it could have been laughter. 'Are they mocking us?'

Snorri brandished his axe in challenge. 'Not for long, cousin.'

His next blow cleaved a skull in two, the second caving a chest as the rat reared up at him. Snorri killed a third with a thrown dagger before something leapt onto his back and put him on one knee.

'Gnhhh… Cousin!'

Morgrim finished one off with a hammer blow to the jaw, and broke its back as it fell mewling. He then kicked ash from the sundered lantern in the snout of another, before using his shield to batter the rat that was clawing and biting at Snorri's back.

Scurrying and scratching rose above the din of blades and bludgeons hitting flesh, the squeals of dying rats.

'Bloody vermin,' Snorri raged, throwing another rat off his arm before it could sink its teeth in.

A score had become two score in a matter of minutes.

Morgrim smashed two rats down with his shield, staved in the head of a third with his hammer. 'There are too many. And big, much bigger than any rat I've ever seen.'

'Nonsense,' Snorri chided. 'They are just rats, cousin. Vermin do not rule the underway, we dawi are its kings and masters.'

Despite his bullishness, the prince of Karaz-a-Karak was breathing hard. Sweat lapped his brow, and shone like pearls on his beard.

'We must go back, get to the tunnel,' said Morgrim. 'Fight them one at a time.' He was making for the cavern entrance from whence the dwarfs had first come, but it was thronged with the creatures. A mass of furry bodies stood between them and the relative safety of the tunnel.

'We can kill them, Morgrim. They're only rats.'

But they were not, not really, and Snorri knew it even if he would not admit this to his cousin. Something flashed in the half-light from the slowly fading lantern that looked like a hook or cleaver, possibly a knife. It could not have been armour, nor the studs on a leather jerkin – rats did not wear armour, or carry weapons. But they were hunched, broad shouldered in some instances, and some went on two legs, not four. Did one have a beard?

'The way back is barred, we must go forwards,' said Morgrim, the urgency in his tone revealing just how dire he thought the situation to be.

Reluctantly, Snorri nodded.

The two dwarfs were back to back, almost encircled by rats. Eyes like wet rubies flashed hungrily. The stink of wet fur and charnel breath washed over them in a thick fug. Chittering and squeaking wore at the nerves like a blunt blade working to sever a rope.

'Remember Thurbad's lessons?' Snorri asked. A slash to his cheek made him grimace but he cut down the rat who did it. 'Little bastard, that was a knife!'

Morgrim's voice suggested he was in no mood for an exam.

'Which one, cousin? There are many.' He kept the rats at bay with his shield, thrusting it against the press of furred bodies trying to overwhelm him. His hammer was slick with gore and he had to concentrate to maintain his grip, thankful for the leather-bound haft.

'Choose your battlefield wisely.'

'Our current situation would suggest we did not listen very well to that particular lesson, cousin.'

Snorri grunted as he killed another rat. Dwarfs were strong, especially those that descended from the bloodline of kings, but even the prince's fortitude was waning.

'We can't fight a horde like this in the open,' he said, swiping up a piece of broken wood with his off hand.

Morgrim was trying not to get his face bitten off when he said, 'And you could not have thought of this *before* we were surrounded?'

'Now is hardly time for recriminations, cousin. Do you have any more oil for that lantern?' he asked, preventing any reply from Morgrim who didn't bother to hide his exasperation.

'A flask.'

'Smash it.'

'What?'

Each reply was bookended by grunts and squeaks, the swing and thud of metal.

'Smash it, cousin. There.' Snorri pointed. 'Next to the stairway.'

'What stairway? I can see no–'

'Are you blind, cousin? There, to your left.'

Morgrim saw it, a set of stone steps leading further into darkness. The prospect was not an inviting one.

Snorri was still pointing with the piece of wood. 'We can – arrrggh!'

Morgrim dared not turn, but the sound of his cousin's pain made him desperately want to.

'Snorri?!'

'*Thagging* rat bit off my fingers… Throw the *chuffing* flask, Morgrim!'

It was risky to stow his hammer, but Morgrim did so to

take the flask of oil from his belt and toss it. The heavy flask sloshed as it arced over the bobbing rat heads and smashed behind them in a scattering of oil and clay fragments.

Despite his wounding, Snorri still clutched the piece of wood in his maimed hand and thrust it into the dying embers of the lantern fire the dwarfs had rallied next to. Dried out from the many centuries down in the abandoned hall, it flared quickly, a spattering of spilled oil and the moth-eaten rag still attached to it adding to its flammability.

Snorri didn't hesitate – his grip was already failing – and hurled the firebrand into the expanding pool of oil. It went up with a loud, incendiary *whoosh*, throwing back the rats clustered around it. Clutching their eyes, they squealed and recoiled, opening a path to the stairway.

Once he was sure his cousin was behind him, Morgrim was running. He didn't bother to pull his hammer, and even threw his shield into the furred ranks of the rats to buy some precious time to flee. Snorri outstripped him for pace, his armour lighter and more finely crafted, and he reached the stairway ahead of Morgrim.

'Down!' shouted Snorri.

Still running, Morgrim replied, 'What if the way isn't clear?'

'Then we're both dead. Come on!'

The dwarfs plunged headlong down the stone steps, heedless of the way ahead, the way behind bracketed by flames. As swiftly as it had caught light, the lantern oil burned away and went from a bonfire to a flicker in moments.

The rats were quick to pursue.

Halfway down the stairs, which were broad and long, Snorri pointed with his maimed hand. Even in the semi-darkness, Morgrim could see he had lost one and a half fingers to the rat bite.

'A door, cousin!'

It was wood, probably wutroth to have endured all the years intact and bereft of worm-rot. Iron-banded, studs in the metal that ran in thick strips down its length, it looked stout. Robust enough to hold back a swarm of giant rats, even rats that wore armour and carried blades.

Snorri slammed against it, grunting again; the door was as formidable as the dwarfs had hoped. Morgrim helped him push it open, on reluctant, grinding hinges.

The rats were but a few paces away when the dwarfs squeezed through the narrow gap they had made and shut the door from the other side.

'Hold it!' snapped Snorri, and Morgrim braced the door with his shoulder as the rats crashed against it. He could hear their scratching, the enraged squeals and the squeaks of annoyance that could not have been a language, for rats do not converse with one another. Frantic thudding from the other side of the door made him a little anxious, especially as he couldn't see Snorri any more.

'Cousin, if you've left me here to brace this door alone, I swear to Grimnir I'll–'

Carrying a broad wooden brace, Snorri slammed it down onto the iron clasps on either side of the doorway.

'You'll what?' he asked, catching his breath and wiping sweat from his glistening forehead.

Off to seek easier pickings elsewhere, the din from the rats was receding.

Snorri smiled in the face of his cousin's thunderous expression.

After a few moments, Morgrim smiled too and the pair of them were laughing raucously, huge hearty belly laughs that carried far into the underdeep.

'*Shhh!* We will rouse an army of grobi, cousin...' Morgrim was wiping the tears from his eyes as his composure slowly returned.

'Then we'll fight them too! Ha! Aye, you're probably right.' Snorri sniggered, the last dregs of merriment leaving him. Wincing, he looked down at his hand and became abruptly sober. 'Bloody vermin.'

'I have never seen the like,' Morgrim confessed. He pulled a kerchief from a pouch upon his belt.

Snorri frowned at it. 'What's that for, dabbing your nose when you get a bit of soot on it? Are you turning into an *ufdi*?'

Morgrim's already ruddy cheeks reddened further. ''Tis a cloth,' he protested, 'for cleaning weapons.'

'Of course it is,' Snorri muttered as his cousin proceeded to wrap it around his bleeding hand. His smirk became a grimace as Morgrim tied the cloth a little tighter than necessary.

'For now, it will suffice as a bandage,' he said. He looked at the dark stain that was already blossoming red all over the kerchief. 'It's a savage bite.'

'Aye,' Snorri agreed ruefully, 'I've half a mind go back in there and retrieve my fingers from its belly.'

'Bet you would as well.' Morgrim was exploring their surroundings, looking for a way onwards and preferably back to a part of the underway they knew. 'That *would* be half-minded,' he mumbled, attention divided. 'Ha, ha!' he laughed, turning to face his cousin. 'Half a mind, to go with half a hand.'

Snorri scowled. 'Very funny. Haven't you found a way out of here yet?'

'There's a breeze...' Morgrim sniffed, venturing forwards. Without the lantern, even with the sharp eyes of a dwarf, the darkness was blinding. 'Coming from somewhere–'

Splintering rock, a loud *smack* of something heavy hitting stone and then a grunt arrested Morgrim's reply.

It took Snorri a few moments to realise this *was* Morgrim and his cousin had fallen into some unseen crevasse.

'Cousin, are you hurt?' he called, only for the darkness to echo his words back at him. 'Where are–'

Hard, unyielding stone rushed up to meet him as Snorri slipped on the same scree that had upended Morgrim. Daggers of hot pain pierced his back as he went down and he cracked his skull before the ground slid from under him and he fell.

Another thud of stone hitting flesh, this time his, like a battering ram against a postern gate. He felt it all the way up his spine and his left shoulder.

Groaning, Snorri rolled onto his right side and saw Morgrim looking back at him with the same grimace.

'That bloody hurt,' he said.

Morgrim eased onto his back, looked up at the gaping crevasse above. Dust motes and chunks of grit were spilling down from above like rain.

'Must have fallen thirty, forty feet.'

He pushed himself up into a sitting position.

'Feels like a hundred.' Snorri was on his back, rubbing his swollen head.

'Nothing to damage there,' said Morgrim. He tapped the helmet he wore. A pair of horns spiralled from the temples and a studded guard sat snug against the dwarf's bulbous nose. 'Should wear one of these.'

'Makes you bald,' Snorri replied, prompting a worried look on his cousin's face. A small stone struck Snorri's brow and he grimaced again.

'See,' said Morgrim, getting to his feet and helping his cousin up. 'Enough lying down.' Once Snorri was vertical again, he brushed the dirt off his armour and checked he still had his hammer. 'We need a way out.'

Without the lantern, it was hard to discern exactly where they had fallen. Doubtless it was one of the lower clan halls of Karak Krum, but there was precious little evidence of that visible in the shadows that clung to the place like fog.

Snorri sucked his teeth.

'A pity you chucked our lantern oil.'

Morgrim bit his tongue to stop from swearing. Instead he looked around, sniffed at the air. 'I smell soot,' he said after a minute or so, then licked his lips. Another short pause. 'Definitely soot.'

Snorri frowned, and went to recover his axe from where he'd dropped it when he fell. 'All I can smell and taste is grit.' He spat out a wad of dirt, hacking up a chunk of phlegm at the same time. 'And rat,' he added.

Morgrim's face darkened. 'No rat I have ever encountered spoke or carried a blade.'

'That is because rats can't do such things.' Snorri tapped him on the forehead and made a face. 'Perhaps you need a tougher war helm, cousin.'

Morgrim wasn't about to be mollified. 'I know what I saw and heard.' His face grew stern, serious. 'So do you. There is more than grobi and *urk* in these old tunnels. Who can say what beasts have risen in the dark beneath the world?'

Snorri had no answer to that. He hefted his axe and gestured roughly north. Even when lost, if a dwarf is underground his sense of direction is usually infallible.

'Nose is telling me it's that way.'

'What is?' asked Morgrim, though his cousin was already moving.

'Something other than this thrice-cursed darkness.' He paused. 'And your talking bloody rats,' he added, before stomping off.

Groaning under his breath, Morgrim followed.

⟨ CHAPTER TWO ⟩

Whispers in the Dark

SNORRI AND MORGRIM knew there was something in the Ungdrin Ankor, vermin maybe, but definitely an enemy the dwarfs had not faced before. Tales abounded, they always did, told by drunken treasure hunters. Few dwarfs, barring the credulous and the gullible, beardlings in the main, believed such tall stories. But myths made flesh were hard to refute. Morgrim was reminded again of the stories of his father, of the glowing rock unearthed by Karak Krum's miners. He brought to mind the faces of the savage creatures they had just escaped and decided there was something alarmingly familiar about them.

The two dwarfs spent the next few minutes in silence, listening for any sign of the rats' return.

After passing through a vast open cavern, its narrow stone bridge spanning a bottomless pit and its ceiling stretching into darkness, Morgrim asked, 'How is your hand, cousin?'

Snorri kept it close to his chest, taking the axe one-handed as he walked. Blood stained the metal links of his armour where it had bled through the makeshift bandage. Regarding the wound, he sneered, 'Think you need thicker pampering cloths.'

Morgrim ignored the gibe, reading the pain etched on his cousin's face. 'Looks in need of a redress.'

They had left behind the chasm chamber with its narrow, precipitous span and walked a long gallery with a high ceiling. Errant shafts of light cast grainy spears in the darkness from clutches of *brynduraz*. Such a rare mineral was worthy of mining and Morgrim had wondered then whether the clans of Karak Krum had left willingly – or moved at all. Long stalactites dripping with moisture that reflected the brightstone made the dwarfs duck occasionally, and a chill gave the air a bite.

'Hurts like Helda just sat on it wearing full armour,' Snorri complained, wincing as the ruddy cloth was re-tightened.

Morgrim laughed out loud.

Helda was one of many would-be consorts that Snorri's father had attempted to *arrange* for the young prince. She was of good stock, *too* good in Snorri's opinion given her impressive girth. A dwarf lord was said to be worthy to marry a *rinn* if his beard could wrap around her ample bosom at least once. Snorri doubted Helda would ever find a mate able to achieve that feat. If she did it would be a longbeard and past the age when siring an heir was amongst the dwarf's concerns. In fact, one night Helda would likely test the poor sod.

Her father, the King of Karak Kadrin, was a strong ally of Karaz-a-Karak and had offered a sizeable dowry from his personal coffers to secure the union but Snorri had objected and then declined. Comely as she was, he had no desire to bed such a walrus and continue the Lunngrin bloodline. Besides, he had eyes for another.

'She was a broad girl,' admitted Morgrim, wiping tears from his eyes as he finished binding the wound anew.

'As an alehouse, cousin.'

'And a face like a troll.'

'Trolls are prettier.'

Morgrim was holding on to his sides, which had begun to pain him, when he saw the light. It was faint, like a distant fire or a partly shuttered lantern.

And it was moving.

'Hide!' he hissed. Both dwarfs moved to the opposite edges of the gallery and hugged the walls.

Snorri gestured silently to his cousin, asking him what he had seen.

Morgrim nodded to the lambent glow in the distance. The reek of soot had grown stronger too.

Dawi? Snorri mouthed.

Morgrim shook his head.

Not this deep.

Karak Krum was a tomb in all but name. It only harboured creatures and revenants now. It fell to the dwarfs to find out which this one was.

The blade of Snorri's axe caught in the light from the brightstone, signalling his intention.

Nodding slowly, Morgrim drew his hammer and followed his cousin as he crept along the opposite side of the gallery. All the while the patch of light bobbed and swayed, but never got any closer. Tales were often told to scare beardlings of cavern lamps or *uzkuzharr*, the 'dead fires' of dwarfs long passed who were slain in anger or because of misfortune. Such unquiet spirits did not dwell with the ancestors, nor did they eat at Grungni's table, but were destined to walk the dwarf underworld. Jealous of the living, they would lure young or foolish dwarfs to their deaths, drawing them on with their light and their promises of gold. Often these dwarfs were found at the bottom of chasms or crushed to death under a rock fall.

Snorri and Morgrim knew the stories, they had been told them too during infancy, but now they were faced with such an apparition made real. The dwarfs kept it in their eye line at all times, using the eroded columns at the sides of the tunnel that held up the ceiling to hide behind. The tunnel led them to another room. It was small and had once possessed a door, which stood no longer. Only rusted hinges and wooden scraps clung to the frame.

It was a temple, obvious from the icon of Grungni carved into the wall, and had no other visible exits. A figure clad in a simple tunic, hose and chainmail was kneeling down inside. Old, if the bald pate and greying locks were anything to go by, he was muttering whilst casting rune stones onto the ground in front of him. A lantern was strapped to his back via some leather and metal contrivance and shone brightly without need of a flame. Its light gave him an unearthly lustre. Seen side on, he appeared to be conversing quietly with someone out of view.

Snorri mouthed, *Not alone*, and the two dwarfs crept closer until they could hear what the old dwarf was saying.

'*Dreng tromak, uzkul un dum?*' the old dwarf asked. 'Are you sure? Nah, cannot be that.' His low, sonorous tones made Snorri think of slowly tumbling rock.

'*What?*' Morgrim hissed, but Snorri pressed his finger to his mouth to silence him.

Casting the stones again, the old dwarf muttered, '*Dawi barazen ek dreng drakk, un riknu…*' It was Khazalid, the language of the dwarfs, but archaic to the point where it was almost incomprehensible. 'Not what I was expecting,' he said, looking up at his companion, who was still obscured from sight. 'Any ideas?'

Morgrim had reached the very edge of the temple and gestured to the old dwarf's 'companion'.

It was a stone statue of Grungni.

'He's mad,' hissed Morgrim, frowning.

Snorri nodded. He recognised some of the old dwarf's words, which now seemed prompted by their arrival. *Death* and *doom*, he knew. Also there was *destiny* and *king*.

Uzkuzharr lure their victims with promises, and their malice is as old as the earth, the words of his mentors returned to him.

'*Uzkul un dum.*' The old dwarf nudged a rune stone with his knuckle, arranging it above another. '*Dreng drakk… riknu…*'

The markings were ancient, wrought from chisel-tongue and hard to define.

Suddenly, the old dwarf turned, fixing them with a narrowed eye.

'I see a dragon slayer in my presence,' said the old dwarf, reverting to more common Khazalid. 'One destined to become king.' His eyes were slightly glazed, as if perhaps he was still unaware of their presence.

'Ears like a bat!' hissed Morgrim, hammer held ready.

Hackles rose on the back of Snorri's neck. His tongue felt leaden, and he tasted sulphur. He hefted his axe in two hands, glad when his voice didn't quaver. 'Stand, creature. Make yourself known.'

In the glow of the lantern, the strange dwarf looked almost hewn from stone, no different to the statues of Karak Krum's fallen king and queen. Snorri had heard Morek the runesmith speak in whispers of dwarfs that dabbled in magic, the wild unpredictable kind not bound to metal, of the slow petrification of their bodies and the cruelty it bred into their souls.

Not all dwarfs honoured the ancestors any more. Not since the Coming of Chaos in the elder days. Snorri knew his history, of legends about clans that fled the Worlds Edge Mountains to a land of everlasting fire and who swore fealty to a different god entirely, a father of darkness.

No dwarf in their right mind would venture this deep alone. Snorri and Morgrim were only there by misadventure, but the old dwarf had clearly come here deliberately. Perhaps he sought to profane the temple. Perhaps it was not a dwarf at all but some unquiet spirit of the lost dwarfs of Karak Krum.

Snorri's skin felt suddenly cold and he suppressed a shiver. He edged forwards, caught a reassuring glance from Morgrim who was just behind him.

Axe at the ready, Snorri called out, 'I said, rise and make yourself known. You are in the presence of the prince of Karaz-a-Karak.'

'I see a great destiny,' said the old dwarf, both cousins in his sight but looking right through them. 'A king one day.'

Snorri partly lowered his axe without thinking. Another step brought him within a few short feet of the old dwarf.

His uttered a choked rasp.

'*My* destiny? King?' The desire in his eyes and his tone betrayed him.

'One who will lift the great doom of our race, he who will slay the drakk...' said the old dwarf, half lost in his prophetic reverie and, muttering the last part. '*Elgidum...*'

'Drakk?' Snorri's axe went up again. 'What drakk, old one? Is there a beast in these tunnels?' He glanced around, nervously. Morgrim did the same.

'I see nothing, cousin,' he hissed, but was deathly pale and clutched his hammer tightly.

Anger burned away Snorri's fear like fire banishes ice, and he returned to the old dwarf.

'Who are you? Speak now or I will–'

'You will what, brave prince?' asked the old dwarf, regarding him properly for the first time, groaning in protest as he struggled to his feet in the light. 'Kneeling is a young dwarf's game,' he mumbled under his breath. 'Would you stab an unarmed dawi, then?'

Like a veil had lifted from his eyes, Snorri balked as he recognised Ranuld Silverthumb, Runelord of Karaz-a-Karak and part of the High King's Council.

'Lord Silverthumb, I...' He kneeled, bowed his head.

So did Morgrim, who caught a flash of azure fire in the runelord's eyes before he looked down.

Ranuld sighed wearily, 'Arise, I have no desire to strain my neck and back further by looking down on you pair of *wazzocks*.' He scowled at the two dwarfs who got up apologetically. 'And sheathe your weapons,' snapped the runelord. 'Did you think me one of the *dawi zharr*, mayhap? Or an *uzkular*? Ha, ha, ha!' Ranuld laughed loudly and derisively, muttering, 'Wazzocks.'

Snorri flushed bright crimson and fought the urge to hide his face.

'What was that prophecy you spoke of?' he asked.

Lord Silverthumb grew angry, annoyed. 'Not for ears the likes of yours!' he snapped, and a shadow seemed to pass across his face. Snorri thought it looked like concern, but the runesmith was quick to recover and wagged a finger at them both.

'Choose your own fate. Make your own. Destiny is just about picking a path then walking it.'

Shaking his head, Morgrim asked, 'What are you doing down here in these ruins, lord? It's perilous to venture here alone.'

Ranuld gaped in sudden surprise, glancing around in mock panic.

'Danger is there?' he asked. 'From what, I dread to know? Might I be stabbed in the back by my own kith and kin?' He scowled again, his face wrinkling like old leather, and sneered scornfully. 'I came here in search of magic, if you must know.'

The look of incredulity on Morgrim's face only deepened. Snorri was also perplexed, his silence inviting further explanation.

Ranuld raised a feathery eyebrow, like a snowfall upon the crag of his brow. 'And you two are supposedly from the blood of kings. Bah!' He stooped to retrieve his rune stones, chuntering about the thinning of dwarf stock and the dubious practice of *krutting*, when one consorts with a goat.

Snorri got over his awe quickly. 'What do you mean? How can you simply *look* for magic? It isn't like a lost axe or helmet. It can't be touched.'

Ranuld looked up wryly as he put the last of his rune stones into a leather pouch and drew its string taut. 'Can't it? Can't you?' Straightening up, grimacing as his back cracked, he jabbed a gnarled finger at the prince like it was a knife.

'I am... um–'

'No lad, you are Snorri, son of Gotrek, so named for the Whitebeard whose boots your beardling feet are unworthy of, let alone his name. I do not know who *um* is.'

Snorri bit back his anger. He had stowed his axe, but clenched his fists.

'Venerable one,' Morgrim stepped in calmly, 'we are not as wise as you–'

'But have a gift for stating what is obvious,' Ranuld interrupted, turning his back on them and taking a knee before the shrine. 'Never any peace,' he grumbled beneath his breath, 'even in lost years. Overhearing words not meant for ears so young and foolish...' Again, he frowned.

Morgrim persisted, showing all proper deference. '*Why* are you looking for magic?'

Finishing his whispered oath to Grungni, Ranuld rose and grinned ferally at the young dwarf.

'*That* is a much better question,' he said, glancing daggers at Snorri. '*This*,' he said, rubbing the dirt and air between his fingers, 'and *this*...' he smacked the stone of the temple wall, 'and *this*...' then hacked a gob of spittle onto the ground, just missing Morgrim's boot, '*is* magic. Some of us can feel it, beardling. It lives in stone, in air, in earth and fire, even water. You breathe it, you taste it–' Ranuld's face darkened, suddenly far away as if he was no longer talking to the dwarfs at all, '–but it's changing, we're changing with it. Secrets lost, never to return,' he rasped. 'Who will keep it safe once we're gone? The gate bled something out we couldn't put back. Not even Grimnir could do that.' He stared at the dwarfs, his rheumy eyes heavy-lidded with the burden of knowledge and all the many years of his long life. 'Can you feel it, seeping into your hearts and souls?'

Morgrim had no answer, though his mouth moved as if it wanted to give one. 'I... I do not...'

As if snapping out of a trance, Ranuld's expression changed. As fiery and curmudgeonly as he ever was, he barged past the two dwarfs and into the long gallery. The runelord was halfway down when Morgrim shouted after him, 'Where are you going now?'

'Didn't find what I was looking for,' Ranuld called back without turning. 'Need to try somewhere else.'

Morgrim began to go after him. 'It's fortunate we found you, old one. Let us escort you back to the underway.'

'Ha!' Ranuld laughed. 'You're lost, aren't you? Best help yourselves before you help me, *werits*. And find me, did you? Perhaps I found you? Ever consider that, beardling? And this *is* the underway, wazzock.'

'No part of it I know.'

'You know very little, like when it's a good time to run, for instance,' Ranuld replied, so distant his voice echoed.

'Wha–'

A low rumble, heard deep under their feet, felt through their bones, stalled Morgrim and he looked up. Small chunks of grit were already falling from the ceiling in vast clouds of spewing dust. Cracks threaded the left side of the gallery wall, columns split in half.

Morgrim had spent enough time in his father's mines to know what was about to happen.

'Get back!' He slammed into Snorri's side, hurling the dwarf off his feet and barrelling them both back inside the temple.

The roof of the long gallery caved in a moment later, releasing a deluge of earth and rock. Thick slabs of stone, weighed down with centuries of smaller rock falls, speared through the roof from above and brought a rain of boulders with them. A huge pall of dirt billowed up from the sudden excavation.

Though he tried to see him, Ranuld was lost to Morgrim. It wasn't that he was obscured by falling debris, rather that the runelord simply wasn't there any more. He had vanished. It was as if the earth had swallowed him. As the storm of dust and grit rolled over them, Morgrim buried his head under his hands and prayed to Grungni they would survive.

Blackness became abject, sound smothered by an endless tide of debris. Stone chips, bladed flakes sheared from a much greater whole, cut Morgrim's face despite his war helm. He snarled but kept his teeth clenched.

Tremors faded, dust clung to the air in a muggy veil. Light prevailed, from above where the ceiling had caved in. It limned the summit of a pile of rocks no dwarf could ever hope to squeeze through.

Snorri coughed, brought up a fat wad of dirty phlegm and shook age-old filth from his hair and beard. Clods of earth were jammed in his ears, and he dug them out with a finger.

'Think most of Karak Krum just fell on top of us.'

'At least we are both alive, cousin.'

Snorri grunted something before spitting up more dirt.

Morgrim wafted away some of the dust veiling the air. 'What about Lord Silverthumb?'

'That old coot won't die to a cave-in, you can bet Grungni's arse he won't.'

Morgrim agreed. For some reason he didn't fear for the runesmith. The old dwarf had known what was going to happen and left them to be buried. If anything, he was more annoyed than concerned.

Barring the mucky overspill from the cave-in, the temple was untouched. Its archway still stood, so too its ceiling and walls. Grungni sat still and silently at the back of the room, watching, appraising perhaps.

Morgrim touched the rune on his war helm and gave thanks to the ancestor.

Snorri was already up, pulling at the wall of rock that had gathered at the only entrance to the temple. It was almost sealed.

'Did you also bring a pick and shovel when you picked up the lantern, cousin?' he asked, heaving away a large chunk of rock only for an even larger one to slam down violently in its place. A low rumble returned, the faint suggestion of another tremor. Motes of dust spilling from the ceiling thickened into gritty swathes.

'Leave it!' Morgrim snapped, reaching out in a gesture for Snorri to stop what he was doing. 'You'll bring whole upper deep down on us. It'll flood the chamber with earth.'

Snorri held up his palms.

'Buried alive or left to rot in some forgotten tomb,' he said, 'neither choice is appealing, cousin. How do you suggest we get out?'

'Use a secret door.'

'Would that we had one, cou–'

Snorri stopped talking when he saw Morgrim hauling aside the statue of Grungni. Behind it was a shallow recess in the wall that delineated a door. It was open a crack and a rune stone had been left next to it that caught Morgrim's attention. He pocketed it and gave the door another tug.

'Get your back into it,' Snorri chided.

'How about yours?' he replied, red-faced and flustered.

'I'm wounded,' said Snorri, showing off his half-hand.

Morgrim spoke through gritted teeth and flung spittle. 'Get your chuffing arse over here and help me move this thing.'

Together, they dragged the door wide enough to slip through. Musky air rushed up to greet them, the scent of age and mildew strong enough to almost make them gag. A long, narrow darkness stretched before them. The gloom felt endless.

'We can stand here,' said Snorri, pulling out his axe, 'or we can go forwards. I vote for the dark.'

'Aye,' nodded Morgrim, and drew his hammer.

They had gone only a few feet when Snorri asked, 'What did he mean?'

'About magic? Chuffed if I know.'

'No, about my destiny. It being great and "lifting the doom of our race" and "he who will slay the drakk"? Those words were meant for me, I am sure.'

'Agreed,' said Morgrim, 'but you're the son of the High King of Karaz-a-Karak, of course your destiny will be great.' Morgrim led the way, following veins of gemstones and ore in the tunnel walls.

Snorri snorted, his disdain obvious.

Morgrim barely noticed. 'Feels like we're going up… Does it feel like we're going up?' He stopped, trying to get his bearings even though there was supposedly only one way for them to go.

'A great doom…' said Snorri. 'Are we headed for war, do you think?'

'Why do you sound as if you want a war? And against whom will you fight, eh, cousin? The urk and grobi tribes are diminished, dying out, thanks to your father. Ruin left the land long ago. Will you fight the rats, the vermin beneath our halls? Our enemies are dead. Don't be so quick to find others to take their place. Peace is what I want, and a mine hold of my own.'

'Fighting is what I am good at, cousin.' Snorri peered down the haft of his axe, all the way to the spike at the top. 'I can kill a grobi at a thousand yards with a crossbow, or at a hundred with a thrown axe. None are better than I with a hammer when used to crush skulls. In that, in the art of killing our enemies, my father and I are very alike.' He lowered the weapon and his eyes were heavy with grief when he met Morgrim's gaze. 'But he has already defeated them all and left no glory for me. I stand at his shoulder, nothing more than a caretaker who will sit upon a throne and rule a kingdom of dust.

'So when you ask why I want war, it is because of that. As a warrior I am great but as a prince of Karaz-a-Karak, I am nothing. At least before my father.'

Morgrim was stern, and a deep frown had settled upon his face. A small measure of respect for his cousin was lost.

'You are wrong about that. Very wrong, and I hope you learn the error of it, cousin.'

Grunting, unwilling to see Morgrim's pity or think about his father's shame, Snorri walked on.

'Ranuld Silverthumb is the most vaunted runelord of the Worlds Edge. If he says a doom is coming then we must prepare for it.' He thumped his chest, stuck out his pugnacious chin. 'Dragon slayer, I was so named. King because of it. *That* is a legacy I wish to inherit, not one of cowing to the elgi and the whims of other vassal lords.'

Morgrim fell silent, but followed. The old *zaki* had said many things during his casting.

One word stood out above the others.

Elgidum.

It meant *elfdoom.*

━ CHAPTER THREE ━

Shadows on the Dwarf Roads

MURDER WAS ALWAYS better conducted under moonlight. This night the moon was shaped like a sickle, curved and sharp like Sevekai's blade as he pulled it silently from the baldric around his waist. Unlike the moon, its silver gleam was dulled by magwort and edged with a verdant sheen of mandrake.

Fatal poisons, at least those that killed instantly, were a misuse of the assassin's art in Sevekai's opinion. Debilitate, agonise, petrify; these were his preferred tortures. Slaying a victim with such disregard was profligate, not when death inflicted upon others was something to be savoured.

Crouched with his shadowy companions behind a cluster of fallen rocks that had sheared from the looming mountainside, Sevekai considered something else which the moon was good for.

Stalking prey…

It was a bulky cart, high-sided and with a stout wooden roof to protect whatever was being ferried. Two stocky ponies pulled the wagon, its wheels broad and metal-banded to withstand the worst the dwarf roads had to offer.

In truth, the roads were well made. An army could march

across them and have no blisters, no sprains or injuries to speak of at the end of many miles. Dwarfs were builders, they made things to last.

Some things though, Sevekai knew, would not endure.

As the trundling wagon closed, four guards came into view. Like the driver, they were dwarfs with copper-banded beards and silver rings on their fingers. Fastened to a hook next to the driver hung a shuttered lantern that spilled just enough light to illuminate the road ahead. The dwarf had kept it low so as not to attract predators. Unfortunately, no manner of precaution could have prevented this particular predator crossing his path.

Sevekai took the driver for a merchant – his rings were gold and his armour ornamental. It consisted of little more than a breastplate and vambraces. Each of the guards wore helmets, one with a faceplate slid shut. This was the leader.

He would die first.

Heavy plate clad their bodies, with rounded pauldrons and a mail skirt to protect the thighs and knees. No gorget or coif. Sevekai assumed they'd removed them earlier in the journey. Perhaps it was the heat of the day, a desire for cool air on their necks instead of stinging sweat. So close to home, they had thought it a minor act of laxity.

Sevekai smiled, a cold and hollow thing, and silently told his warriors, *Aim for the neck.*

The hand gesture was swift, and heeded by all.

Most of the dwarfs carried axes. One, the leader, had a hammer that gave off a faint aura of enchantment. Sevekai was not a sorcerer, but he had some small affinity with magic. Some had remarked, his enemies in fact, that he was lucky. Not just average good fortune, but phenomenal, odds-defying luck. It had kept him alive, steered him from danger and heightened his senses. For a murderer, a hired blade whose trade was killing other people, it was an extremely useful trait to possess.

Other than the hand weapons, a crossbow with a satchel full of stubby quarrels sat within the merchant's easy reach. It was leant against the wooden back of the driver's seat with the lethal end pointing up. That was another error, and would increase the merchant's reaction time by precious seconds once the ambush was sprung.

Six dwarfs, three of them.

The odds were stacked high against the stunted little pigs.

Cloud crawling overhead like ink in dirty water obscured the moon and for a few seconds the road turned black as tar.

Sevekai rose, as silent as a whisper in a gale, his shrouded body dark against darkness. The sickle blade spun, fast and grey like a bat arrowing through fog, and lodged in the guard leader's eye-slit as the wagon hit a rock and jumped.

With a low grunt, the dead dwarf lost his grip on the side rail and pitched off the wagon. To the other guards, in what few breaths remained to them, it would have looked as if their fellow had fallen off.

'Ho!' Sevekai heard the merchant call, oblivious to the fact there was a black-clad killer arisen in his midst and but a few feet away. Hauling on the reins, the dwarf drew the wagon to a halt with a snort of protest from the mules.

That was another mistake.

In the time it took for the merchant to turn and ask one of the other guards what had happened, one of Sevekai's warriors had crossed the road. Like a funeral veil rippling beneath the wind, the warrior crept along the opposite side of the wagon and rammed his dagger up to the hilt in a guard's neck. Sevekai couldn't see the kill, his view was obstructed by the bulky wagon, but he knew how it would have played out.

Kaitar was a late addition to his band, but a deadly one.

Two guards remained. One had dismounted to see to his leader; the other looked straight through Sevekai as he searched for signs of ambush.

You have missed… all of them, swine.

Sevekai drew back his hood for this dwarf, let him see the red and bloody murder flaring brightly in his dagger-slit eyes.

The dwarf gasped, swore in his native tongue and drew his axe. One-handed because of the rail, he should have gone for his shield. It would have extended his life expectancy by three more seconds. That was the time it would have taken Sevekai to close the gap, draw his falchion and dispatch the dwarf with a low thrust to his heart.

Instead he threw his second blade, already clutched in a claw-like grip.

Bubbling froth erupted from the dwarf's gullet, staining his lips and beard a satisfying incarnadine red. He gurgled, dropped his axe and fell face first into the dirt.

The colour spewing from the dwarf's neck reminded Sevekai of a particularly fine wine he had once drunk in a lordling's manse in Clar Karond. Generous of the noble to share such a vintage, but then he was in no position to object given that his innards had become his *out-ards*. Hard to take umbrage when you're fighting to keep your entrails from spilling all over the floor.

The last guard fell to a quarrel in the neck. It sank into the dwarf's leathery flesh and fed a cocktail of nerve-shredding poison into his heart. Death was instantaneous but then Verigoth was an efficient if predictable killer.

That left the merchant who, in the brief seconds that had been afforded to him, had indeed reached and gripped the crossbow in his meaty fist.

Sevekai was upon him before the dwarf had drawn back the string.

'Should've kept it loaded,' he told the snarling pig in a barbed language the dwarf wouldn't understand. The message Sevekai conveyed through his eyes and posture was easy to translate, however.

You shall suffer.

He cut the dwarf beneath the armpit, a slender and insignificant wound to the naked eye.

After a few brief seconds during which the merchant's grubby little hands had constricted into useless claws and a veritable train of earthy expletives had spat from his mouth, the dwarf began to convulse.

Sudden paralysis in his legs ruined the dwarf's balance and he collapsed. Eyes bulging, veins thick like ropes in his cheeks and forehead, the dwarf gaped to shout.

Sevekai leapt on the dwarf like a cat pounces upon a

stricken mouse it has nearly tired of playing with. Before a single syllable could escape the lips, he cut off the beard and shoved it down the dwarf's throat. Then he stepped back to watch.

The dwarf bleated, of course he did, but they were small and pitiful sounds that would scarcely rouse a nearby elk, let alone bring aid of any value or concern. From somewhere in the low forest a raven shrieked, emulating a death scream the dwarf could not make.

'Even for a race like ours, you are cruel, Sevekai.'

'It's not cruelty, Kaitar,' Sevekai replied without averting his gaze from the convulsing dwarf merchant. 'It's simply death and the art of crafting it.'

Teeth clenched, upper body locked in rigor, choking on his own beard, the dwarf's organs would be liquefying about now. With a final shudder, a lurch of defiant limbs still protesting the inevitable, the dwarf slumped still.

Sevekai knew he had no soul, save for something cold and rimed with frost that inhabited his chest, and he regarded the dwarf pitilessly. Despite the artistic flourishes, this was simply a task he had been charged to perform. The theatrics were for the benefit of the others to remind them of his prowess as an artful killer.

Satisfied with the deed, he addressed the night: 'Leave no sign,' and the two assassins on the road stepped back as a slew of arrows thudded into the dwarf corpses.

Pine-shafted, flights woven from swan feather, the arrows were not typical of Naggaroth. Not at all.

When it was done, four more warriors dressed in similar black attire stepped into view.

Sevekai was stooping to retrieve his sickle blades, replacing them with elven arrow shafts, when Kaitar asked, 'And this will fool the dwarfs?'

'Of course, they won't bother to look for subterfuge. They *want* a fight, Kaitar,' Sevekai explained.

'What of the poisons?'

'Gone before the bodies are found.' Sevekai looked up as he punched the last arrow through the dwarf leader's eye. 'If you hear hooves, what do you think of?'

'Horses,' said the deep-voiced Verigoth, a smirk on his grey lips. Like the others, he'd descended from the ridge to appreciate the carnage.

Sevekai smiled, colder than a winter storm. 'And when you think of arrows?'

Now it was Kaitar's turn to smile. 'Asur.'

⤞ CHAPTER FOUR ⤝

What lies Above…

'IT'S AS MYSTERIOUS to me as it is to you, cousin.' Morgrim looked behind them, but saw only darkness. 'How far have we walked?' Taking off a leather gauntlet, he ran his hand along the wall of the tunnel and then licked his fingers. 'Tastes familiar.'

'Zaki,' said Snorri, using the Khazalid word for 'mad wandering dwarf'. During the long walk in the dark, his mood had improved and the dour silence between them ebbed until all was well again. Destiny, his to be specific, was still on the dwarf prince's mind, however. 'You are probably right, cousin. The old fool was likely senile.' He tilted his head, thinking. 'Then again, the words of a runelord are not easily ignored. Are we still lost?'

Pain flared in Snorri's jaw. He grimaced, staggered by a sudden blow. Glaring at his cousin, he asked, 'What was that for?'

Morgrim was big, even for a dwarf. His father was bulky too, from a lifetime spent in the mines. Broad of shoulder, stout of chest and back, he had a chin like an anvil and a head like a mattock. Snorri was leaner, though still muscled, and surrendered half a foot in height to his cousin.

Bare-knuckled, strength for strength he would not prevail against him.

'It was either that or I hit you with the hammer,' said Morgrim.

'I'm just glad you didn't butt me with that bloody helmet of yours.' Snorri rubbed at his chin, wincing at the slowly swelling bruise. 'Take my bleeding eye out with one of those horns. Big buggers. What was it, a stag?'

'Beastman. Much larger than a stag, cousin.' Morgrim smacked his fist into his palm. 'Are you done talking about destiny, or do you need some more sense knocking into you?'

Snorri held up his half-hand; the bandage was dark crimson but the wound had clotted. He slowly nodded.

'Me one-handed, weakened from blood loss and being almost buried alive... Reckon you'd have a decent chance of beating me.'

'Aye,' said Morgrim, unconvinced it would be any sort of contest, and slapped his hand against the wall. 'See this?'

Snorri did.

'I know what stone is, cousin.'

Morgrim glowered at him. 'Use your eyes, *wattock*. I know this place. We are no longer lost.'

Snorri frowned, and regarded their surroundings.

'How can that be? We've not long been...' His voice tailed off, claimed by the darkness which was lessening by the second. Ahead, the crackle of brazier fire resolved on a breeze redolent of shallow earth and the upper world.

A dwarf's nose can discern much in the subterranean depths. He can tell the difference between the deep earth where he makes his hold, that which harbours veins of gold or precious minerals, and shallow earth, the loamy soil best for crops and farming. Unless he is one of the *skarrenawi*, those who 'live under sky', a dwarf has no interest in such things, but he knows earth and can tell it apart.

Other smells, carried by the breeze, drifted into being. There was grass, leaf, stone dried by the sun, the scent of animals and warm water.

Morgrim nodded as he saw the recognition in his cousin's expression. 'It's the *Rorganzbar*.'

'Cannot be,' said Snorri. No matter how hard he stared at the way they had come, he couldn't find the doorway through which they had entered the tunnel. 'We were far from the northern gate.'

'During the fight, we could have got turned around?'

Snorri raised an eyebrow, dubiously. 'And ended up over fifty miles in the wrong direction? Are you sure that helmet of yours didn't take a heavier hit when the cave collapsed? Perhaps you hurt your fist on my jaw and the pain of it has addled your mind?'

'How else would you explain it?'

Taking a last glance at the darkness behind them and the firelit shadows now glowing ahead, Snorri said, 'I cannot.'

The Rorganzbar was the name of the northern gates that fed into the upper world from the Ungdrin Ankor. Such passageways were falling out of use, for dwarfs had little need for what lived above ground, but they were fashioned anyway during times when trading with other races was more common. Elves thronged the Old World now, returned after a war, some matter of kinstrife the dwarfs did not really understand. So too did the skarrenawi, the dwarfs of the hills who had chosen to eschew solid earth and stone for the promise of sky and the warmth of the sun. *Elgongi* some mountain dwarfs called them, 'elf-friends'.

It was meant as an insult.

As they reached a vast stone gateway, the truth of where they were could not be denied. Runic script along the tall, square pillars of the northern gate confirmed Morgrim's suspicions.

'*Rorganzbar,*' read Snorri, hands against his hips. 'Well, I'll be buggered.'

NUMENOS HAILED THEM with a shout. Gifted with tongues, the black-clad warrior made it sound like the screech of a crow.

Sevekai found the scout at the summit of the ridge, crouched low in his chosen rookery. He was gesturing for them to climb up and meet him.

A quick glance around at the ambush site revealed that all was in readiness. Blades and quarrels had been gathered, corpses left with asur arrows in their bellies instead. Stowing his own weapons, Sevekai ran up the craggy ridge in long, loping strides. The others followed silently in his wake.

As he crested the rise, he went low and hunkered down behind a cluster of fallen rocks. Numenos was waiting for him, the slit of his mouth curved upwards like a dagger.

'Fresh meat,' he hissed, and pointed higher up the mountainside, through a gap in a patch of sparse forest, where a second pathway wended above the one where they had laid their ambush.

Two walkers, dwarfs and nobles judging by their attire. They were armed, but looked as if they had already been in a fight, and they were alone.

Killing merchants in cold blood was one thing, murdering the sons of some thane or king was another entirely. It went against orders, and Sevekai was nothing if not a dutiful soldier.

'Tempting, but too risky. The dwarfs will look more closely at their deaths.'

The black-clad warriors were peeling away from the summit of the ridge, back into the night, when Kaitar crept up behind Sevekai and gripped his shoulder. It was light, like a breath of wind brushing against him at first, but with a fearsome strength.

Sevekai snarled but his wrath died in his throat when he looked into Kaitar's eyes. They were fathomless black, as deep pits of cruelty as he'd ever seen.

'Two scalps like that are worth a hundred wagons,' he purred without insistence, like he was stating an irrefutable fact.

Despite his earlier misgivings, Sevekai could see the sense in his words and the eagerness for spilling more blood in his followers. He wondered briefly if Kaitar was trying to usurp his leadership but could see no concealed blade, no desire for command in his eyes. He only exuded a frightful ennui, something dark and shrivelled that Sevekai couldn't reach.

He turned to Numenos. 'How many more asur shafts remain?'

'Enough to stick two stunted pigs.'

Sevekai held his gaze then nodded. Licking the dryness from his lips, moistening his throat so his voice wouldn't catch, he said to Kaitar, 'We kill the nobles.'

FASHIONED OF HEAVY stone, the door to the Rorganzbar needed at least two dwarfs to push it. From the outside it was hard to find, even for those looking for it. Crafted in such a way that it blended in with its surroundings, only a dwarf who knew the exact place and correct height at which to stand could ever hope to find the way into the underdeep through the Rorganzbar.

Snow, light for the time of year, dappled the crags and grassy heaths as the dwarfs stepped outside. The door closed behind them, shut by its own weight in a clever piece of dwarf engineering.

Before them, a long and narrow path that wound around the foothills of the mountains. Above, the towering peaks of the Worlds Edge so high they were lost in thick cloud. Amongst them was Karaz-a-Karak, hold hall of the High King and their home.

It would be a long walk back.

'See that crag over there?' Morgrim pointed. 'The one shaped like a tooth?'

Snorri nodded, mastering a sense of agoraphobia washing over him. A lifetime spent living under the earth where there was no sky apart from the vaulted chambers of the ancestors and the great hold halls had bred a fear of the upper world and all its vastness.

'I see it, cousin,' he gasped, not used to the crispness of the air.

'That's Karak Varn, and in that deep depression where the mountains and hills thin…' He gestured again. Snorri nodded. 'Black Water,' said Morgrim. 'We head south from here, and try to pick up the Silk Road then the Dwarf Road down from Black Fire Pass. Follow it all the way back to hearth and hold.'

'Where I hope there's meat and beer waiting for us and a fire to warm my feet.' Snorri laughed, as the two began to walk. 'You have been ranging with Furgil, I see.'

Thane of pathfinders, Furgil knew the roads and byways of the overground world well, better than any in Karaz-a-Karak. An expert tracker, he was seldom below the earth and spent much of his time under sky instead.

'You'd do well to heed some of his wisdom, cousin.'

Snorri shrugged. 'For a skarrenawi, he is not so bad, I suppose. But what need have I for trees and sky?' He kept his eyes down on the road, on the earth, but his gaze drifted.

Hills undulated below, covered with thick forests of fir and pine, hardy even in winter. Elk and goats watched the passage of the dwarfs nervously from shadowed arbours and brush-choked glades. Deep within the forest, near to the low road, a crow cawed. This close to the mountain there were tors, thickly veiled with rock. Throughout the ages, much of the mountainside had slipped, creating crag-toothed valleys and boulder-strewn fields.

Snorri was glad to feel the solidity of the road underfoot. Strong and flat, it wended around the mountain out of respect. By contrast, the lands beyond it were wild and ragged. This was the domain of the skarrenawi, dwarfs who had left the mountain long ago to find fortune and sovereignty amongst the foothills. Their gilded cities had a dwarf aesthetic. Squat structures of stone and petrified wutroth, resilient to the elements and fortified against attack from beasts and urk or grobi, they had stood for centuries. Outposts dotted the lands of the low hills and plains but the larger cities were few. Kazad Kro was chief amongst them but there was also Kazad Mingol and Kagaz Thar.

Three kings were there of the skarrenawi, but Snorri's father believed there would be more before the century was out.

In truth, the prince knew little more about them. His father had often remarked on how numerous the skarrenawi had become, of their flourishing trade with elves and men from distant lands he did not remember the names of. They were distinctly un-dwarfish names and so Snorri had no interest in them.

'Have you ever visited the hill forts?' asked Morgrim, following Snorri's gaze.

'Once. My father brought me to a council with Skarnag Grum, though I think he just wanted to remind the fat noble of who was High King. Two hundred hearthguard and retainers travelled with us and father was carried upon his throne.'

'Are they like us?' Morgrim asked. Though he knew Furgil, he had never been to the hill forts.

'They are dawi... of a fashion. Their skin is lighter and softer. Fairer haired, too, and with shorter beards, but they are decent forgesmiths and can drink almost as well as a proper hall-dweller. Though I cannot fathom why any son of Grungni would prefer sky over earth. It is unnatural.'

'Perhaps they will soon outnumber the dawi of the mountains and establish more forts.'

'Ha!' Snorri shook his head ruefully. 'Between the elgi and the skarrenawi, the lands beyond the Worlds Edge will be thronged. It already feels crowded as it is.'

Morgrim nodded, 'I know many amongst the clans, my father included, who think the elgi have encroached too far into the empire. Some believe we would be better–'

'*Hsst!*' Snorri held up a clenched fist. He stooped, looking up into the sky where the clouds conspired to obscure his view. Thunderheads were boiling and a low rumble echoed dully above them.

'''Tis a storm, nothing more.'

'Nah, there is something else...' His eyes narrowed and he turned his ear to listen. 'Can't you hear it, a smack of something hitting air?' He released his axe, and met Morgrim's questioning gaze. 'Wings, cousin.'

Morgrim's brow furrowed. He heard it too.

'Something big...'

'And strong enough to defy the wind.'

Unslinging his hammer, Morgrim searched the sky but the growing storm was thick.

'Perhaps old Silverthumb was right about that drakk.'

Snorri scowled. 'Unless dwarfs have learned to fly, we need to leave the road. Now.'

⟜ CHAPTER FIVE ⟞

Sky Ship

THE GREAT ROCK *Durazon* commanded an unparalleled view over the lands neighbouring Barak Varr. Below the flanks of the mountain, several miles down, tributaries ran like veins of crystal, bleeding from the nearby Black Gulf in shimmering ribbons of azure. They fed valleys and farm-land, filled the wells of the lower deeps and birthed three mighty water lanes – Blood River, Howling River and Skull River.

Heglan Copperfist, so named for his father who had dis-covered a vast seam of the ore and made his fortune trading it with the other clans, had sailed all three rivers. An engi-neer, Heglan had constructed the *grubark* he used to ply these waters himself and travelled as far as Karak Varn and Black Water.

Now his mind was occupied by an entirely different enterprise, one that forced his gaze upwards.

Great birds of prey circled in a platinum sky. Screech hawks and crag eagles, the majestic griffon vultures or talon owls, the red condor or the diminutive flocks of peak falcons, Heglan knew them all by size and appearance. Amongst his studies in engineering and the lessons of his guildmasters was an interest in ornithology. Some in the guild believed it to be an unhealthy one.

For as long as he could remember, ever since he was a beardling and his grandfather Dammin had taken him to look out at the wider world from the Durazon, Heglan had believed a ship could be made to fly. Not by growing wings or some such aberration, but by sailing the clouds.

Here, many hundreds of feet up in the high peaks, he would do just that.

Few dwarfs ventured onto the Durazon. Though it was over a hundred paces across, it ended in a crag which led to a sheer, vertiginous drop that for a people who lived most or all of their lives underground was uncomfortable. Not so for Heglan; he relished the sense of freedom he felt standing on this rock that jutted from the flanks of the Sea Hold.

'Sun stone' was its literal name and an apt one at that. The rock was wide and flat, perfect for what Heglan needed, and turned gold in summer when the sun was high and pierced the cloud veil. Winter was ending and the rising sun was obscured by storms rolling in from the south-west. Better days for flying would certainly come but with the guild's patience almost exhausted, Heglan had no choice but to demonstrate his invention now. Frowning at the spreading path of darkness creeping towards them, he just hoped the weather would hold.

From the lofty heavens and the avian beasts he so envied, Heglan's eyes were drawn downwards.

Arcing from peak to peak, resolute against the rigours of weather and war, were the skyroads. It was whilst crossing the passage from Barak Varr to Karak Drazh that inspiration first struck like a hammer swung by Grungni himself. Stone-clad bands that crossed the mountains through belts of thickening cloud and raucous gales, the skyroads had stood for thousands of years. Ever since the earliest days of the dwarf empire these lofty conduits had enabled those brave enough or surefooted enough to traverse between the holds.

Few did, because most believed a dwarf's place was below the earth. Unlike the underway, however, the skyroads were not the lair of monsters. Great eagles and other flying beasts were a menace but stocky watchtowers punctuating the long spans provided warning and protection. Trolls and greenskins couldn't touch these vaulted pathways.

Some engineers had even built ships to travel across them, great propeller-driven longboats that carried cargo and dwarfs by the score. Wind shear made widespread use of these 'sky ships' untenable as many had been torn off the skyroads in a strong gale and dashed on the ground far below. But despite its dangers, upon such a bridge a dwarf could literally walk the skies.

For Heglan it was as close as he could come to doing just that.

Until today.

'Quite a sight, aren't they?' said Nadri, breathing deep as he regarded the monolithic skyroads.

'Aye, they most certainly are, brother.'

'I have heard standing upon them a dwarf can see the entire kingdom, from Karak Azgal in the south to Karak Ungor in the north.'

Like his brother, Heglan inhaled a full breath of the high mountain air and closed his eyes, remembering.

'Indeed he can, but such a magnificent vista will pale compared to what I have in mind.'

Nadri clapped Heglan on the shoulder.

'Ever with your head in the clouds, eh, Heg?'

Unlike his brother, who wore a leather apron with a belt of tools fastened around his ample waist, Nadri was more finely attired as befitted a merchant guildmaster. His tunic was gilded and he wore a small travelling cloak fashioned from the very best *hruk* wool of the mountains. His leather boots were supple and tan. The many rings upon his fingers shone in the occluded winter sun.

Nadri stroked his ruddy beard. It was well preened and beautifully studded with silver ingots that bound up locks of his hair.

'Father would have been so very proud,' he said, and gripped Heglan's shoulder a little tighter.

Lodri Copperfist was dead, slain by urk over a decade ago

during one of the High King's purges of the mountains. Grief had brought his only sons closer, despite the very different paths they had taken.

'He loved the skyroads, Nadri. Just like grandfather.' Heglan's beard was unkempt, more brown than red and tied together at the end with a leather thong. Most casual observers would not think them kin, but the bond between the siblings was stronger than gromril.

For a moment, Heglan was overtaken by a wistful mood. In his mind's eye, he soared through the heavens with the wind on his face, buffeting his beard as he flew. Birds arced and pinwheeled beside him, the sense of freedom overwhelming...

Burgrik Strombak brought him back to the ground with a stamp of his foot.

'Earth is where dwarfs are meant to be,' he said, a pipe stewing between clenched teeth. 'Under it or over it, but never flying above it.'

The engineer guildmaster cut a formidable figure. Two mattock-like fists pressed against his broad waist and a thick leather belt filled with tools crossed his slab chest. Strombak knew engines like no other dwarf of Barak Varr. Most of the sea wall defences on the side of the hold that faced the Black Gulf were his design. A circular glass lens sat snug in his left eye, which he used to scrutinise the young engineer before him.

'What about the sea, master?' asked Heglan, bowing deferentially. 'Dawi can sail the seas too, can they not?'

'You ask me that question in a Sea Hold. Have you hit your head, Heglan Copperfist?'

Heglan bowed again, deeper this time. 'I only meant that the horizons of our race have broadened before and will again.'

Scowling, Strombak leaned in close. 'You are fortunate King Brynnoth can see a military use for this machinery of yours.'

Heglan shook his head. 'No, master. Its intended use is for trade, prosperity and peace, not as an engine of war.'

'We'll see.'

Strombak sniffed contemptuously and stomped over to where Heglan's creation was docked. It had taken sixteen mules and twice as many journeymen to get it up the Merman Pass and onto the Durazon.

It was a ship, a vessel of dark lacquered wood and gilded trim. Incongruous as it was, sitting on the mountain plateau atop a curved ramp, the small wheels attached to its hull arrested by stout wooden braces, it was still magnificent. If he thought so, Strombak did not give any indication.

'And sea is not air, though, is it,' grumbled the old engineer, chewing on his pipe and feeling the smoothness of the wooden hull beneath his grizzled fingers. 'Wood is stout,' he said, 'that is something at least.'

As well as the braces against its wheels, the ship was also lashed to iron rings driven deep into the rock so it wouldn't sway in the wind. A small vessel, it could take five passengers including its captain, but had a hold that would accommodate twice that again in wares for trade. Presently, twenty casks of *grog* sat in the ship's belly from the brewmaster's guild, bound for Zhufbar.

Spry for an old dwarf, Strombak clambered up the ramp and tugged on the rigging.

'Strong rope,' he mumbled. 'Might hold in a decent gale.'

Strombak pulled out the pipe and chewed his beard. It was black with soot from his workshops and resembled a fork in the way the strands of it were parted by bronze cogs and screws. A leather skullcap covered his bald pate, which he revealed when he removed the cap to wipe his sweating brow. Runes of engineering, telemetries and trajectories, parabolic equations and yet more esoteric markings lined his skull in knot-worked strands.

He paced the length of the ship, appraising its rudder and sneering at the absence of sweeps. Sails jutted horizontally from the sides and with the effigy of a dragon carved into the prow it had the appearance of some alate predator, albeit one fashioned from wood and metal.

Sat astern was a small tower, where its captain was already installed and at the wheel. Three large windmills surmounted masts that stuck out from the deck, angled slightly so as not to be perpendicular to the ground.

'Never have I seen a more awkward-looking ship,' Strombak muttered. He turned away, as if he'd seen enough, and addressed Heglan. 'You'd best get on with it. Guilders are waiting.'

Behind the engineer guildmaster were three other dwarfs of the engineers' guild, the high thane of Barak Varr himself and his retainers, and a contingent from the merchants' guild who had funded the enterprise. Every one of the assembled nobles and guilders, some thirty-odd dwarfs, was silent.

Nadri stepped back and joined his fellow guilders.

Heglan licked his lips to moisten them. He glanced at the ship's captain to ascertain his readiness. A vague nod didn't do much for Heglan's confidence at that moment.

'*Tromm*,' he uttered, crafting a deep bow to the lords as he gave the traditional dwarf greeting for veneration of one's betters and elders. 'High Thane,' he added, rising but turning to the entire assembly. 'With your permission, Lord Onkmarr.'

The high thane nodded dourly.

King Brynnoth was away in Karaz-a-Karak attending a council of the High King and had left Onkmarr in charge as regent until his return. Unlike Brynnoth, who had a ribald manner and was as gregarious as any king of the dwarf realm, Onkmarr always seemed slightly put upon. Perhaps it was the fearsome rinn he had taken as his wife. Certainly, his posture was more stooped, his humour more acerbic, ever since he had made a union with her.

Premature age lines furrowing on his brow like cracks in weathered rock, Onkmarr looked as if he wanted nothing more than to return to his hall and his business. Especially if that business was sitting by his fire, seeing to the affairs of the hold and staying out of his wife's way. With the exception of Nadri, the entire assembly appeared eager to get Heglan's demonstration over with.

'Go on, Copperfist,' grumbled Strombak, 'make your oaths and hope they're good ones.'

Heglan nodded, clearing his throat to speak.

'Thanes and masters of Barak Varr, vaunted guilders, we stand on the precipice of a momentous discovery. Ever have the dawi been lords of the earth–' nods and muted grunts of approval greeted this proclamation, '–and the clans of Barak Varr are lords of the sea too.' This brought further bouts of agreements and much chest puffing, especially amongst the engineers. 'But now, with this innovation,' a word that elicited grumbles of disapproval and reproachful glances, 'we can be lords of the sky too.'

Heglan stepped back so the attention of the dwarf nobles was on the ship. He whispered behind his hand to the captain.

'Turn the propellers…'

Having missed his cue, the dwarf in the tower pulled at some levers and the three windmills attached to the masts began to rotate.

'Skryzan-harbark,' Heglan declared. 'The first ever dawi airship!'

Six burly dwarf journeymen in short sleeves and leather aprons were on standby next to ropes that fed to the braces impeding the vessel's wheels. Another two stood ready with axes to cut the lashed sails.

At a sign from Heglan, the sails were freed and the wooden stops removed.

Creaking wood made him wince as the ramp took the weight of the ship and it rolled onto the curve. Propellers were beating furiously now as the captain tested the rudder experimentally as he pitched towards the edge of the cliff.

It got a decent run up, needing to gather speed before the Durazon ended and all that sat beneath the ship was air.

'Grungni, I beseech you…' muttered Heglan, hiding his fervent oath from the other dwarfs as the airship plunged off the end of the ramp at pace. It rolled on for almost fifty feet, wheels spinning, propellers turning like mad. And with sails unfurled, Heglan's creation launched off the edge of the rock and soared like an arrow.

He fought the urge to shout for joy, content to clench a fist in triumph at the skryzan-harbark's inaugural flight instead.

Surprised but approving mutterings issued from the throng of guilders and nobles in a rumbling susurrus of speech as they beheld the flying ship.

'Valaya's golden cups, lad,' breathed Strombak, unable to hide the fact he was impressed. 'I did not think you would do it. The ship is small, but if you can get this to work we can enlarge it.'

Bowing his head, Heglan's voice was low and deferential at such high praise. 'Tromm, my master. This is just a trial vessel. I have plans for bigger versions.'

Clapping the young engineer on the shoulder, Strombak stepped back to discuss the incredible ship with his fellow guilders.

Disengaging himself from the other merchants, Nadri joined his brother and slapped him heartily on the back. 'It is a marvel, Heg, a true wonder to help usher in a prosperous new age.'

Heglan barely heard – he was watching the realisation of a dream.

'See how the sails billow and catch the wind?' he said. 'And the way it achieves loft and forward motion.'

'It is...' Nadri's smile turned into a frown, '...listing, brother.'

At the same time a look of horror was slowly creeping its way onto Heglan's face.

A heavy gust of wind, driven hard and fast through the peaks, pitched the airship to one side. The sails bulged like an overfull bladder, straining against the rigging, and the dragon prow listed awkwardly as if the ship was drunk on too much grog.

'*Compensate, compensate...*' Heglan urged the captain, who was lost from view but evidently struggling at the controls.

Ugly and portentous, the sound of snapping rigging resolved on the breeze and a deep crack fed down one of the masts. The ship began to turn on its axis, pulled and buffeted by the wind.

'Grimnir's hairy arse, no...' Heglan could see the danger before it unfolded fully but was powerless to avert it. He would have run to the edge of the Durazon in the vain hope that his proximity to the ship would somehow guarantee its continued flight if Nadri hadn't held him back.

Buoyed on the harsh thermals whipping up from below, slewed by the biting wind, the ship lurched. The dragon bit upwards, briefly righting itself before yawing dangerously the other way. Pulled back and forth at the whim of the elements, there was nothing the captain or Heglan could do. With a loud crack, made louder and more resonant as it echoed around the peaks, one of the masts snapped. It split in half and speared the deck, releasing a fountain of dark beer from the grog in the hold. Like a lance in the belly of a beast, the skryzan-harbark was wounded. At the same time, one of its sails sheared in half, plucked from its bearings and scattered like sackcloth on the wind.

'Girth of Grungni, no.'

But all the sworn oaths of the dwarf ancestors couldn't stop the encroaching storm from ripping Heglan's dreams apart. Utterly helpless in his brother's arms, all he could do was watch. Like a pugilist that had taken too many licks, the vessel was thrown about and battered by the storm. Slowly the airship began to lose height and sank deeper and deeper into the valleys below. Cloud partly obscured it but soon parted to reveal crags, encroaching from the lower peaks and jutting spurs of rock. Bitterly, Heglan wished he had the foresight to launch the skryzan-harbark over the sea-facing aspect of the hold. Pitching into the waters of the Black Gulf, the vessel could be rescued. Hitting one of the lower peaks or the hard earth of the plains, it would be smashed to splinters.

Below the jagged fingers of rock, the thick spires of stone that could impale the airship and rip it right in half as it fell, were boulder-strewn heaths. Scattered farms dotted the landscape but it was largely barren aside from old burial mounds and trickle-thin streams. Plummeting now, loft decreasing more swiftly with each passing moment, but no longer spinning, the airship slipped through the forest of crags and spires.

Only earth awaited it, packed tight and resilient by the winter. It would be like hitting the solid rock of the mountainside.

Heglan cursed again. Foolish sentiment had got in the way of prudence. Heart ruling the head, it was a mistake he had made before. Nostalgia to release the airship from the Durazon and honour his grandfather Dammin's memory had left him undone.

He wept openly at the thought, but could not take his eyes off the vessel he had so doomed. Striking the edge of the last crag, just the smallest of nicks, the hull was torn open in an explosion of splintering wood.

Every blow brought a wince to Heglan's tear-streaked face.

'Valaya, please be merciful...'

But the ancestor goddess of healing was not listening. Her gaze, deep within the earth, did not extend to sky and cloud. Thunder and storm were Grimnir's domain, and he was ever wrathful.

Entangled with the rigging, the other sails ripped open and dragged much of the hull with them. Deciding upon discretion rather than valour, the dwarf captain at the wheel leapt from the tower and hit the ground a few seconds before the stricken vessel. He landed with a heavy bump, but otherwise survived unscathed.

The same could not be said for the skryzan-harbark.

Prow first, the airship ploughed an ugly furrow into a rugged patch of farmland. Its proud dragon head smashed upon impact, split down its skull as if killed by some mythical dragon slayer. The hull broke apart like a barrel divested of its bands, and the ship's three masts jutted at obscure angles like broken fingers.

Bruised, in both pride and rump, the dwarf captain looked down at the wreckage that had finally settled in the valley and then up at the Durazon. Too far to see anything, he limped off furtively.

Heglan's wrath almost overflowed. He hoped the dwarf below would feel its heat as he looked on disconsolately.

Impelled by what was left of their perpetual motion, two of the propellers still spun. The rudder flapped like a dead fish, hanging on by one of its hinges, the stern jutting up in the air in an undignified fashion.

Free of Nadri's grip, Heglan sank to his knees and held his face in his hands.

'I am finished,' he breathed, letting his fingers trawl down his cheeks, pulling at his beard in anguish.

'*Dreng tromm*,' muttered Nadri, shaking his head. 'I am sorry, brother. I really thought it would work.'

'It should have worked, but I didn't take into account the wind shear, the vagaries of weather or that wazzock, Dungni.'

Adding insult to already stinging injury, the grog from the sundered hold began to leak through the jagged gashes in the wood. It reminded Heglan of blood. His magnificent machine was dead, his dream was dead, so too his tenure as an engineer of Barak Varr.

Strombak was not kind with his reproach as he stomped over to him.

'Gather it up, all of it,' he growled under his breath. 'You have disgraced this guild with your invention and your enterprise. Such things are not for dawi! Tradition, solidity, dependability, that's what we strive for.'

Heglan begged. 'Master, I... Perhaps if–'

'If? If! There is no "if". Dawi do not fly. We live under earth and stone. Do not tread in the same shameful footsteps as your grandfather. Dammin was thrown out of the guild, or is your memory so short that you've forgotten? Keen to endure the Trouser Legs Ritual too are you, Heglan son of Lodri?'

The rest of the assembly was leaving, chuntering about the wilfulness of youth and foolhardy beardlings. First to go was the high thane, already descending the Merman Pass on his palanquin-shield. He left without word or ceremony, pleased to leave the draughty plateau no doubt and enjoy the fire in the hearth of his hold hall.

Unable to rise from his knees, Heglan answered Strombak with his head bowed, 'No, master. I only wish to be an engineer of the guild. I am a maker, a craftsman. Please don't take that from me.'

The scowl on Strombak's face could have been chiselled on, engraved much like the runes on his tools, but it softened briefly before Heglan's contrition.

'You're not without skill, Heglan. A decent engineer, aye. But you're wayward, lad.' He gestured to the sky, 'Head up in the clouds when it should be here–' he stamped his boot upon the rock, '–in the earth. We're not birds or elgi, we're dawi. Sons of Grungni, stone and steel. You'd do well to remember that. Not like your grandfather. He *was* gifted–' Strombak's voice became rueful, '–but he squandered it on foolishness and invention.'

Heglan remained silent throughout his chastisement. Strombak left a long pause to glare at him, measuring him as he would a windlass, crank or a mechanism, to see if what he was saying was sinking in. He grumbled something inaudible, an expression not a word, then sighed deeply.

'Another misstep and you'll be cast out, sworn to secrecy about all you know of our craft.' Jabbing a leathery finger at Heglan, he said, 'Change your ways or change your profession! Barrel makers and hruk shearers are always looking for guilders. Now,' he added, drawing in a long breath that flared his nostrils, 'gather up that mess and use it to fashion something that works, something tried and tested. Tradition, not progression, lad – *that* is the dawi way.'

Heglan nodded – there was little else he could do – and was left alone with Nadri.

On the Durazon, the winter sun was dying as the storm from the southern peaks eclipsed it. Black clouds were gathering, billowing like wool across the sky and full with the promise of thunder.

Wearily, the engineer picked himself up. It felt as if he'd been beaten by a mob of urk.

'Bloody Dungni, son of Thok!' he spat, his shame giving way to anger. If his glare could kill then the dwarf captain sloping back towards the outer gate of the hold would have died at once. 'Drunken bloody *bozdok*. The clod handles a ship like a grobi grabbing at a hruk. Grungni's arse, I'll see this lodged with the reckoners.'

Nadri looked on grimly, at Dungni and the wreck scattered like kindling across the lowland.

'Stoke that furnace, brother. A dawi without fire in his gut is no dawi at all,' he said, and whistled at the devastation. 'Not much to salvage?'

'Ruined, brother,' said Heglan his voice barely louder than a whisper. 'There is nothing left. Nothing.' He seemed to sag, sinking lower than when he was on his knees. 'Bugger.'

A muted cough broke the brief silence that had fallen between them. Nadri turned at the thinly veiled signal.

'Krondi?' he said, addressing one of the merchants who had also remained behind but who was anonymously waiting at the gate to Merman Pass.

'My thane.' Krondi bowed deeply. He was a grizzled dwarf, who had seen much battle in the wars of the High King against the urk. Fair-bearded, he never really fit into the mould of a merchant but had been part of the guild for almost a decade. 'We are expected in Zhufbar in just over two weeks.'

'Aye,' said Nadri, 'and a stop to make at Karaz-a-Karak beforehand. I am well aware of our commitments, Krondi.'

Krondi bowed. 'Of course, my thane.'

Nadri narrowed his eyes at the other merchant. 'Is our passenger ready to travel?'

'He is. Our wagons stand ready to depart at your word.'

Nadri looked down at the wreck in the valley again. 'Then it would not do to keep him waiting,' he said to himself beneath his breath before regarding Krondi again. 'Ride on ahead and pass on my assurances to the king's reckoners that he'll get what he's owed. Gildtongue has never reneged on a bond of trade, tell them.'

Though Nadri's family name was Copperfist, he was known as 'Gildtongue' by his fellows in the merchant guild on account that his every word turned to gold. So successful was he as a trader that he had holdings and wealth that some kings would envy. Of course, in Karaz-a-Karak the hoard of any merchant would always be bettered by the High King.

'I need you to leave me two carts with mules and drivers, Krondi.'

Krondi bowed again and left down the Merman Pass without further word.

'You risk much by not making full delivery, brother,' said Heglan. 'Don't let my failure drag you down.'

'Don't be a wazzock, Heg. By Valaya's golden cups, I'm helping you pick up the pieces of your ship. There is no argument to be had.'

Heglan looked about to protest, but there would be no changing Nadri's mind and so he capitulated. He cast a final glance at the wreckage, the vessel into which he had poured his craft, his sweat and his heart.

'I could have made it fly,' he uttered, the strength of his voice stolen by the wind.

Nadri tried to be consoling. 'You did, brother.'

'That wasn't flight, it was a slow fall.'

'Don't be too disheartened, Heg. At least you are still of the guild.' Nadri was heading towards Merman Gate. From there, they'd travel the winding pass all the way to the upper hold gate, just above the first deep.

Heglan waited until Nadri had passed under the Merman Gate and was out of earshot.

'I *will* make it fly, brother,' he said beneath his breath. 'For Dammin and Lodri Copperfist, I shall do it.'

Heglan and Nadri were already back inside the hold, through the fastness wall and more than halfway down Merman Pass when a bell tolled. It was a warning signal from the sea wall at the other side of Barak Varr.

THROUGH THE GLASS lens the waters of the Black Gulf undulated like a desert of obsidian. Tiny breakers, errant spumes of white foam, exposed the lie of that misperception. In the storm darkness it appeared endless, stretching to an infinite horizon. In truth, it was vast and the Sea Hold of Barak Varr was its only bastion-port.

A flotilla of *ghazan-harbarks*, six in all, plied the gulf. A signal had roused them and together they looked for enemies.

Nugdrinn Hammerfoot perched on the prow of one of the ships, and scoured a small stretch of the Black Gulf that was lapping at the flanks of the Sea Hold. He had a brass telescope pressed to his left eye and peered hard through the lens. Three beacons were lit in the watchtowers, which meant three dwarfs had seen something approaching the gate. A warning bell was tolling, warring with the persistent ringing in the captain's ears, but thus far the horns had stayed silent.

Cessation of the bell and the clarion of horns meant danger approached and the many defences of the sea wall would be levelled at the intruders. Batteries of ballistae and mangonels stood sentry upon the wall, as well as a hefty garrison of Barak Varr quarrellers. If the ghazan-harbarks were the hunters then the warriors on the sea wall would be the spear to slay whatever predator was lurking in the darkness beyond their lanterns.

'Bori, bring the lamp forwards,' he said, one meaty fist wrapped around a length of rope to steady him, one clutching the telescope to his remaining eye. The other was patched, a small oval of leather studded with the ancestor badge of Grungni.

O'er earth and sea, the great miner sees all, Nugdrinn would often say and tap his eye-patch. In other words, just because he only had one eye didn't mean he wasn't watching. 'Shine it here, lad.' He pointed with the telescope. 'Here. Quickly now.'

Nugdrinn had been a sailor all of his life. Born and raised in Barak Varr, there was no ship he could not sail, no ocean he dared not face. Unlike many dwarfs, even those of the Sea Hold, he was at peace with a stout hull and the waves beneath him, so whilst on the gulf his instincts could not be more honed. They were telling him something was out there, lurking in the dark.

Nugdrinn wanted to know what it was.

Lantern light washed over the water, casting it in ruddy orange. It was as if a fire was burning beneath the waves, just about to emerge and swathe the Black Gulf in conflagration.

Beasts lurked in the deeps, way down in the cold ocean darkness. Tales abounded of tentacled kraken and vicious megaladon, the dread black leviathan and the unearthly Triton. Such stories were spun by drunken sailors looking to enhance their reputation or angling for a pint of grog at the listener's expense, but Nugdrinn knew first hand there was some truth to them.

Out in the deep ocean he had seen… *shadows* lurking just beneath the waves, too vast and grotesque to be some mundane predator. Issuing from miles below, he had heard the call of beasts, abyssal deep and full of malice.

One moonless night, many years ago in the waters of the far north, he had witnessed the hide of some gargantuan beast slowly disappearing beneath the waves. Returning from Kraka Drak and the snow-clad fastness of the Norse dwarfs, the holds of their three grubarks brimming with the gold of the northern huscarl-king, Nugdrinn had glimpsed the monster from a distance. By the time he had the telescope to his eye, the beast had sunk beneath the water but several sundered ships were left in its wake.

It was a chill night. Frost clung to the deck, resolved as a ghostly pale mist in the captain's breath. Ice cracked as the dwarfs' ships ploughed through it. Nugdrinn's teeth chattered and not just from the abominable cold. It took several minutes to find the courage to sail close enough to the scene of devastation to look for survivors. It took less time for them to discover there were no crewmen amongst the broken hulks. Only blood remained, and carnage.

Stooping to hook a broken piece of debris that carried the clan's sigil so he might bring word of their demise to their kin, Nugdrinn saw a great blackness through the gaps in the floating remains of the ship. Too late, he recoiled but by then the beast had scented his fear. It came crashing out of the waves stinking of old blood and the cold dank of death. With its single gelatinous eye, the beast fixed on Nugdrinn. Its first bite took apart the grubark, tore a great cleft from the hull and doomed it. Under such incredible pressure, the deck violently split apart and sent a dagger-sized splinter into the dwarf's eye. Nugdrinn screamed but had enough about him still to try and scramble back up what was left of his ship before a second bite claimed his foot.

Half blind, Nugdrinn roared. He bit his lip, used the pain to stop himself from passing out. Blood gushing from the ruined stump of his left leg was already freezing, sealing up the wound. A deeper cold was spreading through Nugdrinn's body when the other dwarfs attacked. Crossbow bolts, some with their tips drenched in oil and then lit, hailed the beast. Thick-bladed throwing axes gouged its flanks. Piercing its blubbery hide, the barbed quarrels drew a bleat of pain from the beast's puckered maw, which was champing up and down on the rapidly disintegrating hull. A noisome stench rolled from its gullet, redolent of putrefaction and the slow rot of the half-frozen dead.

A second barrage of axes and quarrels forced the beast under but it had claimed Nugdrinn's foot and his eye.

Anger and a desire for retribution kept him alive until the dwarfs reached Barak Varr some months later. A mattock head was forged by Guildmaster Strombak to replace the piece of his limb he had lost and so Nugdrinn became 'Hammerfoot' to ever remind him of what he owed the beast.

The memory of that night still brought a tremor to his hand that made the view through his telescope quiver, if only slightly. Nudgrinn took a stronger grip of the rope, glad his rune axe was looped to the belt around his waist.

'Is it you, daemon?' he asked the water. 'Has the gulf spewed up a monster from the watery hells of Triton's cage?'

The water didn't answer.

Instead, the amber glow of the lantern crept across the waves until it found something to alight on.

Nugdrinn snapped shut the telescope and pulled out his axe. He'd fight the beast one-handed, lashed to the prow.

'Come forth then,' he bellowed, vying against the roar of the water that was in a foaming frenzy with the wind peeling off the northern peaks. 'And I'll take from you what you took from me in recompense.'

His ghazan-harbark pitched and yawed but Nugdrinn barely noticed. Adrift on rough water was akin to walking to the experienced captain. His face was slick with spray, little diamonds of seawater clinging to his beard. A rime of salt layered his upper lip and he licked it.

'I taste blood on the water, fiend,' he promised. 'I'll open up yer belly and release those poor lost souls you devoured. I'll cut yer until your entrails spill into the black and are swallowed whole by the briny deep. Come forth!'

For such a monster to be found so close to Barak Varr was unheard of, but Nugdrinn wasn't about to shame the ancestors by doubting it.

A shadow, half-revealed in the lamplight, became more distinct as its identity was unmasked at last.

Nugdrinn lowered his axe, and let his ire cool.

'Douse the lamp,' he said. His heart thundered, and his breath quickened in his chest.

It was wood floating on the gulf. Just a piece of hull, a chunk of stern or prow, some vessel broken out in the deep ocean and washed up on the shores of Barak Varr.

It was nothing. Yet, as the urgency and fervour fled his veins and left him cold and trembling, Nugdrinn could not shake the feeling that there had been something out in the gulf.

But the bell tolled on and no horn was heard on the rough black waters.

'Douse the lamps,' Nugdrinn said again, retreating back to the deck and wondering what they had missed.

BLOOD MAGIC WAS never predictable. It was a roiling mass of archaic forces drawn together through murder and slaughter, a hound brought to the leash but never fully at heel. Dhar, the Dark Wind, was capricious but the deeds that could be wrought through its manipulation were great and terrible. Drutheira knew her art well, however, and had practised much. She knew, as all sorcerers must, that dark magic always required sacrifice. The dead druchii warrior with her throat cut, spilling arterial crimson all over the deck, was testament to that.

Most of the blood from the corpse had been wasted, but there was enough to fill a ritual bowl in the middle of the deck. From it tendrils of ruddy smoke quested like the tentacles of some abyssal horror. They enveloped the raiding ship, occluded it from sight. Thus clouded could the dark elves pass by the watchtowers of the dwarfs and gain passage through the Black Gulf into the rivers of the Old World proper.

Two other witches, Malchior and Ashniel, completed the coven. Lesser sorcerers both than Drutheira, they channelled their mastery into her and she became a conduit that articulated the power of the whole. Sweat dappled her brow, intense concentration written upon her face as she maintained the casting all the way through the gate markers that led them north. As one the triumvirate muttered their incantations through taut, bloodless lips as the other warriors looked to the sea wall and hoped the enchantment would hold long enough for them to pass by.

At the stern of the raider ship, a dark elf stood ready behind the vessel's reaper. The single bolt thrower would find itself quickly outmatched by the battalion of ballistae arrayed against it, so too the twenty or so warriors armed with spear and shield at the ship's flanks. Their fate was in the hands of Drutheira and her witches.

Slowly, agonisingly so, the sea wall faded from sight and the dark elves left the Sea Hold behind them with the dwarfs unaware of them ever having been present in their waters.

Drutheira let out a pained breath, the evidence of her body's trauma revealed in the dark flecks on the hand that she used to cover her mouth.

The others sagged, visibly drained. Ashniel wiped a trickle of crimson from her mouth, whilst Malchior staunched his bleeding left nostril with a black cloth he then secreted back into his robes.

'*Dhar* is a hard mistress,' he remarked, coughing into his hand. When he wiped it away quickly with his sleeve there was blood on his palm.

'Does the sight of blood on your own skin upset you, Malchior?' Ashniel was young and impetuous, but possessed rare magical talent. She also delighted in taunting Malchior.

'I am perfectly sanguine, my little dear,' he replied in a sibilant voice, a savage and murderous glint in his eyes. 'But I would much rather it was your blood.'

Bristling at the obvious threat, she spoke through a dagger-curved grin. 'I could flay the flesh from your bones, here in this very ship.'

Malchior did his best to appear unmoved. 'Ah, the boldness of youth. Such overconfidence for a whelp...'

'Whore-killing dog!' she hissed, summoning a nimbus of dark magic and shaping it in her talon-like fingers.

'Cease your bickering,' snapped Drutheira, dispelling the casting with a curt slash of her hand, 'and know that I am a harder mistress than the Wind of Dhar.' Her wrath faded as quickly as it had appeared, and she narrowed her eyes like a predator to its unwitting prey. 'Save your strength. Both of you. We are not finished, not yet.'

That revelation brought a sneer to Ashniel's blade-thin lips. Malchior tried to hide his dismay behind a viper's charm but failed.

'Whatever our mistress requires,' he purred with a small bow.

Ashniel showed her acquiescence by turning the sneer into a mirthless smile. Drutheira had seen harpies with more humour and resolved to kill the little witch once this was done.

She glanced down at the brass bowl around which the coven was sitting. Together they formed a triangle with Drutheira at its apex. Crimson steam rolled off the sloped interior of the bowl and once it cleared only a residue of the vital fluid remained.

'Vaulkhar,' she called, as if summoning something as mundane as wine or meat, 'I need more.'

The vaulkhar nodded and gestured to two of his crew. A third, who paled when the captain's cold gaze fell upon him, drew his sword but was subdued before he could put up much of a fight. Disarmed, forced to kneel over the bowl, he screamed as Drutheira drew her ritual knife and cut his throat.

Blood, hot and fresh, spilled into the sacrificial vessel.

'Communion…' uttered Drutheira, her voice laced with power, and the three began to chant.

Bubbles rose on the surface of the dark pool as if it were boiling, but no heat emanated from within. Instead an image began to resolve as the fluid thickened. Scarred as if by fire and contorted into a rictus of pure agony, a face appeared in the morass. It had been noble once, now it was ravaged and hellish. Opening its mouth in a silent scream, the face arched back and was consumed.

The bubbling subsided, replaced by ripples, slight at first but growing with intensity as the seconds passed. A pair of tiny nubs, like the peaks of two mountains surrounded by a lake, protruded from the pool. Nubs became horns and the horns crested an ornate helm of jagged edges and bladed ornamentation. It was a barbed piece of armour, sharp and cold. Dripping with blood, its entire surface drowned in viscous gore, a head emerged from the deep red mire.

Unlike before, furnace heat radiated off this manifestation that pricked the skin and brought a grimace of pain to Drutheira's face.

'Dark lord,' she uttered, bowing her head in deference.

Though fashioned magically from congealed blood, her master was no less terrifying. He glowered at the coven, his malice as palpable as the gore-slicked deck beneath them.

At first his words were too thick to understand, spoken in an ancient and evil tongue Drutheira could not translate. Slowly, inexorably, it began to make sense.

'*Tell me of your progress,*' commanded the bloody effigy.

'We cross the borders of the Sea Hold, lord and are even now headed northwards.'

'*And the dwarfs are unaware of your presence?*'

'We passed their defences undetected. The stunted swine could not tell us from the ugly noses on their faces,' she added, allowing a pang of hubris to colour her reply.

'*Don't underestimate them,*' the face snarled, and Drutheira recoiled from its hate and power as if struck. '*Snorri Whitebeard was no fool, and had power. His descendants are worthy of you, sorceress.*'

'No, of course not,' she whispered, abruptly cowed. 'All is as you bid it, lord.'

'*An alliance must not be made between elf and dwarf. They must destroy one another utterly.*'

'It will be as you will it.'

'*See that it is.*'

Rivulets were streaking down the effigy as the magical communion lost potency. Like wax before a strong flame, the blood was slowly melting back into the pool from whence it emerged.

'What is your command, lord?' asked Drutheira, concealing her relief at the spell's ending.

'Our allies are already abroad. The shade Sevekai and his band await my orders through you. Together, enact my plans I have given to you. See the asur undone by their own nature.' As the face sloughed away, its words became slurred and indistinct. The horns had already gone, collapsed into the pool along with much of the jagged helm. Even the eyes had bled away to nothing, the head caving in shortly after until only the mouth remained. 'Yours is but a piece of a much greater plan. Sevekai is to be your scout, your herald. Use him. Fail me and you need not return to Naggaroth…'

Like the final exhalation of breath from a corpse, the voice gurgled into nothing but the threat remained as real and immediate as a knife perpetually at her throat.

Drutheira swallowed, imagining the caress of that steel, and drew on hidden reserves of strength to speak.

I am drained, she said into the minds of her coven. Her eyes were closed. To the warriors aboard the raider ship it would appear as if she were meditating.

We all are, Ashniel replied, as precocious as ever.

Drutheira kept her annoyance at the interruption from her face.

That is why when we reach the shore we will kill every elf aboard this ship and steal the vigour from their blood.

Storm clouds billowed across the mainland, presaging the chaos to come.

At the prow of the ship, the vaulkhar snarled orders to the crew. Unbeknownst to him and his warriors, the coven shared a conspirators' smile.

Malekith had spoken and they would enact his will or they would die.

⫷ CHAPTER SIX ⫸

Master of Dragons

A GREAT ROAR echoed across the peaks. It split the storm in two like a jag of lightning cuts the sky in half and leaves a ragged tear behind it.

Sheltered beneath an overhanging spur of rock, the dwarfs kept their eyes on the heavens. Morgrim's ached from not blinking.

'I still don't see anything.' He had to shout against the wind, which had grown into a tumultuous gale. Drifts peeling off the mountains skirled through the pass and swathed the rocky clearing where they hid in grubby grey-white.

Flecks of snow clung to Snorri's beard like ugly, malformed pearls. He spat through clenched teeth. 'If it is a drakk, I will spill its heartblood and paint the ground red with it.'

Angular runes on his axe blade began to glow as he summoned their power with a muttered oath.

'Two dwarfs with fate on our side against a beast that can raze entire towns with its breath and lay siege to a hold single-handed,' said Morgrim. 'I'd say the odds are with us, cousin.'

Snorri did not reply. His gaze was fixed, the grip around the haft of his axe like stone.

The whip of battered air drew nearer, a low and steady *thwomp* of vast, membranous wings driving against the gale. To maintain such a rhythm, the dragon must be incredibly strong.

Morgrim cried out as a shadow seen through cloud darkened the sky.

'It comes!'

A crack of lighting flared behind it and framed the beast in silhouette.

'Gods of earth and stone...'

The dragon was massive.

Snorri edged from beneath the craggy overhang, squinting against the snow hitting his face. He spat out a lump of frozen mulch and snarled, 'I'll turn its skin into a scale cloak...'

The dragon breached the clouds, tendrils of mist rolling off its muscled silver torso. A long, serpentine neck ended in a snout like a blade, fanged and drooling iridescent smoke. Unfurling its wings, the beast's shadow eclipsed the dwarfs and the entire clearing where they were standing. Like two metal sails, its mighty pinions shimmered as star-fire. Talons like sword blades extended from its feet, and eyes akin to flawless onyx glittered hungrily as it saw the morsel before it.

'Make a tankard of its hollowed out skull...'

No dwarf, however skilled, could hope to defeat such a monster.

Morgrim grabbed for Snorri to haul him back but missed. 'Cousin, wait!'

'Destiny calls!' shouted Snorri and roared as he lifted his axe.

It was the single bravest and most foolish thing Morgrim had ever seen.

Thinking of all the things he had wanted to achieve and that would now be denied him, he sighed, '*Bugrit...*' and then charged after Snorri.

Pressing against the rock, Sevekai prayed to all the dark gods that would listen.

The beast had speared through the storm like a streak of ithilmar, bellowing with such intensity it put the elf's teeth on edge. Heart thundering in his chest, he dared a glance around the edge of the rocks where he and his warriors had gone to ground as soon as they had seen the dragon.

Killing the dwarfs now would be impossible, but then also hardly necessary given what they faced.

Kaitar was crouched beside him but seemed unmoved by the terrifying monster in their midst.

'Was the fear siphoned out of you as an infant, Kaitar?' asked Sevekai. 'Or are you simply too dull-witted to realise how imminent all of our deaths are?' He was about to withdraw, the dwarfs were good as dead anyway, when Kaitar put a hand on his chest.

Sevekai glared daggers at the elf but didn't raise a hand against him.

'A little hasty, I think,' he hissed, nodding towards the dragon.

As THE BEAST landed, its claws pulverising rock, it lowered its head, revealing an elven warrior mounted on its back.

Silver-helmed with lance in hand, he looked like a prince of the ancient days when Malekith and Snorri Whitebeard both still walked the earth. Behind the dragon visor concealing his face, the elf lord's eyes glittered like emeralds.

Fastened to an ornate saddle of white wood and bone was a shield depicting an unsheathed sword. He bore the same device attached to the crown of his war helm.

He raised his hand, voice resonating through the mouth grille of his silver dragon mask. 'Hail, dwarfs of Everpeak,' he said, using rudimentary Khazalid and referring to Karaz-a-Karak by its common name.

Morgrim lowered his hammer, but not completely. Snorri was less keen to relent and maintained his belligerence before the monster.

The elf noble leaned forwards in the saddle and whispered to his beast, although his words carried on the storm.

'Easy, Draukhain.'

'State your business, elfling,' Snorri demanded.

The elf lord stowed his lance, its crimson pennant flapping in the fierce wind. Bowing, he raised his visor. Despite his ostensible geniality, he still sounded imperious.

'I am Imladrik of Caledor, Master of Dragons and Prince of Ulthuan, Lord of Oeragor. I bear you no ill-intent, lord dwarfs.'

Despite the offer of peace, Snorri was pugnacious. '*Dragon master*, eh? I slay dragons, elfling.'

Imladrik raised a gauntleted hand. The knuckles were fashioned as scales, the fingertips like talons.

'I am an ally to you. I mean no harm,' he assured them.

'Be calm,' Morgrim hissed to his cousin through clenched teeth, looking sidelong at the creature drooling sulphur and smoke.

Snorri hissed back, 'I won't be cowed by this elgi and his beast!'

'No, but you may be eaten, cousin!'

'A lot of titles for an elgi,' Snorri scoffed. 'I'm surprised you can remember them all. And you should be more concerned about who wants to harm who, elfling.'

Morgrim tried not to groan, but put a hand on his cousin's arm until he lowered his axe.

'You are far from Oeragor, Prince Imladrik,' he said, eager to defuse the situation once he'd calmed Snorri down. 'I am Morgrim, son of Bardum, thane of Karaz-a-Karak, and this–'

Snorri stepped forwards and thrust out his chest.

'I am Prince Snorri Lunngrin of Karaz-a-Karak, heir to the dwarf kingdom. You are upon my sovereign soil, elgi.'

Imladrik bowed, betraying no hint of reaction to the goading Snorri was attempting.

'I meant no offence, my lords. Through the storm, I saw travellers on the road. Once I realised you were dwarfs, I decided to descend and see if I could offer you a ride. It is a long way back to Everpeak, and since it is where I am bound…'

'Indeed it is a long way,' Morgrim agreed, thinking how his feet would ache after such a trek, and looked at his cousin who had yet to take his eyes off the dragon.

'A ride, eh? On the back of that beast? Is that what you're suggesting, prince?'

'It is faster than going on foot,' Imladrik replied without condescension.

The storm was dying out, the winds abating and the snows thinning until they were little more than errant drifts carried on the breeze. In the north-east, the sun was rising again, easing some warmth back into a cold winter's morning.

'It seems Kurnous favours us, my lords,' the elf prince added, gesturing to the improving weather. 'But I still think you'll reach Everpeak faster on Draukhain's back.'

Morgrim turned to his cousin and whispered, 'I have never ridden on the back of a dragon.'

'With good reason.' Snorri looked askance at the beast. 'They are fell and dangerous creatures. Not to be trusted, much like their masters.'

Elves were possessed of incredible hearing and Imladrik had heard every word exchanged between the dwarf nobles, but if he thought anything of it he did not show it. He merely smiled impassively and waited for them to make their decision.

Morgrim was insistent. 'I have no desire to walk back to the hold when I can as easily fly.'

'And I have no desire to be devoured by some beast of the lower deeps whilst my back is turned!'

Morgrim smiled.

'You are afraid.'

'I am not. I am scared of nothing. I am the son of the High King, a destined dragon slayer I might add.'

'Then ride the dragon and we'll be back in the hold hall before supper,' said Morgrim. 'I for one would like to get out of this thrice-damned cold and feel a fire on my skin, have meat in my belly.'

Snorri licked his lips at the prospect of meat. It had been a while since he tasted beef, smelled roast pork or elk. Stonebread was fortifying but it lacked flavour, in fact any taste at all.

'And what of beer?' Morgrim pressed. 'I would drain the brewhouses dry with my thirst.'

At the mention of ale, Snorri began to salivate and had to wipe his mouth.

All the while, the elf prince looked on.

'I've heard Jodri has uncasked a golden reserve and plans to serve it to the kings at the *rinkkaz*.'

'Which is another matter, cousin,' said Morgrim. 'Your father is expecting you at the council of kings.'

Snorri's expression darkened at mention of the High King. 'Aye, isn't he always.' He turned to Prince Imladrik. 'Very well, elfling, we shall accept your offer of transportation but mark me well,' he said, pointing rudely with an accusatory finger, 'any falsehood will mean the death of both you and your ugly beast.'

Imladrik bowed again, as he would in court. 'As gracious as you are direct, my dwarf prince.' At some unseen, unheard command, Draukhain went down on its forelegs and laid its neck upon the ground so the dwarfs could climb aboard its back. 'There is room enough on my saddle for two.'

'Does he trawl the skies often, looking for wayward travellers below?' Snorri muttered behind his hand. He kept his rune axe loose in the sheath in case he needed it in a hurry.

'I doubt it, cousin, but I do know if you try his patience further we will be going back to Karaz-a-Karak charred to our very boots. Now shut it and get aboard!'

Snorri grumbled some expletive but reluctantly followed Morgrim as he approached the dragon.

DESPITE HIS FEAR, Sevekai edged forwards to try and better hear what transpired between the dragon rider and the dwarfs. An elf of Ulthuan, especially a prince, this close to the dwarf kingdoms was unusual. That he flew alone without his army or any retainers was stranger still.

Whatever the reason, it did not appear that the dwarfs were imperilled after all and that meant Sevekai still had a duty to perform. He silently drew a sickle blade from his baldric.

Verigoth interceded. 'What are you doing?' he hissed.

Sevekai bit back savagely, 'Don't question me, druchii! I've gutted people for less.'

'Perhaps Verigoth is right, brother.' Kaitar slipped between them, a finger on Sevekai's blade hand.

He sheathed it, incredulous that this was the second time Kaitar had touched him and the wretch still wasn't dead.

'We can get closer, listen in. Even if we cannot kill the nobles or their asur ally, we can discern their plans.'

Verigoth and the others looked no more enthusiastic about this plan than the previous one, but probable death was at least preferable to certain death.

'If we are discovered,' hissed Sevekai, glancing at the dragon then back at Kaitar, 'our dark lord's plans could be jeopardised, and I have no desire to engage the interest of the beast.'

Kaitar grinned, a faint resonance to his voice Sevekai hadn't noticed before. 'Then we creep softly and silently, like shadows.'

'Like shadows,' repeated Sevekai, eyes locked with Kaitar's.

Slowly, the dark elves detached themselves from their hiding place and began to creep closer.

MORGRIM HAD ALREADY mounted the beast by the time Snorri was ready to do the same. Though he had agreed to ride upon the dragon's back, the dwarf prince kept his distance.

'Be careful, cousin,' he said, as Morgrim climbed a length of white hemp lowered by the prince. It was thin and Snorri had expected the rope to snap, but it proved equal to Morgrim's considerable mass.

'Must be bound with steel,' he muttered, but detected an aura shimmering off the rope.

Imladrik gestured to him, offering the saddle as one would welcome a stranger in their house. 'Your turn, my prince.'

It was then Snorri realised he had no desire to ride this beast, to fly amongst the clouds. The very thought of it brought an unpleasant acerbic tang to his mouth, but he swallowed it down, knowing he could not be outdone by his cousin.

'We are hall dwellers, not dragon riders,' he grumbled, cinching his belt up and reaching for the proffered rope.

The faint tang of spoiled meat, the scent of dust and ancient fire-baked plains, quite incongruous in winter, suddenly tainted the breeze.

Inches from grabbing the rope, Snorri's fingers seized. A second later and Draukhain reared up, its bulk smacking the dwarf onto his rump. It roared, spitting a plume of flame into the air and swinging its head around as if searching.

'Grimnir's teeth!' Snorri scrambled to his feet, reaching for his rune axe. 'Never trust an elgi! Never trust a drakk!' he spat, ripping the shimmering blade from its sheath.

Flung back in the saddle, Imladrik was trying to steady the beast. He muttered words of command and reprimand, but in a language neither dwarfs, nor most elves, could understand.

Morgrim was pitched off the dragon's back. He rolled, grabbing at the beast's spines to try and arrest his fall, and ended up dumped on the ground next to its thrashing tail. An errant flick caught his helm and he staggered, trying to back away. Like Snorri, he had drawn his weapon.

Not understanding what was happening, together the dwarfs circled the beast.

Snorri's expression was murderous as he briefly met his cousin's gaze. There was more than a hint of self-satisfaction in his eyes.

'You offer us safe passage on your drakk,' he said to the elf, 'and then it tries to kill us!'

'Lords, please.' Imladrik was still struggling to calm Draukhain, though his verbal goads had lessened. Instead, intense concentration was etched on his face as an entirely different war of wills played out.

'What is he doing?' whispered Morgrim, swinging his hammer around in a ready grip.

Snorri wasn't listening. His teeth were clenched. 'If dawi were meant to fly, Grimnir would not have taught us how to kill wyverns and drakk. Any creature with wings is no friend to a dawi,' he spat.

Ignorant of the dwarfs circling him and his mount, Imladrik closed his eyes and began to sing. A soft, lilting refrain echoed across the clearing. Though the elf's words rarely rose above a whisper, they were resonant with power and potency. Each syllable was perfectly enunciated, every string of incantation precisely exacted.

At first Draukhain resisted, reacting to whatever it was that had ignited its predatory wrath. But slowly, as the pattern repeated and Imladrik wove the dragonsong tighter and tighter around it, the beast was soothed and its head bowed. Anger still burned in the black pits of its eyes, but it was fading to embers.

When he was done, Imladrik sank a little in his seat as if his armour was suddenly heavier. When he removed his war helm, his face was gaunt and dappled with beads of sweat.

'My sincerest apologies,' he began, a little out of breath, 'He has never done that before, except in battle. Something enflamed his anger, I don't know what.'

'Perhaps it was a hankering to taste dwarf flesh,' Snorri chided. 'I warn you, my meat is bloody tough!' He brandished his axe meaningfully. 'And my *rhuns* are sharp.'

Mortified, Imladrik put his palms together in a gesture for peace and calm. 'Please, it was a misunderstanding.'

Snorri wasn't about to back down. The beast had accepted Morgrim without complaint, but railed against his presence. It was a matter of wounded pride now, a sin that the prince of Karaz-a-Karak had in abundance.

'And if we'd have been aloft when another "misunderstanding" took place? What then, eh? Cast to the earth like crag hawks pinioned by a quarreller's bolt, left to be dashed on the rocks as a red smear.' He thumped his chest. 'I am dawi born, stone and steel. If you wish us dead then fight us face-to-face, you dirty, thagging elgi.'

It was a step too far. Morgrim knew it and went to say something but no words could take back his cousin's insult.

Imladrik paled, and not from the exertions of his dragonsong. He had to bite back his anger, covering it with a low bow. His eyes glittered dangerously when he rose again, as hard as the gemstones they so closely resembled.

'I deeply regret this, and offer apology to you both. I shall convey the same remarks to you father, the High King,' he said to Snorri alone, 'but you have much to learn of elves, young prince. Much indeed.'

Obeying a snarled command, Draukhain speared into

the air and emitted a roar of sympathetic anger. With a few beats of its mighty wings, both dragon and elven prince were gone, lost to the cloud and the endless sky.

'That was foolish,' said Morgrim. He had followed the dragon's searching gaze to a cluster of rocks outlining the clearing but could see nothing amiss amongst them.

'Foolish was it?' Snorri turned, but when he saw the look on his cousin's face his vainglorious pride deserted him. He muttered, 'Perhaps I did speak out of turn.'

'Your words were callous, cousin, and ill-considered.'

Snorri looked to his boots, then to his half-hand. His anger, self-directed, rose again. 'My father has said something similar to me often. Are you going to rebuke me constantly as he does, cousin?'

'I...' Morgrim met Snorri's hurt gaze and knew the prince was just lashing out. The High King was a hard taskmaster, tougher on his son than even his most veteran generals. It would be difficult to bear for any dwarf. In the end, Morgrim relented. 'No cousin, I will not. But without wings to take us back to hearth and hold, we have a long journey ahead of us. I don't think we'll make the rinkkaz. Your father will be wrathful, I fear.'

'Let him,' the prince snorted. 'I would rather walk the road in my boots, facing urk and troll, even my father's anger, than risk life and limb on the back of a drakk.' He stomped off down the path, slinging his axe onto his back and swearing loudly with every step.

Morgrim decided not to reply and fell in behind him to let his cousin vent.

The return to Karaz-a-Karak suddenly seemed much longer and more arduous.

CROUCHED IN A thicket of dense scrub, Sevekai fought to catch his breath. When the dragon had reared up, he had fled with the others back down the ridge.

The ambush site was close by, as yet undiscovered.

Killing dwarf merchants in the darkness was something he had a taste for, but he was no dragon slayer. In truth, the creatures terrified him. Even those slaved to the will of the druchii he treated with wary apprehension. It had taken him all his willpower to stay hidden when the beast had bayed for their blood.

Verigoth was still shaking and took a pinch of *ashkallar* to calm his nerves. The narcotic was fast-acting but the tremors still remained.

'Did it see us?' he asked.

Sevekai shook his head, reliving the moment in a waking nightmare.

'We'd already be dead if it had,' he breathed. His gaze fell on Kaitar, who was watching them all impassively. 'Are you not disturbed at all, Kaitar?'

He shrugged, as bizarre and incongruous a gesture as he could make in the circumstances.

'We are alive. What is there left to fear?'

Numenos had taken out his blades to sharpen them and calm his shattered nerves. Though his body still trembled, his hands were steady. It spread slowly up his arms, to his neck and back.

'Is it ice or blood you have in your veins, druchii?' he asked, glancing up from his labours to regard Kaitar.

'Neither,' Kaitar answered with a laugh.

Watching the exchange keenly, Sevekai couldn't tell if he was joking or not.

Mirth changed to murder with the shifting of the breeze on Kaitar's face. 'We should go back and kill those two dwarfs.'

Sevekai shook his head. 'That door is closed to us.'

'The beast is fled,' Kaitar pressed.

With a flash of silver, Sevekai's sickle blade was at Kaitar's throat. His voice was thick with threat. 'I said no.'

Kaitar raised his hands, showing Sevekai his palms in a plaintive gesture.

'As you wish.'

Glaring at him for a moment longer, Sevekai lowered his blade and returned it to its place on his baldric. He addressed the warband. 'The storm is abating,' he said, gesturing to the breaking cloud. 'We will need fresh attire by the time the dawn breaches it.'

Before sailing to the Old World, his mind was implanted with Malekith's sorcery. Into Sevekai's mental pathways, he had poured memories of the secret trade routes of the dwarfs, those learned many years ago when he had befriended their High King. Snorri Whitebeard was long dead, so too Malekith's affinity for dwarfs. Only cruelty remained, and a desire for vengeance against those who had wronged him and cast him from his rightful throne.

Sevekai felt these desires vicariously like hot knives in his mind as he sifted through the scraps of memory he needed to fulfil his mission. Failure was not something he dared countenance. Killing the dwarf lords would have garnered favour but his spine was not up to the task of returning to the clearing. An image resolved in his mind's eye, a sheltered passageway of rock and earth, high hills and scattered forest. He had never seen the trail before yet it was as familiar to him as his own hand, or the blade he wielded with it. A second vision revealed a face: a woman, a sorceress, and a name to go with it.

Drutheira.

She was to be their overseer. Sevekai scowled inwardly, and wondered if she had requested this duty. It would not surprise him in the least.

'We move now,' he said.

They needed to find elves first, some asur to kill and steal from before they ambushed again or met up with the sorceress.

It would be as it was before, only this time they would be brazen and leave a survivor.

'Follow me,' said Sevekai, the route burning brightly like a torturer's fire in his head. 'We have elves and dwarfs to kill.'

SNORRI AND MORGRIM were skirting the foothills when the dauntless peaks of Karaz-a-Karak towered above them through mist and cloud. Monolithic ancestor statues tall as the flank of the mountain loomed into view, silently appraising the nobles with stern stone countenances.

Shading his eyes from the sun, Morgrim looked up in awe. 'I see Smednir and Thungi, sons of Grungni and Valaya.'

Several hours had passed since their encounter with Imladrik and his dragon, but the memory of it remained – as did the burning insult Snorri felt at the beast's sudden change in temperament. But to the prince's credit, he kept it hidden.

Snorri followed his cousin's gaze, then looked further across the mountain to an eagle gate, one of the lofty eyries through which the honoured brotherhood of the Gate-keepers kept watch on the upper world. Beneath and beside the chiselled portal hewn into the very mountainside were more dwarf ancestors.

'And there is Gazul and your namesake Morgrim, at Grimnir's side.'

All of the ancestors, their siblings and progeny were rendered as immense cyclopean statues around the flank of Karaz-a-Karak. Crafted in the elder days, they reminded all of the Worlds Edge of the hold's importance and closeness to the gods.

With the hold in sight, the mood between the cousins began to improve.

'More than once, I thought we were bound for the under-earth and Gazul's halls,' said Morgrim.

'Bah, not even close, cousin. You fret too much.' Snorri slapped him on the back, grinning widely. He thrust his chin up, breathed deeply of the imagined scent of forges and the hearth he would soon enjoy. 'Lords of the mountain, cousin. Both of us. Ha!'

Morgrim's own declaration was less ebullient. 'Lords of the mountain, Snorri.' He looked down at his cousin's ruined hand. 'And with the wounds to prove it.'

Snorri sniffed. 'A scratch, Morgrim, nothing more than that.' When his eyes alighted on a figure waiting on the road ahead, his smile faded. 'Oh bugger…'

'Eh?' Morgrim was reaching for his hammer when he came to the same realisation as Snorri. 'Oh bugger.'

Furgil Torbanson, thane of pathfinders, stood in the middle of the road with a loaded crossbow hanging low at his hip on a strap of leather. At the other hip he carried a pair of hand axes in a deerskin sheath. In place of a helmet, he wore a leather cap of elk hide, three feathers protruding from the peak. Lightly armoured, most of his attire was rustic, woven from hardy wool and dyed in deep greens and browns as befitted a ranger.

He was not a dwarf given to saying much, but his eyes gave more away in that moment that his tongue ever would. 'You have been missed, lords of Everpeak.'

Four other rangers blended out of the foothills. Dressed in the same manner as Furgil, they also carried various pots and pans about them. One also had a brace of conies tied to his belt, another had a pheasant.

'Are we having a feast?' Snorri ventured hopefully.

'No young prince, we are not,' said a stern, unyielding voice from farther up the road. When a hulking, armoured warrior, much larger than the rangers, stepped into his eye line, Snorri groaned. 'Thurbad,' he muttered, nodding to the captain of the hearthguard. 'I take it my father sent you to bring me back?'

'He did.'

Thurbad's brown beard was resplendent where the rangers' were scratchy and unkempt. His gromril armour shone, though the cloak around his shoulders achieved much to conceal it. A chest plate inscribed with a dwarf face glowered at them both from within the folds of the ranger cloak. His honorific was 'Shieldbearer', a name he had earned time and again in service of his liege-lord.

'And I also assume that my father is not happy with me?'

Thurbad's chin, much like the rest of his granite face, was like a slab of rock.

'He is not.' He looked down, noticed the prince's bandaged hand and frowned.

'Lost some fingers to a rat,' Snorri explained.

Thurbad's frown deepened.

'It was a *big* rat.'

'You'll go to a temple of Valaya and have your hand seen to before going to the High King,' said Thurbad. His tone made it clear there would be no argument.

'And after that I'll feel my father's wrath?'

Thurbad's jaw twitched then clenched at what he saw as disrespect.

'Yes, young liege, then you will feel the High King's fury like a furnace fire has been lit under your arse. Follow. Now.'

With a curt word he dismissed the rangers, who were led by Furgil into the wilds.

Armour clanking, Thurbad stalked away. Not far from the road, a cohort of hearthguard was waiting.

Morgrim waited until Thurbad was out of earshot before he spoke. 'Not quite the welcome home we had envisaged, cousin.'

'I would almost rather be back with the drakk,' Snorri moaned, dragging his feet after Thurbad and his warriors.

⤛ CHAPTER SEVEN ⤜

Hearth and Hold

THURBAD LEFT THEM as soon as they had passed through the great gate and were safely inside the outer entrance hall of the upper deep. A vast echoing chamber had greeted the dwarf nobles, a very dark and sombre place with its gloom leavened partly by immense brazier pans aloft on chains suspended from the vaulted ceiling. The glow of fiery coals cast a lambent light across statues, inscribed columns and yawning archways. It barely reached the ceiling, the creeping tongues of fire lapping less than halfway up the columns, but cast enough of a glow to make the inlaid gemstones sparkle like a firmament of lost stars embedded in a stony sky.

At the back of the chamber, across a sprawling plaza of stone slabs, was the *Ekrund*. This monstrously broad stairway was the outer marker that led to the lower deeps and the hold proper. Stout-looking Gatekeepers, the same brotherhood who watched the eagle gates, glared like stone golems from their posts, barring the way below to the uninvited.

At its flanks, half hidden in shadowy alcoves, were the hearthguard. Though ostensibly the bodyguard of dwarf nobles, the warrior veterans were arrayed in force to safeguard the many retainers and dignitaries the kings and regents of the other holds had brought with them as part of their entourages.

Treasure keepers, shield carriers and lantern-hands, oath-makers, lorekeepers, reckoners, banner bearers, weaponsmiths and gold counters, muleskinners and their mules, wheelwrights, bards, brewmasters, cooks and consorts all hustled together more than a thousand strong. Like any regal lord a dwarf king had need of many servants, but such retainers were never admitted to the great halls. Despite the masses, the grand entrance hall was not even close to full. Yet dwarfs favoured closeness to their kith and kin, and so the entourage of each king and regent chose to stand together.

They were watched keenly by quarrellers, the king's own, from a lofty perch of stone overlooking the entire chamber. Both Snorri and Morgrim knew that two hundred and fifty of the Eagle Watch were tasked with the safeguarding of the outer entrance hall. There were no better marksmen in the realm, not even the rangers.

As soon as the nobles had set foot inside the hall a doleful voice had boomed out, resonating through a speaking horn.

'Prince Snorri Lunngrin, son of Gotrek, of clan Thunderhorn,' it announced, and then 'Morgrim Bargrum, son of Bardum, of clan Ironbeard,' shortly afterwards. This had continued, until each and every one of the new arrivals was accounted for, named and recorded.

All had bowed, even Snorri, to the speaker and showed their respect as one.

'Tromm,' they intoned.

Standing behind a pulpit of stone, raised above ground level by a thick dais, was one of Karaz-a-Karak's lorekeepers. A thick, leather-bound tome sat on the lectern in front of him and he called the names of each and every visitor, be it dwarf, elf or otherwise, that entered or left the entrance hall. This he then recorded in his book for the later use of reckoners or chroniclers. With all the retainers currently in residence, there was little wonder the lorekeeper was hoarse.

'And so we are named,' said Morgrim as the hearthguard departed.

'Are you not seeing me to the temple then, Shieldbearer?' Snorri asked of Thurbad.

The hearthguard captain did not look back. 'I've charged your cousin with that duty, my prince.'

'Let it be known that Thurbad Shieldbearer did make grudgement against the heir of Karaz-a-Karak,' said Snorri in a petulant tone under his breath.

'You'd be wise not to bait him, cousin.'

'Aye, I reckon my next lesson in axecraft or hammer throwing will be a hard one.'

'I have no doubt at all.'

Morgrim gestured to the myriad retainers thronging part of the hall. He noted some bored but stoic faces.

'The rinkkaz must be well attended and many hours old.'

'It will last for days, cousin,' Snorri moaned, striding purposefully towards the Ekrund, 'days. You had best get me to my priestess. I think I'll have need of some fortification before seeing my father again,' he said with a wink.

'I do not envy him, cousin,' said Morgrim, 'not at all.'

AT THE ENTRANCE to the temple of Valaya, the dwarfs parted ways.

Snorri regarded his bandaged hand. The blood had long since clotted, making a mess of the wrappings Morgrim had used to staunch the bleeding.

'You are not half bad as a nurse, cousin. Shave your beard and perhaps they'd have you at the temple if the miners' guild doesn't work out for you.'

'I see your humour has returned,' Morgrim answered dryly.

'Only, if you do, make sure you don't tend *my* battlefield injuries. I would rather it be a rinn that bathe my cuts and clean my wounds. One in particular, in fact.' A flash of mischief lit up Snorri's eyes at this last remark.

'Ah, and now I see why.'

'She has been waiting for me, I am sure.'

Morgrim groaned, removing his horned helmet to massage his forehead in exasperation.

'Tenacious as ever then?'

'Would you not be with a rinn like that? She is no Helda.'

'*That* we can agree on. You do know that priestesses cannot be betrothed to any dwarf, noble or not?'

'Who is talking about marriage here, cousin?'

The Valkyrie Maidens, temple warriors of Valaya, glared scornfully at the prince from behind their half-faced war helms but Snorri seemed not to notice.

Morgrim rubbed his eyes, as if a persistent headache he thought gone had suddenly returned to haunt him.

'I bid you farewell and good luck,' he said. 'I'll go and find what news there is to be had of the hold. Try and keep it in your trousers.'

Snorri grinned. 'I make no promises.'

'Do you ever wonder, cousin, whether the reason you want her is because you cannot have her?'

'There is nothing I cannot have, cousin,' said Snorri, laughing as he was ushered silently through the gate and into the temple. 'I am the prince of Karaz-a-Karak!'

'You are a fool.'

Elmendrin's scowl was fiercer than some ogre chieftains Snorri had met. She was slowly removing the makeshift bandage, and regarded the chewed nubs of his fingers beneath. 'They were bitten off?' she asked, reaching for a salve and bidding an attendant to bring a bowl of clean water.

'I was rat hunting in the lower deeps of Karak Krum,' Snorri explained, smiling broadly and looking into Elmendrin's eyes. 'Sapphires do not sparkle as brightly,' he said in a low voice.

They were more like steel as the priestess pierced the prince with a gimlet gaze.

'Rats?'

Snorri's brow furrowed and he tried to gesture with his arms.

Elmendrin snapped at him. 'Sit still!'

'But they were big rats, massive, and carrying blades.'

She scowled again. The expression seemed near fixed in

Snorri's presence. 'Vermin do not bear weapons. I see no hero before me, I see the spoilt son of a king with a swollen ego.' She examined the hand further. 'At least your cousin has bound it properly. The wound has clotted.'

Carefully, she began dabbing the stumps of Snorri's fingers with cloth and ointment. He winced, receiving another reproachful look from the priestess.

'It stings,' he complained.

Elmendrin rolled her eyes and continued cleaning the wound.

The temple of Valaya was a simple enough chamber. A place of healing, it contained baths and ranks of cots. But it was also a place of worship and the statue of the ancestor goddess stood proudly at the back of the room, overseeing the work of her handmaidens. Valaya was depicted wearing robes, over which was a skirt of chainmail. She bore no helm, though she was a warrior goddess, and her long plaits fell either side of her ample bosom. Her hands were clasped beneath her chest and a gold circular plate sat in front of the statue, engraved with the goddess's rune.

Low lantern light painted the temple in hues of deep red and orange. The air was thick with the smell of unguents and healing incense. There were also several large beer barrels filled with the kind of restorative no dwarf would ever refuse or doubt the medicinal properties of.

Several priestesses roamed about, bringing fresh water from the wells or salves and balms from the stores. There were a few other injured dwarfs being tended, miners mostly, but due to the size of the chamber the prince had Elmendrin all to himself. A fact he intended to make the most of.

'I have many scars,' he said, 'from the many battles I have fought in.'

Elmendrin kept her eyes on her work. 'Indeed.'

'See here,' said the prince, twisting to show off a jagged red mark down his left side. 'See...' he repeated. With an exasperated sigh, Elmendrin looked up.

Snorri smiled. 'From an urk cleaver, wielded by a chieftain. I cut off his head and mounted it on my banner pole.

During the wars of my father, I killed many urk and grobi, milady. See how it has made my arm strong…' Shirtless, his armour resting at the side of the cot where he was sitting, Snorri flexed his bicep and was gratified by the bulge he saw.

Elmendrin was unimpressed.

'I do not know,' she said, turning back to tending Snorri's hand, 'why you have removed your upper garments when it is just your hand that is injured.' Wound cleaned, she began to rebind the ruined fingers with fresh bandages, muttering imprecations to Valaya as she did so.

Snorri leaned in to whisper in her ear, 'Would you like me to remove the lower garments too?'

Elmendrin met his gaze, their lips not quite touching. The prince's confidence eroded with the sudden prospect of intimacy. She purred, 'Not unless you wish to be a prancing ufdi for the amusement of your father's court, a bard with the voice of a beardling.' She held a pair of prising tongs, the kind used to extract chips of wood or metal from a wound, and held them close to the prince's crotch.

Snorri paled. 'Not the *dongliz*…' he said, and recoiled.

She smiled humourlessly, set the prising tongs down. 'I thought not.' Elmendrin finished tying off the bandage, binding it over tightly and bringing another wince to the prince's face. 'There, it is done. May Valaya bless you and keep the wound from festering. It'll be a while before you can shoot a crossbow again, my prince.'

Snorri examined the finely tended wound, 'Aye, you might be right at that. My sincerest thanks, milady,' he said with genuine affection.

Despite her prickly veneer, Elmendrin blushed and turned away to wash her hands. Heat was radiating off her skin and she felt a tightening in her stomach.

'I am sorry, I–' Snorri began, slightly flustered. 'What I mean to say is I–' He reached out to touch her shoulder, admiring the way her violet robes framed her stout body and the flaxen locks bound into a ponytail that draped down her back.

She was broad chested, with a short stubby nose and strong cheekbones, a fine rinn and a worthy wife of any king. But it was her fire that Snorri so admired, her kindness and poise lacking in some dwarf women, some of whom had greater and longer beards than their dwarf men. He had spoken none of this to Morgrim, for to do so would damage the image he had worked to cultivate in his cousin's eyes. But here, alone with Elmendrin, he had no need for such disguise.

Alas, he also found that words deserted him.

'Do not speak further, my prince.' Her head was bowed when she faced him, but she met his gaze furtively.

'Let us not be prince and priestess,' he said, swallowing his sudden anxiety. 'Rather, we could be Snorri and Elmendrin.'

Elmendrin was about to answer, her lips framing a word, when another voice intruded.

'I heard of your wounding, Prince Snorri,' said a warrior in the garb of a reckoner. He wore chainmail over a leather hauberk and pauldrons of black leather, and carried an iron helmet in the crook of his arm. A small leather book along with several scroll cases was fastened to his broad belt. There was room for an axe too, or hammer, but its loop was empty. No weapons of any kind were allowed in the temple of Valaya. It was a sanctuary devoted to healing and protection, not a place to shed blood in anger. 'But I did not realise it went beyond your hand. Were you also stabbed?' the reckoner asked.

Annoyed at the interruption, Snorri stood up and started to dress. As he hauled on his overshirt, he replied, 'Just my hand, Grimbok.'

Forek Grimbok was removing his leather gloves, tucking them into his belt with the rest of his trappings, when he said, 'Then why is it you need to remove your garments and armour?' He looked to Elmendrin, sketched a quick bow. 'Sister.'

'Forek,' Elmendrin replied.

The reckoner was lean, with a thin face for a dwarf and an aquiline nose. His black beard was neatly trimmed and tidy, but still retained its length. His accent was cultured, for as well as reckoning for the king, he was also a gifted ambassador and negotiator.

Snorri met Forek's iron gaze without flinching. 'I asked the lady Elmendrin to rub salts and salve into my back and neck. When fighting all day in your armour, a dwarf tends to develop a tightness in the shoulders that requires the tender mercies of the priestesses. But I doubt you would be aware of that given the reckoners' deeds are generally confined to seeking recompense from other dwarfs, or am I wrong?'

Forek's face reddened at the obvious slight but he didn't bite, not yet. 'I serve your father, the High King,' he said, 'as do you, Prince Snorri.'

Snorri laughed. 'You and I are not so alike as that, reckoner.' He strapped on his armour, attached his vambraces. 'I assume you're here to take me to him.'

Livid with barely contained anger, Forek's next words almost came through clenched teeth. 'Indeed I am. You have much to explain.'

'Not to you, Grimbok,' said Snorri, flashing a smile at Elmendrin that elicited a scowl from the priestess.

Forek gave her a warning glance, escorting Snorri from the temple in silence.

'I know you covet my sister,' he hissed once they had their weapons and were headed for the Great Hall.

Snorri kept his eyes forwards, nodding to the clan warriors and guilders they met along the way. 'It's the only thing I like about you, Forek.'

'What, my sister?'

'No. Your boldness. One day it's going to get you in trouble.'

'Threats do not become a prince of Karaz-a-Karak, my lord.'

Snorri laughed, loud and hearty like they were two old friends sharing a joke. 'It's not a threat.'

Anything further would have to wait. Thurbad Shieldbearer waited at the end of the corridor, muscled arms folded across his chest. He had removed his vambraces and torcs banded his brawny skin instead.

As Snorri approached, he stepped aside without a word and the iron-banded doors into the Great Hall opened with an ominous creak of hinges.

⟨ CHAPTER EIGHT ⟩

Arrows and Blades

A BEAD OF sweat creeping down his back, a half-glimpsed shadow at the periphery of his vision, a waft of noxious odour, the scent of perfume gone before it was fully resolved. Furgil recalled the sensations he had experienced when they'd found the nobles on the Old Dwarf Road.

He knew these mountains, knew the hills and even the forests though he loathed their shaded arbours and sinister groves. In the wilderness, the lands beyond the hold halls of the mountains or the fortresses of the hills, there was much to be wary of. Danger lurked in every crag and narrow pass, in each wooded glade and weathered hollow. Creatures made their lairs in such places, hungry primitive things that preyed on the isolated and the lost.

Never venture into the wild on your own.

Save for the rangers, it was a rule many followed. But death was a patient hunter and all it took was a moment of recklessness, a wrong turn on the wrong trail, and all the guards and precautions would not matter.

Even during times of peace, these were untamed lands. The Old World would never know true peace. Its citadels and bastions of civilisation, whether they were above or below ground, ruled by elf or dwarf, were merely lanterns in a dark and turbulent sea. Some were even less than that, merely candles guttering in the storm. Furgil had known of many outposts, isolated hamlets and villages where a stake wall, a watchtower and a warning bell were poor defence against being consumed by the darkness.

Beasts and greenskins, giants, trolls and even dragons had descended upon such tenuous places and wiped them from existence.

Knelt with his hand upon the earth, a fistful of dirt clenched to his palm, the thought of unending peril did not bother Furgil. It was the way of nature. It was balance and order, albeit a brutal one. He understood it and that made it tolerable to the dwarf.

But something else lurked in the shadows, something that was not part of this order. It was a foreign object, a thing that had made the ranger's skin crawl and his beard bristle. Ever since he was a beardling, Furgil did not like to be watched.

Out on the Old Dwarf Road, he had sensed the presence of several watchers, of eyes regarding them with harmful intent. If asked, he could not explain how or why he knew this. It was a survival instinct he had cultivated whilst ranging the wild lands beyond the dwarf kingdoms, and it had saved his life on more than one occasion.

Almost without thinking, he touched the scar that ran from his neck all the way down to his chest. Invisible to a casual observer, Furgil felt the evidence of the wound with every breath. The beast responsible was dead. Its gutted carcass was a trophy in his private chambers, a reminder of always listening to instincts, especially when they screamed danger.

Furgil felt that sensation anew now and got to his feet. The earth had a strange aroma, the scent of narcotic root and dank metal. There was another smell too, old and ashen. Throwing the fistful of earth away, he dusted off his hands and descended the slope beyond the ridgeline into the heavy forest below.

A fourth smell intruded on the others. It clung to the

breeze like a plague, filthy and rank. It was piss and dung, mould and the stink of wet canine fur. Once off the road, their spoor was not hard to find. It wasn't as if they were trying to conceal their tracks.

A talisman hung around Furgil's neck. It carried the rune of Valaya and he beseeched for her protection as he entered the wooded glade. The deep forest triggered a sense of disquiet in the ranger. East of Karak Norn was the Whispering Wood, the Fey Forest. He had never entered that place, nor would he unless his life or that of an ally depended on it, but he had seen what was bred within its arboreal borders. Such a beast now adorned Furgil's wall, a many-antlered creature with too many eyes and reeking of musk, fever sweat clinging to its hide like a second skin…

It was no fell beast the ranger now tracked, though. The snuffling of canine muzzles and the shrieking, clipped speech of greenskins were proof of that. Nor were these the watchers he had felt earlier, for they were much subtler creatures.

The rest of his rangers had disbanded across the hills, searching for the watchers too. Furgil was alone.

He sneered, 'Grobi…' when he saw what was waiting for him in the wood.

Three greenskins and their mounts, mangy malnourished wolves, had dragged something off the road and were now worrying at it with tooth and claw.

Silently, Furgil unslung his crossbow and released the studs that looped his hand axes to his belt.

He didn't kill the creatures straight away, but waited to ensure there were no scouts or any lagging behind. Only when he was certain he had all of his prey in his sight, did he bring the crossbow up to his eye and shoot.

A bolt through the head killed the goblin instantly. It collapsed off the back of its wolf, much to the amusement of its fellows who thought it was drunk. When they realised it was dead, they looked up from their feast and began to chatter nervously, drawing crude blades and cudgels. By then, Furgil had loaded another bolt and sent a second rider to meet the first. This time the bolt tore out the goblin's throat and it died slowly but in agony.

A third bolt – and by now Furgil had given away his hiding place – killed a wolf. Its death howl sent a shrill of fear through its brethren, who reacted by snarling at the dwarf.

A flung hand axe killed a second wolf, as it sprang at the ranger without its rider.

The last died when his second thrown axe caved in its flank and sent spears of shattered ribcage into its soft organs.

Rider and mount parted in a fury of curses and flailing weapons. More or less unscathed, the goblin got to its feet, jabbing at the dwarf belligerently with its sword. When it realised its cousins were dead and so too their wolves, it shrieked and fled.

Furgil didn't run after it. Calmly, he slipped a bolt into his crossbow and drew a bead on the goblin's back. Obscured through thick woodland, scampering erratically and at pace. He counted the yards in his head. Nigh on two hundred by the time he had the stock to his cheek and sighted down the end of the bolt.

A difficult shot for most dwarfs.

Not for Furgil. Even the Eagle Watch was in awe of the ranger's skill with a crossbow.

The goblin pitched forwards moments later, the barbed tip of a quarrel sticking out of its eye.

With all the prey dead, Furgil recovered his weapons and went over to see what they'd been gnawing on. He left the quarrel he used to kill the last goblin, resigned to picking it up later in favour of examining whatever carrion had nourished the wolf pack.

The meat was badly mauled, but he caught scraps of tunic, a piece of bent-out-of-shape mail and even a broken helm. Judging by the chewed-up boots, the amount of ragged limbs, he estimated three bodies. Snagged between the wolves' jaws was some ruddy and blood-soaked hair. In the slack mouth of another, tough and leathern flesh.

Kneeling by one of the corpses, a scowl crawled across the ranger's face. His fist clenched of its own volition.

They were once dwarfs.

Furgil was picking through the bodies, searching for talismans, rings or other icons that would identify the dead, when the crack of kindling behind him made his heart quicken. Cursing himself for a fool, his hand got as far as the crossbow's stock when he felt the press of cold steel at his neck.

'Twitch and this dirk will fill your flesh up to the hilt,' uttered a deep voice in the ranger's ear.

A smile creased Furgil's lips as he recognised the speaker.

'You've spent too long in the mountain, brother,' said the voice again, as the blade was lifted from Furgil's neck. 'It's made you rusty.'

'Has it?' Furgil turned around and looked down at the throwing axe in his other hand, poised at the ambusher's crotch.

Rundin smiled broadly, revealing two rows of thick teeth like a rank of locked shields.

'But I have more friends than you do,' he said, sheathing his dirk as four hill dwarfs emerged out of the forest.

Furgil lowered his axe. 'Never did like the deep wood,' he said, and made Rundin laugh.

'That is true enough. Up you get,' he said, clasping the ranger's forearm in the warrior's grip and heaving him to his feet.

The two embraced at once, clapping one another on the back and shoulder like the old friends they were.

Rundin was a slab of a dwarf, broad and muscular like a bear but also lean enough that he had a light, almost lupine, gait. Tanned skin spoke of days spent beneath the sun, roaming the wilds, and a mousy beard unadorned with ingots or rings suggested a down to earth temperament.

'Been too long, son of Torban,' said Rundin, adjusting the thick belt around his waist. Scabbards for several dirks, daggers and long knives were fastened to it, and another belt that sat across his barrel chest had a sheath for the great axe on his back.

With a look, Rundin dismissed the other hill dwarfs who melted away silently. 'Unwise to leave our backs unwatched,' he said.

Furgil nodded, his mood suddenly serious. 'The truth of that sits before us, brother.'

He gestured to the carrion feast, bidding Rundin to kneel down beside him as he continued his investigation of the corpses.

'Dawi?' The leather hauberk he wore creaked as Rundin crept down beside Furgil. He lifted his leather helm – there was an iron raven icon on the band around the forehead – to wipe away a lather of sweat.

'I'd say merchants by what remains of their garments and trappings.'

'Agreed. Though this one wears heavy armour and there are calluses from haft work on the hand.'

'Dreng tromm…' Furgil breathed, and shook his head. He looked up. 'They did not meet their end here.'

'Aye, did you see it too?'

'That I did, brother.'

Easily missed amongst the carnage, the broken shaft of an arrow protruded from one of the dead dwarfs. It was buried deep into his back. The other half was snagged to his mail jerkin, partly concealed under the dwarf's body. It had swan feathers and the shaft itself was fashioned from white pine.

'Elgi,' said Rundin, face darkening.

'Aye. We need to find that ambush site.'

A bird call echoed from beyond the forest borders.

'One of your men?' asked Furgil, rising.

Rundin nodded.

It seemed they had already found where the dwarfs had died.

THREE MORE DWARFS grew cold on the road.

They were face down in the dirt, surrounding a sturdy wagon with two dead mules. Some still clutched weapons in their hands. Drag marks in the earth, scattered stones at the edge of the road revealed where the three the goblins had taken had come from. Unlike their clansmen in the deep wood, the others were more or less intact. Decay had yet to set in, so the deaths were recent. Judging by dwarfs' cold skin, the stiffness of their limbs and fingers, Furgil reckoned they had been dead a few hours.

Arrows stuck from their backs, same white pine shafts,

same swan-feathered flights. No goblin could loose with such a bow. Definitely elves.

The thought brought a concerned expression to Furgil's face.

'Elgi slaying dawi?' He released a long breath through his nostrils, trying to imagine the rationale for what he was seeing. 'Hard to countenance, brother.'

Rundin and Furgil were not brothers, though their bond of friendship was strong, if not stronger than some siblings. They had shared the same clan once, several years ago. Both were Ravenhelms, though Furgil had been stripped of that honour by King Skarnag Grum and thrown out of the lands of the hill dwarfs upon pain of death.

Unbaraki, the king had denounced him. It meant 'oathbreaker' and there was no greater insult that could be levelled at a dwarf.

Furgil had spoken out against Skarnag, for his greed and his isolation of the hill dwarfs. A seat on the high council had given the thane of the pathfinders a voice. With it he had condemned himself to banishment and shame by a bitter, petty king.

Fortunately for Furgil, the High King of the Worlds Edge Mountains agreed with the pathfinder and so he returned to the mountain from whence his clan had departed many centuries before.

Worst of all was that Rundin knew it and had said nothing in his friend's defence. Furgil had warned him not to, for then there would be no one to ensure the prosperity of the hill dwarfs. Loyalty to a corrupt ruler was the price Rundin paid, but devotion would only go so far.

In the solitude of their own thoughts, both dwarfs remembered this thorn between them. It had long since been removed but the memory of it was still bleak.

Furgil paced around the wagon.

'Five heavily armoured guards and a merchant guilder at the reins.'

Sweeping quickly across the scene, crouching and darting as he gathered further signs and markers, Furgil described what had happened.

'No fight occurred here, no battle. The dawi were killed quickly, without mercy. See how the crossbow is loaded but this satchel is full of quarrels. And here… The warrior's axe is still looped to his belt.' He gestured to the wagon itself. 'Unused shields still clasped to the sides.'

Rundin was crouched down, both hands resting on his thighs.

'An empty wagon this close to the hold means they were returning home. Why attack a caravan without wares to steal?'

'I don't think they were merely thieves,' said Furgil, though he had also noticed the little white bands around the dead dwarfs' fingers from stolen rings, the red-raw marks on their wrists where gilded bracelets had been forcibly removed.

Looking up from examining one of the dead guards, Rundin asked, 'What then?'

Furgil touched the swan-feathered shaft of an arrow. It had punched right through the dwarf's platemail as if it were parchment.

'This was cold murder, but I know of no elgi that would ever do such a thing.'

Rundin frowned, remembering something. 'From the watchtowers of Kazad Mingol there have been reports of black-cloaked strangers abroad on the hills. None have yet managed to get close enough to challenge them. When I read the missives that arrived at Kazad Kro, I assumed it was just because of the increased trade with the elgi.'

'Feels different,' said Furgil, suddenly glad that a ring of four hill rangers surrounded them. 'On the Old Dwarf Road, I felt… *something*.'

'Like being watched.'

Furgil met Rundin's gaze. The recognition in the warrior's eyes sent a chill down the ranger's spine.

'Just so.'

The earlier storm had almost passed, but the sun beaming down through the winter sky was neither warming nor comforting. Furgil stood up, deep in thought, his face creased with concern.

'Can you return the bodies to Karaz-a-Karak, Rundin?' he asked.

'Of course, brother. Are you not going back, then?'

'Not yet. I have to find out who these watchers are and what, if any, role they played in this slaughter. Dead dawi on the Old Dwarf Road this close to Everpeak is brazen, but I must go back to the High King with more than just questions and suspicions.'

Rundin got to his feet. 'Need some company?'

Furgil eyed the deep wood, his gaze sweeping across the ridgeline, the low hills, rivers and the crags. They could be anywhere, travelling under any guise. Killing a dwarf on the threshold of his own domain took skill; killing six who were armed and looking for danger took something much, more dangerous than that.

The ranger was about to break one of his own rules. He plucked an arrow from one of the bodies, placed it carefully in his satchel for when he'd need it later.

'No. I'll travel faster on my own.'

THE RAIDER SHIP was several miles behind them, sunken to the bottom of the river bed, its crew likewise. Weighed down by their armour, over a dozen exsanguinated bodies would putrefy and succumb to the slow rot of the dead.

Drutheira and her coven had been swift about the murder of the vaulkhar and his warriors. Gorged but not yet slaked, the witches' power swelled with the stolen blood. The way north would be long and not without peril, but there was much to do beforehand. Not least of which was finding Sevekai and his warriors.

Its presence burned into Drutheira's mind as if by a brand, a settlement was visible on the next rise. Fortified with an outer wall, tower and gate, it was a permanent outpost. Elf and dwarf banners hung from its crude battlements, fluttering on a low breeze blowing in off the distant gulf.

Malchior had not walked far when he began to moan. 'I am not a pack mule, Drutheira.' He adjusted the rough satchel on his back and it clanked with the swords and spears within. 'Could we not have stolen some horses? What merchant travels on foot anyway?'

Malchior no longer had the pale skin of a druchii, nor did

he wear the arcane trappings of a sorcerer. A white skullcap enclosed his head, and a skirt of light lamellar mail clad his body. There were vambraces, shin greaves, calfskin boots and a travelling cloak that attached to small pauldrons on his shoulders. Healthy sun-kissed skin described a rough but noble face.

He still wore a viper's smile, no enchantment could conceal that, but his appearance was already different from the one that had sailed into the Black Gulf from Naggaroth.

'And why must I be the beast of burden when *she* carries nothing?'

Ashniel had undergone a similar transformation, but wore a circlet instead of a skullcap with a diadem at its centre. Her distaste at the pearl-white robes beneath her breastplate was obvious in the sneer on her face. She grinned darkly at Malchior's displeasure, though.

Drutheira flashed a deadly glare at Malchior. 'Because I need her abroad in the settlement, doing the dark lord's work. You are welcome to explain to him why you disagree with that.'

Malchior fell silent, but Ashniel was unafraid to show her disgust.

'My skin crawls with this pretence.' She too carried nothing save for the jewelled athame at her waist and the small flask concealed beneath the belt of her robes.

'Silence,' hissed Drutheira. Her own disguise was akin to that of her coven, albeit more impressive and ostentatious. She had no skullcap or circlet, but wore a gilded cuirass and a velvet cloak with ermine trim. She'd kept her raven hair, masquerading as a noblewoman with two servants. Her eyes were on the outpost and the guards occupying its tower and in front of its gate. Dwarfs *and* elves; it was a strange sight to behold such apparent harmony. Each of them carried either a bow or crossbow.

'We can be seen from this distance. Do not fail me here,' she warned them both, her voice changing mid-sentence. Gone were the barbed tones of the druchii and in their place the more lyrical, lilting cadence of the asur.

'Besides,' she said, allowing the slightest dagger of a smile.

'What need have I of horses when the two of you carry all of my wares and do my bidding?'

Malchior hid his sneer behind a bow, though Ashniel was more brazen and showed her displeasure openly. Drutheira could not have cared less.

'Remember your roles,' she said, hiding her contempt for the nearest guard behind a warm smile. She purposefully kept her eyes off the archers in the tower, as not to do so would arouse potential suspicion. 'We are weaponsmiths, servants of Vaul from across the sea and the rugged hills of Cothique.'

'Must we play as rural peasants, Drutheira?' whined Malchior. 'Why not vaunted nobles of Saphery or Lothern?'

'Because nobles of Ulthuan would not be caught dead in a hole like this,' she said through her teeth. 'And they would certainly possess horses. Of course, if you want to be flayed then by all means please continue complaining.'

Malchior spoke no further, but gave a deathly glance to Ashniel who didn't bother to hide her amusement.

As she approached the gate Drutheira tried to ignore the nocked bows, the ready swords and axes loose in their scabbards. She made the rune of *sariour* with her empty hands, adding a shallow incline of the head in mellow greeting.

Sariour symbolised the moon, its aspect that of a crescent. Especially to merchants and traders, it meant 'fortune' and would be taken as a positive sign by the guards. But like most elven runes, it had a darker interpretation too. For sariour also signified 'evil deeds' and 'destruction'. The obvious duplicity, the plain threat it embodied amused Drutheira greatly as they passed through the gate and into the settlement without incident.

It was as much a backwater as its exterior suggested but large, with at least a hundred elves and dwarfs trading with one another from wagons, stalls and pitched tents. A few less ephemeral structures could be found farther from the gate. One, an ale house, was wrought from stone. A blacksmith's was little more than a stone hut, but its anvil and furnace were in constant use. There were also barrack houses and inns, little more than huts themselves but a roof and four walls for weary travellers who needed a night's rest in a bed and not on the hard ground of the road.

An impromptu market had grown up around a bell house that Drutheira assumed was the domain of some kind of alderman or outpost captain. There were several other structures too, fashioned from wood and at the periphery. Some of these were of elven design and bore such devices as rampant Ellyrian stallions and the rising phoenix of Asuryan.

Above the archway framing the gate a sign swung in the wind on two lengths of chain. *Zakbar Varf* was written in chiselled runescript. It meant 'Wolf Hut' or 'Wolf Wall'. Drutheira decided that 'hut' was a more accurate description of the place.

A dwarf trader with a cadre of guards and wagons in tow and not long arrived himself aroused her attention.

'This way,' she muttered. As she was walking towards the dwarfs who were unhitching their wagons and stretching the stiffness from their backs, she gripped Ashniel's arm. Drutheira's eyes held the fiery intensity of flaming coals.

She hissed, 'You know what needs to be done?'

Ashniel nodded slowly.

'You have everything you need?'

Again, she nodded.

Drutheira held the young witch's gaze a moment longer, saw the hatred and ambition in her almond-shaped eyes.

She released her, taking a mote of pleasure in the grimace of pain Ashniel failed to conceal.

'Good,' said Drutheira.

Like a shadow retreats from the approach of the sun, Ashniel crept away from the others and blended into the crowd.

Silently, Drutheira conveyed a final order to Malchior and the two druchii closed to speak to the dwarfs.

'Greetings, traveller,' she said to the dwarf merchant, smiling politely.

He had a grizzled face, more at home on a battlefield than a trading post, and his fair hair showed up the grease and dirt. He grunted a reply of sorts.

Drutheira tried not to sneer. Fortunately for her, the dwarf was busy with his wagons and paid little attention.

'Are you here to trade, ah…?' She invited.

'Krondi,' said the dwarf, handing a barrel of something to one of his fellow traders. There were runes scorched into the hard wood that Drutheira didn't understand. 'Krondi Stoutback.' He turned and firmly shook her hand.

'Astari.'

Such physical greetings were not common amongst elves and Drutheira was unable to hide her surprise and discomfort.

'Apologies for the muck,' said the dwarf, misunderstanding. Belatedly, he wiped the palms of his hands on his tunic. 'Been a long way from Barak Varr. On the road like on campaign, grime tends to get ingrained. Easy to forget it's there.'

Drutheira smiled again and fed some sorcery into the gesture.

'That's perfectly all right. *Barak Varr?*' she asked, struggling a little with the pronunciation.

'The Sea Hold,' Krondi explained, pointing roughly south with a leathery finger. Under the nail was black with dirt and Drutheira fought to hide her disdain.

She also remembered the bastion the dwarf spoke of, and its defences. She masked her interest with another question.

'You were a soldier then? A warrior for the king, perhaps?'

'Aye, milady,' said Krondi, warming to the elf as his companions unloaded the wagon. Drutheira noticed one dwarf, far off at the head of the wagons, remained seated. He was also hooded and kept to himself, more than most dwarfs usually did. Not a merchant, nor a guard. This was something else. She tasted power and resolved to keep her distance.

'I fought for the High King,' Krondi went on proudly, 'and my own king, Brynnoth of the Sea Hold.'

Gently putting her arm around him, hiding the urge to gag, Drutheira led the dwarf to where Malchior was waiting. She briefly searched the bustling crowds for Ashniel but the witchling was nowhere to be seen. Allowing a half-smile she said, 'Here, then you'll know the value of a good blade.'

Krondi began to detach himself, waving Drutheira off.

'Not here to buy,' he said, shaking his head as if trying to dispel an itch, 'but to rest and pick up provisions, possibly sell, before heading on.'

She made a hurt expression, her eyes mildly pleading. Again, she used a little sorcery to enhance her charms. 'At least look at what I'm offering before you dismiss me, Lord Stoutback.'

Krondi laughed. 'I'm no lord, but I'll take a gander at what yer peddling.' He nodded to Malchior who simply bowed and then unrolled his satchel. Unbeknownst to the dwarf, he was incanting silently beneath his breath.

As the leather satchel was unfurled, a rack of stunning ithilmar weapons was revealed. Jewelled daggers, short swords and spear tips were arrayed in rows. There were shimmering axes, both for felling and throwing, and a few smaller pieces of armour.

One in particular caught Krondi's eye.

'Is that…?' He breathed and looked again, closer. 'Gromril?' There was a glint in Krondi's eye as he met Drutheira's, but also something else. Anger?

'How did you come by this?' It was less of a question and more of an accusation.

'A gift,' said Drutheira, drawing closer. Her eyes shone with power. 'I take it you're interested then?'

Krondi went back to the gromril blade. It was a sword, an uncommon weapon amongst dwarfs, who preferred hammers and axes. There were no runes, but the star-metal it was forged from was unmistakable.

'How much?' he asked, his gaze fixed on the blade.

'Only a fair price. Does anything else catch your eye?'

'I'll take everything. All of it,' he said gruffly.

Drutheira smiled thinly, and bade Malchior to wrap up the leather satchel.

'You have made a considerably wise decision.'

SHE MET ASHNIEL on the outskirts of the settlement, away from prying eyes and ears.

'Were you successful?'

'Of course.' Ashniel presented the athame dagger. Its blade was fire-blackened and the pearlescent gemstones had dulled to the lustre of bare rock. She then showed her mistress the flask, empty of its contents.

'You used all of it, on the ale *and* wine?'

An evil smile curled Ashniel's lips. 'Even the water.'

'Then there's nothing further for us here.' Drutheira looked to the distant horizon and the storm rolling across it. She could almost hear the thunder of hooves.

SEVERAL MILES FROM Zakbar Varf, a host of riders dismounted from a barge. They were hooded and twenty-five strong. Three more such bands were alighting from their own ship nearby. In a hidden grove, a few miles from the trading settlement, they would gather. Sharpening their blades and spear tips, they would wait for nightfall and then ride out.

➤ CHAPTER NINE ➤

Rinkkaz

OVER EIGHT HUNDRED dwarfs crowded the room and still it echoed like a tomb.

The Great Hall of Karaz-a-Karak was the single largest chamber in the entire hold. A small town could fit into its vastness. A vaulted ceiling stretched into a gem-studded darkness overhead and columns broad enough to be towers punctuated miles-long walls against which monolithic statues of the ancestors glowered. There was a stern austerity to the hall, despite its roaring hearth and the dusty banners that stirred gently on the hot air.

Three runes arranged in a triangular formation and confined by a circle of copper and bronze sat in the middle of the dwarf gathering. Each rune was wrought from gold and when the light caught them in a certain way they shimmered with captured power. They were devoted to the chief ancestors: Grungni's rune of oath and honour; Valaya's of hearth and hold; and Grimnir's of wrath and ruin. Each described an aspect of the dwarf race, their very essence which made them sons and daughters of the earth. If lore and legend was to be believed, the magic within the runes had been put there by the ancestors themselves. It was latent power, but would protect the dwarfs when needed.

Gotrek Starbreaker looked upon those runes now and tried to remember their lessons.

A dry, rasping voice uttered from parchment lips intruded on the High King's thoughts.

'Such a rare gathering of kings and thanes is a strong sign of a liege-lord's strength, even though they bicker like beardlings.'

The voice put Gotrek in mind of forgotten halls, lost holds and leatherbound tomes caked in dust.

Looking down from his throne, he met the rheumy eyes of the oldest dwarf in Karaz-a-Karak, he of the longbeards who was simply called 'the Ancient'.

'Tromm, old one.' The Ancient was wise beyond reckoning, his age uncounted and unknown except by the High King's Loremaster. 'Should it not concern me that my vassal lords snap at each other like jackals?' he asked in a sideways fashion. He needn't have been so surreptitious, for the dwarf nobles were not paying any attention.

The rinkkaz was a sacred oath that bound all kings. Barring recent death, war, plague or invasion, the council of kings was observed by all of the dwarf holds and occurred every decade. But it was also a chance to settle old scores or revive grudges that were never truly forgotten. For every rinkkaz, which often lasted several days, the incumbent High King would allow a period of *grudgement* for the other kings to vent some spleen. It made later discussion swifter and more amiable.

Gotrek was patient. He had to be. The Ancient never answered quickly and always considered every word. He would often say, at length, it was why he had lived for as many centuries as he had. In the end his breath came out of his wizened mouth like a pall of grave dust.

'Better they bite at one another than sharpen their teeth on your hide.'

Leaning over, Gotrek whispered conspiratorially, 'They would find it leathery and tough if they did, old one.'

The Ancient laughed at that, a grating, hacking cough of mirth that brought up clods of phlegm.

Gotrek slapped him on the back, loosening whatever was lodged in the old dwarf's throat, and received a nod of thanks. He regarded the throng in front of him.

No fewer than seven dwarf kings, not including the High King himself, were in attendance. If a king could not be present at the rinkkaz then a delegate, an ambassador, lord or high thane, even a regent, was sent in his stead. Only the kings of the hill dwarfs were absent, a fact that was noticed by all.

'Yet again, Skarnag makes his insolence plain to the realm...' muttered Ranuld Silverthumb. The runelord was seated on the opposite side of the High King, wisdom and knowledge to his left and right. Only the captain of the hearthguard was closer, but the imposing figure of Thurbad was absent for the moment. 'Wazzock.'

Since their expatriation from the Worlds Edge Mountains, Skarnag Grum and his fellow lords had not once attended the rinkkaz.

'He might surprise us yet,' muttered Gotrek, though without conviction. His gaze strayed to the distance, where he could just make out the bronze doors to the Great Hall, but he wasn't about to hold his breath in expectation of them opening.

Bedecked in his finest runic panoply, a staff of wutroth and banded gromril clenched in his left fist, a helm of gilded griffon feathers upon his beetling brow, Ranuld cut as stern a figure as his liege-lord.

'I'd suggest we march on Kazad Kro and bring the rinkkaz to his gates if it were not for my weary back and legs.' Ranuld grimaced as he said it, and Gotrek smiled to himself. The runelord was much more hale and hearty than he let on. 'Besides,' he added, thumbing over his shoulder, 'the Ancient would never make it.'

A snorting, nasal dirge was coming out of the old dwarf's mouth. None in the hold could snore so loudly.

Ranuld frowned, waggled a finger in his ear. 'Like a boar rutting with an elk.'

Gotrek stifled a laugh then asked, 'Did you find what you were looking for in the old halls?'

The runelord shook his head, 'No, my High King.'

Ranuld Silverthumb was amongst the High King's royal retinue and occupied one of ten seats reserved for the high council. At Gotrek's edict, all of his advisors were present including his Loremaster and Grudgekeeper, both of whom scribed in leatherbound books cradled on lecterns in front of them, thick parchment pages cracking as they were turned. As well as the Master of Engineers, who sat with a thick belt of tools around his waist, there was also the Chief of Lodewardens, he who was responsible for the mines and therefore much of the hold's wealth and prosperity, and the Chief of Reckoners who ensured that grudgement was meted out and reconciled on the behalf of the clans of Karaz-a-Karak, including the royal clan of Thunderhorn, against other clans and other dwarfs if needed.

Disputes were commonplace for a race that valued honour so highly and held grudges so easily. Dwarfs would seldom forgive; and they would never forget. Therefore a record and a means of settling disputes was needed in order for their culture to function without constant wars breaking out between the clans. As High King, Gotrek was fierce but also wise. He had mediated many grievances between his clan lords and those of his vassal kings. His rise to power was not only assured through the greenskin purges of his early reign, but also the agreements he brokered between the northern and southern kings when the former encroached on the latter's territory by mistake. Blood was shed, for dwarf clans are not above fighting one another, but not so much that the warring nobles could not be reconciled.

Many years later the grudges on both sides were still remembered. It was echoed by the fact that all the northern kings sat on Gotrek's left and the southern kings his right. He wondered absently where the kings of the hill dwarfs would have sat, should they ever have graced his hall with their presence.

Gotrek had made his disdain for Grum's insolence plain to all, and only current matters prevented him from taking steps to redress it. From atop his Throne of Power, seat of the High Kings since before Snorri Whitebeard's days, he glowered. Clan bickering had turned to matters of the realm. It was a subject that had cropped up often during the rinkkaz, and Gotrek felt its unwelcome weight upon him like a cloak of anvils.

Ever since they had returned to the Old World, the grumbles from the other kings had been the same.

Elves.

No one wanted war with them, but then no one especially wanted peace either. Of all the liege-lords of the dwarf realm, it was Gotrek who had extended the hand of friendship most readily. Like his forebears, he recognised the nobility and power of the elves. There was also the honour of heritage and ancestry to uphold. For was it not Snorri Whitebeard himself who had made an ally of the Elf Prince Malekith and even called him friend?

Who were they not to maintain such a fine tradition?

'They encroach too far onto my lands,' griped Thagdor. As he puffed up his chest, the King of Zhufbar clanked in his ceremonial armour. The majority of the kings and their delegates were smoking pipeweed. Thagdor was no exception, and a palpable fug of their combined exhalations clung to the lower vaults of the massive chamber in an expansive cloud. Together with the smoke issuing from the roaring fire in the High King's mighty hearth, it muddied the air, obscuring the many warriors Thagdor had brought with him.

A traditionalist, fond of engineering and with a thriving guild, Thagdor was just slightly paranoid. Zhufbar had been besieged by greenskins many times, in the early days before Gotrek had made his war against the creatures and all but eradicated them. It had made Thagdor wary of constant attack, his back perpetually up. A hundred hearthguard had accompanied him into the great hold hall; a hundred and fifty more awaited him above in the entrance hall.

'Every time I step beyond my halls for a stroll, there's a bloody elf wandering about,' he went on. 'I am fed up with it, Gotrek.'

No lord other than Thagdor ever called the High King by

his first name during a rinkkaz. There was none more down to earth than the lord of Zhufbar and this extended to the way he greeted his liege-lord, so it was tolerated.

There were mutterings of agreement from Brynnoth of Barak Varr and the fierce-looking Luftvarr of Kraka Drak at this proclamation. The former resembled a sea captain more than a king, with a doubloon eye-patch and a leather cloak festooned with sigils of sea monsters and mermen. Brynnoth had a long, plaited beard that flared out at the ends where it was attached to tiny hooks that tied to his armour.

Luftvarr wore furs and pelts, in keeping with the Norse dwarfs who had to travel vast distances to reach such proceedings. His scowl was legendary, said to have killed a stone troll at fifty paces. His beard was rough and wild, his helmet crested by two massive mammoth tusks. Ringmail swathed his muscular body and his arms were bare apart from knotted torcs just below the elbow.

'And what of the rats in the lower deeps?' said King Aflegard of Karak Izril. The Jewel Hold was well known for its wealth and its deep mines. Rich veins of ore ran through its hewn halls, much to the envy of the other liege-lords present.

King Bagrik of Karak Ungor, the farthest of the northern holds of the Worlds Edge Mountains from Karaz-a-Karak, nodded in agreement with Aflegard. He was called 'Boar-brow', an honorific earned because of the mighty pelt he wore over his back and shoulders, beneath which was a red and gold tunic armoured with a coat of silver mail.

Aflegard was as bejewelled as his hold and wore a great many rings and bracelets. It made him appear slightly effete, especially given his silk garments and the fact he was known for trading openly with elves. Every rinkkaz he protested about the rats, claiming them to be more numerous, larger and cleverer with each passing decade. Thus far, his concerns had fallen on deaf ears.

'I have seen them too,' said Thane Brokk Stonefist of Karak Azul. He was no king, not even a high thane, but had been trusted to come in his liege-lord's stead. As militaristic as his king, Brokk's attire was functional and war-ready. His armour was thick plate. He carried a pickaxe and wore a miner's soot-stained features. 'Heard them even,' he added. 'Rats that walk like you or I, noble kings. Rats that can–'

'Bollocks, laddie!' A raucous bellow broke through the fog. King Grundin of Karak Kadrin was on his feet and swearing readily. 'We should be more concerned about the return of the urk and grobi. Ach, there are fekking hundreds of the wee little bastards roaming beneath my halls. What's to be done aboot them, might I ask?'

Grundin's loyalty to Karaz-a-Karak was beyond doubt, but a little needle still persisted between him and Gotrek on account of the High King's son's refusal of his daughter Helda.

'Perhaps you should look to your own ironbreakers to clear your underhalls of the vermin, as we all have,' countered Aflegard.

'Ye dirty little scutter!' Four of the High King's hearth-guard had to hold Grundin back from crossing the hall and lamping one on Aflegard's bulbous nose.

'Enough!'

One word, not shouted, but with raised voice, silenced the room.

A grumbling hubbub persisted, but it was impossible to stop a dwarf king from muttering his displeasure.

Gotrek looked down on his vassals and scowled.

'You are kings of the Karaz Ankor, not bickering grobi chieftains. I invite you into my halls, let you eat my meat, drink my beer to discuss important matters of state, not settle old scores.'

Grundin shrugged off the guards with a curse or two then bowed a quick apology. Chuntering, he sat back down.

An impressive feast had been arrayed for the kings, who sat in a semi-circle before their liege-lord, a host of retainers behind them. Adjacent to the Great Hall, through two low archways chiselled with runes and gems, were a pair of large feast halls. Racks of stout wooden tables with short-legged stools and benches sat within. Soon they would be brimming with food and ale.

The vassal lords had been fed already – some still carried their tankards – but the second course was being readied. Roast boar, elk, thick slabs of beef and even fowl were being prepared and cooked for the edification of the High King's guests. The look on Gotrek's face at that moment suggested he wanted to spit on their food and throw them out of his house.

'But what of the elgi problem, my liege-lord?' asked another voice, one that was more cultured and refined than the rest. He had seated himself away from the crowds, at the edge of the semi-circle, so that Gotrek had to crane his neck to speak to him or risk looking as if he was showing disrespect.

Sinking two heavily ringed thumbs into his gilded belt, King Varnuf of Karak Eight Peaks asked, 'Well, my High King?'

Regarding the ostentatiously attired dwarf with his gems and his indecently large crown, Gotrek answered through clenched teeth.

'There are elgi who are guests of this hold, I'd remind you,' he said. 'Not a thousand paces from this very hall in fact. And once the rinkkaz is done with, I'm expecting you all to eat with them too.' He glared at Varnuf before he could interrupt. 'I'll tell you why we tolerate the elgi, why they are allowed to roam in our lands and trade with our merchants. It's very simple. Peace.

'For thousands of years we dawi have fought. We've dug our holds, we've honoured our ancestors, killed urk and grobi and drakk by the score. But now we have peace. For once, our hearths are safe and our wars a distant memory. I could no more expel the elgi than I could oust you all from your own halls.'

That spurred a sudden bout of vociferous complaint, amidst threat of grudgement and invocation of the reckoners.

'Don't be soft in the head,' Gotrek snapped, silencing the ire of some of the more belligerent kings. 'I mean the elgi are staying. They are our allies, and they've given me no reason to believe otherwise.'

'Their ways are not our ways,' Thagdor protested. 'I want 'em off my hills and out of my chuffing sight.'

'You're welcome to move them yourself, Thagdor,' said Gotrek, 'but know that I won't raise a finger to help you and I'll make damn sure none of your fellow kings do either. I won't jeopardise peace.' He shook his head. 'I won't.'

Further grumblings greeted this remark but the High King would not be swayed.

His gaze alighted on Varnuf who said nothing, but merely sank back into his seat. His face was lost in smoke and shadow until the tip of his pipe flared and threw a glow upon a stern and envious countenance.

Ever had the Vala-Azrilungol, the 'Queen of the Silver Depths', been a rival to the majesty and splendour of Karaz-a-Karak. Its halls were vast and impressive, its wealth immense. Varnuf considered Eight Peaks as a rival to Karaz-a-Karak, and himself a worthy replacement for the current High King. He would not do so through dishonourable means, for this was not the dwarf way, but he would also not shirk from the Dragon Crown should it be offered to him.

Gotrek had neither the will nor the strength to continue the argument. It was draining, and he slumped back in his throne.

'The elgi stay. This is my final word.' He surveyed the room with his gimlet gaze, 'And any who gainsay it had best take up their axe and be ready to fight their king.'

⫷ CHAPTER TEN ⫸

The Hammer of Old

AFTER LEAVING SNORRI to the tender ministrations of a certain priestess, Morgrim didn't return to his clan holdings as he originally intended. To reach the southern halls of Karaz-a-Karak, even via the mining routes, would take too long and he had no desire to face his father. Not yet.

His mind was occupied by other thoughts.

Morgrim believed in fate, he believed in a reason for everything and everything for a reason. So when Ranuld Silverthumb pronounced a great destiny for his cousin, he was certain of its fulfilment. This in turn troubled him. His concern was twofold: first at what lengths Snorri would go to in order to ensure he attained his prophesied greatness as quickly as possible and second, what that meant for him.

If he was lucky, a dwarf would live a long life; but children were rare and in order for his name to live on, his legacy to endure, it was by his deeds that he would often be remembered. Morgrim had no wife, and no aspirations to find one. He did not wish to be a general or even a king, though his position as the prince's cousin could afford him such a title. Like his father and his father before him, he was a miner. It was a life and profession that suited him, that suited many dwarfs, but one thing about it bothered him.

How would he make his mark?

Such aspirations had never worried him before, but some of Snorri's rampant ambition had rubbed off he supposed. Death had been close in the dilapidated halls of Karak Krum. He'd felt it like a cold breath on the back of his neck. Yes, he and Snorri had laughed about it, but Morgrim saw the look in his cousin's eyes that mirrored his own.

Both of them could have been killed in that lonely place, left to be gnawed upon by rats. Morgrim did not want that as his epitaph. Like any dwarf, he wanted to be remembered.

Perhaps then that was why he now found himself in the Hall of Kings, standing before one of the greatest liege-lords Karaz-a-Karak had ever known.

Every previous incumbent of the Throne of Power was honoured in this echoing gallery of jewel and stone. Thorik Snorrison, slayer of the *ngardruk*; Gorim Ironhammer, he who discovered the mines of Gunbad and Silverspear; and Gurni Hammerfist, he who was father of Gotrek and defeated the orc warchief, Huzkalukk with only one hand. Legends all, but it was the alcove-chamber of Snorri White-beard that was the largest and most venerated.

An immense statue of the High King of the Karaz Ankor, rendered in his full panoply of war and hewn from flawless marble, stared out into the darkness of the deeper hall.

The Hall of Kings was a place of veneration, of quiet imprecation to the spirits of the great ancestors. Some came to beseech wisdom, others fortune and better times. Occasionally, dwarfs would speak their grudges before these effigies of stone or swear oaths of vengeance or fealty.

Morgrim did none of these things, for he did not come to the Hall of Kings on his behalf but rather he came to plead for another.

'Tromm, High King Whitebeard,' he uttered, bowing his head sombrely to remove his helm before taking a knee in the shadow of the cyclopean liege-lord of Karaz-a-Karak. 'I come to you on behalf of another. Though he carries your namesake, and proudly, he does not have your temperance.'

Breathing deeply, he said. 'Let him heed the wisdom of his ancestors. By Grimnir, he has courage but let him be brave enough to not let pride ruin a father's love and respect. Let him find inner counsel against reckless abandon. Let him live to see his destiny realised. For this I make my oaths to the gods, to hearth and hold.'

Morgrim raised his eyes, returning the great horned war helm to his head.

Hard marble stared back at him.

The ancient king had not stirred. No magic had animated his stern countenance, which was as unyielding as winter earth. His jaw was still fixed. His fists were still clenched.

But Morgrim hoped his words were heeded anyway. Oaths made, he began to appreciate the rest of what lay inside the alcove-chamber.

Though his weapons and armour were locked away in the treasure vaults of the lower deeps, protected by rune seals and stern-faced ancestor guards, there were other artefacts of Snorri Whitebeard's reign. Banners describing his conquests and deeds swathed each of the chamber's three walls. Trophies of the terrible monsters he had slain were hung up on spikes of iron between them.

Some of the scaled flesh of Gnaugrak was missing, supposedly cleaved off to fashion a wondrous cloak given as a gift to one of Snorri's vassal lords. It was said it had taken the king and over fifty of his ironbreakers to impale the dragon's heart. On the opposite wall, the spiked head of a massive orc chieftain. Preserved in oils and unguents, the greenskin still leered, though the gums around its shattered tusks were slowly succumbing to rot. It neighboured a crushed giant's skull and beside that was a flayed troll carcass, doused in fire-salt to prevent regeneration. Morgrim doubted that even without the salt, the beast would ever be able to re-knit its skin and bones, or grow its organs anew. Stranger things had happened though.

Bones of other creatures, griffons and shaggoths, great tuskors and iron-hided manticores, fimir and wyverns described a bloody legacy that stretched into centuries. But it was to the broken hammer, incongruous amongst the grisly trophies, that the dwarf's eye was drawn.

'What must it have been like to live in such days?' he wondered aloud, reaching out for the weapon.

Its power had been drained long ago, during one of the last great battles of the age. A jagged cleft raked down the head and split the haft, evidence of where a daemon's evil had broken it. Tentatively, Morgrim went to trace his finger down the hammer's mortal wound, imagining it reforged before he took his hand away.

'A different time...'

Morgrim turned sharply at the voice in his ear. What he saw standing in the entrance of the alcove-chamber, almost fifty paces away, was a friend.

A look of incredulity crumpled Morgrim's face as he recognised the warrior before him.

'Drogor?'

The dwarf was dressed in furs and lizard hide, a bronze pauldron over one shoulder and a helmet with a flanged crest in the crook of his right arm. On his left side was a mace, also bronze, with a heavy gem affixed to the pommel. He looked weather-beaten, his skin sun-kissed and a peaty brown, but he wasn't old. White, wiry hair ran a ring around his balding pate and his long moustaches drooped like the exhausted tentacles of some leviathan cloud. His beard was bound in a bronze ringlet, etched with the snarling visage of a serpent. A cloak of exotic feathers cascaded down his back.

Drogor was staring intently at the statue and the hammer above it in what Morgrim took to be reverence. At mention of his name, the dwarf smiled and nodded.

'By the ancestors, I thought you were dead!' Rushing over, Morgrim clapped his errant friend in a firm embrace, slapping his back and shoulder.

'I went south with my clan, Morg,' said Drogor, coughing as Morgrim crushed the air out of him. 'I didn't venture north to the Wastes.'

'Of course... I just didn't expect to see you again.' He shook his head in disbelief. 'There's been no word from Karak Zorn in many years, and last we heard...'

At this remark, Drogor nodded grimly.

'Aye, there are worse things than sun and jiggers the size of your fist in the endless jungle. Ziggurats that claw at the sky, and beasts…' He shook his head, as his gaze was drawn far away as if back beneath the sweltering canopy. 'Like you have never before seen. Creatures of tooth and scale, of leather pinion and tusk, chitinous bone plates that repel crossbow bolts like paper darts.'

Drogor's hand was shaking, and Morgrim clutched the fingers to steady it.

'It's all right, old friend,' he said, his voice soothing, 'you are returned to Karaz-a-Karak, but I am surprised you are back at all. How long did you travel from the Southlands to get here? How many long years has it been?'

Clans Bargrum and Zarrdum had been staunch allies for many decades, across two generations without bloodshed or a grudge made. Miners and fortune hunters, the Zarrdums had left Karaz-a-Karak over twenty years ago and gone south to be reunited with their cousins in the sunny climes of Karak Zorn.

Finding his composure again, Drogor said, 'We were many months travelling on perilous roads. Fifty of us ventured out, our pack mules brimming with saurian gold. Of that expedition, I alone remain.'

'What happened?'

Drogor's expression darkened further. 'Having survived the jungle with just under half of my father's warriors, we reached the borders of Karak Azul.' His eyes narrowed, remembering 'Foolishly, we thought we would be safe in the shadow of the mountain but we were wrong. An ambush, old friend. Archers, hidden in the crags and raining steel-fanged death upon me and my fellow dawi. It was a slaughter.'

Morgrim's jaw clenched at such perfidy. 'Cowards…' he breathed, an undercurrent of anger affecting his voice. 'How did you survive?'

At this Drogor hung his head. 'To my shame, I ran and hid.'

'Dreng tromm… Mercy of Valaya that you lived. There is no shame in retreating from certain death.'

'Then why is it that I wish I had died with my kin?'

Morgrim gripped the shoulder of his old friend, and exhaled a deep, rueful breath.

'Come with me,' he said, after some thought. 'I must meet my cousin outside the Great Hall but then we can find an alehouse and drink to the honour of your slain clansmen.'

Nodding solemnly, Drogor said, 'I don't think I have ever met your cousin, the great prince of the Karaz Ankor. I much look forward to it.'

'I warn you,' said Morgrim as he left the alcove-chamber, 'he takes a little getting used to.'

Drogor smiled. 'We have time, old friend.'

⊰ CHAPTER ELEVEN ⊱

Return of the Prince

DURING TIMES OF WAR, a king's duty to his hold and his peoples is very clear. Conflict against a different race, a different creed unites clans, it brings cultures together. It was no different for the dwarfs. But Gotrek had fought his wars, or so he hoped. He had defeated the greenskins, harried them to the point of extinction and brokered peace between all the clans of the Karaz Ankor. The dark days were over, at least for a while, and had been for many years.

So, why then did he feel so tired?

It was with a weary reluctance that he dragged himself from his bed or to his feast halls, or even the alehouses of the chief brewmaster. War made a king lean, sharp like the razored edge of an axe blade. Gotrek felt blunt like a hammer, but without its purpose and directness.

Though he didn't want to admit it, especially to himself, peace was wearing him out. Despite his protestations to the other kings who still argued and fought him and each other, he would prefer war but was wise enough to realise the folly of that desire. Weary of constant negotiation and compromise in the search for harmonious co-existence with the elves, he just wanted a good clean fight to blow away the dust he felt gathering between his bones. It provoked a maudlin mood in the High King.

I am atrophying, becoming a living ancestor bereft of his tomb.

In the minds of some, he had invited an enemy onto their shores, to camp and build cities outside their holds. Tempers were already frayed. It wouldn't take much of a spark to ignite something more serious than mere discontent and pugnacious bellyaching.

War was easy. It was simple, the need obvious. Survive or die. Kill or be killed, they were hackneyed words but with good reason. Truth shouted loudly from every syllable. Give him greenskins or giants, even dragons run amok in the underway, even the Grungni-damned rat creatures he was hearing so much about of late. But not elves, not them, and not peace. At least not one as fragile as this. It was as if their very natures fought against it, that no matter how he reasoned, no concession would ever satisfy the lords of both races.

Looking over to the only two empty seats on the high council, below and in front of the Throne of Power, Gotrek sagged. One was for his queen, beautiful Rinnana, who had died some sixty-three years ago whilst giving birth. Perhaps that was why the weight fell so heavily upon his shoulders? Shared, it would be halved. As it was, it was an anvil big enough to forge a sword for a giant.

'*My love…*' he murmured, and prayed to Valaya to bring him fortitude.

The other empty place brought a scowl to the High King's face. His errant son was wayward yet again.

As if summoned by the thought, a creaking sound invaded the penumbral gloom of the Great Hall as the massive bronze doors yawned open. A quartet of figures entered, striding quickly, armour clanking, down the mosaicked walkway that led all the way to the ancestor runes and the Throne of Power.

There was a shallow enough gap in the semi-circle of nobles for the late entrants to pass through. None spoke, not even to grumble, during the many minutes it took for the dwarfs to cross the hall. All looked, though, sucking on their pipes thoughtfully, glaring through exhaled smoke.

Thurbad led the small throng, his face as grim as a thundercloud. He stopped when he reached the ancestor runes and took a knee. Slamming a fist against his armoured chest, he waited for the High King to bid him rise and then announced who he had escorted into the chamber.

'Tromm, High King,' he said, bowing his head before meeting the king's gaze again to add, 'Prince Snorri Lunngrin of Thunderhorn.'

'Tromm, Thurbad.' Gotrek nodded his respect to the captain of his hearthguard. 'You may take your place.'

Snorri stepped forwards from between a pair of silent warriors, crafting a shallow bow that smacked more of rote than respect.

When he continued forwards, the High King raised his hand.

'Not you, my son,' he said, fierce and cold as winter storm. 'You have not earned the right to be by my side.' He nodded to the back of the semi-circle where room had been left for Skarnag Grum. 'That's your place, back there.'

Snorri looked over his shoulder, and frowned.

No one spoke. Even the Ancient's snoring had dulled to a low susurrus of heavy breathing.

'In the seat of the skarrenawi? Thagging hill dwellers?'

The frown became a scowl.

Gotrek mirrored it, only his was born of centuries of grudges. He had perfected it, forged it into a weapon to make all but the staunchest vassal lords quail.

'Sit down,' he said, snarling the words through his teeth. 'Now, and disrespect me no further.'

Snorri glared, every inch his father's son, about-faced and planted himself down in the seat reserved for Skarnag Grum. It took a few minutes to reach the back of the throng, and silence was with the prince during every step. He didn't speak to the lesser nobles around him when he sat down, he didn't even look at them. His eyes were on his father, arms folded and brow jutting to display his displeasure.

Like any good father who is trying to teach a lesson to

his son, Gotrek ignored him and turned to his Loremaster instead.

'Missives?' he asked, requesting any letters or messages from the more distant holds unable to attend the rinkkaz.

Clearing his throat, the Loremaster's stentorian voice boomed without need of a speaking horn.

'From Krag Bryn, King Drong does send word of elves setting up a colony on the borders of his lands.'

This brought renewed consternation from certain vassal kings, especially Bagrik of Karak Ungor, which Gotrek silenced by slamming his fist upon the arm of his throne.

Turning to a fresh page, the Loremaster continued, 'At Silver Pinnacle, King Borri Silverfoot of Karaz Bryn makes a detailed record.' The Loremaster waited for permission to relay it, which Gotrek gave him with a nod.

'"More of the grey men were sighted in the southern reaches today, wandering lonely upon the hills and fens that border our hearth and hold. As their numbers grow, so too does my concern at their presence. A dark cloud lingers over the barrows and cairns beyond our walls, where a party of rangers went missing several weeks past. I have instructed the gates to be shut and sealed, the guard doubled at night. No more dawi shall leave my halls come the fall of darkness. Fell winds blow across my lands that reek of death, even in the deep earth we can smell them and are reminded of our own mortality. I pray to Valaya they will soon abate."'

The Loremaster looked up from his reading.

'There is nothing further, High King.'

A perturbed look creased Gotrek's brow. Beyond sending a message of support, there was little else he could do for the Lord of the Silver Pinnacle.

'Carry on,' he breathed, still deep in thought.

'Karak Zorn makes mention of riches in the far south where the sun is hot enough to cook a dawi in his armour. Several have fallen to exhaustion and wells have dried up across the hold. Forays into the deeper jungle have encountered "saurian beasts". A gathering of these creatures is mentioned and an attack upon the hold itself.'

The crease on Gotrek's brow deepened. It seemed the dwarfs were assailed by enemies familiar and unknown. At least Karaz-a-Karak and the Worlds Edge were mercifully spared from fighting.

Shutting his great leatherbound tome, the Loremaster looked up. 'That concludes all of the missives, High King.'

'Tromm, Loremaster.' Gotrek switched his attention to the assembled lords, regarding his son with a reproachful glance.

Some of the kings and thanes had caught the waft of cooked meat, the malty flavour of hops from freshly uncasked ale. Several licked their lips, stomachs groaning in anticipation.

'Business is concluded,' he declared. 'The feast halls are prepared. Eat. Drink.' He shooed them off, as if tired of seeing their faces.

None took offence, but rather tromped off in their masses to the nearby feast halls, drawn by the emanation of smells.

Snorri was left alone, sitting before his father and the high council. The young prince was surprised to see Ranuld Silverthumb amongst the venerable dwarfs and glowered when the runelord winked at him.

'Leave us,' Gotrek said firmly, but with an underlying weariness.

It took many minutes for the council to depart, during which time Snorri locked his gaze with that of his father. Should the two of them ever attempt a staring competition, a victor would be tough to predict and the contest itself would last for days, perhaps even weeks.

When they were properly alone, the sounds of merriment echoing distantly from the feast halls, Gotrek beckoned his son to him.

Fighting to keep his temper, he rasped, 'Where were you?'

Snorri's nostrils flared and he licked his lips. 'Father, I have been on the road for many hours. My stomach is empty. Can we not discuss my absence before there is nowt but scraps at the feast table?'

'Answer me!' Gotrek rose to his feet, hands clutching the arms of the throne; their knuckles white, he gripped so hard.

Snorri was about to when Gotrek raised his finger, stopping him. 'And I warn you, boy, give me any more of your flippancy and I will come down off this throne and beat some respect into you. I swear to Grungni, I will do it,' he said, settling back down and speaking more calmly. 'Now where were you?'

Snorri swallowed back a lump of trepidation in his throat. 'In the Ungdrin Ankor, in the hold halls of Karak Krum.'

The anger returned to the High King's face, manifesting as a flush of vermillion to his cheeks and nose. His beard bristled.

'That place is forbidden to the dawi.'

'Morgrim and I, we only–'

'With good reason!' Gotrek bellowed. 'There are dangers in the dark beneath the world, fell creatures we dawi have no interest or business in provoking.'

'Provoking?' said Snorri, becoming bolder. 'The Karaz Ankor is our sovereign territory. We dawi are masters of earth and stone, is that not what you have always told me?'

'Aye, it is, but–'

'Then what do we have to fear of the dark, father? Whatever lurks in the ruins of Karak Krum should be mindful of us, not the other way around.'

Gotrek was shaking his head, descending the throne. 'You have much to learn, my son. And do not think I won't have words with your cousin and his father too, though I know whose idea this little adventure was.'

'I venture beyond our borders because you will not. Every day parts of our hold are surrendered to urk and grobi who have returned in number since the purge. Beneath the halls of Karak Krum, I saw rats, father. Rats! They walked on two legs and spoke with one another.' Snorri brandished his bandaged hand like a badge of honour. 'We barely escaped with our lives.'

'Precisely why you must do as I bid, as your king bids.'

'Ignoring the enemies at our gates won't make them disappear, father. We are besieged, if only you would look beyond your fragile peace with the elgi to see it. Or are we to look to them for our protection now? Resting on past laurels, what would my mother think?'

Gotrek raised a fist. His teeth were clenched tight as a sprung trap.

Despite himself, Snorri flinched.

'I am your father, Snorri, but you should choose your next words very carefully indeed.'

Snorri bowed, and knew he had gone too far. 'Tromm,' he uttered. 'I am sorry, father. I didn't mean it.'

Unclenching his hand, letting his arm fall by his side, Gotrek sighed and turned his back. 'Yes, you did.'

'Please father, I…'

'It's all right,' said Gotrek, waving off his son's protests like they were flies. 'Do you not think the same thoughts have entered my head?' His eyes lingered on Rinnana's empty seat. 'How I miss her…'

When he faced Snorri again, there were tears in Gotrek's eyes but he mastered his voice to stop it from cracking as he put both hands on his son's shoulders.

'One day the throne will be yours,' he said, staring into Snorri's eyes, 'and I would have it that you're ready to rule when that day comes. Being king is not about warring and killing, it is about keeping your realm and maintaining peace for as long as you can. It is the hardest thing you'll ever need to do as king. Killing is easy. Any fool can make war and slay his enemies. Keeping a realm once it is intact is much more difficult. Don't be so eager to take up axe and hammer, my son. It might be a while before you can put them down again and I can tell you they grow very heavy in that time.'

'I *am* ready, father,' Snorri said in a small voice, 'if you would but see it. There is none amongst all the champions of the holds that can best me with axe or crossbow. Nothing scares me, nothing. I would purge the very Ungdrin Ankor of monsters to prove that I am a leader, a worthy successor.'

Gotrek let go, and began to pace.

'Have you got chuff in your ears, for I can think of no other reason why you have heard nothing I have said.'

'Father, I have–'

Gotrek stabbed a finger in the direction of the feast halls.

'Sitting in there, Varnuf of Eight Peaks covets my throne.

He would not seize it or try to take it from me by nefarious means, but nonetheless he believes he would be a better High King than I. He wants war with the elgi because it is popular amongst the other kings, and he also seeks to undermine me at every turn. We dawi are honourable, but we are also envious, greedy creatures. One always wants what another has, be it his gold or his armies, even his hold.'

'Then declare grudgement against him. Tie your beards together and fight Varnuf. Show him who the High King of the Karaz Ankor is. I'll do it now, father. Challenge him in your name.' Snorri began to turn.

'No! Do not suggest it. Do not even dare. If the only way a king can maintain order is to pummel his fellow lords into submission, his would be a short rule. Stand down or I shall put you down, by Grungni I swear it.' Such was the intensity in Gotrek's eyes that the prince shrank from it and was rooted to the spot.

Snorri rallied quickly. 'Can I do nothing that meets your standards, father? Without chastisement and being brought to heel? Ever do my achievements fall short. What must I do to earn your respect?'

Gotrek sighed again, like he was a bellows and all the air was escaping from within him.

'Not this.'

'Then what? What must a son do to gain his father's favour? He who vaunts all others above him out of spite?'

Gotrek had no answer. He dared not speak in case in his anger his words betrayed him.

'You are a great king, my liege.' There was a grimace of inner pain on Snorri's face as he spat the words. 'But you are a poor father.'

He turned around and stalked from the Great Hall.

Breathing hard, heart pounding in his chest, Gotrek watched him go.

It was several moments before he could speak again. When he did, it was to ask a question of the shadows.

'Why won't he heed me?'

From the darkness, a smoke-wreathed figure answered.

'He is still young, and burdened with the weight of expectation,' said Ranuld Silverthumb. Hidden from sight, he watched the prince keenly. 'Do not be too hard on yourself, my liege.'

Gotrek's shoulders slumped and he broke out his pipe to draw deep of its calming embers. 'I am striving to leave him a legacy of peace, of a lasting realm unfractured by war and death. Yet he is more belligerent than ever.'

'Were you so temperate when you mustered your armies during the greenskin purge? Or when you knocked Grundin and Aflegard's heads together? What about the time when you journeyed to Kraka Drak and fought King Luftvarr for his fealty?' Ranuld emerged from the darkness to add his smoke to that of his king's. 'You have fought your wars, my liege. Not only that, you won them all and have carved a great legend for the book of deeds. When Grungni calls you to his hall, you will sit at his table.' He gestured to Gotrek's departing son with his pipe. Snorri had only just reached the doors and slammed them on his way out. 'Not so for Snorri Lunngrin, now Halfhand.'

Gotrek laughed. 'Is that what they're calling him now?'

'His cousin thought of the name.'

'A worthy honorific, I suppose. He said there were rats in the deeps of Karak Krum, who walk on two legs not four.'

'And who speak.'

Gotrek turned to Ranuld Silverthumb, but the runelord was not mocking him.

'And who speak, yes.'

'It was a rat that gnawed off your son's hand.'

The silence held an unspoken question that the runelord answered.

'There *are* creatures in the deeps of Karak Krum, but they are not rats. At least, not as we know them.'

'I'll have the ironbreakers look into it. Borin can muster the lodewardens and seal up the underway. No dawi will set foot in there again.'

Ranuld said nothing. His mind was far away, lost to some unfathomable thought.

'He'll need a gauntlet for that hand,' said Gotrek.

'My apprentice shall fashion one under my tutelage.'

Gotrek half-glanced over his shoulder, one eyebrow raised. 'And the other?'

'*Az* and *klad* as you requested, my liege. But it will take some time. Master runes always do.'

Gotrek's gaze returned to the distant bronze door of the Great Hall.

'I hope he is worthy of it.'

'That, my liege,' said Ranuld, slowly disappearing back into the darkness, 'is not up to you.'

⇥ CHAPTER TWELVE ⇥

Old Magic

MOREK HAD BEEN listening to the rinkkaz from an alcove behind his master. Dutifully, he remained silent throughout the summit with his head bowed.

As Ranuld Silverthumb returned to the shadows he strode past his apprentice, uttering a single word.

'Come.'

Morek followed, marvelling at how the statue of Smednir slid aside as his master worked the earth runes on the hidden doorway it concealed. Like many of the lesser ancestors, Smednir dwelled in the penumbral darkness that haunted the edges of the Great Hall. Few knew of the statue's presence, let alone the existence of the hidden passageway that lay behind it.

Lost in thought as he counted the six hundred and thirty-four steps of the spiral down into the first of the deeps, Morek started when his master spoke.

'You are prepared for what is before you, runesmith.'

From Lord Silverthumb's tone, it was difficult to tell whether it was a question or even one that he wanted answering.

'I am, master.' The feebleness of his own voice surprised Morek.

Ranuld Silverthumb barked back at him.

'I know you are, wazzock. I have made certain of it, sure as steel.'

Morek fell into silence again at the sudden rebuke, which only earned further reproach.

'Have you no tongue, zaki? Bitten off by a grobi hiding under that last step was it?'

Morek resisted the urge to look back to see if there actually was a greenskin crouched under the last step. Their echoing footfalls, clacking against the stone, seemed louder in that moment.

Smoothed by the rivulets of water trickling from some underground lake or stream, the walls of the stairwell were also chiselled with runes of warding and disguise. None but a runesmith, or someone who was accompanied by one, could enter this place and not lose his way. By their natures, dwarfs were secretive but there were none more clandestine about their craft than the runesmiths. Other than its enchanted sigils, there was little else to distinguish the long, winding, descending corridor.

It was wide, massive in fact like so much of the subterranean Karaz Ankor. There were precious few sconces with lit braziers and those that did grace the coiling tunnel did so with a flickering, eldritch flame.

Occasionally, the hewn face of Thungi, lesser ancestor god of runesmiths, would glare at them from some sunken reliquary or shrine. Lord Silverthumb seemed to ignore it but his lips moved in silent oath-making as he passed by the patron of their guild and profession. Morek felt cowed by every stony glance, feeling more unready and unworthy than his master surely already believed. After the four hundred and fifty-eighth step, he found his voice again.

'No, master. But I am unsure of what you want me to say.'

Lord Silverthumb grumbled another insult under his breath, hawked and spat as if the stupidity of his apprentice left a bitter taste in his mouth.

'Aren't you wondering,' he said, 'why I brought you to the rinkkaz?'

'I… um…'

'You are the second ufdi to refer to yourself as "um" in as many days.' Ranuld Silverthumb came to an abrupt halt, bringing Morek to a stop too. So sudden was it that the apprentice nearly tripped and fell trying to avoid clattering into his master, who stood in front of him like a craggy bulwark and glowered.

'Come here,' he snapped, and seized Morek's chin in an iron grip that had more in common with a vice than a dwarf's fingers. Even the gnarled leathern skin of the runelord chafed and the apprentice barely stifled a yelp.

Lord Silverthumb pulled open Morek's eye, using thumb and forefinger to check the sclera. His own eyes narrowed as he made an observation.

'Are you a doppleganger wearing the flesh of Morek as a dwarf would wear a coat of mail? Hmm, well? Speak, fiend, if that's what you are!'

Ranuld Silverthumb let him go, carried on walking.

'No,' he said, 'I think you are him.'

Morek shut his open mouth, an answer no longer needed.

His master continued. 'I shall tell you then why I brought you.'

Scents and sounds wafted and emanated from below as they closed on the deep. Morek discerned metal, the heady aroma of soot, the tang of heat pricking his tongue. Hammer rang on anvil, creating a monotonous but dulcet symphony that had oft been used to send beardlings to sleep. But there was something further... Old stone, dank, but which had seen and endured more than one age of the slowly turning world. Every time Morek placed his hand upon it to steady himself when a step was too broad to descend safely without being braced he felt the resonance within the rock, the sweat and earth of the dwarfs who had also once traversed this passage. Magic was thick in the air, and not just on account of the runes engraved into the walls. It saturated the corridor, bound to the rock, to the earth.

'Master?' Morek ventured after a few minutes of silence.

Lord Silverthumb scowled, flashed a scathing glance in his apprentice's general direction. 'What is it now, wazzock? Always talking... chatter, chatter, chatter,' he said, mimicking a flapping mouth with each of his hands. 'You're no better than a rinn.'

Reddening beneath his beard, Morek said, 'Why did you bring me to the rinkkaz, master?'

Lord Silverthumb sniffed either with regret or rueful derision, Morek couldn't tell which.

'Do you know how old I am, Morek?' he asked.

'I... um...'

'Again with this "um". Our noble ancestry has been watered down to a clutch of would-be lordlings and princes who when confused can only think of "um". You and the prince, "ummers" both. Must be chuffing catching or something.'

Ranuld Silverthumb had lit a pipe and was blowing intricate smoke rings in the shape of runic knotwork through the flickering half-darkness. 'I am venerable,' he said, and now he sounded weary, thin like old parchment or a threadbare tarp stretched too wide over its frame. 'The oldest living runelord of the Karaz Ankor. Knowledge is my legacy and I am to bequeath it to you so the greatest secrets of our craft do not die with me. But I am yet to be convinced if such power is for your generation of dawi. If I pass on my wisdom to you, I will be putting god-fire into your hands, Morek. Are we not too belligerent, so that such a thing would destroy us? But if I don't, and allow this power to fade, to be consigned to dust and memory, then the dawi will fade as well. One is a slow demise, the other a flare of fire, ephemeral but bright.'

The talk of mortality and destruction sent Morek into a grim quietude. He got the impression of a great weight upon his master, a burden of which he had confessed but a little. Of course, he knew there was much below the forge halls, in the lowest deeps of Lord Silverthumb's chambers, that he had never been privy to. Giving of knowledge, especially that which comes also with power, implied trust – but not only in the wisdom of the receiver, but also in his ability to keep such power safe and for what it was intended. How many had fallen to corruption and ruin where the pursuit of power was concerned?

Known as 'Furrowbrow', after his father and his clan, entire harvests could have been planted in the deep ripples lining Morek's forehead at that moment.

Ranuld Silverthumb seemed not to notice his apprentice's dilemma.

'The High King has asked for a weapon and armour for his son. A gift if he is worthy of it, and token of his father's esteem. Gotrek Starbreaker too, you see, has a legacy to hand down. All of us, we dwarf lords, carry that burden. You will forge them, az and klad, inscribe the master runes and speak the rites.'

Morek briefly bowed his head. 'Tromm, master. It is a great honour.'

'No, apprentice, it is your *duty*. To me, to your king, to your race. Legacy, lad, is all we veterans have left to us in the end.'

The last fifty steps were descended in silence until Morek asked just before they reached the lower deep, 'You were gone for several days, master… Did you find what you were looking for?'

Lord Silverthumb shook his head. 'No, lad, I didn't. Old magic is getting harder to find.' He scratched his beard as if pondering why. Unable to reach an answer, he carried on. 'But I fear the world is changing because of it. Something lurks in the air, the earth. I fear it will change us, that it *is* changing us even now.'

Morek frowned and the furrows deepened. 'Old magic?'

Ranuld Silverthumb shrugged. 'Magic is magic, I suppose. It's what's done with or can be harnessed with it that makes some of it feel old. We dawi know magic. Its dangers are known to us too, so we trap it within stone and steel in order to control it, lest it control us and we become as stone.'

Morek didn't fully understand, but chose to ask no further questions. His master had answered; he had to fathom its meaning for himself.

They were walking the slab-stoned passage that led to the iron forge where the clattering of hammers sounded and bellows wheezed in time with every strike of metal against metal. Bordering the threshold of the forge hall, Lord Silverthumb's expression darkened as a cloud passing over the face of the sun.

'Trouble is coming. It's been coming for thousands of years but we'll see it in our lifetime, Valaya have mercy. A great doom, lad, and a terrible darkness from which there may be no light.' With the premonition bright like azure flame in the runelord's eyes, he retreated into himself but spoke his inner monologue aloud. He rasped, voice barely rising above a whisper, 'A gathering must be made, a conclave of the runelords.' He shook his head, his faraway eyes no longer seeing the fuliginous dark of the forge or the lambent orange glow of embers at its yawning cavern entrance. 'Won't be easy. Some might be dead, others lost or asleep. Some can sleep for years at a time. It feels like an age since I last slept… Ancestors, all of us. Too old, too thin and past our time. Been centuries since the last conclave, but the wisdom of the ages can no longer be left to slumber. I fear it will be needed in the end…'

Ranuld Silverthumb blinked once and his voice returned to as it was before. 'What are you staring at, wazzock? Look like you've seen one of those talking rats those two ufdis were blathering about.' He snapped his fingers and made Morek jump. 'Wake up, *wannaz*. Now,' he added, heading into the forge, 'Snorri Lunngrin, now Halfhand, needs a gauntlet fashioning. Find him before you begin the rune rites, examine his wound and see what's to be done.'

Morek was half agape, unable to follow his master's capricious nature in the slightest.

'Well, go on then, zaki,' said Lord Silverthumb, shooing his apprentice away like he was a beardling. 'Bugger off and find the prince. And do it fast, the anvil calls.'

Ranuld had brought him all the way down to the *grongaz* only to dismiss him and send him back up its steps again. He was about to ask why but his master was gone, swallowed whole by soot and shadow.

Scratching his head, more furrow-browed than ever, Morek went to look for Snorri Halfhand.

* * *

FOR RANULD, THE dark brought with it a sense of peace. Even with the hammers of the grongaz flattening and shaping, he found tranquillity in his own domain. Breathing deep of the soot and ash, of the metal and the heat, he sighed.

The words spoken in the ruins of Karak Krum had come unbidden. They were also not meant to be heeded, but fate had other ideas it seemed. Briefly, he hoped he hadn't begun a landslide with his trickling rock. Deciding it was done and could not be undone, he sagged in his ceremonial armour and began removing it. Unbuckling straps, uncinching clasps, he walked over to a stone effigy of a dwarf's body. There he released the breastplate, followed by the rest of the cuirass. Resting it reverently on the armour dummy, he took off his helm and did the same with that. Then he grabbed a leather smock, stained with the evidence of forging, streaked black and scorched with burns. He passed through a dark chamber, beyond his forging anvil. No other smiths were present, Ranuld was alone. The sound of hammers echoed from the upper deeps, from the foundries and armouries above. Passing a weapons rack, he took up his staff and looped a hammer to his belt.

Smoke parted before him and the firelight of the forge itself cast deepening shadows, pooling in his craggy features. Through a narrow aperture in the stone, he crossed a small corridor to a door hewn from petrified wutroth. Ranuld merely presented his staff and a sigil hidden upon the door's surface glowed. With the scrape of rock against rock, the portal parted wide enough for the runelord to enter. A muttered incantation and the solid door closed behind him again, sealing off the new chamber like a tomb.

It was dark within, darker even than the rune forge, and no sound reached its confines. Warmth radiated from inside, even standing at the threshold. Lifting his staff, Ranuld ignited the first braziers set into the flanking walls. Like ranks of fiery soldiers they came alight, first six then ten then twenty then a hundred. A chain of fire burst into life down both walls and threw an eldritch glow upon the contents.

'*Duraz a dum…*' he intoned, releasing a breath of awe.

No matter how many times he had seen them, they never failed to impress him.

Six immense anvils sat in front of Ranuld, arranged in two ranks of three. Silver flashed in the brazier light, the anvils capturing the potency of the magic used to ignite them and using it to set their own runes aflame.

Ranuld read each and every one, careful to speak them in his mind and not aloud. The rune hammer in his belt hummed with the proximity of the artefacts, and the runelord patted the weapon to calm its spirit.

Anvils of Doom were one of the single most powerful weapons the dwarfs had in their arsenal. Legend held that Grungni had forged them in the elder days, as a means of harnessing the elements. Mastery over lightning, earth and fire were the reward of any runesmith dedicated and skilled enough to mount an Anvil of Doom. Six more resided in each of the major dwarf holds of the Worlds Edge Mountains, presided over by their chief runelords.

Muttering oaths to Grungni and Valaya, Ranuld ran his hand over the surface of one. Its inner glow grew brighter still and a thin veil of lightning crackled across the metal. It fed to the others, leaping from anvil to anvil until all six were wracked by the same storm. Shadows that were impenetrable to the brazier light retreated before the magic and revealed further runic artefacts in silhouette and half-light, immense war gongs and battle horns the size of ballistae. Behind them, at the back of the chamber slumped onto their haunches, were statues. Stone golems, like the other artefacts in the room, were relics of the elder days. Even with the unfettered fury of the anvils crackling loudly before them, the golems did not stir. Magic was leaving them, fading just like the knowledge which had created it.

A last artefact caught Ranuld's eye, a massive war shield turned on its edge and polished to a mirror sheen. Runes circled around a plane of pellucid silver in which the runelord could see his own image reflected back at him. He tried not to linger on the thought that he looked older than he remembered, so much so that he almost didn't recognise himself any more.

'A great doom, indeed,' he muttered, recalling his earlier vision, and recaptured the lightning of the anvils back into his staff where it would dissipate harmlessly.

Approaching the shield, he spoke an incantation under his breath and the silver shone, rippling like a pool.

Only the *Burudin* were capable of harnessing its power. There were eight ancient lords of the rune that yet lived in the dwarf realm and one of those belonged to the expatriate hill dwarfs of the upper hold-forts. Over the centuries, many had perished through war or old age. Ranuld had known each and every one, just as he knew their like would not return and he like the remaining Burudin would be the last of an era.

Feldhar Crageye, Negdrik Irontooth, Durgnun Goldbrow, these were the ancients that Ranuld sought next. Agrin Fireheart was second in venerability only to Ranuld. He had already answered the summons and was on his way from Barak Varr, but more were needed.

Ungrinn Lighthand, Jordrikk Forgefist, Kruzkull Stormfinger… Leagues upon leagues separated the distant holds but through the shield that would be as nothing. Ranuld wondered how many more would heed the call and come to the conclave. With regret, he realised that some would not, that some would already be dead. Old magic was leaving the world, never to return. And like all who are privy to secret knowledge, he feared what would happen when it did.

⟨ CHAPTER THIRTEEN ⟩

Reunions

EVEN AS THE bronze doors slammed violently in his wake, Snorri felt the first pangs of regret. His ire, so quick to rise in the Great Hall, cooled quickly when faced with the quiet introspection of what he had done and said.

Bringing the name and memory of his mother into the argument was low. He regretted that, but couldn't retract it.

Pride and the slightest undercurrent of persistent annoyance kept him from turning around and apologising immediately, but a lot of those words, although harshly given, were true.

Gotrek Starbreaker was Lord of the Underdeep, High King of all the dwarfs, and he cast a long shadow. Snorri felt eclipsed by it. He had wanted to tell his father about the prophecy he had heard, of his foretold greatness, how he had fought the ratkin in their warrens and the threat they might mean for the hold, but instead he had chosen to swagger in and expect his place to be waiting.

Being discarded at the back of the assembly, in the seat reserved for the hill dwarfs of all creatures, had been a barb too hard to excise before they had exchanged words. Now they could not be withdrawn, as every dwarf knows. In any other circumstance, a grudge would have been made against Snorri but a father was not about to do that to his son.

Instead he would endure his wrath, and hope that like his own it faded.

Neither, of course, would admit they were in the wrong. It was not the dwarf way.

In the end, Snorri was glad the flickering darkness barely leavened by the ensconced braziers hid his face, although he could still feel the cold glare of accusation from the hearthguard that had been waiting outside.

The veteran warriors were not the only ones waiting for him upon leaving the Great Hall. A familiar figure approached from farther down the corridor, moving with long and light steps like a dancer. Warm and welcoming, his face did not mirror the dwarf's even slightly. A scowl distorted Snorri's expression, only partially hidden by his beard. He had at least removed his axe for the audience with his father and looked slightly less belligerent than the last time he had seen Prince Imladrik.

In lieu of his armour, the elf wore pearl-white robes trimmed with the fire-red commonly associated with Caledorian princes. A circlet of silver with a sapphire in the centre replaced his war helm and he carried no visible weapon. Clean and dressed, he had obviously been at Karaz-a-Karak for several hours already, perhaps even days. As the elf walked down the wide corridor towards him, Snorri wondered for what purpose.

No elf would ever be invited to the rinkkaz. Even in the pursuit of peace his father wouldn't break that sacred oath. Imladrik's presence in the hold halls must be for some other reason. Whatever the cause, Snorri found he resented it just as he resented the prince. After the dragon had turned on him, Snorri felt ridiculed and secretly blamed the elf for what happened. It only affirmed what he had always suspected, that you could never trust an elf or its beast.

Though he walked the hold halls unarmed, Imladrik had several retainers who were waiting for him at the threshold of Everpeak. Each was fully armoured, helmed and wore a long sword scabbarded at the waist. Short cloaks of dragon hide hung from their backs, not trophies but rather the honourable leavings of shed scales from the oldest and mightiest of the drakes.

The retinue reminded Snorri of elves masquerading as dragons, hoping perhaps to yoke some element of their obvious power. It drew a sneer to his lips at the sheer hubris of the notion.

Master of dragons and dragon lackeys, thought Snorri, allowing the bitter curl to grow for the prince's benefit. Heading towards the Great Hall, the elf was obviously here to meet with his father. More talk of peace and harmony, no doubt. Snorri's fists clenched.

'We meet again, Prince Lunngrin.'

Snorri didn't return the nod of greeting, nor did he dawdle to exchange pleasantries.

'You will find him in a foul mood, elfling.'

One of the guards stiffened at the flagrant disrespect but Imladrik quietened her with a glance.

'I hope to bear news that will improve it, then.' Imladrik's reply was diplomatic, but fashioned so that he wouldn't seem to be cowed in front of his warriors.

'Doubtful,' Snorri replied, hiding well his desire to know the elf's business. 'He is a curmudgeonly bastard, slow to calm down.'

'I see *you* possess his fiery spirit too.'

Snorri ignored the comment as they passed each other. 'You'll have to leave your entourage outside,' the dwarf said, thumbing over his shoulder at the formidable hearthguard standing sentinel before the doors.

Imladrik stopped as Snorri walked on. A light clanking refrain from his warriors sounded as they did the same, circling the prince protectively.

'Tell me something, lord dwarf,' he said, 'what is it exactly that I have done which offends you?'

Snorri considered walking further. In the end he stopped too but left his back to the elf.

'You left your island and came here.'

'Your father wants peace, so do we,' he called to the dwarf's slowly departing figure.

Snorri's reply echoed back. 'My father wants many things. And not all of your kind desire peace. That's what concerns me, dragon master. You're squatters, nothing more. The Old World belongs to the dwarfs and will do always.'

The elf didn't answer. There was nothing he could say, though it took all of his resolve not to rise to anger as the dwarf wanted. Instead he carried on in silence, ruminating on all he had heard.

'I will not be the last dwarf to speak it, either,' said Snorri to himself, and went to find Morgrim.

ALEHOUSES WERE SOMBRE places, more akin to temples than bawdy drinking holes. Sitting by the roaring hearth, the air thick with the reek of hops and wheat, dwarfs came here to worship. For aside from gold, there were few things the sons of Grungni vaunted as highly as beer. But they were also discerning creatures, and would not put up with swill or any brew which they deemed weak or unworthy of their palate. Grudges, bloody ones, had been made for less than a brewmaster who served another dwarf a poor beer.

As Snorri entered the hall, a dozen pairs of eyes looked up at him, glittering like jewels. Several of the dwarfs acknowledged the prince, uttering a sombre 'tromm' in Snorri's direction. Others were too lost in grim reverie to notice.

A strange gloom pervaded in the drinking hall where scores of dwarfs clasped gnarled fingers around foaming tankards of clay and pewter. It was a half-light, a gloaming that settled upon patrons and furnishings alike. Long rectangular tables filled the main hall, surrounded by stout three-legged stools and broad benches. An antechamber, the brew store, fed off one side of the expansive drinking hall and was festooned with wide, iron-bound barrels. Every barrel was seared with a rune describing the beer's name and potency. Only the ones behind the bar and the alehouse's brewmaster were tapped.

Brorn Stoutnose was cleaning his tankards with a thick cloth behind a low wooden bar. Deliberate, exact, there was ritual to the task he performed and he muttered oaths to the ancestors as he did it. Several other cloths, one for drying, one for polishing, another for wringing, sat snugly beneath a thick belt girdling an impressive girth nurtured by many years of dedicated quaffing. Nodding at the prince of Karaz-a-Karak, he gestured with raised chin to one of the low tables where two dwarfs were in hushed conversation.

'Of all the brew halls in the karak, you managed to find the soberest,' said Snorri.

Morgrim looked up sternly from his tankard, which he'd only half drained, but couldn't suppress a wry grin. 'I see you escaped your father's wrath more or less intact.'

At mention of the High King, Snorri's face darkened. 'Words were exchanged,' he said, and read from his cousin's face that Morgrim knew some of those words were regretful.

'Did you tell him about the rats of the underdeep?'

'The elgi sit at the forefront of his mind, and the precious peace he has fought so hard to win. I even saw that elfling prince on his way to the Great Hall.'

'Imladrik?'

'Yes, but not his drakk. I cannot even imagine where he would have stabled such a creature.'

'Likely it nests in one of the peaks. He must have business with your father.'

'Indeed, but what?' Glancing over to the other stool, Snorri addressed the dwarf sitting opposite his cousin. 'And who might you be?' He took in the bronze pauldron, the sigils on his belt and armour. 'Strange trappings for a dawi.'

Morgrim introduced them. 'This is Drogor…'

'Of Karak Zorn,' said Drogor, rising to offer a hand to the prince. 'My lord.' His eyes flashed in the firelight from the hearth. 'I can see the blood of kings in you.'

Morgrim clapped Snorri on the back, so hard it made the prince's eyes bulge a little.

'This is Snorri Lunngrin, Prince of Karaz-a-Karak.'

Drogor bowed deeply. 'I am honoured, my lord.'

'Karak Zorn in the Southlands?' asked Snorri, ignoring the flattery. His eyes narrowed, only half shaking the other dwarf's hand. 'How is it you are here, yet your king was absent from the rinkkaz?'

'Drogor is only here by the mercy of Valaya, cousin,' said Morgrim.

'My party and I were ambushed south of Karak Azul,' Drogor explained. His eyes dipped slightly. 'I alone lived to tell of it.'

'Dreng tromm,' uttered Snorri, suspicions fading. 'Was it grobi?'

'They were… archers, cousin.'

Snorri regarded Morgrim sternly.

'Elgi?'

Morgrim shook his head then looked at Drogor, who answered, 'Perhaps. The arrows were not crude enough for grobi or urk, though I didn't wait for the killers of my kin to reveal themselves.'

Snorri's gaze was on the table at the two slowly warming tankards of ale, but he wasn't thirsty. When he looked up, his face was creased with concern.

'I'm sorry for your loss, but you should seek an audience with my father and tell him what happened to you and your kin,' he said to Drogor. 'There has been no word of Karak Zorn for years, and then there is the matter of your ambushers.'

The sound of a door opening arrested the dwarfs' attention.

A familiar figure had just entered the alehouse, and was looking around.

'Furrowbrow,' Snorri scowled. 'What does he want?'

When the runesmith's gaze alighted on their table, he began to walk towards them.

'Looks like he wants you, cousin,' said Morgrim.

Folding his arms in a gesture of annoyance, Snorri said, 'Aside from his master, I have never known a more saturnine dawi.'

'He is certainly dour,' agreed Morgrim.

'Why the perpetual frown though, cousin? Perhaps his gruntis are too tight, eh?' Snorri leaned over to speak to Drogor. 'What do you think, Dro…'

But the dwarf from Karak Zorn was gone. Snorri thought he saw him at the back of the drinking hall, disappearing into a pall of pipe smoke, lost to the gloom.

'Let's hope that wasn't because of something I said,' Snorri remarked, and turned to face Morek Furrowbrow.

'My lords,' uttered the runesmith, bowing. Though he was Ranuld Silverthumb's apprentice, Morek was older than both the nobles. Grey hairs intruded on his dun-coloured beard and at his temples. Wrinkles under his eyes suggested a lack of sleep, but also a weight of years yet to burden the other two dwarfs. And then of course there was his forehead and the lines of consternation worn there almost continuously.

Peering past the two nobles, Morek scrutinised the darkness at the back of the hall. The alehouse was over half full and there were many patrons who chose the anonymity of that part of the drinking hall, but Morek's eye was fixed upon one and one alone.

He couldn't say why.

'Who was that dwarf?' he asked.

Morgrim glanced over his shoulder. 'Which dwarf, this place is full of– Ah,' he said, realising who the runesmith meant. 'An old friend, come back from Karak Zorn.'

Morek glanced at Morgrim. 'The Southlands? I thought that hold was cut off from the rest of the Karaz Ankor.'

Snorri chipped in, 'Yes, the Southlands. An expedition made it to Karaz-a-Karak, if you can count one dwarf as an expedition that is. Are you here to see me, runesmith?'

Regarding Snorri askance, Morek said, 'At the behest of my master, I am to fashion a gauntlet for you. Given your injuries, I need to see your hand in order to forge one that fits.'

Snorri showed off his bandaged wound and smiled. 'Well, it won't need all the fingers.'

Morek wasn't really listening. His eyes had returned to the shadows at the back of the drinking hall, but the dwarf from Karak Zorn was gone.

meant the last word as an insult when he cleared his throat and said in a loud voice, 'Let it be known, on this day did–'

'No, no, no,' snapped the king, scowling and slashing a clawlike hand through the air as if to cut Krondi off from speaking further. 'No declarations, no oaths or grudgement.' He exhaled, as if already tired of the exchange when it had barely begun. 'You have come from Zakbar Varf, yes?'

Shocked at the hill king's flagrant disregard for the accepted tradition of voicing a grievance, Krondi nodded mutely.

'And you claim to have been cheated by elgi merchants?'

Krondi found his voice. 'They said they were weapon-smiths, and it is no claim. It's true, my lord.'

'Liege.'

Krondi frowned. 'Your pardon, my lord?'

'I am a king, High King of the Skarrenawi, and thus you will address me as *liege*.'

Taking a deep breath, Krondi said, 'Yes, I was cheated, my *liege*, and as Zakbar Varf is an outpost of the skarrenawi I have come to seek reckoning against the elgi.'

Dutifully silent until that moment, Rundin stepped forwards to speak on the merchant's behalf. 'I believe there is a case for grudgement here, my king, and can have our reckoners ready in the hour.'

Grum shook his head to dismiss the idea. 'Not necessary,' he said, then eyed the other dwarf sternly. 'Explain to me how you were duped, dawi. What did the elgi do that was so heinous you feel the need to disturb me in my hall and demand restitution? Eh?'

Krondi flushed with anger, but kept his temper. In his battlefield days he had killed for lesser slights against his honour. Shucking off a laden pack he carried on his back, he kneeled and unfurled a leather satchel of blades.

Grum recoiled, scowling. 'You dare bring weapons into my hall!'

Rundin interceded again. His hands were raised and he glanced at the darkness behind the throne, giving the slightest shake of the head to the guards Krondi now knew were posted there.

'These are just his wares, my king.' He looked down at the assorted blades, hammers and hafts. 'And a poor lot at that.'

Krondi nodded to the other dwarf, finding him to be honourable and just, much more so than his king at any rate.

'Gold exchanged hands, much of it,' said Krondi, inadvertently piquing the hill king's interest, 'for what was a clutch of battered swords, spears and arrows.'

The weapons were certainly well worn, with chipped blades and blunted heads. Little better than battlefield leavings, it was hard to conceive of why even the most naïve of traders would part with coin for such a sorry cache.

'Did you not inspect them before purchase?' asked Grum, incredulous.

'Of course.' Krondi lowered his voice at an unspoken rebuke from Rundin. 'Of course,' he repeated more calmly, 'but they did not look as this.'

'Then how is it that they do now?'

'What else?' Krondi said, nonplussed at the hill king's failure to grasp his meaning. 'Sorcery. Elgi magic. They enchanted the blades to make them appear to be priceless artefacts.'

Grum tutted. There was more shaking of the head, much stroking of his lank beard. A small gold coin had appeared in his left hand and he was rolling it across his knuckles.

'A bad business,' he conceded, 'for which you have my sympathies.' Grum beckoned to the shadows. Four burly dwarfs in heavy armour and full-faced helms emerged into the hall.

'Agreed,' said Krondi, 'so what is to be done about it?'

The throne bearers were already lifting the opulent hill king and his throne off the ground when Grum turned to the merchant with a confused expression and said, 'Nothing. Fools beget what they beget. I will not waste coin on sending reckoners on a pointless errand. Do I look profligate to you, dawi?'

'Thievery has been done to me!' Incredulous at what he was hearing, Krondi stepped forwards, only for Rundin to impede his path. Instead, he shouted over the warrior's massive armoured shoulders. 'Grudgement must be made…' Krondi scowled as the king was slowly led away and called after him, 'If not against the elgi then against you, Skarnag Grum.'

The hill king raised his hand and the bearers stopped.

'Heed this warning, dawi. Do not return to Kazad Kro and do not threaten me with grudgement in my own halls. Begone, or I will have you thrown out of my gates and off my rock.'

'The reckoners shall hear of this,' Krondi vowed, marshalling his anger but only barely. 'I shall seek the counsel of the High King of Karaz-a-Karak.'

Grum's bearers were moving again, the king's voice growing fainter as they disappeared down the long hall towards his private chambers. 'Do so with my blessing, for Kazad Kro will not hear your grievances further. Rundin,' he called, 'I am retiring to my counting house. Escort the dawi out.'

Rundin was about to oblige when Krondi snarled at him.

'Lay hands on me and it'll be the last thing you do.'

Palms up, Rundin said, 'Leave without a fuss and there'll be no need to.'

Krondi had his back to him when he replied. 'How you can serve a king such as Grum I cannot fathom. All dawi are greedy and selfish bastards, but he is something worse.'

'He is my king,' said Rundin.

'If that is the best you can say of him, you are being loyal to the point of blindness.'

At that Krondi stalked out of the hall.

Rundin was left alone with his thoughts. Silent as a tomb in the grand hall, the distant *chink* of coins being counted in King Grum's treasure room clanged brashly. Beneath it, running as an undercurrent, was another sound. At first it was difficult to place, but Rundin listened hard and was rewarded. Laughter. It was laughter that he heard. Just the odd chuckle, a half-stifled giggle but which soon gave way to raucous hooting and guffawing.

─➤ CHAPTER FIFTEEN ➤─

Wrath and Ruin

SKIRTING THE WORLDS Edge, the caravan of wagons was deep into the mountain passes now. Despite the fact he rode out ahead of Nadri, Krondi could ill-afford the detour to Kazad Kro especially when it had yielded nothing. His coffers were all but empty, wasted by elven treachery, and he felt the sting of that indignity worse than a dagger in his gut.

Driving the mules hard, he was determined to at least ensure his passenger reached Karaz-a-Karak in good time.

Perhaps it was his obsession with achieving that goal, or possibly some residual anger from his meeting with Skarnag Grum though it was days old, that blinded Krondi to the fact that he had strayed into the sights of a predator. Three days out of the domain of the hill dwarfs and he finally realised they were being tracked.

Cursing himself for ignoring the signs and allowing his good instincts to be clouded by selfish concerns, Krondi turned to his charge who was sitting quietly alongside him in the lead wagon.

'We are being followed,' he said. Krondi glanced over his shoulder, but all he could see was the lengthening shadows of the slowly dipping sun. Nightfall was not far off and they were too far away from Everpeak to reach it before the light died completely. Krondi did not want to still be on the road when that happened.

The old hooded dwarf beside him grunted something, appearing to ignite the smoking root in the cup of his pipe with his finger.

Hailing one of the guards riding at the back of the wagon, Krondi said, 'Keep a sharp eye behind us. I don't think we are alone out here.'

Durgi frowned, gesturing to the twenty or so warriors that rode on the four wagons. 'Only a fool would attack such a well-defended caravan.'

'That is what concerns me. A sharp eye, remember,' Krondi told him, pointing to his eye before returning both hands to the reins.

They were approaching a rocky gorge. High-sided and narrow, it would funnel the wagons into a tight cordon, an ideal position for an ambush. Krondi tried to search the highlands at the summit of the gorge for signs of warriors. There were only craggy boulders and rough gorse bowing gently in the wind.

He muttered, 'Something doesn't feel right.'

On the path laid before them the wagons would be exposed but at least they would have room to manoeuvre if needed. Through the narrow defile of the gorge they'd be sheltered from the flanks but vulnerable to an attack from above. Making any sort of camp in this terrain was out of the question, so the two choices remained.

Take the path or travel through the gorge?

Krondi chewed his beard then said, 'These mountains are my home. I know them as I know my own skin. So, why then do I fear them all of a sudden?'

'Do you wish me to answer, beardling?' asked the old dwarf with a voice like cracking oak.

'Something hunts us,' said Krondi, urging the mules to greater effort. 'And anything bold enough to attack a party of over twenty armoured dawi in their own lands is something I do not wish to fight.'

'We won't reach Karaz-a-Karak,' said the old dwarf, 'not before they catch us.'

Krondi turned to the hooded dwarf sitting next to him smoking his pipe. His eyes grew a little wider. 'So I am not imagining it. We *are* being followed.'

'Have been for miles, lad.'

Krondi was incredulous. 'Why didn't you say something?'

'What good would that do? Kill us quicker, maybe. No, better to get closer to the hold, better to let them see us and know us for what we are.'

'Their prey?' asked Krondi.

Now the hooded dwarf turned and there was fire in his eyes, of forges ancient and forgotten, of jewels that glitter for eternity.

'No. We are dawi, stone and steel. And we are not afraid. That is what they will see. Strength, lad. Strength and courage of our ancestors.' The flame in the hooded dwarf's eyes faded and he added, 'Slow down, spare the mules or you ride the wagon train into the ground and do our hunters' job for them.'

Krondi nodded, let his beating heart slow also to a dull hammering in his chest.

'I have fought in dozens of battles, fought the urk and grobi, trolls and *gronti*. I am a warrior, not a merchant.'

'Aye, lad,' said the hooded dwarf, 'but this is not a battle. There's no shield wall, no brother's shoulder to lock against your own. We are alone out here in the rising dark.'

The mouth of the gorge was approaching, forking off from the main path.

'What should I do?'

Supping deep of his pipe, the passenger said, 'It doesn't matter. Either way, we will have to fight.'

Muttering an oath to Valaya, Krondi took the gorge.

THE SKRYZAN-HARBARK WAS ruined. It slumped in Heglan Copperfist's workshop a broken wreck, once a ship and now little more than kindling. Some of the hull had survived intact but the sails had been utterly destroyed, along with Helgan's dreams, in the crash.

Under threat of expulsion from the guild, Master Strombak had commanded him to break the vessel down, strip it for parts, but faced with the reality of that Heglan was finding it hard to imagine such a formerly magnificent creation rendered into anything so prosaic as a stone thrower or heavy ballista. It would be an easy task, Heglan was gifted as an engineer, but that was also why he railed against the fetters of tradition the guild shackled him with.

His entire workshop was littered with designs, plans sketched with sticks of charcoal depicting various flying vessels he one day hoped to build. Incredibly detailed, each parchment schematic was filled with calculations, formulae for wind speed and velocity, theories on loft and chemical equations related to steam and pressure.

Of the engineers, Heglan was the only one to have fitted his workshop with a vast skylight. He had fashioned the glass himself and the massive aperture sat above the wreckage of his airship, letting in the sun to expose its many wounds. Shadows intruded on the scene as Heglan scrutinised through a pall of pipe smoke. Sharp, hooked beaks, arrow-straight wingspans and the suggestion of talons created a fearsome menagerie of silhouettes. Alongside his engineering endeavours, sitting between his many racks of tools, his cogs and half-built machineries, his oils and ropes, nails, bolts, screws, chisels, planes and work benches was his feathered host.

Here Heglan had created an aviary of the creatures of the sky he so wished to emulate. Preserved, meticulously posed and stuffed, there were hundreds. Often he had ventured in the low lands at the edge of the hold or taken a grubark out towards the ocean in the south. Dead birds were a common sight. Heglan had gathered them, studied their musculature, their pinions and the composition of their feathers. A notebook, bound in boar hide, was almost filled to the hilt with his scratched observations and sketches.

'It should have worked,' he muttered bitterly to an uncaring gloom. 'It should have flown.' He approached the wreck. In his tool belt he had a large hammer and a heavy-headed axe for the demolition. Running his hand over the hull, he winced every time he felt a crack or encountered a splinter. Rigging had broken apart like twine, masts snapped like limbs. The stink of spilled grog reeked heavily and spoiled the lacquering of the wood in places.

Shadow eclipsed most of the airship's remains. Heglan kept many of the lanterns doused, lighting just enough in order to work. Cloud obscured the sun and any luminescence that might penetrate the skylight. Heglan preferred it this way. Darkness salved his thoughts and his stung pride.

Nadri had accomplished so much, earning the respect of his guild, his hold and the dwarfs of other holds beyond Barak Varr's borders. Heglan was an engineer, a vaunted profession for any dwarf, but had thus far not achieved his potential. With their father Lodri dead and grandfather Dammin cold in his tomb, it mattered more than ever to honour them. Both brothers felt this keenly, and Nadri had remarked upon it when he had left Barak Varr to try and catch Krondi and the caravans.

'Sons are destined to bury their fathers, Heg,' he had said. 'It's only war that turns that around.'

Heglan had his head in his hands. 'I've shamed them this day with my hubris.'

Nadri gripped his brother's shoulders, made him look up. 'Be proud of what you have achieved. You *honour* them. You will have your moment, Heg. Determination is what made the Copperfist clan what it is this day. Do not forget that. Do not give in to despair, either. We are dawi, stout of back and strong of purpose. We are the mountains, enduring and unyielding. Remember that and you will be remembered, just as they are.'

He gestured to the talisman around Heglan's neck. It was the exact simulacrum of the one that Nadri also wore. Upon it were wrought the names of Lodri and Dammin, a son and father.

Heglan nodded, relieved from his torpor by his brother's words of support.

'But do this one thing for me,' said Nadri, releasing Heglan's shoulders to make his point clear with an outstretched finger.

'Name it, Nadri.'

'Heed Strombak, do not go against your master's will and risk expulsion from the guild. Do that for me, Heg.'

Heglan went to protest, but the look in his brother's eyes warned him to do so would earn further reproach. Reluctantly, he nodded.

Nadri nodded too, satisfied he'd been heard. 'Good,' he said, and clapped him on the shoulder. 'I'm bound for Karaz-a-Karak. Krondi will meet me there and we'll be on our way.' He glanced at the ruined airship, squatting in a forlorn heap inside the workshop. 'I wish I could stay and help you with this, but I am already late.'

They clasped forearms, and Heglan embraced him.

'What would I do without you, Nadri?'

'Likely go mad,' he laughed as they parted.

After that, Heglan had bidden him farewell. Dismissing the journeymen dwarfs who had helped retrieve the broken ship, he had been left alone. There he had stayed in seclusion for two days, pondering Nadri's words and those of Master Strombak.

Almost on the last of his smoking root, he chewed the end of his pipe and regarded the broken ship through a veil of grey. Three days and he had not lifted a finger to break the ship apart. This part of the workshop was sealed, a vault where Heglan could craft in secret and not be disturbed. Other machineries could be fashioned to demonstrate his commitment to his master. This, the plan forming in Heglan's mind inspired by the drawings on his workshop walls, he need never know about.

For the first time in three days, he gripped the worn haft of his hammer. Ever since his grandfather Dammin had shown him the proper way to use one, Heglan had regarded it as a tool to create, not destroy.

Purposefully, he strode towards the wrecked skryzan-harbark.

'I am sorry, brother.'

A dwarf would fly and Heglan was determined to be the first.

* * *

SWEAT LATHERED THE flanks of the mules. The beasts were gasping, shrieking with fear as Krondi drove the head of the wagon train like all the daemons of hellfire were at their heels.

For all he knew, they actually were.

Of course, daemons did not clad themselves in midnight black, nor did they carry bows, nor did they wear the countenances of elves...

'Curse the thagging elgi and all their foetid spawn!' Krondi shrank into his driver's seat, hunched as tight as he could be and still lash the mules.

Arrows whickered overhead. On the road behind them, three guards lay dead with shafts in their backs. More protruded from the sides of the wagons, jutting like the spines of some forest creature.

Dwarfs armed with crossbows tried to reply in kind but the bouncing wagons, now driven into a frantic charge through the ever-narrowing gorge, made aiming difficult. Even on foot, at full sprint, the elves not only kept pace but were also more accurate.

Durgi took one in the eye. He spun, a rivulet of blood streaking his face like a long tear, before he fell.

Another guard – it looked like Lugni but he died so fast it was hard to tell for sure – gurgled his last breath and also slumped off the wagon. Glancing over his shoulder, Krondi watched their bodies smack off the road like dead cattle and swore an oath to Grimnir towards their vengeance.

Several of the surviving guards were wounded. Some had arrows in their shoulders, others cuts or grazes from near misses. At least all four of the wagons were still intact but the road through the gorge was hard, better suited to travellers on foot than mules and iron-banded wheels.

Krondi cursed himself for a fool again. Then he cursed the elves.

'This road joins the *dawangi* pass to Kundrin hold,' he said to the hooded dwarf, pointing at a fork in the gorge. 'It's little more than a track but we can lose them in there and make for Thane Durglik's halls. Once we have sanctuary behind his walls, we can go back out and hunt these cowards down.'

The hooded dwarf nodded, but didn't stir beyond that. His head was bowed and he was muttering beneath his breath. Krondi did not recognise the words, for they had the arcane cadence of magic.

From the brief glances he'd had and the shouted reports of the guards farther back on the wagon train, Krondi reckoned on six raiders. Twenty dwarfs against six raiders was an uneven contest but the elves had them at range, at the disadvantage of terrain and could pick them off. There was also no guarantee that there weren't more raiders lying in wait. No, to stand and fight was foolish. Better to run and find safe haven. Though all evidence pointed to it, they did not seem like mere bandits either and this was what disquieted Krondi the most.

He was reining the lead mule in, turning the bit so its head faced towards the fork he wanted to take, when a shadow loomed overhead, crouched down at the summit of the high-sided gorge.

A dwarf yelled 'Archers!' before he was cut off by an arrow in his heart. It punched straight through the breastplate, came out of his back and impaled him.

'*Ghuzakk! Ghuzakk!*' Krondi urged the mules that gaped and panted with the last of their failing strength.

The fork that would take them out of the gorge and to the winding trail that led to Kundrin hold was closing.

From above, steel-fanged death came down like rain. Though the dwarfs raised shields, several of the guards were struck in the leg or shoulder. One screamed as he was pinned to the wagon deck by his ankle. When he lowered his shield, a second shaft pierced his eye and the screaming stopped.

A terrible, ear-piercing shriek was wrenched from the mouth of one of the mules on the leading wagon. Moments later the poor beast collapsed and died, unable to go any further. Its companion slumped down with it, similarly exhausted. Krondi was pitched forwards and clung to a hand rail to stay in his seat. Abandoning the reins, for they were no use to him now, he instead concentrated on keeping his shield aloft to ward off the relentless arrow storm.

It was studded with shafts in seconds, several of the barbed tips punching straight through the wood mere inches from his nose.

'Thagging bastards!' Krondi leapt off the wagon as it slewed to a halt and nosed into the dirt road with only the collapsed bodies of the mules to slow it. The hooded dwarf beside him made the jump at the same time. Miraculously, the arrows had yet to hit or even graze him.

'Old one,' Krondi called to him, 'here!' Sheltering beneath a rocky overhang, he gestured to the hooded dwarf, who followed.

Despite the furious attack, several of the guards yet lived and were making their way from the wreckage of the other three wagons to join up with Krondi. Two tried to raise crossbows against the archers but were struck down before a bolt was even nocked to string. Of the rest, three out of the original twenty-strong band made it into cover.

An injured dwarf, Killi, was crawling on his belly towards them just a few feet from the safety of the overhang. One of the other guards went to drag him the rest of the way but Krondi hauled him back.

'No, they'll kill you too,' he snapped.

A moment later, three arrows thudded into Killi's back. Then it stopped.

There was no sight of the elves above or those on the road behind. As if an eldritch wind had billowed through it to carry their enemies away, the gorge was deserted.

Krondi knew they were still there watching. Either they had run short of arrows or they were waiting to see if the dwarfs would venture from safety.

'No one moves,' he told the survivors.

Dwarfs can stay still for hours, even days. During his service in the armies of Gotrek Starbreaker, there was a dwarf Krondi knew, a real mule of a warrior. Lodden Strongarm was his name, a veteran of the Gatekeepers who had stood guard on the same portal into the Ungdrin Ankor for many years. Krondi knew him because he had been the warrior sent to relieve him from his post when the previous incumbent of that duty had died in battle. Three weeks Lodden had waited, unmoving by the gate. He only stirred to sip from a tankard of strong beer or to nibble from a chunk of stonebread, the only victuals he had to sustain him. Like the mountain, Lodden had stood guard and would not shirk or grumble for he had no one to grumble to. Finally, when Krondi had come to take Lodden's place, the old Gatekeeper had grown long in beard, his skin dusted with fallen debris from the mountain to such an extent he looked almost part of it. He didn't voice complaint when Krondi arrived, but merely nodded and returned to the hold.

Waiting was easy for dwarfs. They were mostly patient creatures. This was back when Krondi was young and full of fire. Times had moved on since then. Lodden was laid in silent repose in his tomb, whilst Krondi lived on to lament his loss of youth; but he was not as venerable as the hooded dwarf, whose voice broke through his maudlin reverie.

'Draw your blades,' he rasped, the sound of old oak carrying to every dwarf beneath the overhang. 'They are coming for us.'

Those who still had axes showed them to the failing light.

Krondi drew his hammer, the weapon he had carried since he had been a Gatekeeper. Never in all the years he'd spent campaigning had the haft ever broken.

Darkness filled the gorge as the sun faded, drowning the dwarfs taking shelter at its edges in a black sea. Like shadows detaching themselves from the darkness of falling night, the elves emerged six abreast and filled the narrow road.

From the other side came four more, only this quartet still had arrows nocked and bows unslung. To Krondi's eyes the slender necks and white pine shafts of the bows looked incongruous in the hands of the black-garbed killers.

'There is more to this than mere thievery and murder,' he murmured.

The hooded dwarf answered, a staff of iron appearing suddenly in his gnarled hands. 'They cannot allow us to leave this place,' he said. 'A great doom is coming...'

From the group of six an elf came forwards, evidently their leader. He said something in a tongue unfamiliar to

Krondi, though he could speak some elvish, and the four archers fell back.

So they wish to cut us then.

At least it was a better end than dying at the tip of an arrow.

When the six drew long serrated knives from their belts, Krondi knew his earlier assumption was true.

One of the other dwarfs piped up, 'If we fight them, the others will shoot us in the back!'

'Thagging elgi scum!' spat another.

Krondi knew them both. They were brothers, Bokk and Threk. He briefly wondered if their father had any more sons to continue his name.

'Make a circle,' said Krondi. For the old veteran campaigner, memories came back in a red-hazed flood of similar last stands. On each of those previous occasions, fighting beasts or greenskins, dwarf tenacity had won out and he had survived. Somehow this time, it felt different.

The dwarfs obeyed Krondi's command, coming together and raising shields. Only the hooded dwarf stood apart, and Krondi was content to let him. He hadn't asked who the dwarf was and why he needed to be ferried to Karaz-a-Karak, but he'd seen enough, felt enough to realise he was not just some mere warrior.

'Like links in a shirt of mail,' he told the other dwarfs, 'we do not part, we do not break. Stone and steel.'

'Stone and steel,' echoed all three in unison.

Seemingly amused by their antics, the leader of the elves bade some of his cohort forwards. Four night-clad warriors advanced with slow but deliberate purpose.

Krondi saw the glint of stone-cold killers in their eyes, and knew the last stand had been a mistake. It was far too late to do anything about that now. Closing his eyes for a moment, he made an oath to Valaya and then Grungni.

Let me die well, he beseeched them. Finally, he added a remark to Grimnir too, *and let me take some of these whoresons with me.*

Four elves attacked as one, shrieking war cries.

Ugdrik stepped from the circle, breaking the wall, for

the fall from his wagon had damaged his ear drum and he hadn't heard Krondi's command. Sparks flew for a few moments between his axe and an elven blade but poor Ugdrik was quickly gutted on a long knife, his guts spilling all over the road.

The others fared better. Under Krondi's anvil-hard leadership, they repelled the first proper elven attack against their wall. Krondi buried the head of his hammer in the skull of one, which made it three apiece.

Frustrated, the elven leader sent his other warrior into the fight. In the warrior's eyes, Krondi beheld a fathomless abyss of darkness and suppressed a tremor running through his body at the sight. The leader of the elves then hailed his archers to return and waded in himself, a sickle blade held low and by his side.

Seemed the elves did not fight fairly after all, which was no more than Krondi expected.

In a few seconds, what was a short skirmish became a dense melee through which it was tough to discern anything except flashing steel and the reek of copper. Bokk died swiftly, two jagged knives in his back and neck. His fountaining blood bathed Threk in a ruddy mire. He roared, threw himself at one elf, cut him down and wounded another, but a third slit open the grief-maddened dwarf's neck.

It left only Krondi, the leader and the hollow-eyed warrior.

One of the elf archers went for the hooded dwarf. Embattled himself, Krondi heard a low *whoomf!* of crackling, snapping air, followed by a sudden burst of heat that pricked his bare skin. Screaming came swiftly on its heels. Burning flesh filled his nostrils with a noisome stench.

The hooded dwarf was chanting again, though this time he was much louder. It sounded like an invocation. Between his words, the yelled orders of the elven leader grew more frantic.

Then Krondi realised who he had in his midst and that they would not die after all.

Arrows were loosed by the three remaining archers, but the shafts broke as if they struck a mountainside.

In a momentary respite as the elves' resolve began to fail them and they retreated, Krondi saw the hooded dwarf had one gnarled hand outstretched in front of him, clenched into a claw. Rings upon his fingers glowed brightly in the night gloom and as he brought them into a fist another flight of arrows snapped as if he had been holding them.

Out of shafts, the archers drew blades too and rushed the dwarfs.

Casting aside his cloak, the once hooded dwarf revealed his true identity.

Agrin Fireheart, Runelord of Barak Varr, stood in his armour of meteoric iron. His incantation reached a crescendo as he threw off his disguise and, as he bellowed the last arcane syllable, he brought his iron staff down hard upon the ground. Runes igniting upon the stave which filled with inner fire, a massive tremor erupted from the point where Agrin had struck.

The elves were flattened, their murderous charge violently arrested by the runelord's magic.

A shout split the dark like a peal of thunder. It took a moment for Krondi, lying on his back like the elves, to realise it had come from Agrin's mouth.

Like a dagger blade bent by the smith's hammer, a jag of lightning pierced the sky and fed into the runelord's staff, so bright that the arcing bolt lit up the gorge in azure monochrome. With sheer strength of will, he held it there, coruscating up and down the haft in agitated ripples of power like he was wrestling a serpent.

One of the elves was trying to rise, take up a fallen arrow and nock it to his bowstring.

Agrin immolated him like a cerulean candle. The elf burned, grew white hot... There was a flare of intense magnesium white and then he was gone, with only ash remaining.

Thrusting his staff skywards again, thunderheads growling above him, Agrin was about to unleash a greater storm when a spear of darkling power impaled him.

Slowly he lowered his staff and the clouds began to part, losing their belligerence. A smoking hole, burned around the edges, cut through the runelord's meteoric armour.

It was just above his heart.

Agrin staggered as another dark bolt speared from the shadows at him. Krondi cried out, railing at the imminent death of the beloved runelord of his hold, but Agrin was equal to it and dispelled the bolt with a muttered counter.

His enemies revealed themselves soon after, three robed figures walking nonchalantly through the gorge. A female led the sorcerous coven, sculpting a nimbus of baleful energy in her hands. Krondi was no mageling, but he had fought them before and even he could tell that the female was the mistress. The other two were merely there to augment her powers.

She unleashed the magicks she had crafted and a vast serpent fashioned from bloody light painted the gorge in a visceral glow before it snapped hungrily at the runelord.

Once more Agrin foiled her sorcery, a rune of warding extinguishing on his staff as he brandished it towards the elemental. She shrieked as the enchantment failed, recoiling as if burned, and pressed a trembling hand to her forehead before snarling at the male sorcerer in the coven as he went to help her.

Despite the fresh tipping of the scales against then, Krondi felt renewed hope. He didn't have long to appreciate it as the leader of the elves came at him with a pair of sickle blades. The other was still grounded and watched eagerly from his prone position.

From the corner of his eye, Krondi saw Agrin assailed by dark magic as the three sorcerers vented their power as one. Runes flared and died on his staff as the iron was slowly denuded of its magical defences. Outnumbered, the runelord was finding it hard to retaliate, just as Krondi could only fend off the silvered blades of the elf leader intent on his death.

'Submit,' the elf snarled in crude Khazalid through clenched teeth, 'and I'll kill you quickly.'

Krondi was shocked at the use of his native tongue but knew that some elves had learned it, or tried to.

'Unbaraki!' he bit back, invoking the dwarf word for

'oathbreaker', for these bandits or whatever they were had broken the treaty between their races and sealed the deed with blood.

'Your oaths mean nothing to me, runt. I'll cut your coarse little tongue from your mouth–'

Krondi finally struck his enemy. In the elf's fervour he had left an opening, one an old soldier like Krondi could exploit. Ribs snapped in the elf's chest, broken by a hammer blow that the dwarf punched into his midriff.

Mastering the pain, the elf rallied but was on the back foot as the dwarf pressed his advantage. Laughter issued from somewhere close, though it sounded oddly resonant and was obscured by the near-deafening magical duel between Agrin and the coven.

Like he was swatting turnips with a mattock, Krondi swung his hammer with eager abandon. Kill the elf now, bludgeon him with sheer fury and power, or he would be dead like the others. He couldn't match the elf for skill. Krondi knew this but felt no shame in it, as his father had taught him humility and pragmatism, so that left only brute strength.

His resurgence was only momentary. Dodging an overhead swing intended to break his shoulder the elf weaved aside and trapped the hammer between the razor edges of his sickle blades. With a grunt the elf cut in opposite directions, shearing the haft apart and disarming the dwarf.

Looking on despairing at his sundered hammer, the weapon that in all his years of loyal gatekeeping had never broken, Krondi scarcely noticed the twin blades rammed into his chest.

'–and then gut you like a fish,' the elf concluded, a grimace etched permanently on his face from the crushed ribs in his chest.

Krondi spat into it, a greasy gob of blood-flecked phlegm that ran down the elf's cheek and drew a sneer to already upcurled lips. The dwarf slid off the blades, life leaving him as he hit the ground. He was on his side and tried to claw at the earth, to catch some of it in his numbing grasp and know he would be returning to the world below and his ancestors. Through his muddying vision that crawled with black clouds at the edges, though the storm had long since cleared, Krondi saw Agrin on his knees.

Teeth clenched, the runelord was defiant to the last but the wound he'd been dealt when his guard was down was telling upon him. It was to be his end.

Agrin met Krondi's gaze across the litter of dwarf and elf dead.

'A great doom…' he mouthed before three tentacles like the arms of some kraken forged of eternal darkness impaled him and then tore him apart. Even meteoric armour couldn't spare the runelord that fate, and so another ancient light of the dwarf race was snuffed out.

Krondi slumped, his final breaths coming quick and shallow. A chill was upon him now, but he heard singing, the crackle of a hearth and the voices of dwarfs he knew but had never met. They were calling his name, calling him to the table where his place was waiting. But as he descended, leaving the world above to embrace those that came before, Agrin's words lingered and seemed to travel through Gazul's Gate itself into the dwarfen underworld.

A great doom…

SEVEKAI SLUMPED, THE pain in his chest from the two broken ribs besting him finally. He scowled at Kaitar who was still lying on the ground, though now more reclining than upended by the dwarf's crude magicks.

'Why did you not aid me?' Sevekai's tone was accusatory. He still held the bloodied sickle blades unsheathed.

'Don't threaten me, Sevekai,' said Kaitar, rising and dusting off his tunic. 'You wanted to kill the runt, you said as much to me with your eyes. If it proved tougher prey than you had first envisaged that is no fault of mine.'

'I heard you laughing when he struck me.'

'From sheer surprise that the runt landed such a blow. You grew overconfident, but it gave you the focus you needed to finish it.'

Sevekai wanted to kill Kaitar. He *should* kill him, plunge his sickle blades into his heart and end the impudent little worm, but he didn't. He told himself it was because they had lost too many of their number already but that wasn't the truth, not really. The truth was that he was afraid of the warrior, of the fathomless black in his eyes, the kind of ennui only shared by converts of the assassin temples, the devotees of Khaine.

Cursing in elvish, Sevekai let it go and turned to the slain dwarfs.

As before on the Old Dwarf Road he was careful, ensuring there was nothing in the murders that would suggest anything other than asur involvement. He suspected most of the stunted creatures wouldn't be able to tell druchii from asur anyway, but it still paid to be careful. Couple this most recent carnage with the acts of killing and sabotage happening all across the Old World and the prospects for continued peace looked bleak. It should have satisfied him. It did not.

Touring the massacre he was genuinely dismayed to see the charred corpse of Numenos amongst the dead, if only because it meant he'd need to find another scout from whoever was left. Including Kaitar and Sevekai himself, only five of the shades remained. Enough to do what still needed to be accomplished but preciously short on contingency. There were other cohorts, of course there were. Clandestine saboteurs were hidden the length and breadth of the Old World.

In his private moments, the few he was afforded and only when he was certain the dark lord wasn't watching, Sevekai wondered at the sagacity of the plan. Unfolding perfectly at present, it would allegedly do much to further druchii ambition but Sevekai could not see that end, not yet. His doubt troubled him more than the thought all of this might come to naught.

'You appear conflicted, Sevekai,' a female voice purred from in front of him. Masking his emotions perfectly, Sevekai averted his gaze from the blank stares of the dead and met her equally cold expression.

She *was* darkly beautiful, wearing a form-fitting robe of midnight black. Her skin was porcelain white but she carried a countenance that was hard as marble with a stare to rival that of a gorgon. Hair the colour of hoarfrost cascaded down her slender back as she near paraded in front of him, her spine exposed in a long, narrow slit down robes that also barely cupped her small breasts. She was lithe and ravishing but sorcery had stolen what youth and immortality had given her. Ashniel, her little protégé witch, had the same snow white hair, but did not carry the subtle weight of age about the eyes, neck and cheekbones.

Lust and wariness warred ambivalently in Sevekai, for the last time he had shared her bed he had left with a blade wound from a ritual athame in his back. Not lightly did one consort with Drutheira of the coven, especially if you ever questioned her prowess as a lover. It was meant as a tease, a playful rejoinder, but Drutheira was not one for games. Some scars, Sevekai knew, went deeper than a blade.

The sorceress's mood was predictably belligerent.

'You also look weathered, *my love*.' No druchii could say 'my love' with such venom as her. A deadly adder could not achieve the same vitriol should it be given voice to speak. 'Are those ribs cracked by any chance? Has your peerless *talent* with your little knives finally been exposed for the parlour trick it really is?'

'I have missed you too, dearest.' Sevekai's smile was far from warm, and had more in kind with a snake than an elf. 'I expected to see you sooner.'

'Other matters required my attention that I do not have to explain to you.'

Though it pained him, Sevekai gave a mocking bow. 'I am your servant, mistress.'

Drutheira was gaunt from spellweaving, but she was also injured. A red-raw scar like an angry vein throbbed on her forehead.

Sevekai gestured to the wound. 'Seems I am not the only one not to have escaped the battle unscathed.' Her hands were also hurt, burned by the dwarf's bound magic.

Drutheira touched the scar, her hands already healing from the minor incantation she'd silently performed, and snarled. Her mood changed again, sarcasm lessening in favour of hateful scorn.

'Little bastard ripped it from my head.'

'Ripped what?' asked Sevekai, briefly regarding the dwarf's corpse. It was hollowed out, as if long dead and drained of all vitality. Dark magic tended to have that effect on the living.

'The incantation, the spell,' Drutheira replied, apparently annoyed at Sevekai's ignorance. 'It was charnel blood magic and he took it from my mind and destroyed it.'

The others in the coven did not speak, but like jackals they examined every detail of her sudden weakness. Drutheira sensed their murderous ambition, spoken on the Wind of Dhar still roiling through the gorge, and was quick to reassert her dominance.

Malchior, her male suckling, was the perfect example. She thrust her hand at him, turning it into a claw, and Malchior was contorted by a sudden agony.

'I see your thoughts,' she hissed, flicking a scathing glance at Ashniel who quailed despite her ostensible truculence.

Veins stood out on Malchior's forehead like death-adders writhing beneath his skin. He fought to speak, to muster something by way of contrition that would make the pain stop. Instead, he managed to stare. His eyes were oval rings of red, burning flesh. Rage, fear, desperate pleading for the agony to end roiled across his face. Spittle ran down his cheek, drooling through clenched teeth.

'I could churn you inside out, flay the flesh off you,' Drutheira hissed, seizing him by the neck of his robe and dragging him to her until mere inches parted them.

She glared, revealing to him the manifold agonies that awaited him, let Ashniel see it too.

'Crippling, isn't it?'

Malchior barely managed a nod. '*Druth...*' Crimson flecked his lips as he tried pathetically to speak.

She leaned into his ear, whispering, 'Do you see how insignificant you are to me?' before she bit his ear and then looked up at Ashniel.

'Excruciating... Would you like to try?'

The young sorceress was already shaking her head. Malchior was on his knees, retching. Drutheira released him, and he collapsed.

'Never put your hands on me again,' she snarled.

Malchior found the strength to breathe then grovel. He nodded weakly.

'I only meant–'

Drutheira cut him off with a raised fist, the promise of further torture.

Malchior bowed and spoke no more.

'Prepare the rite of communion,' she snapped, sneering at them both. 'Lord Malekith will know all that has been done in his name.'

Dismissed, Malchior and Ashniel went to find a sacrifice. Some of the dwarfs yet lived, if only just. Although slowed, their blood would still be fresh.

'Your apprentices, or whatever they are,' said Sevekai, 'are viperous little creatures. You should be careful, Drutheira.'

She pouted at him. 'Is that concern for my welfare I am hearing, Sevekai?'

His face grew stern like steel. 'What are you really doing here? You need no scout through these lands.'

'Performing our dark lord's bidding, as are you I presume. "To each coven a cohort of shades", you remember now, don't you?' She regarded the runelord's desiccated body. 'Fortunate that I arrived when I did, it would seem.'

'Do not expect any gratitude.'

'Must we fight, *lover*?' she purred.

Sevekai laughed, utterly without mirth.

'I still feel your *love*, my dear. It is a wound in my back that is taking its time to heal.' He winced, his mock humour jarring his damaged ribs.

Drutheira stepped closer. 'Then at least let me ease your suffering…'

She outstretched her hand, but Sevekai recoiled from her touch.

'Don't be such a child,' she chided him.

Still wary, he relented and showed her the side of his chest where the dwarf had struck him.

'Now,' she warned, 'be still.'

A warm glow filled Sevekai, just hot enough to burn but the pain was tolerable. When it abated again, his ribs were healed.

'Miraculous…' he breathed.

Drutheira clenched her fist as he smiled and one of the ribs broke as if she'd crushed it.

Crying out, Sevekai glared daggers at her.

'Hell-bitch!'

'A reminder,' she said, all her genial pretence evaporating into an expression of pure ice, 'that I can do that to you at any time.'

'Duly noted,' said Sevekai. Behind, Kaitar was approaching.

Drutheira's gaze snapped to regard him.

'Who is that?' she asked.

Sevekai thought he detected a hint of anxiety in her voice, even fear, but dismissed it almost at once.

'He is no one. Just a shade from Karond Kar.'

She lingered on the distant warrior for a moment, and Sevekai took her interest for lust. He tried not to feel jealous, but his fist clenched at the slight.

Drutheira was still staring.

'What?'

'It's nothing.'

Sevekai's eyes narrowed. 'Drutheira, are you all right?'

'We are not staying,' she said, turning her attention back to Sevekai.

'You have just arrived. Do you tire of my company already?'

'Yes, I do.' She beckoned him. 'Come forwards.'

Sevekai obeyed and like a striking serpent Drutheira cut his cheek with her athame.

'Whore!'

'Now my blood mingles with yours,' she told him. 'In it you will find your purpose.'

Still wincing from the burning pain of the wound, Sevekai saw a host of hidden roads in his mind's eye. Such seldom trodden paths could only be found by those who were given knowledge of them by their keepers. Malekith possessed such knowledge, garnered long ago from an old friend. Given unto Drutheira by the dark lord, she now passed it on to Sevekai.

'We will accomplish more and be less conspicuous if we are apart. My task requires craft that you don't possess, *my love*.' She smiled like a serpent.

'Beguiling dwarf lords and marking outposts for your riders to burn down,' he smirked. 'Indeed, such craft is required for that subtle work.'

'You have your orders,' she snapped. 'See them done.'

Sevekai was still wiping the blood from his cheek. 'You need not worry about that, Drutheira.'

'Just conceal our presence here if you can,' she said, turning on her heel and heading further into the gorge to find the others.

Kaitar had stopped halfway and was standing amidst the corpses. He was just looking, no expression, no acknowledgement beyond what was in his eyes.

Sevekai hailed the others, suspecting that Drutheira was leaving much earlier than she had initially intended. He wondered if it had anything to do with the warrior from Karond Kar.

They hauled the dwarfs off the road, dragged them into the shadows created by the overhanging rocks. Any that still clung tenaciously to life were quickly ended. Others would find them in time, would see the elven arrow shafts sticking out of their bodies and believe the asur had done this.

A fire would sweep through these lands, Sevekai knew. It would be as embers at first, for every flame must begin with a tiny insignificant spark. Soon this would become a blaze, a conflagration that would consume the elves and the dwarfs, drown them in a bloody war from which there would be no return.

⚔ CHAPTER SIXTEEN ⚔

Let it not be War

GOTREK REGARDED THE broken shaft of the arrow.

Elven.

Definitely elven.

Even a beardling could tell from the white pine, the swan feathers and exquisite fletching. No other race used arrows this good, and the dwarf High King wasn't afraid to admit that.

'And you found this on the road not far from the karak?'

The ranger nodded.

In the shadows behind the High King, the only other dwarf in the room kept his arms folded. Thurbad had listened, and listened grimly, to Furgil's report.

'In the body of a dead dawi…' the ranger added. '*Several dead dawi, my lord.*'

Few dwarfs could range alone in the mountains and the wild lands beyond and return to their hold unscathed. Furgil had achieved that feat but was bowed by the news he brought like a heavy burden on his back as he met Gotrek Starbreaker in his private chambers.

'How many?' The High King still hadn't taken his eyes off the arrow and ran his fingers over the broken shaft in his hands as if some secret would be revealed to him in the process of examining it.

It wasn't.

'Six, my lord.' Grimly, the ranger recounted what he had seen in the woods, the merchant and his guards, the precise nature of the attacks, how there had been no retaliation from the murdered dwarfs. 'It was an ambush in our own territory,' he said, without really needing to.

'Those are our secret trade routes you describe, Furgil. Few who are not dawi know of them.'

'Some of the elgi do, my lord.'

Gotrek's face was set like chiselled stone but the play of emotions visible in his eyes was as turbulent and unsettled as an ocean storm. Returning the arrow, the High King sat down at a broad-legged writing desk. It fitted well with the room's rustic aesthetic, which was mainly comprised of simple wood and stone. This was a chamber for thinking, not entertaining. Solitude was its main function.

Since the rinkkaz, he had dispensed with his regal finery too and wore a simple tunic and leggings. A mail shirt clad his back and chest but he was otherwise unarmoured. He said nothing as he pored over the reports of the reckoners sitting in front of him on his desk. Like his chief scout's, the High King's face was grim.

'According to these–' he picked up a handful of the parchments to help illustrate his point, '–there have been several further acts of disorder in addition to the murder and treachery you describe, Furgil.'

Though he tried, the ranger could not conceal his shock. 'This has happened elsewhere?'

Gotrek nodded, reading off one of the reports.

'A trading outpost sacked and razed not four days ago.' He leafed to another. 'Here, reckoners make claim on behalf of Hugnar Barrelgirth of nefarious dealings that left the merchant out of pocket. Another makes reference to sorcery used to befuddle and extort an honest dawi trader. As of yet,' said the High King, his eyes rising from the parchments to regard Furgil, 'there have been no further deaths.'

Furgil sighed, 'Dreng tromm,' wringing his cap in his dirt-stained hands.

Gotrek returned to the messages from his reckoners. Almost forgetting Furgil was still present, he hurriedly dismissed the ranger.

'Thank you for bringing this to me, Furgil. You have my authority to double all of the ranger patrols on the trade routes. Keep a sharp eye for me, lad.'

Furgil nodded and was gone, leaving the High King alone with Thurbad.

'Thoughts?' he asked the captain of the hearthguard.

'Someone is trying to break down the peace we have with the elgi.'

'Not unexpected, especially when our accord with them is on such fragile ground.'

'Their settlements expand as trade between us grows,' said Thurbad. 'It was only a matter of time before the other thanes objected.'

'Eight Peaks and Ungor pledge their allegiance to "difficult times ahead".' Gotrek held up a pair of missives he had retrieved from the pile amongst the scratchings of the reckoners.

'Very politic of them both,' Thurbad observed. 'They must be seen to support you if they then want to go on and usurp you.'

'Indeed.' Gotrek had taken out his pipe. Upon touching his lips the cup flared into life, casting the rune of *zharr* engraved on it into sharp relief.

'But the attack on the trade routes is troubling. How many know of those roads?'

'Not many, or so I thought. It dates back to the old pact, the one during Snorri Whitebeard's days.'

'The elgi prince, their ambassador?'

'Malekith, aye.'

'Where is the elgi now?'

'Dead, disappeared? I have no idea, Thurbad. The records pertaining to him ended when he left the Karaz Ankor two thousand years ago. They are practically myth.'

'Someone knows.'

Gotrek got up out of his chair and walked over to where a huge map of the dwarf realms was hung up on the wall like a grand tapestry. The map was old, torn in places, burned at the edges and curling slightly. The dark ink etched upon it in certain areas was not so old. In fact, it was very recent.

'I cannot justify sanctions against the elgi for a few acts of disorder.'

Thurbad joined him at the wall.

'Are you asking me or telling me, my king?'

Gotrek left a pause to consider. 'Telling. But I need you to ensure the hearthguard are all armed and ready to act immediately should they be required.'

Thurbad bowed. 'Always, my king.'

Returning his attention to the map where not only the dwarf holds and settlements were depicted, but the elf ones too, he said, 'I hope this is just a spate of disorder, that these are just the rash acts of a few dissenters.'

Gotrek was a wise king. Unlike some, he realised the stark differences between elves and dwarfs would always result in a difficult peace, but unlike others he wasn't willing to go to war with them over it. Fighting the elves for the Old World would harm both races. It was foolish. Despite all of that, he was deeply troubled by everything he had seen and heard.

He pointed to the map with his pipe.

'How many elgi do you think are in my realm, Thurbad?'

'Too many to count easily, my king.'

From the sheer number of settlements, outposts, even cities, Gotrek knew it must rival the dwarf clans. Though he would not speak it to Thurbad, for the briefest moment he wondered if he had made a grievous error in being so genial to the elves. He wondered if he had allowed an enemy to creep into his hold halls invited and now that enemy was unsheathing his dagger to plunge it into the king's back.

Releasing a long plume of smoke that obscured the crude depictions of holds and cities on the map with an all-consuming fog, he said, 'Have the guildmasters instruct our forges to begin stockpiling weapons and armour.'

'Are we headed for war, my king?'

It was a reasonable question, but one Gotrek chose to answer with flippancy so as not to alarm his captain of the hearthguard unduly.

'Don't be an ufdi, Thurbad. There will be no war between elgi and dawi. There *must* be no war, but I will have our armouries full anyway.'

Slamming his clenched fist against his breastplate, Thurbad left to make his preparations.

The High King was alone.

Gotrek traced a gnarled finger along the sketched trade routes on the map and then the roads and byways to and from the elven settlements.

'Too many to count,' he murmured, echoing Thurbad's words. He prayed to Grungni. 'Let it not be war, noble ancestor. Let it not.'

ACT TWO

A Great Betrayal

⊰ CHAPTER SEVENTEEN ⊱

A Clash of Arms

SWEAT SOAKED HIS eyes but he dared not blink. A roar filled his ears, muffled by plate, so loud he could barely hear his heavy-beating heart. Steel clashing against steel was a constant drone. The stink of blood, of piss and dung lingered in his nostrils, unfettered by his nose guard. Heat like a second skin cleaved to his body, stealing away breath. Fire burned nearby, the acerbic tang of it on his tongue, the reek of smoke and soot, the crackle and snap as the flames went about their purifying work.

This was battle against a hardened foe, with limbs already numb from the killing that lay around him in chopped-up heaps. Greenskins by the score, too many to tell, too few to matter. But this was no goblin or orc before him with blade aimed at his chest.

When an attack came, it came like lightning on a clear day. Fast and utterly by surprise. Morgrim snarled in pain, the force of the blow's impact against his shield so hard it jerked his shoulder.

No time to think, just time enough to hurt.

A second strike, overhead and two-handed, kept him on

the defensive back foot as he used the haft of his warhammer to parry.

Weather it, endure.

Battered relentlessly, though there was precision and skill to each carefully crafted attack, the dwarf knew he would soon run out of battlefield in which to retreat.

He is stronger than he looks…

So did Prince Imladrik.

The elf was a blur of silver, every thrust and lunge, slash and cut choreographed in a deadly dance for which Morgrim was his unwilling partner. In the brief exchange, several blows had already penetrated the dwarf's armour. A gash below his eye throbbed. His breath was forced and ragged.

The elf was winning.

Corpses lay all about them, putrid and stinking, their spilt blood just as dangerous underfoot as any blade. Broken spear hafts jutted from the earth like bones reaching from the grave. Each was deadly as a lance if fallen upon. Smashed shields added to the general battlefield detritus. Through his dimming view, Morgrim saw the silhouettes of other figures moving in the battle fog but they couldn't help him.

The dwarf was alone in this.

It was a mercy the elf was not riding his dragon. Should the beast have been involved, it would be a much shorter contest. As it was, Morgrim was hardly making a decent fight of it. Defeat looked all but certain.

He lashed out, caught the elf just below his knee and drew a cry of pain from the prince's mouth. Fevered shouting around the battlefield intensified. Though muffled through his helm, the sound of the elf's discomfort brought a smile to the dwarf's lips. Morgrim roared his defiance, tried to press the slim advantage fate had provided, but Imladrik was a consummate swordmaster and recovered quickly. A dazzling series of ripostes aimed against the dwarf's left side made him overcompensate with the shield, left him exposed on the right. Morgrim narrowly avoided being disarmed as the elf swept his longsword in under the dwarf's guard and tried to hook the hammer away. Twisting his wrist, Morgrim barely caught the blade against his hammer's haft. Shavings of wood and metal cascaded where the elf's weapon bit. He fashioned his resistance into a shoulder barge that caught Imladrik in the chest and drew out a grunt. A hard shove to follow up pushed the combatants apart, and they regarded each other across the charnel field through the eye-slits of their war helms.

Morgrim's, horned and wrought of dwarf bronze, was not only lower but was also bowed compared to the elf's upraised helmet of glittering silver ithilmar.

'If you wish to concede,' gasped the dwarf between breaths, 'then I'll ensure your honour remains intact when my hammer falls.'

Though he hid it well, Imladrik's breathing was laboured too. He lifted the dragon visor of his helmet with a gauntleted hand.

It was the same armour he had worn when they had first met outside Karaz-a-Karak. How different things were now.

'Amusing,' the elf replied. Sweat dappled his forehead. Just a little, but Morgrim saw it catch the light in little pearls of perspiration.

So he does tire.

That at least was some encouragement.

Prince Imladrik went on, 'I would offer you the same courtesy but think you would probably not take it.'

'Aye.' Morgrim spat a wad of phlegm onto the ground. There was a little blood in it from a cracked tooth. 'You'd be right about that, elgi.'

'Thought so,' said Imladrik, lowering his visor before he took up a fighting stance. 'I'll make it quick,' he added with a metallic resonance to his voice.

Shrilling a war cry, the elf leapt into the air – a feat made all the more remarkable for its suddenness and the fact he was wearing a full suit of armour – and launched a piercing thrust that would have split Morgrim's shield and armour as one.

Reacting more on instinct than with purpose, Morgrim hurriedly sidestepped and caught the bulk of the blow against his shoulder. It stung like all the fires of Grungni's forge and he barely held on to his shield. A hammer swing smote air but the elf was gone. Eyes darting, Morgrim caught a silver blur in his peripheral vision but was too slow to prevent the longsword splitting his shield in two. It was hewn from stout oak, banded by iron, and still the elf's sword cut it apart as if it were rotten wood. Such was the power behind the blow that Morgrim lost his footing and his hammer. On his back, barely catching breath, he went to grab the weapon's haft when he felt the chill of elven steel at his neck.

Morgrim slumped, let the hammer go and accepted his fate.

'Grimnir's hairy balls,' he spat, baring his neck. 'You have me, elgi.'

Imladrik's eyes were diamond sharp within the confines of his war helm.

Morgrim growled, 'Finish it, then.'

The elf's belligerent mask slipped.

The dwarf smiled, then broader still.

'Well met, Prince Imladrik.'

Withdrawing his blade, the elf lifted his dragon visor. He was smiling too. Sheathing his longsword with a flourish, he bowed and proffered the dwarf his hand.

'A close match, Thane Morgrim. There is little to choose between elven speed and dwarf tenacity, I think.'

Grunting, Morgrim got to his feet with Imladrik's help.

In the stalls surrounding the arena battlefield the gathered crowd were cheering them both, but Morgrim failed to feel their acclaim.

High King Gotrek had commissioned a vast auditorium of stone and wutroth to be built in honour of a grand feast and series of games that were meant as a way of healing the frayed relationship between the elves and dwarfs in light of the recent 'troubles'.

Known as the *brodunk*, a festival of worship to honour Grimnir and the art of battle, the union of dwarf and elf on this day was hoped to be an auspicious one. In times such as these, with peace hanging by a skein of civility, it needed to be. There were other festivals: *brodag* honoured Grungni and brew-making, whereas *brozan* was the celebration dedicated most to Valaya and the bonds of brotherhood between the clans. In retrospect, perhaps it would have been a better choice to try and coincide the feast with the ancestor goddess's feast day instead.

Upon hearing the news of the caravan attacks and the destruction of Zakbar Varf, many of the thanes had demanded retaliation. Bagrik of Ungor, though now returned to Karak Ungor to meet with ambassadors of Tor Eorfith, had called for calm. He had no wish to disaffect his elven guests before they had even arrived. King Varnuf had kept his own counsel, doubtless seeing where the most favour would fall, whilst Luftvarr and Thagdor demanded retaliation. Thagdor was absent from proceedings but had set up camp close to Karaz-a-Karak to keep closer eye on what Gotrek would do next. Never one to miss out on celebrating a good fight, Luftvarr had stayed. In any case, the journey back to Kraka Drak was a long one. Above all else, the Norse dwarf king was a pragmatic one and would always prefer warm food in his belly to an arduous trek north with only trail rations for sustenance.

Temperate as well as wise, High King Gotrek had resisted the call to arms. Ambassadors from the elven court in the Old World, of which Prince Imladrik was the highest rank-ing noble, had assured the dwarfs these were isolated acts of malice to try and undermine peace. They too attended the brodunk. Afterwards, Gotrek had echoed Bagrik in call-ing for calm and so the axes of his vassal lords remained sheathed for now, but the mood was fractious.

It had taken several days of hard dwarf labour to bring the brodunk into being. More than ever Gotrek was con-vinced of its need and hoped it would reignite camaraderie and genuine bonhomie between the races. The hold was kept running with a bare minimum of miners and crafts-men, the rest were petitioned to create the stage required for the grand feast.

Mules pushing great, rounded millstones had flattened the ground. Stonecutters, rockbreakers and lodemasters dragging stone from the mines, fashioning pillars and walls, flagstone plazas and wooden stalls had worked days on end to bring the High King's desires to fruition. Many grumbled but respected their liege-lord enough to keep their misgivings private. It was no easy thing to put this burden on his clans, on his hold, but Gotrek did it because he believed lasting peace would only be maintained with sacrifice and toil. These, at least, were not strange concepts to a dwarf.

Flags and banners were nailed up, most bearing the solemn iconography of the dwarfs – the forge, the hammer and axe, the faces of their ancestors – but others depicted dragons, eagles and horses, the imagery of their elven guests.

Mouth-watering aromas emanated from feast halls where dwarf cooks and brewmasters slaved to create victuals for their kin and guests alike. Fluttering in a light breeze coming off the nearby mountains, pennants on the roofs of tented pavilions carried the runes of the elven houses present for the festivities. Other tents sewn together with rough dwarf fabric had the faces of the ancestors stitched in gilded thread and carried banner poles surmounted by clan icons of bronze, silver and gold.

Coal pits provided warmth and light, for the arena was outdoors in order to better suit the elves, a concession which had earned favour from the visitors but not the more truculent dwarf kings. Grundin of Karak Kadrin had been particularly vociferous on this point. There were roasting pits in which boar and elk were prepared for feasting later. Shields describing the clans and warrior brotherhoods festooned the walls of the structure, which was based on a large central arena with several smaller ones attached to it via a series of open tunnels. Even when building an auditorium meant to be open to the elements, dwarfs could still not deny their natural instincts to be enclosed.

At first the elves had balked at the solidity of the auditorium, its stout walls, viewing towers and gates. To the elves it was not so different from a fortress. Certainly, the regal quarters afforded to the dwarf kings in particular were well fortified. Indeed, if attacked, it was highly likely the dwarfs could muster a garrison and defend it like one.

Yes, the clans of Everpeak had gone to great efforts to fashion a stage worthy of their king. It was a pity then that the first major contest upon it had ended in defeat for the dwarfs.

Through the brazier smoke at the edge of the mock battlefield, Morgrim could tell there were more elves than dwarfs rejoicing at the display. One in particular, a stern female wearing crimson scalloped armour, gave Imladrik a nod, which the prince returned. She didn't linger, merely waited long enough to show her quiet applause for his victory before disappearing into the crowd. As was typical of their race, the elves were restrained in celebration but the sense of triumph they evinced was palpable.

It was like a slap in the face for Morgrim. Shame reddened his cheeks and he was glad his helm obscured them. Not daring to look towards the High King's royal pavilion where Snorri and his father were watching, he kept his eyes on his hammer and pretended to tighten the leather straps around its haft.

Imladrik appeared to sense what the dwarf was thinking. 'There's no shame in this. If your shield hadn't broken, if you'd have swung when you tried to dodge... Well,' the elf admitted, 'things could have turned out very differently. If it matters at all, you pushed me to the limit of my endurance, Morgrim.'

They clasped forearms in the warrior's greeting, something not usual amongst elves but common in the dwarfs, resulting in another cheer. Over thirty dead greenskins and one troll, chained to a lump of stone, littered the arena. It was the warm-up act, according to the High King. From their faces, some of the elves had found such wanton butchery in the name of 'entertainment' distasteful.

'You treat them with such disdain,' said the prince, echoing the apparent mood of his kin.

They stood in the middle of the battlefield together, deciding to allow the more raucous spectators to calm before leaving the arena. Armourers from both sides were heading towards them to help them out of their trappings, take their weapons and ensure they were cleaned and readied for the next bout.

Morgrim shrugged, barely glancing at the disappointed faces of his own retinue. 'They're just vermin. Good sport for our axes.'

Imladrik nodded, but Morgrim saw in the elf's eyes that he didn't really understand.

'Grobi are dangerous,' the dwarf said, nudging one with his boot, 'but only in large numbers. True, they have a certain low cunning that–'

A shout from behind the dwarf arrested his explanation. A moment later and a flash of metal glinted off the sun as it sped past the elf. Imladrik avoided the blade out of instinct but need not have bothered. It would have missed him, barely. Instead it struck the shoulder of a goblin that had played dead amongst the corpses. A broken spear tip slipped from the creature's scrawny hands as it collapsed back into the heap of carcasses it had crawled from.

Striding towards them, breaking from the retinue of armourers he had accompanied, Snorri Halfhand's grin was wide and slightly smug.

'Should watch your back, elfling,' he called to the prince, adjusting his weapons belt where a second throwing axe was attached by a leather loop. 'I won't always be there to save your skinny arse.'

He slapped Morgrim on the back, harder than he really needed to.

'Wanted to make him feel better, eh, cousin?'

Snorri didn't wait for an answer and stomped past them. Taking a knee down by the dying greenskin, he muttered with mild surprise, 'Still some life in this one…'

Imladrik turned to the dwarf prince, bowing his head. 'You have my gratitude, lord dwarf. If you had not–'

The *schlukk* of Snorri's axe as it was wrenched from the goblin interrupted him.

'Didn't catch that,' said the dwarf, half looking over his shoulder at the elf. 'Busy getting my axe back.' Looping it back onto his weapons belt, he regarded the greenskin again and thrust a gauntleted finger into the wound.

The wretched creature squealed and squirmed under the dwarf's touch, which only made Snorri dig deeper, a half-snarl contorting his lips. He wasn't dressed for battle, but carried his hand axes anyway. Instead of pauldrons, a regal blue cape armoured his shoulders. A tunic sat in place of a breastplate or suit of chain. His vambraces were supple leather. Morek's mastercrafted gauntlet was the only piece of metal on his body.

Forbidden by his father as punishment for his defiance, Snorri would not be competing.

When the goblin shrieked and crimson geysered from its ugly mouth, Imladrik went to intercede and end the greenskin's suffering swiftly but Morgrim put a hand on his arm.

'This is barbaric,' hissed the elf. 'The creature is no further threat.'

Morgrim simply shook his head.

'Don't be fooled,' said Snorri, and elf and dwarf prince met eye-to-eye with the dying goblin between them. As he withdrew gory metal fingers from the wound, the goblin snarled but Snorri caught its wrist in a steel grip and twisted it before the greenskin could shove a piece of broken blade into his stomach.

It yelped but Snorri kept going until he'd broken the wrist. Then he wrapped his thick fingers around its head and yanked it round to snap its neck.

'See,' said Snorri to Imladrik alone, 'can't be trusted not to stab when your back is turned, no matter how dead you think they might be.'

Though he trembled with anger, Imladrik maintained his composure.

'Your cousin fought well,' he said, his jaw still taut. 'With honour.'

Morgrim was nodding when Snorri interjected and said, 'He doesn't need your false magnanimity, elgi,' before stomping off back towards the royal pavilion.

'My apologies for my cousin,' said Morgrim in a low voice. 'He doesn't realise the effect of his words on others sometimes.'

Imladrik glared at the prince's back as he watched him go.

'It is of no consequence.' He drew his sword, saluted and then sheathed it quickly. 'You honour your kin enough for both of you, Morgrim Bargrum. Tromm...' he intoned, bowing once more before returning to the elven tents with his armourers.

Morgrim went after Snorri but noticed something glinting in the battlefield earth. It was a piece of silver scale, cut from Imladrik's armour. Watching Snorri depart, he was suddenly glad that the father had banned his son from taking part in the games.

An elf death, accidental or otherwise, was the last thing peace needed.

⫸ CHAPTER EIGHTEEN ⫷

Wise Words

SNORRI CALLED, 'COME, cousin!', as he tramped across the arena towards the royal pavilion.

A massive stone ancestor head loomed over them, the great god Grungni. Enormous emeralds hewn from the lowest deeps glittered in his eyes and a set of broad steps unfurled from his wide-open mouth like a stone tongue.

Within, lit by the flickering flame of braziers, was the High King of Karaz-a-Karak.

Bedecked in his finest royal attire, a red tunic with a skirt of gleaming gromril mail, matching cloak trimmed with ermine fur and the Dragon Crown of Karaz fixed upon his brow, Gotrek cut a powerful figure sat atop the Throne of Power. Alongside the king, fitting easily in the ancestor's gaping maw, were several of his elders but only those who were capable of leaving the hold and staying awake for the festivities. There was also a place at his side for his son.

Gotrek was in a saturnine mood, rattling heavy rings against the arm of his throne as he awaited the prince's return.

As if sensing his father's displeasure and perhaps even seeking to aggravate it, Snorri slowed as he got closer to the royal pavilion.

'Did you mean to hit him, cousin?' Morgrim asked as he caught up.

'Didn't realise I had,' said Snorri, feigning surprise.

'You are the best axe thrower in all of the karak.'

Snorri smiled wryly. 'It was only a nick, nothing to trouble a master of drakk that is for sure.'

'If he noticed it…'

'Then he is not saying, cousin. Let it go.'

'I cannot.' Morgrim paused. What he asked next wasn't easy. 'Are you deliberately trying to scupper peace with the elgi, cousin?'

His smile faded and Snorri stopped in the middle of the field. He dismissed the dwarf armourers tagging along behind them.

'Why so serious, Morg? It was a jest, a polite reminder that dawi rule these lands, not them.'

'Not *them*? You speak as if they're already our enemies.'

The silence that followed suggested Snorri thought precisely that, to a lesser or greater degree. After a few moments they walked on.

All the humour bled out of the prince, his mood now matching that of his cousin.

'A band of elgi was killed for trespassing on dawi soil a few days ago. I heard my father talking to Furgil about it.'

'Murdered?' Morgrim sounded shocked.

Snorri glanced at him. 'They were uninvited and unannounced, cousin. Given the recent attacks on the caravans, the burning of Zakbar Varf, is it any wonder?'

'Dreng tromm…' Morgrim shook his head. 'It's worse than I thought.'

'Trade has all but ceased with them. More and more of the elgi are going to the skarrenawi now because King Grum has no sense of honour.' Snorri hawked and spat. 'He is barely half dawi as it is, and now he makes himself an *elgongi* to rub in further salt to already stinging wounds.'

'You learned all of this from your father?'

'Aye,' said Snorri, 'as well as speaking with some of the other lords. King Varnuf and King Thagdor have sanctioned heavy embargoes on trading with the elgi. If these "troubles", as my father calls them, continue they will enact outright bans.'

Morgrim's eyes narrowed. 'Aren't Varnuf and Thagdor against your father's petition to keep the peace?'

Snorri nodded. 'By listening to my fellow dawi lords, I'm not going against my father, Morg.'

'But if commerce breaks down between our races, it will lead to but one road after that,' Morgrim warned.

They were nearing the pavilion now and would soon have to part. Morgrim's armour needed tending and Snorri was expected by his father.

The prince's steady gaze told Morgrim he knew what road that was.

'And, cousin?'

'And?' Morgrim was incredulous. 'And? Think of the cost, Snorri, in lives and livelihoods.' He kept his voice low in case others were listening in. 'War will devastate our lands, our clans.'

'Nonsense, cousin. We will expel the impudent elgi with barely any dawi blood being shed. They are merchants and squatters, Morg. Barely a decent warrior amongst them.'

'What about Imladrik? He just bested me in single combat.'

'Bah, you just let him—'

'I let him do nothing. I fought him, as hard as I could, and still he beat me.'

Snorri dismissed the notion with a snort, regarding the broken shield the armourers were taking back to the distant forge.

'For an elgi he has a strong arm, I suppose.'

'You underestimate him, cousin.'

'No, Morg.' Snorri fixed him with a gimlet stare. 'He over-commits when he thinks he has victory, looking for a quick finish. He has no patience, not like a dawi. You should've used that against him, found an opening just before his killing thrust. Then you would not have been beaten.' He shook his head slowly, impressing the import of what he was going to say next. 'He would not have defeated me. I would have broken him apart.'

The two dwarfs parted ways, an uneasy silence between them.

Morgrim's armour needed tending, so did his wounds and battered pride. It was a pity there was no salve in the tent for his unease at his cousin's demeanour. To some it would appear as if the prince believed they were already at war.

As he gave one last look towards the royal pavilion, he noticed Drogor seated within amongst the high thanes and masters. Snorri must have invited him. They had been spending much time together of late, but Morgrim thought no more of it as he headed for the forge.

LIANDRA'S FACE WAS a mask of displeasure when Imladrik parted the door of the tent wider and descended into what was known as the 'rookery'. It was dark inside and the air smelled of earth. Though the shadows were thick, they suggested a vastness belied by the apparent closeness of the tent's confines. The ceiling also was incredibly high, even with the sunken floor. Guttering candles did little to lift the gloom, but then elves did not need light to see and nor did the creatures the rookery harboured. It had to be this way, drenched in shadow, to placate these denizens and keep them quiescent.

Imladrik heard their snorting, the hiss of their breath and the reek of sulphur that came with it. Like an itch beneath his skin, a heat behind the eyes, he felt their frustration and impatience, the desire to *soar*. Only through sheer will, born of years of practice and dedication, could the prince shake off his malaise. Otherwise, it would have consumed him as it had consumed lesser elves before him.

Armourers had removed his breastplate, tasset and rerebraces. A servant had also left two missives on the table beside him.

'Letters from home,' said Liandra without looking down. 'I received word from my father, also.'

She glanced at an elf standing nearby clad in silver armour, half cloaked in darkness. He went unhooded, carrying a helmet with a purple feather at its tip under his arm.

This was Fendaril, one of her father's seneschals. Bowing to them both, Fendaril left the tent.

'There was no need to dismiss him.'

'Fendaril has other business. Because I'm occupied by this farce, I need him to return to Kor Vanaeth. He has fought in his bout.'

'Very well.'

They were alone.

Setting down his dragon helm on a nearby stool that was altogether too low for an elf's needs, Imladrik silently began to read.

'My brother sends word from Ulthuan,' he said. 'Druchii raids continue.'

'Lord Athinol brings similar tidings.'

Imladrik read the second letter more quickly, before tucking them both into his vambrace. Trying to occupy himself, he started to unbuckle his leg greaves.

'Your son, he is well?' asked Liandra, and Imladrik saw a slight nerve tremor in her cheek as she guessed at the second sender.

'He is.'

'And her also.'

'Yes, her as well.'

Imladrik's scabbard, which contained the sword Ifulvin, was placed reverently on a weapons rack nearby. Lances were mounted on the rack and each of them had names too, etched in elven runes upon their shining hafts.

'Are you going to stare at them all afternoon, Liandra?' the prince asked, changing the subject to ease the tension. Pulling off a boot, he relished the kiss of cool spring water on his bare skin as a servant poured some from a silver ewer.

'I am glad you bested that dwarf,' she said, eager to turn the conversation to more comfortable ground too. Her eyes did not move to regard Imladrik. She lingered at the entrance to the rookery, at the summit of a short set of earthen steps, and peered through a narrow slit in the heavy leather flap. She was fixated on the royal pavilion at the opposite end of the field, the king and all his retainers looking on.

She sneered, 'He was a crass little creature, all dirt and hair. When I first heard that dwarfs live in caves under the ground I scoffed, but now I see the truth of it.'

'I fought a warrior, Liandra. A noble one possessed of a fine spirit. Morgrim Bargrum is a thane of vaunted heritage – you should not be so disparaging.'

'You obviously see something which I do not.' She glanced at him, 'Anyway, I salute your victory, Imladrik.' Liandra raised her sword, which the prince noted was unsheathed.

Despite her caustic demeanour, even in the darkness of the rookery Liandra's stark beauty shone like a flame. Her hair was golden but not akin to anything as prosaic or ephemeral as precious metal – such a thing would fade and give in to the ravages of entropy in time. Rather, it was eternal and shimmered with an unearthly lustre. Threaded with bands of copper like streaks of fire, she had it scraped back and fastened it in place with a scalp lock. Pale as moonlight, her skin was near silvern and her eyes were like sapphires captured from the raging waters of the Arduil.

She was beautiful.

Imladrik had always thought so and the very fact spoke to his poetic soul, much as he tried to deny it. His desires were not for war and battle, though he possessed great martial skill and as brother to the Phoenix King of Ulthuan, it was almost expected. Imladrik wanted peace, which he had. Only it felt like his hands were an hourglass and the fragile accord between the elves and dwarfs grains of sand slipping through it. No matter how hard he tried to seize them they would worm their way between his fingers. Grip too tightly and the glass would shatter, spilling their contents anyway.

Not so Liandra. She desired battle, *ached* for it. Fierce-hearted, especially as she was now clad in her ceremonial dragon armour, she was happiest with a sword or lance in her mailed fist. The blood red of the armour's finely lacquered plates, edged and scalloped, only enhanced her ethereal beauty.

Imladrik removed his other boot before giving her his full attention.

'Petty pride is not worthy of a princess of Caledor,' he told her. 'And you have not even greeted me properly yet,' he added.

Liandra turned and bowed, a gesture that Imladrik reciprocated. There was no physical contact, no handshake or embrace of any kind. It was as if an invisible veil of propriety existed between them that no sword or spear could ever part. Briefly, Imladrik found he was envious of the more tactile ways of the dwarfs, the open and flagrant, even sometimes crass, mores of social greeting in their culture. Elven stiltedness had its place in court. It was dignified, but all too cold between old friends. Perhaps he had spent too long amongst dwarfs, learning their ways as Malekith once did before his fall.

'Congratulations again on your victory,' she said, interrupting his thoughts but only exacerbating the formality of their exchange further.

Imladrik inclined his head. 'Thank you.'

'But it is not pride that makes me glad you defeated the dwarf and showed all of these mud-dwellers our true strength.'

'Do not speak of them like that.' Imladrik was on his feet, and still looked imposing despite the fact he was barefoot and had no armour.

The beasts in the deep shadows of the rookery stirred but he calmed them with a glance. None present, not even the largest, would dare oppose the Master of Dragons.

'*Vranesh!*' snapped Liandra, an eye on the darkness briefly too before she replied. 'I heard them talking, heard what they think of us, our people.'

Pouring a goblet of wine, Imladrik sighed. 'As did I, but that is no reason to hate them, Liandra, not if we are to achieve harmony between our two races.'

'I do not want harmony. I do not like these *dwarfs* or their ways, nor do I understand why you seem to have such an accord with them.' She moved away from the entrance, down the steps and away from prying eyes. 'All this talk of murder, of ambushes in the night, it is just that. Talk. Likely, it was made up by the dwarfs to justify attacks on elves.'

Imladrik looked at her shrewdly. 'And is that what you

think, Liandra? Or are these the beliefs of your father?'

'Not only my father, but my brothers also,' she snapped, raising her voice. 'Why wouldn't I believe them?'

'Because they are thousands of miles away on Ulthuan, fighting the remnants of Malekith's forces in the mountains where you wish you could be right now.'

She was on the verge of another outburst when her anger ebbed. 'I am a warrior of Caledor, Imladrik. By my father's side is where I should be.' She lowered her voice, unable to meet the prince's gaze. 'And is it any wonder that I want to kill druchii after what they did, after...' She faltered, but recovered quickly. 'I am here under sufferance, that is all.'

'You're here because your father, despite his misgivings, believes that peace is something worth fighting for and not over. You are his ambassador, a feat beyond the skills or patience of either of your brothers.'

'Do not besmirch them,' she warned.

Candlelight limning the edge of its saurian body, the beast a few feet away from Liandra growled in empathy. It clawed at the earth with its long talons.

Imladrik was not cowed. He had nothing to fear from Vranesh, upraising his palms to placate the princess not her beast.

'I merely speak plain fact and the truth as I see it, Liandra. Just as I see the dwarfs are a noble race who value heritage, tradition and honour.'

'Honour? Really?' She stooped to retrieve a length of thick iron chain that trailed along the ground and into the darkness. 'Where is the *honour* in this? The dignity?'

'The dwarfs built this rookery for us. They cut the earth to allow us–'

'They dug a hole, Imladrik. A *hole*. And then they filled it with chains and shrouded it from the sky. Insult is too light a word, confining noble creatures such as this. The dwarfs should be grovelling at their feet.'

'The High King has organised this brodunk for us, the least we can do is concede to his wishes to see our mounts kept hidden. We are on his lands, these are his people. I can understand his concern.'

Liandra scoffed. 'You even use their tongue like it is your own. Are you sure you aren't turning native on us, Imladrik?'

'I will pretend you did not say that to me, and attribute it to the fact you miss your father and brothers. The dwarfs *are* a good people. We have much to learn from each other. We are just different, our kind and theirs.'

'As mud is to air and sky.'

She mounted Vranesh, getting a foothold in the stirrups and propelling her body up into the saddle. Liandra turned to Imladrik, looking down from her lofty position as the roof of the rookery tent was hauled away by ropes like a tarp from the back of a cart and the light flooded in. A host of dragons, drakes and wyrms of all stripe and hue were revealed, chained to the ground and muzzled. Draukhain was amongst them, easily the largest and most magnificent, lowering his neck under the gaze of his master. All did, recognising Imladrik's mastery and the potency of his dragonsong. Few were left amongst the asur who commanded such respect amongst the dragons. Certainly, none bore his archaic title.

'It is no wonder that blood has been spilled between us and them,' said Liandra. 'The only surprise to me is that it took this long.'

Not waiting for a reply, Liandra whispered a harsh word of command and Vranesh took to the skies. The chain fastening its ankle to the ground broke apart as if it were brittle bone, and the muzzle shattered likewise as the beast uttered a feral roar.

Imladrik watched her disappear into the clouds, an ill-feeling growing in his heart.

'I am sorry, though,' he whispered, but wanting to say it out loud, 'about your mother.'

━◄ CHAPTER NINETEEN ►━

Father and Son

DROGOR CLAPPED SNORRI on the shoulder from where he sat behind the prince. Since he'd entered the royal pavilion, his father had said nothing to him and this was the first act of recognition the prince had received since taking his seat… aside of course from the High King's toady, Grimbok. Preened and plucked as ever, the reckoner had been particularly obsequious during the brodunk and cleaved to Snorri's father's side like a limpet. Like a narrow-eyed crag-hen, he scoured the clans watching the tournament, his dirty little book of reckoning ever chained to his belt. In fact, he had only averted his gaze from the crowds to give both Snorri and his new friend a withering glare as the prince had joined the royal party.

Mouthing the word *ufdi*, Snorri had ignored him after that, including his muttered rejoinder. Drogor had laughed. It was a burbling sound that rattled in his gut, but was not so loud that it woke or roused any of the High King's guests that were sitting with him.

Since making his acquaintance in the drinking hall, Drogor had been Snorri's near-constant companion over the past few days. Regaling him with tales of Karak Zorn, of scaled monsters that lurked in the torpid jungles of the Southlands and of ziggurats of pure gold that stretched all the way to the sun, Snorri had found his company a welcome respite from Morgrim's continual lectures about duty and the decency of elves. Several were sat with the High King and did not look best pleased by the fact. Snorri ignored them too.

As Prince Imladrik was the Elf King of Ulthuan's representative, he was afforded a seat in the royal pavilion but had yet to sit in it because he was still taking part in the brodunk. Along with the presence of the elves, this was another reason for Snorri's distemper.

At least Morgrim had stopped urging him to heal the rift with his father, which was some small respite, but then he had barely seen him to talk to at length. Other, more conciliatory voices had the prince's ear now.

'Saw what you did out there,' Drogor whispered. 'That axe throw…'

'Heh.' Snorri grinned, enjoying the quiet acclaim. 'Yes, a little closer than I had intended.' Given who was sitting nearby, he lowered his voice still further. 'The elgi moved quicker than I thought.'

'Not close enough to my unpractised eye, my lord.'

'I think drawn blood might have put a dampener on the brodunk, Drog.'

A brief pause suggested Drogor thought that would be no bad thing at all.

'You should be out there competing against the elgi, my lord.'

'Aye, but I am not.' Snorri half turned so he could see the other dwarf. 'And stop calling me "my lord". It's overly formal. Use "my prince" instead,' he said with a wry smile.

Drogor chuckled, but the smile he wore didn't quite reach his eyes, which glittered like endless dark pools in the dim light of the pavilion. He leaned in closer, pointing across the field to the elven rookery.

'See there,' he hissed, 'the elgi rinn lurking in the darkness?'

Snorri nodded.

'Not stopped glaring at you or your cousin since she

clapped her narrow little eyes on you. What do you think she is saying?'

Surprised that Drogor could even see that far, let alone know it was an elf female that was looking at them, Snorri squinted but couldn't tell much of anything.

'How I am supposed to know.'

'It doesn't look friendly. She scowls, like she just stepped in something.'

'Perhaps our rugged earth disagrees with her.'

'That or the fact she is surrounded by dawi,' said Drogor. 'I see the same expression in many elgi faces.' He glanced askance at the elven lords in the royal pavilion. They appeared too self-absorbed to pay much attention to the High King, let alone any other dwarf sitting with them. 'I do not think they can be trusted.'

Now Snorri turned all the way around, earning a reproachful glance from his father who was trying to look interested in the brodunk but who had a host of other matters on his mind.

'What are you saying, Drogor?' Snorri asked.

'That elgi and dawi should not mix. We are too different.'

'Aye, as solid rock to an insubstantial breeze.' Supping on his pipe, he returned his attention to the battlefield.

'Bad enough having skarrenawi around.' Drogor pointed at the champions taking part in the next event, an elf and a hill dwarf Snorri had heard of.

The prince clenched his teeth a little.

'They are not so bad.'

Rundin Ravenhelm was well known to him. Skarnag Grum had made him his captain and chief reckoner. He seldom left Kazad Kro, on account of the king's paranoia no doubt. This, then, was a rare occasion. Obviously, Grum had sent him here as his champion to uphold what little honour the hill dwarfs had. Snorri felt his annoyance at his father for barring him from the brodunk anew – he would have dearly liked to measure himself against this Ravenhelm.

'Perhaps not,' hissed Drogor and shrank back into the shadows.

Snorri watched as the elf and hill dwarf readied their weapons, the former carrying a silver longsword and wearing an eagle-winged helm, while the latter bore a finely crafted rune axe and went unhelmeted in lacquered black leather armour.

'He is bold, for certain...' muttered the prince and could not help but admire the hill dwarf. Half turning again, Snorri was about to reply to his friend but Drogor was gone.

THE AIR WAS hot and thick inside the iron forge, drenched with the smell of soot and ash. Morgrim breathed deep of it, letting it fill him like a balm. In the murky depths, he found Morek casting an eye over his warhammer.

After a few words of incantation, a silent rite performed in the air, the runes of the hammer glowed and were still again.

'What are you doing here, runesmith? Surely the karak has enough metalworkers and foundry dwarfs to run the forges for the brodunk?'

It was true. There were several other dwarf smiths roaming the gloomy confines of the forge, working the bellows and hammering out the dents from the armour and blades of all the combatants. Morek Furrowbrow was the only runesmith.

'I am here at my master's behest to deliver the gauntlet to Prince Snorri and ensure its fit was a good one.'

'I saw it earlier. A fine piece of craftsmanship indeed, but why do you linger now?' Morgrim sat down on a stone bench and began to take off his armour. It was a slow process, made slower by the fact that every piece coming off his body was accompanied by renewed pain at the battering Imladrik had given him.

'I merely wanted to watch some of the bouts. Seemed wasteful not to lend my skill in the forge tent. Master Silverthumb will summon me as soon as he is ready. Then I shall commence my master work.'

Morgrim nodded, satisfied with the runesmith's explanation.

Morek gripped the hammer's haft to test the leather bindings, swung it around his wrist a few times gauging its balance and heft. His deftness surprised Morgrim. There was not only forge-skill in the runesmith's hand. He had the hammercraft of a warrior too.

'All is well?' asked Morgrim.

Through the tent flap, the clash of arms sounded again as the next bout began.

'Solid as ever, the *rhuns* on the blade potent as the day they were wrought.'

'You wield it better than I.'

'I doubt that.' Morek set the hammer down. 'But I've spent my entire life around weapons. I know something about how to use them.'

'Indeed you do.'

Morgrim was removing his war helm. Stinging sweat made him blink and he ran a gnarled hand through his soaked hair. Summoned from the healing tent, a priestess of Valaya had entered the forge and waited nearby to provide ministration. Once he was done smoothing his scalp, he beckoned her.

'It availed me little though, I'm afraid,' Morgrim told the runesmith as the priestess dabbed his facial cuts with a damp cloth from a bowl of water. 'I hope I did not dishonour its craft.'

Morek shook his head. 'Not at all. I saw you fight. The elgi is a fine warrior.'

'You are one of few other dawi at this brodunk that thinks so.'

'I know metal and flame, and nothing of the politics surrounding elgi and dawi,' the runesmith confessed. 'I saw a little of the rinkkaz but much of it was beyond my grasp to negotiate. Certainly, I do not envy the High King in his task. As dawi, we pride ourselves on tradition and heritage. It is one of the cornerstones of our culture. Tradition it seems must be eased if we are to maintain peace, but many of the lords are stubborn. My master is concerned with legacy and what is left behind for others when he and his kind are gone. I think perhaps that the High King is too.'

Morgrim eyed him shrewdly. 'You understand more than you think, runesmith.'

Looking up from tending a piece of battered armour, Morek was about to try and mend Morgrim's shield but discarded it as scrap.

'You'll need a fresh shield.'

'With a shoulder and arm to go with it,' Morgrim replied, wincing as his pauldron was removed along with the padding and chainmail beneath, an ugly purple bruise revealed beneath all three. 'He hits like a hammer.'

Once he was no longer armoured, the priestess approached with a bottle of rubbing alcohol to ease Morgrim's suffering. He stopped her before she could apply it.

'Waste of grog that, milady,' he said, and gently took the bottle from her. 'Use salts instead.'

She did.

Grunting as he eased the stiffness from his back, Morgrim drank a belt of the dirty liquor and grimaced at the taste.

'Packs a kick like a mule.'

'You are as unrefined as that ale, Morgrim Bargrum,' Morek informed him.

'I am.'

The bruise on Morgrim's shoulder was ripening nicely as the priestess applied the salts.

'Do you have another bout?' asked Morek.

'Anvil lifting.'

'Not even the sense you were born with.' He laughed. It was an all too rare expression in the runesmith that lifted the furrows of his countenance.

Outside the forge tent, a resonant shrieking rent the air as the dragons took flight. Morgrim watched them ascend, fear and awe warring for emotional dominance within him. Through the peeled-back leather flap, it was difficult to see much but he fancied he could make out Imladrik's beast and the prince saddled on its back. He was like a glittering arrow of silver fire, behind the flight of dragons at first but quickly gaining on the leader before overtaking her and assuming the tip of their formation.

Though he had humbled him in front of his king and peers, Morgrim bore no grudge against Imladrik. The elf had fought fairly and honourably. Again, as he had so many times in recent days, he found Imladrik to be even tempered and moral. Unlike many elves who could be haughty and arrogant, even disdainful, there was much to like about him. It was just a pity that Snorri could not see it.

'An anvil lifting an anvil, eh?' he said to Morek, reaching for happier thoughts and looking back over his shoulder.

The runesmith wasn't listening. Something else, or rather someone else, had got his attention. The frown returned to his brow as his face clouded over.

'Is that your old friend?'

'Who?'

'The dawi from Karak Zorn.'

Morgrim looked but couldn't see Drogor amongst the crowds.

'Possibly, though he's been spending more time with my cousin of late.'

Morek turned to him. 'With the prince?'

'Yes, my *cousin*. That's what I said.' Morgrim tried to find Drogor again but it was like looking for chalk dust in an ancestor's beard. 'Is something wrong?'

Morek was leaving.

'My master will be waiting.'

Left alone with the priestess, Morgrim sighed. 'I'll never understand runesmiths.'

A COMMANDING VOICE got Snorri's attention. 'Son of mine,' said Gotrek Starbreaker, not even deigning to glance at the prince, 'see here a lesson in axecraft.'

Even as the High King spoke, goblins were scurrying into the arena armed with knives and cudgels. Furgil and his rangers had rounded up the creatures, caging them until this very moment.

Sitting a short distance from the High King, Forek Grimbok was busy speaking with the elven lords. Using a mixture of elaborate hand gestures and a halting dialect, the reckoner described to them what was about to happen next. As Snorri listened to the crude bastardisation of Elvish and Khazalid tumble and crash off Forek's tongue like weighted anvils, he smiled. For a dwarf, Forek sounded like a very good elf.

The reckoner need not have bothered with the convoluted explanation. It was a waste of effort. Snorri could have explained the outcome of the fight with a single word.

Slaughter.

The elf and the hill dwarf had unsheathed their weapons and went to opposite ends of the arena, the former releasing his longsword with a perfunctory flourish, whilst the latter merely fastened a tight grip around the haft of his axe. Both combatants looked determined on what they were about to do. Despite himself, Snorri found himself admiring the toughness of the elf. He seemed less airy than Imladrik, a warrior not a statesman, a slayer not a conciliator.

Perhaps it would not be such dull entertainment after all.

In the middle of the arena were the greenskins, penned off from the two fighters by a cage. Wrought of heavy iron, spikes decorating the points of intersection on the latticed metal, the goblins were well secured. Capering and hooting, biting each other and rolling around in the muck, the greenskins did not seem to understand what was about to happen to them.

Snorri did a rough count in his head and reckoned on close to eighty greenskins on the field. Furgil must have been busy to capture so many for the brodunk.

'All the grobi at once?' he muttered, intending to keep it quiet, but the High King had sharp ears like a wolf's and heard him anyway.

Gotrek jabbed his son playfully in the side.

'Would you balk at such a feat, lad?'

Snorri affected a dismissive air. 'They are just grobi. I could kill a hundred on my own, but since you have banned me from taking up an axe...'

'Ha!' Gotrek's bellowed laughter woke some of the sleepier members of the elder council and sent tremors of unease through the elves, for which Grimbok hastily apologised. 'And that is not about to change because of your petulance. Remember why you are sat here and not out there fighting alongside Lord Salendor.'

'Is that his name, the elgi?'

'Aye lad, and he is a brutal bastard of a warrior. You just wait and see.'

Snorri had already made that same assessment.

'Sounds like you admire him, father.'

'I respect him, as should you. They are not so thin boned and soft of spine as many dawi think.' He eyed the elves again at this remark, as if testing that theory by sight alone. He need not have been so cautious, for the elves did not understand him. True Khazalid was beyond even their most gifted ambassadors. Even so, Gotrek leaned in closer to his son, nudging him conspiratorially. 'Tell me, what do you think of the skarrenawi? You have seen him fight.'

Gotrek pointed at the hill dwarf. He was crisscrossing test swings over his body to loosen his shoulder. Every loud *whomp* of his blade through the air drew a cheer from the small crowd of hill dwarfs that had gathered at the arena side.

'Years ago,' said Snorri, recalling a similar feast time. 'He was decent with an axe.'

'Now I know you are lying, son.'

Snorri was disinterested and had no qualms about giving his father that impression. His gaze wandered over to the healing tents, where the priestesses of Valaya practised their battlefield ministrations.

The High King seemed not to notice and went on, 'Rundin son of Norgil is the skarrenawi king's champion. He shuns the rinkkaz but sends his axe-battler to humble our warriors in the brodunk. Petty, King Grum, very petty,' he grumbled.

'What does it matter if he does? Let me go over there and show him up for the pretender he is. The skarrenawi do not care about us, why should we care about them?'

'Spoken like a true wazzock,' Gotrek said angrily. 'Does nothing I say ever sink into your thick skull, Snorri? The skarrens are our kith, if not kin. They are dawi, albeit of a different stripe. You should care about them, for the day may come when we need them. Relations between our two disparate clans, hill and mountain both, are important. Grum is the problem, not the skarrenawi.'

'Yet you do nothing when he thumbs his teeth at you.'

'Diplomacy is a delicate business, lad,' the High King replied, though he agreed with his son that something needed to be done to bring Grum back in line. Bad enough dealing with elves and the ambitions of King Varnuf, without adding the hill dwarfs to his list of immediate problems.

Snorri scoffed, his gaze drawn back to the healing tents where it lingered in hope.

'Skarnag Grum is an oaf and a glutton, grown fat on excess,' he declared, lowering his voice to add, 'I've even heard rumours of an elf consort.'

Forek, who had evidently been earwigging, nearly spat out his ale and ended up tipping most of his tankard over his finely tailored tunic.

'I seriously doubt that,' said the High King, though there was a glint of amusement in his eye as Forek did his best to apologise to the elves and wipe down his attire at the same time.

'If I could beg your leave, my liege,' he began, coming over. 'I need to–'

'Yes, yes,' Gotrek told him dismissively, 'just go. You don't need me to tell you when to go for a piss, Grimbok, neither do you for this. Away.'

Bowing profusely, crafting a dagger stare at Snorri who was finding it hard to maintain his composure, he left the pavilion to get cleaned up.

'Bit of an ufdi, that one,' Gotrek said behind his hand to Snorri once the reckoner was gone. 'But he's good with words and the hardest bastard reckoner in the Karaz Ankor. Grimbok has settled more debts than any other for this hold.'

Snorri wasn't really listening. His attention was on the healing tents.

'Do not look for her,' said the High King. Though his tone was stern, it was also paternal. 'She isn't there, son.'

Turning away ostensibly to watch the tournament, Snorri feigned ignorance. 'I look for no one, father. My eye merely wandered for a moment.'

'See it does not wander back then.'

Snorri didn't answer but his face was flushed.

'Don't take me for a fool, lad. I know for whom you hold a torch. It is as glaring as Grungni's heart-fire. A pity that Helda was not more to your liking,' he mused briefly, 'a marital union between Karaz-a-Karak and Karak Kadrin would have been very useful about now. Though I trust him to be an ally, Grundin is a thorny hruk at the best of times. If we could have bonded his daughter and his clan to ours...'

'Father,' Snorri implored, 'she was–'

Gotrek waved away his protest. 'The size of an alehouse and with a face like an urk licking dung off its own boots. Yes, I know, lad. But the rinn you want is not for you. She is sworn to Valaya and as such is off limits, even to the son of the High King.' He gestured in the direction of another tent put up nearby. 'Besides, her brother would not look on it favourably either.'

Snorri opened his mouth to protest, but Gotrek silenced him.

'Off limits, lad,' he told him again, but for all that the mood between them was improving. 'Now, let's watch this son of Norgil and see if he's as good as he claims... for a skarren, anyway.'

Father and son smiled together, and Snorri found he was glad of the rare moment of bonding. There had been precious few of them recently.

In the arena, the cage was lowered into a thin trench through some mechanism fashioned by the engineers' guild and the goblins were finally released. Twin war cries in Elvish and Khazalid curdled the air.

Before it was over, there would be much blood.

A FOUL MOOD was upon Forek Grimbok as he entered the healing tent.

Several dwarf warriors taking part in the various games had laughed at him as he strode across the field and the memory of it still simmered. His breeches were wet from the spilled tankard, and it looked as if he'd pissed himself. Their derision only worsened when they realised it was beer that Forek had wasted. One even offered to sup it from his sodden garments, until the fearsome reckoner had glowered at him. At that the half-drunken clanner had sobered up and left quietly with his friend.

Grimbok might enjoy the finer things that life had to offer, he might enjoy the silks the elves brought from far-off lands and keep his beard trimmed, maintain neat and pristine attire, but he knew how to crack skulls too and had done so often during his tenure as reckoner.

It was warm inside the healing tent, and light from suspended lanterns cast a lambent glow over cots and baths. In the centre stood Valaya, a small stone effigy of the ancestor goddess removed with respect from one of the lesser temples and brought here to watch over the wounded. Her rune-emblazoned banners hung from the leather walls.

During the course of the games so far, there had been mercifully few serious injuries to trouble the priestesses. Therefore he was surprised to see his sister Elmendrin tending to the wounded. She was carrying an armful of fresh linen bandages to a wooden trunk.

'Were you planning on wringing that out into your tankard later, brother?' she teased, gesturing to his soiled tunic.

'An unfortunate accident,' Forek replied formally, cheeks reddening. 'I thought you were performing rites in the temple?' he asked, looking around for something to swab his tunic with.

Elmendrin proffered a clay bowl and a sponge she picked from the trunk, which Forek took and proceeded to dab his tunic with.

'Scrub it,' she chastised, showing him how until Forek got hold of the sponge again to save his expensive attire from ruination.

'You are such an ufdi, Forek,' she said, smiling.

A dwarf in a nearby cot sniggered. He had one foot up, exposing a missing toe.

'Never was much of a dancer,' he said.

Forek scowled back before returning his attention to his sister.

'So why are you here, then?'

'Another of the priestesses came down with *kruti* flu, so I took her place.'

The scowl turned into a disapproving frown.

'*He* is here, but I daresay you've already noticed that.'

'Who?' asked Elmendrin as she started to wash a batch of soiled, ruddy bandages in a pewter tank.

'Halfhand.'

She paused, failing to suppress a small smile. 'Is that what they're calling him?'

'I don't need to tell you–'

Elmendrin turned sharply, cutting off Forek in mid-stream.

'No brother, you *don't* need to tell me anything. I am here to perform my duty, not to fawn over the High King's son,' she snapped. 'For good or ill, Valaya has sent me here.'

Forek sagged down onto an empty bench, holding his hand up apologetically.

'Sorry, sister. I am drawn, that is all.'

Indignation became concern on Elmendrin's face and she went to him and sat down.

'You look very troubled,' she said, resting her hand on Forek's shoulder. 'Tell me.'

'I am tired, worn like metal overbeaten by the fuller,' he confessed, using his knuckles to knead his eyes. 'Failing to reckon the many misdeeds done to dawi by elgi has left me ragged. Reports flood in daily of more attacks, more unrest, and our kin grow ever more belligerent.' He met her worried gaze with a look of fear in his eyes. 'I can see but one outcome.'

'But what about the brodunk? Surely it will help salve whatever wounds these troubles have caused between our peoples.'

'Weak mortar to mask the cracks, sister. Nothing more.'

Remembering the other priestesses moving quietly around the healing tent, Elmendrin whispered, 'I had no idea it was this bad.'

'Few do. My every effort is bent towards urging the clans not to retaliate unless they know for certain who the bandits responsible for this perfidy are.'

'Surely the High King can restrain them.'

'Not for much longer. Relations with the elgi are worse than ever.'

She pursed her lips, unsure how to ask her next question. 'And what do you think? About the elgi, I mean?'

Forek looked down at his boots, worry lines deepening the shadows on his forehead. 'I think the world is darkening, sister.'

Elmendrin rubbed her brother's back and held his hand.

'They will be caught. This will stop and the bloodshed will end,' she assured him. 'Elgi do not want to kill dawi, nor dawi kill elgi. It is madness.'

'And yet the killing does not stop. Only the other day, a band of rangers from Karak Varn slew a band of elgi traders bound for Kagaz Thar. Aside from hunting bows, they were unarmed but did not speak much Khazalid and could not explain why they had blundered onto the sovereign territory of the Varn. With all that has happened, what else could they do but kill them?'

Elmendrin rubbed his back harder, fighting back her tears. 'It will pass. It has to. You always see the worst, Forek, but that is just how Grungni made you.'

Forek gripped her hand and she embraced him warmly.

'Not this time, sister.'

He let her go, and her eyes followed him all the way to the flap of the tent. Forek turned just before he left. 'I need to return to the king.' He smiled, but it was far from convincing. 'You're right, sister. All will be well again soon.'

Elmendrin watched him go and the silence of the healing tent became as deafening as a battlefield in her ears.

⫷ CHAPTER TWENTY ⫸

A Herald of Doom

As Snorri watched the fight unfold he began to recognise some of the differences between elf and dwarf in the way that they fought. Despite his obvious disdain for the elves, he had always studied them in war, what little he had been able to garner in these times of peace anyway. Salendor was an odd exemplar of their method.

He fought more like a dancer than a warrior, but with a brutal edge that many elves lacked. His face was an impenetrable mask of concentration. It betrayed no weakness, nor did it show intent. Every blade thrust was measured and disguised, fast as quicksilver and deadly as a hurled spear with the same amount of force.

Goblins fell apart against Salendor's onslaught. Heads, limbs and torsos rained down around him in a grisly flood of expelled blood and viscera. He weaved through the bodies, never slowing, always on the move. No knife touched him. No cudgel wielded by greasy greenskin hands could come close. He was like a cleaving wind whipping through the horde, and wherever he blew death was left in his wake.

Where Imladrik fought with precision, a swordmaster in every regard, Salendor improvised, broke expected patterns and unleashed such fury that many of the goblins simply fled at the sight of him advancing upon them.

The hill dwarf was a different prospect altogether. He brutalised like a battering ram, gladly taking hits on his armour, wearing the savage little cuts of the greenskins like badges of honour. As well as his axe, he fought with elbow and forehead, knee and fist. Rundin reminded the prince of a pugilist, wading into the thick of battle. Utterly fearless, his axe was pendulum-like in the way it hewed goblin bodies. Never faltering, rhythmic and inexorable, it carved ruin into their ranks. Where the elf used as much effort as was needed, the hill dwarf gave everything in every swing. His stamina was incredible.

From what he knew of the son of Norgil, Rundin was not given to histrionics, yet he flung his axe end over end to crack open a fleeing goblin's skull and earn the adulation of the crowd. It was indulgent, and Snorri suspected that Grum had instructed him to entertain with this obvious theatre. It left the dwarf vulnerable but he used a long left-handed gauntlet to parry then bludgeon until he seized his axe and began the killing anew.

Seeing the artifice of the gauntlet reminded Snorri of his own finely-crafted glove. Through it, he recalled the pain of his wounding by the rats beneath the ruins of Karak Krum and of Ranuld Silverthumb's prophecy. Scowling at the memory, he wondered how he was supposed to fulfil his great destiny *watching* other people fight.

Flowing like a stream, Salendor moved through a clutch of goblins. He cut them open with his longsword, spilling entrails, then sheathed the blade and drew the bow from his back in the same fluid motion.

It appeared that Rundin was not the only one told to put on a show.

Arrows seemed to materialise in the elf's hand, nocked and released in the time it took for Snorri to blink. One goblin about to be felled by the hill dwarf's axe spun away from the blow with a white pine shaft embedded in its eye.

At the edges of the arena, a dwarf loremaster announced the kill for the elf. Tallymen racked the count and held up stone placards decorated with the *Klinkerhun* to describe the score.

It was close, but Salendor had the edge by one.

Only six goblins remained.

Beside the prince, the High King shifted uncomfortably in his seat.

'It is tight…' he murmured.

'What does it matter who wins?' said Snorri. 'Elgi or skarren, we lose on both counts.'

That earned a look of reproach from his father. 'I would rather it be a dawi, be that of the mountain or hill.'

'You should have let me fight,' said Snorri, his sudden petulance betraying the better mood that had been growing between him and his father. 'Then the victor would not be in any doubt.'

Gotrek showed his teeth. They were clenched but did not bite. Instead, he fixed his attention on the end of the bout.

Around the arena, the mood was tense but raucous. In tents draped in mammoth hide, Luftvarr hooted and roared with every goblin slain. On the opposite side, Varnuf was more considered and watched keenly over the top of his steepled fingers. Grundin and Aflegard mainly glared at each other, their attention returning to the fight only when prompted by the reaction of the crowd to something particularly noteworthy. Brynnoth, ever the gregarious king, vigorously supped ale with his thanes as they exchanged commentary. The closer it became, the more he drank. It was fortunate that the king of the Sea Hold had an iron constitution from imbibing vast quantities of wheat-rum.

Rundin had pulled one back, but Salendor was quick to riposte, unleashing the last of his arrows to pin a goblin through the heart.

It left four greenskins with the elf still one up. Rundin took two at once, earning a loud bellow of approval from King Luftvarr. Even Grundin clenched a fist. The hill dwarf tackled them before Salendor could run them through with his sword. In using the bow, the elf lord had put too much distance between his quarry and was now paying the price for that.

Swift as a lightning strike, the elf thrust his blade through a greenskin that rushed him in desperation, making it even. One goblin remained, flanked by the two bloodstained champions who looked ready to rush it from opposite ends of the arena.

'The elgi is quick,' hissed Gotrek, glancing up as Grimbok returned to the fold.

'Aye, but the son of Torbad has an eagle-eye when he throws that axe,' the reckoner replied.

Snorri folded his arms and said nothing.

Both warriors advanced on the lonely greenskin, who looked back and forth, scurrying one way and then the other before it realised there was no escape.

'Kill it!' bellowed Brynnoth, banging down his tankard and swilling out some of the dregs.

The goblin shrieked once, clutching its emaciated chest, and slumped down dead, its heart given out.

Silence descended like a veil, settling over the dumb-struck crowd.

Eyes wide, wondering if he had ended the creature with his voice alone, Brynnoth looked down at his tankard and belched.

Some of the elves looked around at him, disgusted and incredulous at the same time.

Both combatants met one another's gaze. The loremasters scoring the bout paused, unsure what to do next. They looked to the High King.

Snorri laughed out loud, his mirth echoing around the arena crowd who were still stunned into bemused silence.

'The grobi kills itself,' he declared. 'Expired by its own fear!'

He laughed again, raucously and derisive. 'Incredibly, both elgi and skarren found a way to lose.'

'That's enough,' snapped the High King. 'You dishonour yourself and the hold.'

'I am merely stating facts, father.' He gestured to the stone placards, the same Klinkerhun inscribed on each now the loremasters realised they had no choice but to score one kill apiece. 'A tie is a win for neither.'

Grimbok began to clap, slow and loudly. When he got to his feet, some of the elder council took up the applause. When the thanes of Everpeak joined in it grew to a clamour. Brynnoth roared with drunken laughter, the king and thanes of Barak Varr hammering their tankards with aplomb. Setting aside their grievance for now, Grundin and Aflegard urged their respective quarters to clap and holler.

Much to Grimbok's relief, elves were celebrating too, not only the ambassadors but those retainers who had accompanied the nobles of their houses. There was a rare mood of camaraderie and community fostered as both races seemed pleased with the result.

From the Norse dwarfs, Luftvarr shouted, '*Runk!*' and his boisterous warriors took up the call.

'Runk, runk, runk!'

The chant spread to other quarters, dwarfs from the other holds echoing their northern cousins eagerly.

'Runk?' one of the elf ambassadors queried to Grimbok.

'It means a thrashing, noble lord,' he explained. 'Such as that given to the grobi by our champions.'

The elf didn't look as if he really understood.

Snorri leaned in, enjoying the swell of aggression manifesting around the arena.

'It also means brawl, ufdi,' he grinned.

The elf ambassador lifted his eyebrows to ask an unspoken question.

'Ahh...' Grimbok began but then cringed as the first punch was thrown.

King Luftvarr decked one of his thanes, a heavy blow that knocked the other dwarf out cold. Seconds later, the entire Norse quarter were fighting.

Drunk, still feeling the vicarious belligerence of watching the brutal combat, dwarfs from other holds started brawling too. Unlike the Norse, it was less brutal, more wrestling than boxing as such.

'Runk, runk, runk!' they bellowed as one, a deafening refrain that set the elves on edge.

Tankards were spilled over, tables upended as most of the onlooking dwarfs revelled in a good, honest scrap.

Musicians began piping, drummers beating out a tune to accompany the brawling.

Grundin was slapping his thighs, supping on his pipe and blowing out smoke rings. The King of Karak Kadrin looked as if he were enjoying this spectacle much more than the bout itself.

Sloshing ale hither and thither, Brynnoth seized a boar-skin drum from one of his musicians and joined the chorus.

Even Varnuf was laughing, though whether in genuine merriment or at the elves' obvious discomfort was difficult to ascertain.

Unsure at the sudden development, Lord Salendor merely bowed to his kin and stalked from the arena. Rundin clapped with the drummers' beat, dancing a little jig much to the roared acclaim of his fellow hill dwarfs and the other mountain clans too.

Throughout it all, Gotrek remained pensive. Like his chief reckoner, he recognised the unease of the elves and dearly wanted the runk to subside, but to do so would harm his standing with his own kin. This was customary amongst the dwarfs and as their High King he would not stop it.

'The elgi, my liege…' Grimbok began. He had sat back down and was no longer clapping. He looked as unsettled as the High King.

'I know,' said Gotrek, impotent to do much of anything in that moment.

'Sire–' Grimbok persisted.

Gotrek snapped, head turning on a swivel to face the reckoner.

'I know!'

'They are leaving, my king.'

Without a word, the elf ambassadors had risen from their seats and were filing out of the royal pavilion with their retainers in tow.

'Should I…' Grimbok was getting to his feet.

'No, sit down,' chafed the High King. 'These are our ways, dawi ways. If the elgi cannot stomach that, then… well, I will not change our customs for outsiders.'

'*Outsiders*, my king?'

'Yes! That is what I said. The elgi are–'

Whatever Gotrek was going to say next remained unspoken when a hearthguard strode up the stone steps of the royal pavilion, interrupting him.

Thumping the left breast of his cuirass, the warrior took a knee and removed his war helm.

'Rise, hearthguard,' said the king. Out of the corner of his eye, he noticed the elves still lingered and were looking at the warrior too. 'You are Gilias Thunderbrow, aren't you?'

'Aye, my king,' the warrior said, standing up. 'Sent by Captain Thurbad with a message from the entrance hall of the upper deep. He bade me come swiftly.'

Around the arena the din from brawling was dying out as all attended to the lone hearthguard. Without his helm, which now sat in the crook of his left arm, to conceal it, the warrior's face was grim.

'Bad news, is it, Gilias?' Gotrek exchanged a dark look with Grimbok, for he already knew the answer to his question.

'Aye, my king,' the hearthguard replied. 'Bleak as winter.'

'Be calm, all of you,' he said. 'This is still my hold and I am still High King of the Karaz Ankor.'

Varnuf's eyes narrowed slightly at that remark. Gotrek expected nothing less.

'Then expel the elgi from our halls and lands, father,' Snorri urged.

'I will not!' roared the High King.

All the dwarfs present, even the other kings, lowered their eyes in acknowledgement of his superiority. All except Snorri.

'They kill dawi by the score, take our gold, cheat our merchants and burn our settlements to the ground and you still wish to treat with them?'

The elf female could contain her ire no longer and spoke out. 'Our people have been slain too. Fort Arlandril was burned and innocent asur murdered. It is not just–'

'Quiet, Liandra!' Imladrik glowered at her, but retained some of his composure to address the High King. 'Liege-lord,' he said, 'this heinous act will not go unpunished. Allow me to send riders to find these bandits and bring them to justice.'

Gotrek was shaking his head. His shoulders sagged, as if defeated.

'It has gone beyond that, my prince. Deaths of merchants are one thing but the slaying of an ancient is something else entirely. I must think on this. Decide upon a course of action.'

Snorri was incensed. 'What is there to think about? Banish the elgi and draw arms against them.'

The stony expressions of Brynnoth and Varnuf suggested they agreed.

Liandra went for her sword again. Several of the elf retainers did likewise and this time Imladrik did not forbid them. Unsheathed elven steel shone brightly in the lamplight.

Only Prince Imladrik stayed his hand.

A ripple went through the hearthguard as they tightened their fists around axe hafts. Above in the higher vaults of the chamber, bow strings were tautened. Thurbad held the warriors in place.

Gotrek met the prince's gaze, and there were storm clouds boiling in the High King's eyes.

'Tell your kin to put up their swords,' he said levelly. 'Tell them to do it now, my prince.'

Imladrik did so, immediately. None argued, for they could see the hopelessness of their situation.

'Please, High King,' Imladrik implored, 'let me–'

'You will do nothing! Nothing!' Gotrek raged. 'This is a dawi matter, now. It shall be dealt with by my hand. Leave.'

Imladrik's face clouded over. 'High King?'

'I said leave. Take your elgi and leave this place. I will guarantee safe passage back to your settlements, but you cannot stay here. Not now.'

Realising there was nothing more to be said, the elf prince bowed and did as the High King had ordered.

Liandra and the other elves followed. The great gate was still open and no one barred their exit. All of the dwarfs watched them go, not taking their eyes off them until the gate was sealed again and sanctity had returned to the entrance hall.

'Why does it feel as if you just gave quarter to an enemy?' said Brynnoth.

Varnuf remained pensive.

'We should have killed them,' muttered Snorri. 'Send a message to–'

Gotrek struck him across the jaw, hard enough to put the prince on his knee.

'Shut your mouth,' snarled the High King, 'and do not dishonour me further with your idiotic talk.'

Snorri was hurt, but mainly his pride. 'Father, I'm… I'm sorry. I didn't–'

'Save your contrition.' Gotrek was shaking his head. 'To think I have raised such a son.' That barb stung worse than any blow ever could. Gotrek turned to Thurbad. 'Gather the rest of the kings, round them all up and bring them here. I will have counsel immediately.'

None opposed him. None dared. With a final glance at his son, who rubbed his jaw painfully, Gotrek stormed from the entrance hall and down into the Ekrund.

* * *

A GRIM AND sombre mood pervaded in the Great Hall.

Agrin Fireheart was dead. Worse than that, he had been slain by elves.

Elves.

It went beyond merely killing. Agrin was a runelord, an ancient, one of the few. His like would not grace the earth again. In one fell and heinous act of callous murder, Barak Varr had lost its closest link to its ancestors.

Gone were the retainers, the guards and lesser thanes; only kings remained. The Grand Hall echoed with their lonely presence, and shadows crowded the small group of dwarfs encircling the High King.

'His body shall be recovered. Furgil and his rangers shall see to it,' he told the only member of the assembly who was not of regal birth.

Nadri Gildtongue bowed. Tears were yet to dry on his dusty cheeks and ran in streaks down his face. In lieu of speech, he chewed his beard. Clothes torn, lathered in mud, stinking of sweat, the merchant cut a sorry and dejected figure.

King Brynnoth nodded to his fellow king.

'Tell them as you told me,' he said to Nadri, indicating the other kings who had only just arrived back at the hold, 'of how you found him and the rest of your kin.'

Nadri nodded, but the words did not come. Grief had thickened his tongue, and the long moments spent waiting for the other lords of the Karaz Ankor to arrive had forced him back to bleak thoughts.

Brynnoth gripped the merchant's shoulder paternally.

'Come on, lad,' he urged. 'All here present need to hear this.'

Swallowing hard, Nadri met his king's steady gaze and found his courage.

'I was three days, maybe less, behind Krondi,' he said. 'We were driving wagons to Zhufbar, but Krondi carried a passenger that was bound for Karaz-a-Karak, so we agreed to meet there and continue on together.'

'Agrin Fireheart was whom your friend was ferrying, yes?' asked Varnuf. For once the King of Eight Peaks seemed without agenda and shared a worried glance with Gotrek.

'Aye, lord,' said Nadri, 'but he did not know. I thought it better if the ancient travelled in secret. It seems my plans were for naught, though.' Face clouding over, he was about to lapse into another deep melancholy when Brynnoth brought him back.

'Keep going, lad.'

Licking his lips, Nadri went on.

'Following Krondi's trail, I became concerned when I reached the ruins of Zakbar Varf. The trading post had been burned, many dawi were dead but, by Valaya's mercy, Krondi was not amongst them.' He wiped an errant tear at the memory. Some of the dwarf kings began to tug their beards in anger. Luftvarr had almost stuffed his entirely into his mouth in order to fetter his Norscan wrath. 'But I moved with haste, eager to make sure of my friend's safety and that of his charge and his warriors.' Nadri's face darkened further and from looking down at his boots forlornly, he met the gaze of the High King who listened quietly. 'Upon reaching the gorge, not twenty miles from the hold gates, I was disabused of that hope.'

All eyes were on the merchant now as a strange air of stillness settled over the kings like a funerary veil.

'At first I saw a guard,' said Nadri. 'He'd lost a boot. It was a few feet from his body. Arrows studded his back, splitting his mail and greaves like paper. They were white-shafted, long and with fanged tips.'

Gotrek weighed in at that point. 'My chief scout found similar arrow shafts at the site of another ambush several days ago.'

'D'ya think these were tha same wee *dreks* that killed this one's kin?' asked Grundin. The King of Karak Kadrin went unhelmeted and his bald pate shone like a coin in the lambent light.

Despite their dispute, Aflegard stood beside him, smoking his pipe in quiet contemplation. Dwarfs were a passionate race that were quick to anger, but slow to forget, and never forgave. No one could hold a grudge like the sons of Grungni. In their language, there were more words for vengeance and retribution than any other. But in this, when kith and kin were attacked by outsiders, they were united. Feuds could wait when others warranted the axe first.

Gotrek nodded. 'It is very likely. Furgil has increased the rangers' patrols and all roads around the karak are watched day and night, but no one has seen these bandits. No one.'

Nadri spoke up. He was shaking his head. 'They were not bandits, High King. What I saw in that gorge was no skirmish. Agrin Fireheart was a master of the rhun. He could wield the elements through his craft.' The merchant clenched a fist as if reliving the final moments of the runelord. 'He brought lightning and thunder to the gorge. Though there were no bodies of elgi, I saw the black marks they had left where Agrin had scorched their skin. No mere bandit could match such a power. Only one thing I know could do that.'

'Sorcery,' uttered Aflegard, the word bitter in his mouth. He chewed the end of his pipe, leaving an indentation in the clay from his clenched teeth.

'Aye, magic of the darkest kind was unleashed against Agrin,' said Nadri, weeping again, 'and he was undone by it.'

And there the merchant's story ended.

Brynnoth patted him on the back, saying, 'Well done, lad. Well done,' in a soothing tone.

Silence fell upon the hall, leavened only by the dulcet crackle of braziers.

Each of the kings looked at one another, their eyes revealing more of their inner thoughts than their tongues ever would.

Luftvarr's were red-rimmed. The King of Kraka Drak was almost apoplectic. Others maintained a more guarded countenance, though it was fairly obvious that Varnuf was waiting for Gotrek to do or say something. His expectant gaze bordered on disparaging before the High King had even spoken.

'Thurbad...' Gotrek intoned to break the quietude.

Like a stone sentinel, the captain of the hearthguard emerged from penumbral shadow.

Gotrek addressed Nadri. 'You'll be escorted safely from

the karak back to the Sea Hold. Thurbad will see to it.'

Brynnoth nodded again to his High King, knowing that he would need to remain behind for further talks. To make a decision in haste now would be foolish, but something would have to be done.

Gently taking Nadri by the arm, Thurbad led the merchant out of the hall and left the kings to ruminate.

'Snorri,' said the High King as Thurbad was leaving. Gotrek did not deign to look at his son. 'You may go too.'

About to protest, Snorri clamped shut his mouth and marched from the Great Hall in barely veiled disgust.

'He's a fiery wee bastard, yer son,' Grundin remarked when the prince was still in earshot.

Gotrek lowered his voice, only looking at Snorri with his back turned and walking away.

'He is a headstrong fool with much to learn.'

'And even more to prove, it would appear,' added Varnuf.

'Not so different from his father during his early reign,' said Brynnoth, to which Aflegard nodded.

'I care not!' Luftvarr had spat out his beard. It spewed out with a spray of sputum. Gobbets still clung to it like dirty little pearls but the Norse king seemed not to notice. 'My warriors stand ready to fight. Elgi have slain dawi in cold blood, and this time a lord of the rhun. No answer to that could ever end in peace, so tell me this, king of the high mountain – when do we make war?'

⤛ CHAPTER TWENTY-TWO ⤜

Legacies

THE SURFACE OF the *dokbar* faded from pearlescent silver to ash grey, its activation robbing it of its lustre and plunging Ranuld into shadow. Like the massive runic shield, his surroundings were a dark mirror to his thoughts. Through the gate between holds he had warned the others. He hoped it would be enough to spare them a similar fate. The magic in the runes inscribed around the dokbar's edge were fading. Soon it would speak no more and his voice would no longer be heard across the leagues.

Much as he had feared, old magic was leaving the world. As the secrets of the old lore diminished, so too did what the dwarfs used to be. Ruin was changing them, as slowly and inexorably as the tide erodes the face of a cliff and exposes its inner core to further decay.

Ranks of gronti-duraz surrounded the runelord but were not good company, no salve to his grief. Still dormant as they were, he alone did not possess the craft to reanimate the stone giants and breathe magical life back into their runes. He needed others to achieve that feat. It was one made harder by what had happened at the borders of Everpeak.

Since leaving the Great Hall after the rinkkaz, Ranuld had remained in the forge but he had felt the passing of Agrin Fireheart like a physical blow. Scattered coals, a fuller lying strewn and uncared for, still littered the floor above. Intent on his work in another chamber of the forge hall, Morek had not heard them fall.

Another light had faded, snuffed out by a great doom that would douse all the lamps should it be allowed to run unchallenged. Ranuld knew not what he could do to stop it, only that he must.

Hope lay in those younger than he and the ancients he had summoned to his conclave. Age and wisdom were giving way to youth and passion. All he could do was help temper this young steel into a blade that would cut through the encroaching shadow.

Weary, Ranuld left the vault and went back to the forge itself, drawn by the sound of hammering.

Morek was toiling at the anvil. Sweat lathered his muscled frame and he wiped a gloved hand against his brow to soak up the worst of it on his face.

'Star-metal is not so easy to shape,' uttered the runelord, causing his apprentice to turn.

A partially formed blade, slowly being cogged into shape and then to be edged and fullered, lay upon the anvil. Morek stared at it forlornly.

'It is unyielding, master.' He sounded breathless; the sinews in his arms were taut enough to snap and his muscles bunched like overripe fruit grown too big for its own skin.

'Like the *karadurak*, it must be coaxed into giving up its secrets,' Ranuld told him. 'Strength is not enough. Any oaf can whack a hammer with enough force to split a rock, it will only respond to skill. And much like splitting everstone, meteoric iron, *gromril*, can only be forged by a master smith. Are you such a dawi, Morek of the Furrowbrows?'

'I think so, master.'

Ranuld scoffed. 'Werit. Think? Think, is it? *Think!*' He bellowed, 'You must *know* it. Az and klad will not forge themselves.'

'Master, I...'

'And to think it is to you who I must pass on all my knowledge… Kruti-eating *wanaz*, I should take the hammer from your hand this instant and use it upon your stupid head! Ufdi!'

'Please don't, master.'

'Wazzock,' spat the runelord. His eyes narrowed on his terrified apprentice then to the slowly bending star-metal he had clamped against the anvil. An axe blade was visible, and once it was finished the runes could be struck. 'Hit it again,' Ranuld told him, watching sternly as Morek worked the meteoric iron.

'Gromril is the ore of heroes and masters. It is only they who can wield it, only they who can craft it.'

Morek kept going, hammering relentlessly, slowly building up a rhythm that Ranuld felt resonate in his very soul.

'It requires an artisan's touch to tame and temper. No mere metal-smith can do it. Let them forge shoes for mules or rivets for scaffolds. Theirs is not the way of the rhun. That is the province of our sacred order alone, of which you are a part.'

Hammering, Morek became entranced and the star-metal began to bend to his will.

Ranuld lit up his pipe, took a deep draw as he sat back to regard his apprentice.

'The rhun is slow, so too the metal that bears it. Many weeks it can take just to make a single ingot. Forge its angles sharp and tight, imbue it with the magic of our elders and become a master.'

The ring of metal against metal was almost hypnotic now. Morek had transcended from the 'now' to a place of creation, the rites of forging tripping off his lips like a chant.

'Aye,' said Ranuld, 'now you *know*, lad. Now you can see.'

Slowly, a smile crept up at the edges of his lips. Morek was learning.

'As one light dies,' he said, 'another ignites.'

EVEN THE SKIES presaged a storm. Grim, black clouds crawled across the sun to blot out the light. Imladrik felt the cold pull at his clothes and seep beneath the plates of his armour. But it was not just the sun's absence which chilled him. The look in the High King's eyes was like ice when he had dismissed Imladrik and the other elves. Suppressing a shiver, he dug his heels into Draukhain's flanks, urging the beast to fly lower.

Karaz-a-Karak was a bitter memory. He cursed inwardly that blades had been drawn in the High King's hold hall and wondered if there was any turning back from the course they were set upon now.

The prince's retainers were on their way back to Oeragor, where he would join them just as soon as he had made this last flight with Draukhain. Others would return to Athel Maraya, Kor Vanaeth and even the vaunted spires of Tor Alessi. After what little he had heard in the entrance hall, Imladrik had decided to track the dwarfs leaving Everpeak. Not those going to Barak Varr but the rangers who had been ordered to recover the bodies of the slain. He wanted to see where it had taken place, and know what had happened in order to make sense of it. One of the dwarfs' runelords was dead. It was unlikely a bandit's arrow had killed him. Imladrik suspected something darker was at work and intended to find out the root of it. The only way to do that was to go to where Agrin Fireheart had died.

The prince's dragon snorted and growled, behaving more belligerently now than when it had been surrounded by dwarfs. It felt the prince's ire and frustration, echoing and amplifying it.

'Peace, Draukhain...' Imladrik soothed, inflecting his voice with a mote of dragon mastery. The beast eased, piercing a layer of cloud.

Below, the rangers were gathering up the bodies of the dead, wrapping them in cloth and placing them reverently on the back of a cart. As funerary transportation went, it was hardly fitting. Imladrik stayed within the lower cloud layer, wreathed in its grey tendrils so if the dwarfs should look up they would not easily see him. The last thing peace needed now was the sighting of a dragon prowling the scene of a foul murder. But then perhaps peace was beyond them at this point. He hoped fervently that this was not the case, and wondered how much his brother knew or cared about what was unfolding on the Old World. Not for the first time in recent weeks, Imladrik wondered if he should return home. The letters he had received at the tournament were still tucked in his vambrace. Their words were burned so indelibly in his mind that he had no need for either any more.

Rising again with a beat of Draukhain's powerful wings, Imladrik found he was not alone when he returned to higher skies.

'Can you smell that reek?' asked Liandra from the back of Vranesh. The beast was small in comparison to the mighty Draukhain but the two dragons recognised each other as kin, snarling and calling to one another in greeting.

Liandra wrinkled her nose. 'It is dark magic. Like a canker on the breeze, the stench is unmistakable. The Wind of Dhar has been harnessed here.'

Though her lips moved, Imladrik heard the words in his mind as though they were standing side by side in a quiet room and not aloft and far apart in a turbulent sky.

He calmed Draukhain, for the depth of the beast's greeting cries would build to the point where the dwarfs below could hear them and think they were under attack.

Liandra frowned. 'What are you doing here?'

'Flying.' Imladrik was in no mood for an inquisition. 'Why did you follow me?'

Beyond his dragonsong, which was potent, Imladrik had no magical craft to draw upon. He had to shout, but Liandra heard him easily enough.

'You can speak normally,' she told him. 'The enchantment works both ways.' She reined Vranesh in a little, for the dragon could smell the dwarfs far below them and wanted to better taste their scent. Like its mistress, the beast neither liked nor trusted the dwarfs. But also like his mistress, he had even less love for dark elves.

Imladrik would not be distracted and asked again, 'Why did you follow me, Liandra?'

'If I said it was to make sure you weren't going to do anything reckless, like try and talk to the dwarfs, would you have believed me?'

'No.'

'Then I did it to find out what you were doing. You entire household leaves the dwarf lands, headed for Oeragor, and yet you, their prince and master, go west after a trail of rangers. I wanted to know why you would do that, Imladrik.'

'And do you?'

'You don't believe that asur did this.'

'No elf of Ulthuan I know uses the Dark Wind. Those that do are rounded up as traitors by the warriors of the White Tower and executed.'

A darkness flashed across Liandra's face at a bitter memory.

'You think it was druchii?'

'You do not?'

They circled one another, the wings of their mounts flapping lazily but their nostrils flaring as the wind grew steadily more vigorous. It was buffeting Liandra's hair, releasing her gilded locks into the air like flecks of brilliant sunshine.

'Storm is coming,' she said, gazing into the heart of a thunderhead growing on the horizon.

Imladrik maintained a neutral expression. 'You didn't answer my question again.'

'I do not think it matters whether the druchii are involved or not. But I can taste Dhar like ashes in my mouth. Whatever was unleashed down there in that gorge left a mark.'

'A powerful sorceress then,' said Imladrik, partly to himself. 'It is worse than I first thought.'

Liandra nodded. 'And something else too, something I cannot quite see.'

Imladrik was keen of sight. He looked through a patch of thinning cloud and saw that the dwarfs had collected their dead and were moving on.

'Would a closer look make it any clearer?'

'I would rather not descend into the gorge,' she told him, and there was a note of fear in her voice.

'The dwarfs are leaving. If we land at the ridge on either side and climb down into the gorge, they would not see us.'

Despite the prince's reasoning, she looked far from certain.

'I would have thought of all people, you would be the most keen to find out if there are druchii abroad in the Old World. It might have a bearing on whatever happens next. You are no friend to the dwarfs but I also know you do not want another war for our people.'

She peered down through the clouds for a few seconds before conceding. 'We must be swift.'

The dragons dived a moment later, Draukhain in the lead with Vranesh a few feet behind. In keeping with Imladrik's plan, they perched on the ridges of the gorge on either side. The elves then dismounted and climbed down. They met in the middle in a scrum of scattered, broken blades and patches of churned earth.

'It was a brutal fight,' said Liandra. She was crouching down, running the earth between her fingers.

'That is plain even to my mundane sight,' said Imladrik. 'What else do you feel?'

She closed her eyes and took a deep breath.

'Dhar saturates this place. It has been tainted by it. Three sorcerers, one much more potent than the others...'

Imladrik kept his voice low, but his gaze was intense. 'How can you tell?'

'Each crafts the wind of magic subtly differently. Such a thing leaves a trail of essence behind it if you know how to look for it.'

'And what of the other thing, the enigma you spoke of?'

She screwed her eyes tighter. Her fists were clenched at her sides. Liandra's already pale skin drained further, leaving her cold and corpse-like. She shuddered, wracked by a sudden convulsion that threw her off her feet and onto the ground where she spasmed.

'Liandra!' It was as if Imladrik's voice was lost through the veil of a waterfall, distant and muffled.

Reaching her side, he shook her hard, pulling her up onto her knees again.

'Liandra!' Rubbing her arms, trying to beat some warmth back into her, Imladrik didn't know what else to do. 'Come back to me,' he urged and was about to strike her when Liandra's eyes snapped open again.

She flushed at the look of concern on Imladrik's face. When the prince recognised it too he backed off.

'Are you hurt?'

She struggled to her feet but refused any help.

'We cannot linger here. It's not safe.'

'Liandra?'

She was already climbing back up to the ridge, finding trails no dwarf ever could and moving with a grace and swiftness that would seem impossible over such rugged terrain. Equally as nimble, Imladrik gave chase.

'Liandra...' He grabbed at her arm, and she snapped it away with a muttered curse.

'Even with a dragon to protect me, I do not want to feel a crossbow bolt in my back,' she said.

'The dwarfs are gone, and I doubt they would shoot us without cause.'

'Did you not see as I did in the dwarf hall? They want retribution for this. Even if their king is wise, they are not. They are a vengeful and greedy people, Imladrik. It is time you realised that. It might not be tomorrow, or even next year, but a war is coming to our people and there is nothing you can do to prevent that.'

Imladrik was about to respond but knew she was right.

Perhaps he had lingered too long in the Old World with the dwarfs. His brother was calling him back. He had received several letters from the Phoenix King petitioning for his return. Standing there looking at Liandra, he also realised something else.

'You hate them, don't you.'

'The druchii,' she sneered, 'yes. They killed my mother, there is much in that for me to hate.'

'No, not just that. You hate the dwarfs too.'

She nodded without hesitation.

And just like that, Imladrik saw how far apart the two of them had become. He wanted harmony, a peaceful accord between their races; Liandra wanted war. Either against dark elves or dwarfs, it didn't matter.

'I did not notice it before,' he admitted. 'I think I was blind somehow, but you are a supremacist, Liandra. Whether from your bloodline or the horrors you have endured in the past, you have become intolerant of every race except for your own.'

'I am my father's daughter,' she answered defiantly. Her face softened and she added, 'You are leaving, aren't you?'

Imladrik looked resigned. 'Yes. With Malekith's forces stirring in the north, my brother has need of me to marshal the warriors of the dragon peaks.'

'I wish I could go back with you, but my father forbids it.'

'Don't be so eager for bloodshed, Liandra. It is not as glorious as you think it is.'

'I only want to be by their side… my father's and brothers'. But if there are druchii here, I *will* find them,' she promised.

'Don't give in to hate, Liandra.' Imladrik paused, unsure of how to ask his next question. He decided to be direct. 'What did you see, when that palsy stole upon you?'

Her face paled a little at the memory.

'I don't know.'

'Nothing born of Naggaroth?'

She shook her head, which only made the prince's frown deepen. Their enemies were gathering, it seemed.

Though she was a little further up the rise, Imladrik was much taller than her and looked down on the princess. As their eyes met, they drew close enough to touch. She gently put her hand upon his cheek. The metal of her gauntlet was cold, but the warmth of the gesture was not.

'You are such a noble man, Imladrik.'

The prince's face darkened as he thought of those who waited for him back on Ulthuan, and the feelings stirring within him as he looked at Liandra despite everything.

'No, I am not.'

'Love is not love when the choice is made for us,' she said, cradling his chin before leaning in to kiss him delicately on the cheek.

He didn't stop her but didn't know how to respond either. She did all the talking for him.

'If this is to be farewell then I would have you know what I think of you, my prince.'

She touched his chest once, her armoured fingers lingering

against his breastplate just where his heavy-beating heart was drumming. Then she carried on up the rise without another word.

Imladrik let her go. He didn't return to the gorge but summoned Draukhain from the opposite ridge, leaping onto the dragon's back as it flew beneath him.

He flew into the storm, his mind troubled. If the dark elves really were abroad in the Old World then the High King of the dwarfs must be told. Arriving at the gates of Everpeak on the back of a dragon after being banished would only create further discord. A subtler method was needed. Reining Draukhain, Imladrik headed west in the direction of his retainers. He needed a swift messenger, one the dwarfs would not try to kill or capture on sight. Praying to Isha, he only hoped he would not be too late.

⤛ CHAPTER TWENTY-THREE ⤜

Skulls

BONE FRAGMENTS PEPPERED Snorri's armour as he shattered the goblin skull with a warhammer.

Kicking off the bone chips still littering the flat rock he was abusing, the dwarf prince went to grab another skull when he saw Morgrim watching him from the archway.

'Quite an impressive collection you've got, cousin,' he said, indicating the fifty or so flensed greenskin heads Snorri had piled up. Several days old, they were the gruesome leavings from the brodunk. The dwarf prince had severed the heads himself. Stuck in the earth next to them, nigh hilt-deep, was a broad-bladed knife. It was flecked with goblin blood. There was no sign of the skin or flesh.

'Threw it over the edge for the screech hawks,' said Snorri, as if reading his cousin's mind. 'I've heard they like the taste of grobi.'

Morgrim closed a heavy wooden door behind him, and stepped out onto a rocky plateau. Surrounded by a low wall punctuated by crenellations, it was one of the eagle gates of Karaz-a-Karak; just without its Gatekeeper, whom the prince had dismissed for some solitude.

Morgrim sucked in the mountain air, relishing its crispness.

'Didn't think you liked the outdoors,' he said.

Snorri lined up another skull and smashed it with a heavy blow, like he was hewing timber for the hearth fire.

'I'm learning to live with it. I'll be seeing a lot of it in the coming months.'

'You think we'll go to war, then?'

Another skull capitulated noisily beneath Snorri's hammer.

'It's inevitable. Every dawi knows it. It's only my father that won't acknowledge it.'

'He doesn't want a war.'

Snorri looked up from his bludgeoning. 'You think I do?'

'You're out here smashing grobi skulls, venting your anger, cousin. I think you have some pent-up aggression.'

'My father talks when he should be strapping on az and donning klad. I am frustrated, Morg. And I don't understand why he cleaves to the elgi so much. What have they ever done for us but cause trouble?' No longer in the mood, Snorri tossed the hammer down and sat on a different rock. He rubbed his shoulder to ease out the stiffness. 'Every day brings news of more murder and theft, yet my father does nothing. He hides in his Grand Hall, bickering with the other kings. Right now the elgi are nothing, just a few thousand warriors and the odd drakk, scattered across disparate settlements. We could defeat them in a month and reclaim the Old World as our own.'

Morgrim picked up where his cousin had left off, choosing a particularly ugly goblin skull to split.

'You make it sound so simple.'

'It is! It's easy, Morg. If an enemy threatens you, take up az and klad, step into his house and kill him. Drogor can see it, why not you?'

Morgrim looked down at the skull he'd just sundered. 'Drogor is not the dawi I remember.'

'You were little more than beardlings when you knew each other. Despite what our ancestors say, dawi can change.'

Morgrim took another skull. 'Not that much.'

'He is a little strange, but I just put that down to his

ordeal to reach the karak or living under hot sun for the last twenty-odd years. Southland jungles are no place for dawi.'

'Aye, perhaps.' Bone fragments exploded furiously across the ground. 'I can see why you enjoy this.' Swinging the hammer onto his shoulder, Morgrim hefted a third skull. This one had belonged to an orc. 'He certainly hates elgi.'

'Wouldn't you if they'd slain your kin? And is that such a bad thing?'

'I do not doubt his cause, but if he turns your mind towards similar thoughts then yes, it is bad.'

Snorri scowled. 'I'm no puppet, Morg.'

Two-handed, Morgrim split the orc skull in twain.

'I know that, cousin. I'm sorry.' He took off his war helm to wipe the sweat dappling his forehead. 'Thirsty work.'

'I have ale…' Snorri pulled a damp tarp off a modest-sized barrel he'd kept in shadow beneath the tower wall. He handed Morgrim a pewter tankard. 'And hoped you would find me up here.'

Taking a long pull of the foaming brew, Morgrim said, 'Tromm, but that is fortifying.'

'*Drakzharr*, one of Brorn's special reserves.'

A companionable silence fell between them as they supped together, the sun on their faces and a light wind redolent with the scent of the earth filling their nostrils.

Morgrim breathed deep as he took a long swig of the liquor.

'Been too long since we did this.'

'Aye Morg, it has. I am sorry too. My father…' Snorri bit his lip to keep back his anger. 'He treats me like… like…'

Morgrim smiled reassuringly.

'Like his son, Snorri. And that means he judges you harshest of all dawi.'

'Why won't he let me show him what I am capable of? I am of the Thunderhorn clan, of Lunngrin blood. I am Whitebeard's namesake, by Grungni, and yet he favours elgi over his own kin.'

Morgrim shook his head. 'No, cousin. He does what he must to hold on to the peace he's fought so hard to create.'

'And what if I want war?' Snorri's eyes were crystal clear

as he said it. 'What if what Drogor says is right and the elgi cannot be trusted? Is it not better to strike first?'

'When have you ever known a dawi to strike first, cousin? Besides, Drogor seems full of bile. Be wary that you do not heed him too much.'

'He is your friend.'

'Not one I recognise.'

'What is it you can see that he and I cannot? You have befriended this Imladrik–' Snorri tried but failed to keep the sneer from his face, '–and of all the elgi, he at least seems honourable, but the rest... this elgi woman and the other, this Salendor...'

'Imladrik is the ambassador of the elgi king, the one who resides across the sea. If anyone speaks for their race, would it not be him? Why do you see the others as enemies? They are acting no different to you, cousin. Your belligerence and mistrust is a mirror which they reflect back.'

Snorri smirked. 'Have you been talking with Morek, cousin? You sound as cryptic as the runesmith and his master.' Finishing the drakzharr, he wiped his mouth and poured another. 'A drakk slayer, one destined to be king. That is what Ranuld Silverthumb prophesied.'

'I remember,' said Morgrim.

'Only elgi ride drakk and they are supposedly our allies. How then must I go about killing one if that will always be true?'

'Nothing with prophecy is ever clear. Even Ranuld Silverthumb doesn't know its meaning and he is runelord of Karaz-a-Karak. Do you think you can decipher it so easily?'

'Times are changing,' said Snorri, looking off into the high peaks where dark clouds had started to gather, wreathing the pinnacles of the mountains like smoke. 'I can feel it, Morg.'

There was a danger of the conversation souring again, so Morgrim sat down, clapping his cousin on the shoulder to dispel any growing tension. 'These are hard times for everyone,' he said, 'but I am still hopeful that a peaceful outcome to the troubles can be reached.'

Snorri paused in his supping, eyes darkening.

'It may already be too late for that.'

Incredulity deepened the lines in Morgrim's face. 'The High King is still in council, so how can that be so when no decision has been made?'

Snorri met his cousin's questioning gaze.

'Varnuf and Thagdor have already mustered armies. They wait in the hills and valleys not far from Karaz-a-Karak. Luftvarr too has over two thousand dawi warriors awaiting their king's return. And I reckon there will be others too.'

'And what do you plan on doing, cousin?' Morgrim had set down his tankard, the ale more bitter than it was previously.

'Several clans see as I do. Regardless of the council's decision, I am marching on the elgi. We attack now or regret our temperance at length.'

Morgrim was on his feet. In his haste he kicked over his tankard, spilling the precious brewmaster's ale. He barely spared it a glance.

'Varnuf is a rival of your father's, so too Thagdor of Zhuf-bar. Luftvarr is just a savage. How can you be thinking about throwing your lot in with them, possibly against the High King's wishes? It is beyond reckless, cousin.'

Snorri stood up too. 'It is reckless to do nothing, *cousin*. The elgi have enjoyed our understanding and flouted our hospitality for too long. We must show them who the true lords of the Old World are. My father *will* declare war. What other choice does he have?'

'And if he doesn't?'

Snorri's eyes were hard as granite. A harsh wind tossed the curls of his beard, making him appear even more belligerent.

'Then I shall declare it for him.'

◄ CHAPTER TWENTY-FOUR ►

War Counsel

No DECISION EVER made by a dwarf came easily. One that must be debated by a dynasty of dwarf kings was near impossible to reach a consensus over.

Debate raged in the Great Hall. Tempers were fraying after the news of Agrin Fireheart's death had got out. The High King had made no attempt to conceal it, but the furore it had created was increasing the number of worry lines upon his brow tenfold.

All of the kings from the brodunk were there. Thagdor had also travelled from his encampment to be at the council. Only Bagrik, who had long since returned to Karak Ungor, was absent. There were other nobles of the dwarf realms, of course: the lodewardens of Mount Gunbad and Silverspear, too busy at their mineholds; the southern kings of Drazh and Azul, too distant. Both Brugandar and Hrallson had sent emissaries for the rinkkaz, both of whom had returned to their holds and not attended the brodunk. There was no time to request the presence of them or their liege-lords. The same was also true of Karak Varn and its king, Ironhandson. Fledging holds, those of the Black Mountains and Grey Mountains, would also not be present and so the decision whether or not to make war with the elves would be decided by but a few.

The King of Zhufbar was unperturbed by that and took his opportunity to speak eagerly.

'We must fight the elgi. What other choice do we have now?' Thagdor asked of them all. 'Dead merchants, theft and thagi across the length and breadth of the Karaz Ankor. Settlements burned, and now rhun lords slain by sorcery. What's next? Besiegement of our holds and lands? Will I wake up tomorrow from my bed to find a host of elgi outside my gates?' The King of Zhufbar paused for breath. 'I bloody won't. I'll kill the sods before it comes to that.'

Luftvarr thumped his chestplate, declaring, 'Elgi cannot be allowed to stay in the Old World. I have warriors, two thousand strong, ready with *az un klad* to kill the elgi traitors!'

The Norse king's declaration was met with rousing approval from Brynnoth who burned with retribution for the slaying of his runelord, but it was Varnuf who spoke up next.

'None of us want war with the elgi…' he began, waving off protests from the more belligerent kings, but eyeing Gotrek in particular, 'but anything less would be seen as weakness on our part now.'

Brynnoth tugged at his beard, unable to say much of anything. His eyes said enough. He wanted blood.

'We should not be hasty,' counselled Aflegard, tucking his thumbs into the jewelled braces he wore across his paunch. 'I can spare no warriors for war, and it would be unwise to attack the elgi before we know who the perpetrators of Agrin Fireheart's death were.'

Grundin stepped in to cut off some of the more pugnacious kings before they could voice further tirades. 'For once, I find myself in agreement with the ufdi king. He's thinkin' aboot his purse, though–' Grundin snapped. 'Ah, shut it ya wazzock!' before Aflegard could open his mouth to deny it. 'We all know ye trade with the elgi. Am no sayin' you're a traitor or even an elgongi, just a miserly bastard, protectin' his hoard.' The King of Karak Izril looked far from placated but Grundin ignored him so he could carry on. 'But I dinny think we should be killin' elgi fer no good cause. Ach, I know that Agrin lies cold. Dreng tromm, I know it, but I canny see how declaring war on the pointy-eared wee bastards is ginny change that.'

Brynnoth glared, unconvinced and swung his murderous gaze over to the High King, who so far had only listened.

'Trade with the elgi ends. Now,' Gotrek declared to all. 'We shut our borders to them until such a time as the fighting stops and we can return to the negotiation table.'

'Negotiation,' said Thagdor, brandishing his fist. 'I'll negotiate with the buggers at the end of my chuffing axe, I will.' He shook his head and the copper cogs attached to his beard jangled. 'There can be no treating with these elgi, none at all. I won't do it,' he said, folding his arms as if that was an end to the matter.

'See this?' Gotrek brandished a slender note in his meaty fist, the parchment too thin and smooth to have been made by a dwarf. 'Written by the hand of a prince and brought to mine by a bird,' he said. 'Can you imagine such a thing? How different are we, the elgi and the dawi?' He laughed without genuine humour. 'As mud is to the sky, I have heard said behind our backs. This Prince Imladrik is an honourable warrior and ambassador to his king. He claims another race did this.' He paused to read a word from the note, finding the pronunciation difficult. '*Druchii.*'

'What is this *druchii*?' asked Thagdor, unconvinced.

None of the kings were.

'A darkling elgi,' said Gotrek, unsure himself. 'Some murderous but distant kinsman, bent on mischief. I do not know.'

'Elgi is elgi!' snapped Grundin. 'Ach, the pointy-eared bastards will say anything to save their silk-swaddled arses.'

Mutters of approval from the other kings greeted the lord of Kadrin's outburst.

'There was betrayal here,' said Gotrek to quieten the murmurs of his vassal lords, eyeing Brynnoth in particular, 'and mark me that retribution will be meted out, but I cannot sanction war against all elgi on account of the deeds of a few, especially when there is any doubt.'

'You may not be able to stop it,' answered Varnuf dangerously.

Gotrek swung his gaze onto the King of Eight Peaks. 'Speak your mind plainly, Varnuf,' he told him, his voice level and laden with threat. His knuckles cracked as he seized the arms of his throne.

'Forces already muster north of Karaz-a-Karak.' His eyes widened and a slight smile tugged at the corners of his mouth, barely visible beneath his long beard. 'And they are making ready to march.'

'Aye,' said Aflegard, ignorant of what was happening between the other two kings, 'and I've heard talk of elgi laying siege to the skarrens too.'

'Ach, that's a lot of shite,' said Grundin, scowling at the effete dwarf. 'You would jump at your own shadow, ufdi.'

Aflegard was puffing up his chest, about to reply, when the High King bellowed.

'Silence! Both of you.' He glared, then returned his gaze to Varnuf. 'Any vassal lord of mine who marches on the elgi will be answerable to me, whether these so-called *druchii* exist or not. Is that plain enough?'

The mood around the Great Hall was fractious. The kings did not look keen to submit easily. Varnuf had read it well and chose then as his moment to act.

'Dawi lie dead and you ask us to do nothing,' he said. 'What will stopping trade achieve? How will shutting our borders and roads stop the killing? It will not. It will send a message to the elgi that we are soft, that they can kill our kith and kin, and that we will let them.' He stood up to address the gathering. 'I won't stand by and allow murder and destruction to continue in my lands, our lands, without response. *Our* lands,' he reaffirmed, nodding to all, 'not theirs, not the elgi's.' He looked at Gotrek, who glowered, and pointed a beringed finger at the High King. 'When you vanquished the urk and grobi–' Varnuf bared his teeth, revelling in the bloody memories, '–rendered them so low that they would never threaten our kingdoms again, I would have followed you into the frozen north itself. A king of kings sat upon the Throne of Power then. He did not fear war. He was stone and steel with the wisdom of Valaya upon his brow, Grimnir's strength in his arm and Grungni's dauntless courage.'

There was regret in Varnuf's eyes and hurt too, as if from a sense of betrayal. 'Now, all I see before me is a scared dawi who no longer has the stomach for a fight. What value has peace, if it is bought and paid for with our deaths?'

A shocked murmur ran around the chamber like a flame as each of the kings shuffled back. Alone of all them, Varnuf stepped forwards. He had unhitched the hammer from his belt.

Gotrek was already on his feet and had done the same. He knew what was coming and couldn't help but think back to what his son had said to him all those nights ago in this very hall.

'Speak the words then. Do it now or by Grungni I shall descend from this throne and crack open your skull, Varnuf of the Eight Peaks.'

Varnuf did not just speak the words, he snarled them. 'Let it be known that on this day, Varnuf of Eight Peaks did pronounce grudgement on Gotrek of Karaz-a-Karak.'

Aflegard stifled a gasp, but only so Grundin wouldn't clout him for it.

The others looked on solemnly, waiting for the High King's answer.

'So be it.' Gotrek unclasped the cinctures and torcs binding his beard, unfurling it like a belt of cloth as he stepped from the dais of his throne and onto the chamber floor.

Vanruf had done the same. Like Gotrek he had also removed his crown.

Both dwarfs wore no armour beyond that which was ceremonial and had no war helms either. Their hammers were not runic, but they were well fashioned from hewn stone and could crack bone easily enough.

Thurbad was not present, so Gotrek turned to another ally to officiate.

'Grundin, come forth,' he said, gripping the full thickness of his beard in one meaty hand and proffering it to the northern king. 'Bind us,' he said, staring into Varnuf's eyes as he too gave Grundin his beard.

'You two are proper wazzocks...' muttered the King of Karak Kadrin.

'Tie it tight,' said Gotrek, the leather grip of his hammer creaking in his clenched fist.

Grudgement was a solemn oath pledged by kings and lords. It was a trial by combat and could also end in death, though no dwarf would ever condone the slaying of his own. This was a matter of honour and for such things a dwarf would shed blood, even kill if necessary. By the binding of beards did both combatants commit to the fight. There could be no flight, though some had tried only to end up with their brains dashed upon rock or their necks severed by a heavy-bladed axe. Only death or the cutting of the beard bond, the *trombaraki*, could end such a duel.

'Hammers then,' muttered Varnuf, swinging a few half circles to loosen up his shoulder.

'Aye, hope you have a harder head than you look.'

'Hope yours is not as soft as your stomach,' Varnuf bit back.

Once grudgement was declared and accepted rank and station counted for naught. Two dwarfs entered this deadly compact and only one would be standing at the end of it. Alive or dead was at the victor's discretion.

Tired of talking, Gotrek nodded to Grundin. The northern king backed away and so grudgement could begin. All the kings had done the same, leaving a small arena for the two dwarfs to fight in.

'It's not too late, Gotrek. Relinquish your throne and I will take us into this war.'

'You're a damn arrogant fool, Varnuf. And there can be no backing out, not once grudgement is pronounced. But you can do me one favour...'

'Name it, your tongue may be incapable of speech after I'm done with you.'

'Stop talking and swing. I have a kingdom to protect.'

Varnuf roared, yanking on his beard and dragging Gotrek towards him. His blow glanced the shoulder of the High King, who grunted but was unbowed, planting his hammerhead into the other king's gut. Beer breath exploded violently from Varnuf's mouth and he almost retched, but managed to smack his haft against the High King's nose.

Blood streaming from his left nostril, Gotrek dropped to a crouch, bringing down with him Varnuf who hadn't properly squared his feet. Rising, Gotrek uppercutted the King of Eight Peaks in the jaw, and Varnuf snapped back immediately because of the beard binding and took a sturdy elbow smash in the cheek. He kneed Gotrek in the stomach, forcing a pained shout, but the High King had fought in many grudgements before and thumped Varnuf hard and repeatedly in the kidneys.

Thrusting his shoulder, Varnuf barged Gotrek onto his heels.

Battered, both kings tried to retreat for a breather but their beards were well tethered and they lurched back into striking range.

Haft to haft they rained a score of heavy blows on one another, hitting so hard as to create a rain of splinters. Varnuf resorted to a punishing array of overheads, which Gotrek parried with both hands braced against his hammer. He grimaced as the last breathless blow fell and he managed to lock their weapons together.

'Let me tell you something about when I purged the grobi and the urk,' Gotrek growled when the two were inches apart and face to face. Sweat was pouring off both kings, sheeting their foreheads and darkening their tunics across the chest and armpits.

'Go on,' hissed Varnuf, straining against his opponent's guard.

'Well,' said Gotrek, 'I didn't do it cleanly.'

The King of Eight Peaks's face went suddenly blank.

'Uh?'

Letting all of his resistance go, Gotrek quickly stepped aside as Varnuf's momentum took him forwards. There was just enough beard length to get behind him and swing his hammer haft into the other king's crotch.

For want of a better word, Varnuf yelped. It was so brief, so small a noise that it was missed by most of the spectators, but Gotrek heard it. Then he exhaled, a long, deep, agonised groan that echoed around the Great Hall and had every king present wincing.

'Reet in the *dongliz*,' whispered Grundin with a pained expression.

'Bugger me,' gasped Thagdor.

Most of the other kings crossed their legs.

Varnuf staggered. His eyes were watering and he tried to shuffle around to face Gotrek before collapsing. He half crouched, half slumped, held up by his bound beard.

Gotrek turned to Grundin, who was standing nearby with an axe.

'Cut it,' he said, and watched as Varnuf fell into a heap. 'Eh,' he added, giving the King of Eight Peaks a nudge so he looked up at him. 'My balls are solid rock. That's why I sit on that throne. That's why I am High King.'

Varnuf nodded meekly, and whispered, 'Tromm.'

Gotrek looked away.

'Brynnoth,' he said, singling out the lord of the Sea Hold. 'You'll have vengeance for Agrin Fireheart. I swear to Grimnir, he will be revenged, but not like this. We will find the truth of this first, if it was these druchii that the elgi prince spoke of.' Then he shifted his attention to the others, regarding each king in turn as he uttered a final edict. '*I* am High King. Gotrek Lunngrin of the Thunderhorn clan, Starbreaker and slayer of urk. My deeds eclipse all of yours combined as does my will and power. Do not defy it. Here in these lands, my word is law. Obey it or suffer my wrath. Defend your borders and sovereign territory. Close your gates and hold halls to the elgi. No trade will pass between us. All dealings with them will cease. An elgi upon our roads will be considered trespass and you may reckon that to the very hilt of our laws, but we do not march.' He shook his head slowly for emphasis. 'We do not go to war. It will ruin us. Ruin the dawi and the elgi for generations.' He let it sink in, let the silence amplify the resonance of his words before adding a final challenge.

'Will anyone else gainsay me?'

None did.

* * *

GOTREK WAS ALONE again as he went down into the grongaz. Amidst the smoke and ash, he discerned the glow of fire and heard the clamour of a single anvil. So he followed the sound. Passing through a solid wall of heat, he found Ranuld Silverthumb watching his apprentice.

'He works a master rhun,' said the ancient dwarf without looking up from his vigil.

'My son's az un klad?'

Ranuld supped on his pipe, took a deep pull. 'Aye,' he said, expelling a long plume of smoke. 'You have given your word on the elgi?' he asked after a moment or two of watching Morek's hammer fall. It was rhythmic, measured. It rang out a dulcet chorus resonant with power. The very air was charged with it. Gotrek's beard bristled, and the torcs and cinctures he had entwined in it grew warm to the touch.

'I have,' he said. 'Though it was not easy to do. My heart says fight, my head says not to. What would you do, old one?'

'I think I am not High King, therefore my opinion is moot.'

'But I value your counsel.'

'Of course you do, I am the oldest runesmith in the Karaz Ankor. My wisdom is worth more than your entire treasure vault, but it still matters not what I think. I see greed amongst our kin, an obsession towards gold gathering and hoarding. It was not always so. Once dwarfs crafted and were not so driven by the acquisition of wealth. What good is a hoard of gold to a dead king, eh?'

'Tromm, old one, but Agrin Fireheart was one of your guild. Would you not see him avenged?'

'Aye, one of the oldest, and his name shall be remembered. I mourn him but do not want revenge against all elgi for his death.' Now he met his king's gaze, showing the hard diamonds of his eyes. 'A great doom is coming, and it is this which I fear. Elgi may be a part of it, though I think it is but a small part. I foresee destinies forged in battle and a time of woes.'

Gotrek looked away, searching his heart and his conscience.

'I must do everything to prevent a war. It will destroy us both. The elgi are not as weak as some suppose them to be, though that is no reason not to fight them. They have been friends to the dawi. I will not cast that aside cheaply.'

'And we have precious few allies in the world when our enemies are amassed around us above and below. You are rare, Gotrek Starbreaker.'

Gotrek raised an eyebrow questioningly.

'We are changing, all of us, dawi and elgi both. You, like me, are hewn from elder rock. Less prone to change. I have seen another who is of similar stock. Stone and steel. He shall become king when you are dead, the slayer of the drakk.'

'I don't understand, old one.' Gotrek frowned. 'My son will be king when I am gone. It is his legacy.'

Ranuld said nothing further, and returned to his vigil.

'Will it be ready soon?' Gotrek asked, listening to the anvil, aghast at the lightning strikes cutting the air with every blow against it.

'He works the magic,' said Ranuld, gesturing proudly with his pipe. 'It will take time, but with patience anything is possible.'

'And should I show patience now?'

'That is something a king must answer for himself.'

⤛ CHAPTER TWENTY-FIVE ⤜

The King of Elves

OERAGOR WAS A fading memory, as was his urgent flight across the Great Ocean, through the veils and on to the verdant pastures of his home. His army had gone ahead, led by the dragons but ensconced in a great fleet of elven galleons. Alone, it had been a hard journey for the prince through a succession of unearthly storms. Something unnatural persisted about the blackened clouds and the roar of the wind. He had hoped to find his warriors again, catch up to them before they reached home but the storm was all consuming. Though it was difficult to tell for certain, shadows lurked within those clouds. Bestial faces, the visages of the daemonic and the monstrous, loomed over Imladrik during his flight. They mocked and cajoled, raged and encouraged. The elf prince shut his eyes and tried to close off the rest of his senses to them.

More than once, Imladrik had faltered until a growl from Draukhain steeled him against the voices. He chanted the names of Isha, Asuryan, Kurnous, invoking the blessings of the elven gods to ward him against the unnatural tempest that had set about them.

It grew angry, and Imladrik had been forced below the

clouds to keep from being struck by lightning or ripped out of the saddle by hurricane winds. He reached the veils surrounding the island with his nerves hanging by a thread. Never had he undertaken such a perilous journey, but after almost two weeks he had reached his ancestral lands alive and intact. And like a dream, the memory of the faces in the storm faded to nothing but a wisp of remembrance that Imladrik would only recall in his deepest nightmares.

Sorcerous mist, the ancient veils of Caledor Dragontamer that still protected his land, parted to reveal an island of verdant pastures, soaring mountains and crystalline rivers. Ports and fleets of ships resolved through the mist, together with sprawling forests and glittering towers. It shimmered, like an image half seen through a haze of heat, though the air was cool and refreshing. Imladrik breathed deep.

At last, he was home.

Ulthuan.

It had been years since he had last set foot upon the magical isle.

He had travelled south borne by Draukhain, across the harbours of Cothique where doughty merchantmen and sailors aboard catamarans pointed up at the sky at the passing of the dragon. From there Imladrik went east, skirting the Chracian mountains and letting Draukhain have his head amidst the cloud-wreathed peaks. Though he couldn't see them from so high up, he knew the vigilant woodsmen of that land would be abroad in the dense forests and narrow passes through the cliffs, ever watchful for invasion.

Imladrik's thoughts had strayed to Liandra and he had to banish them at once. His mind also wandered back to the carrier-hawk, soaring into the mountain fastness of the dwarfs, bringing his message to the High King. He hoped the words would hold some meaning, that a chance yet remained to avert a war. If it brought the dwarfs to the negotiating table then that at least would be something. Perhaps if they were willing to treat, he might be allowed to return to the Old World again and heal two rifts at once.

First he flew over the Phoenix Gate, the great bastion wall that sat on the borders of Chrace and Avelorn, its purpose to defend against invasion from the north across the hills of Nagarythe. It was a monolithic structure of pale stone and encrusted with jewels. The gilded image of the rising phoenix was emblazoned upon its vast and towering gate, a bulwark against attack. Silent guardians patrolled its battlements, grim-faced and clutching their halberds with fierce intent. Its neighbour, the Dragon Gate, was equally magnificent. Bordering Avelorn and Nagarythe, it was well garrisoned by spearmen and archers. The buttressed walls were scaled in keeping with its draconian aesthetic and the effigy of a soaring drake of Caledor was engraved upon the gate itself.

Even seen from high above, the gates were impressive. To Imladrik they looked nigh-on impregnable, which was just as well given the enemy they had been erected to repel. Many were the battles fought against the dark elves beyond their borders.

Once across the Phoenix and Dragon Gates, Imladrik was reunited with his army as he had set down on the plains of Ellyrion where his host were making ready for the next stage of their journey. He didn't stay, for he had business elsewhere, but instead took a steed from one of the horse-masters who had been there to receive him and rode the borders of Nagarythe and Avelorn until he reached his destination.During that time he was regaled with familiar sights, sounds and smells, a cavalcade of sensations that whispered 'home'. Except for Imladrik, this was no longer a place he understood.

This was no homecoming for the prince, it was more like a trial.

DARK ARBOURS DRENCHED in shadows gave way to thicker brush, thorny branched pines and an altogether denser arboreal gloom. These were wild lands, heavily forested, and beasts lurked in the mountains brooding overhead. A small war party moved through the thickening forest, fleet of foot and lightly armoured but wary.

A tall warrior dressed in tan and crimson led the modest group. Leather-clad, he carried a long bow and had a quiver half full of arrows strapped to his back. He was lithe, with almond-shaped eyes and a mane of golden hair tightly bound in a ponytail behind his neck.

Sighting prey, the warrior stopped and signalled silently to his companions to do the same. One was a burly-looking woodsman with thick furs draped over his back. He had drawn a hunting knife and a large double-bladed axe sat in a sheath between his shoulders, haft sticking up. The other laboured under a red hauberk, not as used to the forest as the other two. A short sword slapped against his thigh and three more quivers full of arrows were slung over his shoulder. Despite his shorn hair, which was night black, he was sheened with sweat.

'I see you...' whispered the leader, silently drawing an arrow and nocking it to his bow in a single seamless motion.

Scenting danger, the great stag realised it was being stalked. Raising its mighty antlered head, it snorted the air and the muscles bunched in its legs as it made to flee.

The swan-feathered shaft made almost no sound as it was released into the air. It sped swiftly in a white blur, dagger sharp and lightning fast. It pierced the great stag's heart, killing it instantly.

'Ha!' King Caledor looked pleased with his kill. A fine mist was coming off the beast, a fever sweat that was fading to nothing as the heat of its body expired.

'Flense it, woodsman,' he said to the fur-clad brute, who nodded. 'I want fur, flesh and meat. Spare nothing except for the head, which I shall take as a trophy.'

'See, Hulviar,' said Caledor to the other elf, gesturing to the woodsman who was quickly about his task. 'Chracians do have their uses.'

'Ever since your father's time, they have been the protectors of the king, my liege.'

'Yes, the White Lions,' Caledor sneered, 'but *he* is just some peasant.'

If the Chracian heard his noble lord, he was wise enough not to show it.

'How many is that today?' Caledor asked.

'Seven, my liege. You have denuded this part of the forest.'

Caledor's eyes narrowed and he smiled self-indulgently. 'Indeed, I have.'

The sound of branches snapping underfoot had the king raise his bow again, and Hulviar draw his sword.

'Who goes there?' demanded the retainer.

The woodsman had work to do, and continued with it. Besides, he had been aware of the intruder several minutes ago and knew it was no threat.

'Stand down, Hulviar. I am no great stag to be skewered by my brother's wayward arrow,' came a voice from the gloom.

Another warrior emerged into the clearing where the woodsman was butchering the dead stag.

'Khalnor,' said the warrior, who received a warm nod of greeting from the Chracian.

The king smiled so broadly that it filled his face, if not quite his eyes.

'Never forget a name, do you, little brother?' Handing the long bow to Hulviar, Caledor went over to the warrior and embraced him.

'A lesson you would benefit from learning,' he chastised mildly.

Caledor whispered, 'I can always call them peasant, can I not, Imladrik?'

There was amusement in the king's face that Imladrik hoped wasn't genuine.

'I have returned, brother.'

'For which you have my thanks.' Caledor let him go, favouring his brother with another half-smile, before walking from the clearing.

Imladrik followed. He was still clad in his dragon armour, though he'd removed the greaves and wore only the cuirass and vambraces.

'When I received your missive, I was under the impression that the skirmishes had escalated to something more serious and yet here you are… hunting.'

'It is good sport during this part of the season, brother, and as you can see…' Parting the thick bracken, Caledor stepped into another clearing where several more high elves pored over a map stretched across a white table. It sat beneath a tented pavilion where servants decanted wine and served silver platters of truffles. 'My advisors keep me well apprised.'

Imladrik joined them at once as Caledor slumped upon a plush couch to remove his boots and hunting apparel.

He nodded to the assembled lordlings, greeting them all by name. To a man, they responded in kind, showing Imladrik the same amount of deference as their King.

Though he thought he had kept it hidden, the prince noticed his brother's scowl at the way the other nobles and warriors treated him. Imladrik was beloved.

'He seeks inroads through the Caledorian Mountains and Ellyrion,' he observed, fathoming the situation instantly without need of assistance from any of his brother's advisors.

'Lord Athinol requires reinforcement,' said Caledor idly. 'More swords and spears to watch the passes. Every day more Naggarothi scum penetrate our watchtowers.'

'I am dismayed to hear that,' Imladrik said honestly, 'but unfortunately I bring further bad tidings.'

Caledor frowned, as if sensing his hunting trip was about to be curtailed.

'Relations with the dwarfs have soured.' Imladrik looked up from the map to regard his brother, who was sipping from a silver chalice.

'Hardly a surprise. What of it?'

It took all of Imladrik's composure to bite back his exasperation. 'Our colonies in the Old World are in danger. There have been murders, I believe by druchii, designed to foment ill will between our two races.'

Caledor sat up, but held on to his wine.

'Again, I cannot see how this is of import to Ulthuan. We have our own problems to deal with.'

'There are over eighty thousand elves in the dwarf realm, with more arriving every day. Trade has been completely suspended by their High King.'

'And still I do not see the imperative here,' said Caledor.

'Malekith has been beaten. Sorely. But he is not vanquished. Did you not hear what I said about our borders, brother?'

'I did hear it, but I am talking about the prospect of a full scale war on foreign soil.'

'With the mud-dwellers,' Caledor laughed, loudly and derisively. 'Let them return to their holes and tunnels. Our lands here in Ulthuan are threatened and I have need of generals to protect them.' He nodded to Imladrik. '*You*, dear brother.'

'I do not think this problem should be ignored.'

Caledor rose to his feet, shedding the leather armour for a close-fitting tunic of blue velvet. 'And so why did you return if matters are so dire?'

Though he found it hard to admit, Imladrik was jaded. He thought his years spent in the Old World, living amongst and trading with the dwarfs, had fostered a culture of understanding. That assumption had been dashed when the High King had refused his aid, expelled the elves from his lands and shut his gates.

'My presence there was not helping the situation.' It was a half-truth.

Caledor seemed not to notice or care.

'Let the colonies look after themselves. We have other vassals better suited to that task, do we not?

'There is Lord Salendor of Athel Maraya and Lady Athinol of Kor Vanaeth, amongst others. In them I pledge my trust and confidence, but they do not share my temperance.'

At this remark, Caledor smirked. 'And how is the Caledorian princess?'

'Well, but belligerent as ever.'

'Much like her father then,' Caledor added by way of an aside. 'Tell me, brother, have you seen your wife or have you yet to divest yourself of your army?'

'Yethanial awaits me in Cothique.'

Swilling the last of his wine around the chalice, Caledor tried to appear nonchalant. 'How many did you bring back with you, brother?'

'Ten thousand warriors and a head of fifty dragons,' Imladrik stated flatly.

'Quite a host. And Oeragor, it flourishes?'

'Less well without my presence, but yes.'

'A pity, but the needs of Ulthuan must come first.'

'Of course, brother.'

'What is it they call you again?' Caledor asked, feigning interest in his empty chalice. 'Ah yes, that was it… *Master of Dragons*. Such a curious little honorific and one I have never really understood.'

'It's ceremonial, and a tad archaic. I am the last Master of Dragons.'

Caledor sniffed, mildly amused. 'And they should be mastered, shouldn't they?'

'Our bond with the drakes is a harmonious one, forged of mutual respect.'

'Indeed,' Caledor replied, though he did not sound convinced. His disdain for dragons was well known, his opinion of their servitude to the elves a matter of some consternation amongst the older drakes. Fortunately, it was also one that had yet to be debated.

Imladrik got the sense that Caledor had discovered what he needed to and was rapidly losing interest in their conversation. This was confirmed when he changed subject.

'I want to show you something, Imladrik,' said Caledor, turning his attention to his retainers. 'Hulviar.'

The retainer nodded, evidently prepared for his king's theatrics as he tossed a scabbarded blade which Caledor caught and drew with ease.

'It's a sword, brother,' observed Imladrik, nonplussed.

Caledor showed him the edge, the runes upon the flat of the blade and how it shone in the dappled sunlight coming through the forest canopy overhead.

'Sapherian steel,' he said. 'As light as goose down but deadlier than a Chracian's axe blade. I had it made.'

Caledor turned the weapon in a series of intricate moves, rolling it over in half-swings and switching from hand to hand in a dazzling, but vainglorious display of swordsmanship.

'Impressive,' said Imladrik without much enthusiasm. 'You dropped your scabbard,' he added, stooping to pick up the scabbard from where Caledor had carelessly discarded it.

The king took it and sheathed the sword, obviously upset with his brother's apathy.

'You have had a long journey,' he said, 'and must be tired, which explains your mood, Imladrik. Return to Cothique, see your wife and then come to Lothern and my court. We have much to discuss.' He was already turning his back when he added, 'You have six days.'

Imladrik bowed, albeit curtly and lacking in deference. His brother the king had measured the threat he posed to his rule and had positioned him here to neutralise it. Imladrik cared not for the trappings of rulership. He didn't lust for power or standing and so was happy to oblige.

Mounting his horse at the edge of the deeper forest, his thoughts were troubled nonetheless, but not by that. The maps and charts strewn upon the war table showed the dark elves had made extensive inroads into Ulthuan. Attacks were obviously increasing and together with that, he suspected, was dark elf involvement in the Old World. Imladrik wondered just how spent a force Malekith really was.

A war with the dwarfs would decimate the high elves, take them to the brink of destruction. After that, it wouldn't take much to push them over the edge and into oblivion.

⤙ CHAPTER TWENTY-SIX ⤚

The Gathering Throng

A VAST FORCE of dwarf warriors had gathered on the shores of the Black Water.

Early morning brought with it a dense fog that rolled off the mirror-dark sheen of the lake-filled crater in a grey pall. Cloth banners, topped by icons of bronze and copper, fluttered in the wind. The standards of the brotherhoods were metal only, forged from gold and silver, and sat apart from the clans. The debris of over two hundred extinguished campfires littered the high-sided gorge where the dwarfs had sung songs, supped ale and eaten roast beef and pork, elk and goat the night before. What began as bawdy drinking ditties, the lyrical mottos of the clans and the sombre litanies of the brotherhoods, became a rousing war chant that disturbed crag eagles from their eyries and sent greenskins for miles around scampering in fear of death.

Khazuk! was the cry that pealed across the Black Water, in the shadow of Zhufbar where fifteen thousand warriors had assembled. Several hours later with the sun just reaching up over the peaks, the echo of their belligerence had still to fade.

War was coming to the elves, and the dwarfs would bring it to them.

They merely awaited the order of their general to march.

Snorri paced the edge of the lake, fancying he could discern the shadow of bestial creatures moving languidly in its fathomless depths. He was arrayed in his full war panoply, a winged helm fastened to his belt by its chinstrap, and chuntered loudly.

Most of the other dwarfs couldn't hear him. They were too busy making preparations themselves, sharpening axes, tightening the bindings on hammers, fastening armour plates and tying off vambraces. Colours were unfurled, icons presented to the sky, horns and drums beat in a warm-up staccato. The clan warriors jostled and joked; but the brotherhoods, the longbeards and ironbreakers, the hearthguard and runesmiths, wore grim faces, for they all knew what they were about to undertake.

So did Snorri, and it was this thought as well as respect for his father that warred within him.

'They gave us no choice,' said a voice from behind him.

Snorri started. He had thought he was alone.

'Drogor...' he said, as if just speaking the dwarf's name made him weary.

'But,' said Drogor, coming closer, 'if you were to halt the march, no one would brand you a coward. You were merely fulfilling the wishes of your father and High King.'

'I am not my father's vassal lord, for him to command,' Snorri snapped. 'I have a destiny too.'

'A great one,' Drogor conceded, bowing his head in a gesture of contrition. 'I meant no offence, my prince, only that you should not feel forced into action.'

'We will march, by Grimnir,' Snorri scowled. 'This has gone on long enough. If my father lacks the courage to do something then I, as heir of Karaz-a-Karak, will.'

'Justly spoken, my prince.'

Snorri frowned. 'Drogor, please. To you I am Snorri, not "my prince".'

Drogor bowed again as if at court. 'As you wish, Snorri.' He smiled. 'Shall I see to the preparations of the warriors?'

Snorri nodded. 'Yes, do it. Begin the muster and send runners to Thagdor and Brynnoth, even Luftvarr. I want to speak with all three before we leave Black Water.'

'As you wish.'

Drogor departed just as another dwarf was coming into view, emerging through the lake fog which was thick as pitch.

Morgrim gestured to Snorri's winged war helm. 'Didn't think you needed one.'

'I like the wings. Makes me look important,' Snorri replied, grinning. 'Or perhaps my head has grown soft, cousin.'

'Perhaps it has,' said Morgrim, glaring after the Karak Zorn dwarf. He seemed to blend with the mist, becoming spectral until he was lost from sight completely. 'I hope he is not giving you more bad counsel.'

'He is a dutiful thane and valuable advisor,' Snorri replied with a little bite to his tone.

'*Thane* is it now?'

It had been several weeks since the High King's pronouncement that all trade would be suspended with elves. Armies were mustering too, and the weapon shops of all the holds toiled day and night churning out armour and war engines for what Gotrek hoped would be a stockpile of materiel he would never need to call upon. Short of declaring outright war, it was as far as the High King could go to assert his authority as well as present a clear warning to the elves. His edict had been welcome news, but for many did not go nearly far enough. Snorri counted himself amongst that number and in Drogor found an ally more willing to listen to his concerns than his peace-favouring cousin. Nonetheless, he had wanted Morgrim by his side in this and so here they were, together, if at odds with one another.

'Aye, thane. He has no hold, no clan. I will make him a clan lord of Karaz-a-Karak in recognition for his deeds and loyalty. It is only honourable and right.'

'Then why do you look so troubled, cousin?'

'Because I am about to go to war against the wishes of the High King and am painfully lacking in warriors.'

'You have over fifteen thousand axes, if the loremaster's tallying is accurate.'

'Aye, but none from Eight Peaks and no word from King Varnuf.'

'He was at the council of kings with your father.'

'And, no doubt, my father has convinced him it was not in his best interests to support me. Musters take time, all dawi know that, but three weeks is enough to send a missive or a war party.'

'Perhaps he saw sense as you should do.'

Snorri roared, 'What, to sit on my arse as elgi kill kith and kin with impunity?' Some of the dwarfs nearby looked up as the shout resonated around the gorge, and the prince lowered his voice. 'I can be idle no longer. I said if my father did not declare war then I would. Once it's begun, he will see I was right and have no choice but to call the clans to battle. I know it.'

'I hope you are right.'

'If you do not believe in this then why are you here, Morg?'

Morgrim was already turning his back, disgusted by what he saw as warmongering for its own sake. Snorri wanted to prove his worth and the only way he could see of doing that was to wilfully go against his father and pick a fight with the elves.

Snorri called after his cousin. 'Well? If you don't want a fight then why come here bearing az un klad, eh? Why are you here, Morg?'

'To stop you from getting yourself killed, you ufdi.'

He walked away and Snorri, though he wanted to apologise, to take back his words, could only watch.

With one last look at the stygian depths of the Black Water and the endless darkness within, he went to meet the kings. Heart-sore and weary beyond fatigue, his armour had never felt so heavy.

He did not want to defy his father but what choice did he have? Destiny, his destiny, was in the balance. Snorri *would* be king and this would cement his legacy. Gotrek had purged the greenskins, he would kill the elves.

* * *

TWO KINGS WITH their ceremonial hearthguard awaited Snorri beyond the mist-shrouded shores of Black Water. Brynnoth of Barak Varr was bedecked in scaled armour of sea green. A teal leather cloak, emblazoned with images of mermen and other sea beasts, was cinched to his shoulders by a pair of kraken-headed pauldrons. His war helm bore a nose guard studded with emeralds and carried an effigy of a sea dragon as its crest. Snug in its belt loop was a broad-bladed axe with a toothed edge like the fangs of some leviathan.

Thagdor's armour was less ostentatious. He favoured a simple bronze breastplate over gilded chainmail. His vambraces were leather and sewn with the images of hammers. An open helmet with a slide-down faceplate sat on the table beside him and his hammer was strapped to his back, the haft jutting out from behind a cloak of purple velvet.

From where he'd been stooping over the table, Brynnoth looked up. He scratched the hollow under his eyepatch as Snorri approached.

'My prince,' he said, sketching a short bow.

Thagdor did the same, but was less deferential to the young heir of Karaz-a-Karak.

'So when are we getting bloody going then?' he asked. 'My boots are rough as a troll's arse I've been standing around that chuffing long.' Thagdor thumbed over his shoulder to where a large cohort of dwarfs was gathering. 'I've got nigh on seven thousand beards mustered behind me, lad, and they want a bloody good scrap.'

The sun had risen higher in the last few minutes and was slowly burning away the morning mist, revealing the full glory of the dwarf throng.

Thagdor had brought the bulk of the army and a great many siege engines, but then they were practically on the doorstep of Zhufbar. It was mainly clan dwarfs and miners, but with a strong cohort of hearthguard. Sailed up from the Sea Hold across the Skull River were another five thousand dwarfs of King Brynnoth's throng, many of which were longbeards roused to battle by the tragic death of Agrin Fireheart. The rest came from Luftvarr, two thousand Norse dwarfs who just wanted a decent fight, and the clans that were loyal to Snorri in Everpeak. Others had pledged their allegiance to his cause too. Hrekki Ironhandson of Karak Varn and dwarf throngs from Karak Hirn were to meet them at the edge of Black Fire Pass.

The route was inked out on the parchment map lying on the table. South across the fringe of the mountains, along the hills and rocky tors until reaching the mouth of the pass. From there, with some twenty thousand dwarfs in tow, north-west to the first elven city of Kor Vanaeth. Only by attacking a settlement of some significance would the dwarfs make clear the elves were no longer welcome in the Old World. Snorri meant to sack Kor Vanaeth, to raze it to the ground utterly. It was a long march, one that would take several weeks with mules and trappings, but the prince was patient. He had waited this long for his father to act and been content to watch as the High King did nothing. Now, he would show his mettle and seize the destiny that had been foretold to him by Ranuld Silverthumb.

'We are ready,' he said huskily. It was no small thing to defy his father, but Snorri kept telling himself the dishonour of it was outweighed by the indignity of standing by and letting elves kill dwarfs without retribution.

Brynnoth gripped the young prince's hand. There were tears in the dwarf king's eye. Salt stained his beard and a briny odour emanated off his clothes.

'Thank you, lad,' he whispered. There was fire in Brynnoth's gaze too, fuelling his desire for vengeance at Agrin's death.

Nodding, Snorri slipped free of the sea king's hand and signalled the call to march.

Drums and horns echoed around the gorge, followed by the raucous clanking of armoured dwarfs moving into position.

To the outsider dwarfs might appear stunted and slow, but when properly motivated they are quick and direct. Such a fact had often caused their enemies to underestimate them, and believe them cumbersome creatures when the opposite was true.

'Luftvarr of Kraka Drak,' Snorri called, seeing the Norse dwarf king who looked up at the prince from brawling with his warriors. 'Do you stand with me?'

Brandishing his axe into the sky, Luftvarr roared and his huscarls roared with him, a belligerent chorus that shook the earth from the surrounding mountains.

'Khazuk!' they cried as one, before the king silenced them to speak. 'Luftvarr think this will be a mighty runk… Ha, ha!' His warriors laughed with him and kept going until they were ranked up in the order of march.

'I hope you know what you're doing trusting to those savages,' muttered Brynnoth.

'I can heel them easily enough,' said Snorri, eyeing the berserkers with a wary look. 'Luftvarr just wants to kill elgi, we can all empathise with that.' He tromped off to join the Everpeak dwarfs at the head of the army. Who he saw there when he reached them was unexpected.

Standing by Morgrim's side, dressed in a travelling cloak and wearing a light suit of mail, was Elmendrin Grimbok.

'Come to wish us on our way, priestess?' Snorri uttered coldly, and tried to deny the heavy beating of his heart at the sight of the dwarf maiden. 'War is no place for rinns,' he said, 'despite the warriors you have brought with you.' A small band of ironbreakers, clad in gromril with their faceplates down, stood back from the maiden, together with two more priestesses from the temple. Snorri glared at Morgrim before she could answer. 'I assume you are responsible for this?'

Elmendrin stepped in front of him.

'He merely told me where you would be mustering. I chose to come here of my own accord. The warriors are for the protection of my sisters who insisted on accompanying me.'

'What would your brother say, I wonder?' Though he tried, Snorri could not help it sounding petulant.

'Since he is with your father, trying to find a way to maintain peace with the elgi, I would not know.' She paused, searching for some mote of conscience in the prince's eyes. 'I would speak with you, Snorri Lunngrin.'

'It's Halfhand.' He brandished the gauntlet. 'And I am here,' said the prince, 'so speak. Though be quick, I have an army to lead.'

'So I can see.' She scowled disdainfully, then gestured to where one of the encampment tents had yet to be taken down. 'I would prefer to talk alone.'

Snorri smirked. 'Finally want to get me alone do y–'

'Stop it!' Elmendrin snapped, and there was venom in her eyes that told Snorri his remark had been an unworthy one. 'You are acting like a wanaz.'

He capitulated at once. 'Tromm, I'm sorry. We can talk, but I cannot linger.'

'That's all I ask,' she said, and headed for the tent.

Snorri turned to his cousin. 'Morg…'

'I'll keep them here until you return,' he said, gripping Snorri's shoulder before he left. 'Listen to her. Please.'

Snorri nodded. He caught Drogor's gaze as he went after Elmendrin – he was standing with the Everpeak dwarfs and had an intensity about him that disquieted the prince. Shrugging off a profound sense of urging to expel the priestess, he followed her into the tent.

She had her back to him as he entered the narrow angular chamber. It was gloomy inside and the canvas reeked of sweat and stale beer. Snorri found it embarrassing that she should have to endure this, and felt suddenly crude and ungainly in his armour.

'I would offer you something, but the victuallers have packed it all up. Not even a crumb of stonebread remains.'

'We've recently eaten. It's fine.' She was wringing her hands, clearly nervous.

Snorri wanted to go to her, but knew it was not his place.

'It has been a while since I last saw you,' he ventured awkwardly.

'You had lost some fingers to a rat, if I remember.'

Snorri looked to his gauntlet, tucking it behind his back as Elmendrin turned around to face him.

'It was a *big* rat,' he said, frowning.

She smiled, but all too briefly and all too sadly for it to warm the prince.

'I thought… I mean, I saw you at the brodunk, did I not?' he asked.

'Yes, you did. I was in the healing tent, tending to the wounded. You seemed to be on better terms with your father then.'

Snorri's face darkened and he half turned away. 'My father doesn't know me. He sees only a petulant son, who must be kept in his place.'

'He sees what you show him,' said Elmendrin.

The scathing glance Snorri was about to give her faded when he realised she wasn't remonstrating with him.

'He loves you, Snorri,' she told him.

Snorri sagged, and his pauldrons clanked dully against his breastplate.

'And I him.'

'Then don't be so pig-headed, you stubborn, obstinate fool. Look beyond your own selfishness and see what this will mean. If you make war on the elgi, you will invite devastation on us all and estrange your father into the bargain. Is that what you want? Is that why you are here?'

'It's my destiny.'

'To kill wantonly to satisfy your need to be honoured by your father? Do you think he will clap you on the back and tell you how proud he is of you for defying his will? He will not respect you for this. He will despise you for it. So will I,' she whispered.

Snorri had no answer. In his heart, he thought what he was doing was right. Some small part of him knew it was to serve selfish needs, but he assuaged that guilt with the certain conviction that he was acting on behalf of the greater good. Confronted by the hard truths from Elmendrin, he wasn't so sure.

'Hearth and hold, oath and honour,' she asked. 'Whatever happened to that?'

'Wrath and ruin, that is what we must do in times of war.'

'We aren't at war. Not yet.'

'Not yet, indeed.' Snorri started pacing, exasperated but also conflicted. Elmendrin had a way of clearing his thoughts, easing away the fug of doubt and guilt that fostered his belligerence. 'What would you have me do?' he asked, pointing to the entrance of the tent. 'Out there, fifteen thousand dawi await my command. At Black Fire Pass another five thousand will join us. It is too far gone to turn back now. I cannot.'

'You are the prince of Karaz-a-Karak, what can *you* not do?' She came over to him, touched her fingers to his arm, and drew the gauntleted hand out of hiding from behind Snorri's back. 'Losing a few fingers is one thing, but the consequences of a reckless decision here are far worse. Stay your armies. Show what kind of a king you will be, one who calls for calm when all others are losing their heads, one who is not afraid to take the hard path if it is the best of all roads, a king who puts his people before himself.'

Though Elmendrin was proud, by far the proudest dwarf woman he had ever known, Snorri saw the tears in her eyes and knew she was pleading with him. He willed her not to get onto her knees. He didn't want that.

In the end he sighed. 'Brynnoth will not be pleased, nor Luftvarr.'

Morgrim was waiting at the entrance to the tent. Evidently, the army was waiting but could do so no more. He had overhead the last part.

'I'll tell them both,' he said.

'No, Morg, it should fall to me.'

Snorri was on his way out when he turned back to Elmendrin.

'Though I sheathe my axe today, war *is* coming. My father knows it too, though he would deny it to all but his own heart. Peace cannot endure, but I won't break it. Not yet.'

Then he left and so did Morgrim, who gave a nod to the priestess, left alone in the gloom.

'Thank you, cousin,' said Morgrim, walking by Snorri's side as he went to address the throng. 'For heeding her, I mean.'

'It will do no good,' said the prince. 'None of this will. I meant what I said, war will come. Dawi and elgi are too different, it's only a matter of time before we start killing each other for real.'

'Then why disband the army if that's what you believe?'

'Because she asked me to, and I'm not disbanding us.'

'What then?'

'There is a fortress at Black Fire Pass, large enough to hold a force this size. I plan to garrison it and set up pickets along the mountains.'

Morgrim stopped him. 'You're waiting, aren't you?'

'Isn't that what we dawi do best?'

'Do you really think there can be no peace between our races?'

Snorri favoured his cousin with a stern glance. 'None.'

'And what of the kings? They have holds and will not wait for war to begin.'

'None will march without me. Even Luftvarr is not so bold as to go against my father without the presence of his son. Thagdor will return to Zhufbar, and Brynnoth to Barak Varr. But both will leave warriors in my charge. The Norse will probably go back to Kraka Drak, but I'd prefer to be without the savages anyway. The rest will remain here for as long as it takes, a bulwark against further elgi aggression.'

'So this is a shield wall now, is it? One to keep the elgi out.'

'We'll lock our shields for now, but we will become a hammer when needed and mark me, cousin, it *will* be needed. The only difference now is that when I do eventually march it will be at the head of a much larger throng. Word will be sent to the lesser mountains and when my father sees how many have come to my banner, he will have no choice but to throw in with me.'

They had reached the army, fifteen thousand dwarfs waiting silently for their prince to lead them. Even the Norse were quiet but the scowl on King Luftvarr's face suggested he suspected all was not as it had been before the prince had entered the tent.

An OATH STONE was embedded in the earth in front of the throng, set there by Snorri's hearthguard. These warriors were as dour as any of Thurbad's praetorians but they believed that war was the only answer to the elves and had thrown in with the young prince. Snorri nodded grimly to them as they parted their armoured ranks for him. Just before he climbed the oath stone, he saw Elmendrin's silent departure back towards Everpeak. He watched her for a few moments but she didn't look back, not once. In her absence he felt his anger returning, and found he was drawn to Drogor who waited in the front rank of the Everpeak dwarfs.

'While our axes remain clean, there is still hope for peace,' said Morgrim, wrestling Snorri from the other dwarf's gaze.

Snorri looked down on him before he addressed the army, clutching in his gauntleted fist a large speaking horn handed to him by one of the hearthguard.

'Peace died in that gorge, cousin. It died when Agrin Fireheart was murdered. A wall of shields has risen up in answer. With you by my side or not, Morg, I shall kill the elgi and drive them from the Old World. Whether now or in ten years, war is coming. And I will be ready for when it does.'

ACT THREE

An Inevitable War

~◄ CHAPTER TWENTY-SEVEN ►~

Gold and Grudges

THERE WAS A glint in the eye of the hill dwarf king that only came upon him when he was in his counting house surrounded by his most precious possessions. Of late, they had diminished and it was for this that he scolded his goldmasters.

'Every year for the last eight my hoard has lessened.' Grum cast around, gesturing to the piles of treasure, the ingots, doubloons, crowns, pieces, gemstones, bracelets, torcs, mitres and chains that festooned his counting house. Sets of scales were abundant, all carefully balanced and their amounts meticulously logged in stacks of leather-bound volumes that lined the bookcases on the walls. They were hard to see, not just because vast mounds of accumulated treasure obscured them but because of the sheen that was emanating from all the gold. It hurt the eyes to look upon it, though Grum's were bird-like and narrow as if the mammonistic king was well used to the sight and had evolved to compensate for it.

Uncharacteristically, his eyes were wide at that moment as he thrashed in a fit of conniption.

'It should accrue, not diminish!' He thumped the arm of

his throne with a gnarled, bony fist. 'Explain yourselves! Why aren't you bringing more treasure to my coffers? Why aren't I getting any richer? Eh?'

There was a fever in the king's expression and the chief of his goldmasters balked before it as he made his excuses.

'Since the High King of Karaz-a-Karak suspended all trade with the elgi–' He didn't even get chance to finish his sentence before Grum interrupted with another bout of apoplexy.

'*I* am High King of this city, of the skarrens. I care not for the whims of Gotrek bloody Lunngrin. He is not my lord and master. Let him be concerned with the mountain. If he has taken umbrage with the elgi then that is his business. Our gates remain open to their gold and business.'

In his anger, Grum knocked over a pile of coins with his kicking leg and scattered them across the floor. His gaze followed them for several moments, drawn to the tinkling, glittering pieces inexorably. A little patch of white froth bubbled at the corner of his lip.

'Well then?' he raged, as if coming out of a trance and remembering where he was and the matter at hand.

'Our gates have remained open, High King,' said another of the goldmasters, an enthusiastic understudy wanting to curry favour, 'and we continue to extend invitation to elgi traders to treat with us but they do not wish to trespass onto dawi lands for fear of persecution. The Hi–, er... *King* of Karaz-a-Karak has petitioned greater and greater numbers of rangers and reckoners to patrol dawi borders. Travel is almost impossible.'

'Enough!' snapped Grum, staggering to his feet to dismiss the ineffectual goldmasters. 'Get out, all of you! Especially you,' he added, jabbing his finger at the one who had seemingly lost his tongue. 'Bloody mute! Out!'

Bowing profusely, the three goldmasters backed away and out of the counting house.

'Idiots,' hissed Grum before they were gone, stacking coins as the old familiar veneer slid across his face. Eyes beginning to glaze over, a dumb smile pulling at the corners of his mouth, he almost didn't hear Rundin speaking.

'...are right, my king,' he was saying.

'Uh? What?' Grum asked, slightly dazed. When his gaze fell on his champion and protector, he became more lucid. 'Who are right?'

Rundin was standing by his master's side, arms folded, his expression neutral at all times.

'Your goldmasters, my king. All of the major roads are closed to trade, especially to elgi. What little gold is coming in to Kazad Kro is from the Vaults and the Grey Mountains, but that is not enough to sustain previous yields.'

Grum slapped a page of his ledger, leaving a greasy palm print on the parchment. Scrawled Klinkerhun daubed every leaf in a feverish script.

'I can see that, Rundin. The numbers never lie.' He carried on counting, mumbling, 'Gotrek is a selfish wazzock.'

'My king…' Rundin ventured after a minute of listening to his liege-lord lay one coin atop another.

'There is more?' asked Grum, agitated, licking his bottom lip as he slowly created a gleaming tower of stacked coins.

Rundin nodded. 'Cessation of trade with the elgi these past eight years is because of a much larger problem.'

'I fail to see any larger problem than that which my gold-masters have already presented.' Once again, he returned to his counting.

'War, my king. There is talk of war with the elves.'

Grum's face screwed up like an oily rag. 'Over what, some petty trade disputes? Bah! Gotrek must have been supping from the dragon.'

'No, my king.' Throughout the exchange Rundin's tone had never wavered from stolid and serious, but now he showed his incredulity at just how little his liege-lord seemed to be aware of the greater world. 'Murder and death, sabotage and destruction. The burning of Zakbar Varf was just the beginning. Kazad Mingol bore witness to a skirmish between a band of its rangers and elgi warriors. No fewer than sixteen shipments from Kagaz Thar have gone missing in the last three months alone. Grudges longer than the gilded road running through our city litter our *dammaz kron* and continue to accumulate. And that is not to mention the grievances of our mountain kin.'

'No,' Grum uttered flatly.

'No?'

'I will not have war. It is bad for business.' He gestured to the massive hoard of treasure in his counting house. 'See how it already hurts my coffers? I won't countenance it. War is expensive. It means shields and armour, and axes, provisions. If the elgi are as belligerent as you say then we will shut our gates to all and wait out Gotrek's little feud.'

'I fear it has gone beyond that, my king. We may have no–'

Grum slammed his fist down on the arm of his throne and glared at his champion.

'Are you determined to defy me, Rundin?'

'I would never do that, my king, but if Gotrek Starbreaker declares war upon the elgi then we must, as dawi, answer.'

'Must… *must!* I am High King and shall not bow to him. I do not recognise his authority. Let mountain dawi deal with mountain dawi problems, why should I be dragged into it, why should our people be dragged into it?' Grum's eyes narrowed as he found the leverage he needed to mollify his champion. '*Your* people, Rundin. You wouldn't want to see them ravaged by a war that is not theirs to begin with, would you?'

Rundin bowed his head, knowing he had lost.

'Of course not, my king.'

'You are loyal to me, are you not?' asked Grum, leaning forwards as if to scrutinise the champion's veracity.

'I am, my king.'

'And swore oaths to defend me and protect my rule, yes?'

'I did.' Rundin knew it, he knew it all, but could not bring his eyes up from his boots.

Leaning back, Grum returned to his counting.

'Find me more gold, Rundin. You're good at that. Seek it out in the rivers and hills, bring the elgi back to our table to make trade.'

'As you wish, my king.'

Thumping his chest, Rundin took his leave.

* * *

HE MET FURGIL on the outskirts of Kazad Kro, below the city's rocky promontory. It was a wasteland outside. Gone were the encampments, the bustling market town of trade that had grown up around it. A few disparate, determined traders from the Grey Mountains and Vaults had set up their stalls and wagons but would stay only briefly. Threat of imminent war had chased all others away. Either that or it was the constant patrols of heavily armed rangers that had dissuaded them.

The chief scout of Everpeak looked more grizzled than most. He was not alone and led a large band of rangers. Some had injuries and one of the dwarfs carried two crossbows.

'A skirmish,' Furgil explained, when he saw Rundin regarding the state of his warriors. 'Lost Bori and took some cuts.'

'Elgi?'

Furgil nodded.

'Seems your king has extended invitation to trade still, but hadn't reckoned on the fact that his liege-lord has rangers patrolling the roads and overground routes.'

'He will not fight,' said Rundin, 'if it comes to war.'

'Been eight years, brother, and the killing keeps on rising. We haven't returned to Karaz-a-Karak for months. War will come, Rundin. Too much bad blood running in the river now. We stand on a precipice.'

'Aye, brother. But the skarrenawi will not march.'

'What of Kazad Thar and Mingol?'

'Them neither. King Grum rules both with iron.'

Furgil spat onto the ground. 'Grum rules nothing except that treasure chamber he sits in all day. *You* are the one the skarrens respect, not him.'

'What are you saying, brother?' asked Rundin, a dangerous look in his eye.

'Ah, calm yourself. You know what I'm saying.' Furgil turned on his heel and the other rangers went with him. 'If Grum sits on his arse, Gotrek will be coming for his head when he's done with the elgi,' he called.

Rundin had no reply to that. He let Furgil go, hoping it wouldn't be the last time he saw his friend.

A canker wormed at the heart of Kazad Kro and all the skarrens, it stank to the sky and though he didn't want to admit it, Rundin knew he would have to be the one to cut it out.

GOTREK STARBREAKER HAD never felt so powerless.

For eight years he had cooled the ire of his vassal kings, for eight years he had shackled them to peace. And for eight long, arduous years his efforts had come to naught.

He was drowning, in more ways than one. The sheer amount of parchments, scrolls and stone tablets was staggering. Gotrek's private chambers were full of them. His desk groaned under their weight despite its broad wooden legs. Hunched and grim-faced, he looked almost gargoylesque as he peered over the piles of missives and declarations of grudgement laid out in front of him. The tankard he had supped from was long empty, his pipe cold with its embers long dead. From across the Karaz Ankor, kings, thanes and lodewardens expressed their continued dissatisfaction at what they described as elven 'dissension' and 'belligerence'. Attending to them was not to be a brief task, even for a dwarf.

Trains of reckoners were dispatched daily from Everpeak alone, seeking recompense for misdeeds, and rangers thickened the byways and roads of the hills and lower slopes of the Worlds Edge Mountains until nothing could get through without their prior knowledge.

And still disorder persisted.

Dwarfs and elves were not meant to live together, it seemed.

Some of the disparate clans, those from Mount Gunbad and Silverspear, took the lawlessness as sanction to attack elven settlements, gold-greedy miners looking to fatten their hoards with stolen treasure. Warriors from the distant holds of Karak Izor and Karak Norn had clashed directly with elven war parties in minor skirmishes. Such incidents were few and far between, but as the last decade had ground on the frequency of such skirmishes had worryingly increased.

Gotrek condemned it, sought recompense from the elves, but thus far his messages had remained unheeded. In turn he urged the clans to close their gates and stay within their holds, and forbade any dwarf of Everpeak from violent action.

In the deeps, the forges slaved night and day to fashion weapons, armour and machineries. Thus far, it was stockpiled in the voluminous Everpeak armouries but Gotrek knew the day was approaching when it would have to be broken open and used to furnish his armies.

It had been a desperate hope that forcing distance between the dwarfs and elves would see matters improve or at least not worsen between the two races.

That hope had been dashed on bloody rocks and it was to falter further still.

'And here,' he said wearily, a rasp in his throat from the many hours of reading aloud to his Grudgekeeper who was on hand with the hold's book of grudges. 'At Krag Bryn and Kazad Thrund did elgi come from across the sea and slay the great King Drong the Hard, leaving his queen Helgar without a husband. Let it be known on this day...' Gotrek trailed off, taking a moment's respite to rub his brow.

Seeing his chance, the Grudgekeeper massaged his aching shoulder and flexed his fingers.

For days they hadn't left the chamber. It was the latest stint in what had become a regular accounting of the misdeeds of elves over the last few years. The grudge from Krag Bryn was almost three years old and Gotrek was only just getting to it now. He balked at what else he would find.

'How many more are there?' he asked the statue at the door of the room.

'Three more vaults, my king,' uttered Thurbad in a sonorous voice. 'And there are reckoners gathering in the entrance hall.'

'How many of them?'

The captain of the hearthguard didn't betray a tremor of emotion. 'Almost two hundred.'

Gotrek rubbed his eyes with fingers black from ink. Try as he might, he could not smooth out the worry lines across his forehead. He picked up another missive, waving away the Grudgekeeper who was still waiting for the High King's edict concerning Krag Bryn.

'Bagrik is dead,' he muttered, it not seeming so long ago that the King of Karak Ungor had enjoyed the hospitality of his hold. 'Slain by elgi, his queen now a widow too. Two kings of dawi dead, and a host of elgi lordlings too no doubt.' He seized a fistful of parchments, scattering and displacing others much to the Grudgekeeper's obvious but quiet dismay. 'Grievances the length and breadth of the Worlds Edge...' Gotrek sighed deeply, worn out and tired of peace. 'Is it any wonder my son has left the karak, and garrisons the keep at Black Fire Pass?'

'There is still no word from him, my king,' offered Thurbad, 'but my hearthguard report he has yet not left the fastness. Should I tell them to stop him if he does?'

Two hundred of Thurbad's warriors had left with the prince, ostensibly in support of Snorri's war. In truth, the High King had sent them to keep a watchful eye on his son. The wayward clans of Everpeak, he would deal with later. Their thanes would be punished for their transgression. Such things had waited for eight years, they would stand to wait a little longer.

'I am sorely tempted to join him, Thurbad.' Gotrek paused, as if considering just that, then shook his head. 'I'd rather he had hearthguard protecting him as not. I doubt they could stop him anyway. How many dawi does he have allied to his banner?'

'Almost thirty thousand warriors.'

'Dreng tromm... and he holds?'

'For now, my king. He does.'

Gotrek muttered, 'Perhaps he's learned some temperance after all.' He sighed again, trying to exhale his many worries. 'We stand upon the brink of war,' he croaked in a tired voice that suggested decades, not years, had passed since he ceased trade with the elves.

The two other dwarfs in the room did not answer. What could they say that wasn't a facile reminder that their High King was right?

Gotrek rose to his feet.

'High King?' asked the Grudgekeeper, uncertainly.

'I am done with grudgement for today, Haglarrson. Seal the *kron* and have these grudges gathered up for my later reckoning.'

Haglarrson the Grudgekeeper nodded mutely, still unsure what was happening.

Gotrek directed his attention to Thurbad. 'Dismiss the reckoners. All of them.' He was leaving, and the captain of the hearthguard followed him in perfect lockstep.

They were into the Great Hall, its large and empty vaults echoing with the footfalls.

Gotrek snarled, 'This is blatant transgression by the elgi. They flout any chance at peace with their arrogance! Dawi lie dead and cold in my lands, Thurbad. Tell me how should I make answer to that without dooming us all?'

'I cannot, my king. All I can do is serve the karak.'

Gotrek stopped. He gripped Thurbad's shoulder.

'And a more brave and noble servant I could not wish for, Thurbad.'

'Tromm, my king…' he said, bowing. 'Is there anything further?'

Gotrek nodded. 'Yes, bring me my Loremaster and that reckoner, Forek Grimbok. I have need of his silvern tongue.'

'Should I tell him what it is concerning?' Thurbad asked.

'Tell him I need him to go to the King of the Elves on Ulthuan,' said Gotrek. 'Tell him I need him to prevent a war.'

FOREK GRIMBOK'S HEART pounded like a boar-skin drum. He knelt before the Throne of Power, head bowed, his left arm tucked against his chest.

'Tromm, High King…' he uttered to a largely barren room.

'Look at me, reckoner.'

Forek tilted his head up to meet the gaze of the High King. His mind was reeling already with the task before him. Pride swelled his heart and he tried to master it for fear it would overwhelm him.

'You are my most gifted ambassador. If anyone can

wrench a peace from this mess, then it is you. But make no mistake, Grimbok, I want an apology from the elgi for their transgressions, nothing less.' He waved the robed dwarf on his left forwards. 'My Loremaster has a missive you must present to the King of the Elgi. It is unsealed. Read it, digest its meaning and know my mind before applying the wax. Put it in the elgi king's hands and his alone. Do you understand?'

'I do…' Forek croaked, cleared his throat then tried again. 'I do, my king.'

'Good. It will be up to you to impress upon him that misdeeds have been done unto us by the elgi, but that I am not without forgiveness and such misdeeds can be undone in the eyes of the Karaz Ankor.'

'Yes, my king.' Forek took the letter and secreted it inside his tunic.

'Now rise and let Thurbad tell you of your journey ahead.'

The High King gestured to the captain of the hearthguard, a mass of armoured muscle who was standing by his right.

'Twenty of my best warriors will accompany you,' said Thurbad.

Behind Forek, the hearthguard bristled with strength and threat. Only one amongst them wasn't wearing his full-face war helm, a flame-haired warrior who stepped forwards into the reckoner's eye line. 'Gilias Thunderbrow is their leader and will be your shadow.'

The one Thurbad had introduced as Gilias bowed, before steeping back and donning his war helm.

'A ship will carry you across the Great Ocean and you will have the runelord Thorik Oakeneye in your party. He will meet you at Barak Varr and shall ensure you breach the veils surrounding the land of the elgi.'

With the salient details of the journey revealed, the High King took over again.

'This is our last chance, Grimbok. Of all the dawi of the Karaz Ankor you know the elgi best. Bring me back peace and a measure of contrition with which I can placate the other kings.'

'By Grungni, I swear I will try.'

'You must succeed, Grimbok. Many dawi lives are depending on it.'

'Y-yes… of course, my king. When do I depart for Ulthuan?'

The High King's eyes were like two chips of hardened diamond.

'Immediately.'

THE FASTNESS OF Black Fire Pass was bleak and cold. Known to the dwarfs as *Kazad Kolzharr*, which simply meant *the fortress of black fire*, it was a stout keep of hewn stone with a broad, thick gate bound by strips of iron and sentinelled by a quartet of stocky watchtowers. It offered a peerless view of the mountains and a wide aperture into the lands west, all the way down the Old Dwarf Road.

'I heard Ranuld tell that in ancient days the road was paved with gold and shimmered like fire in the sun.'

'Poetry isn't really my strength, cousin.'

Snorri's mood was as bleak as the weather and their surroundings as Morgrim joined him on the wall.

The dwarf prince was peering into the west through a spyglass at the arrow-sharp pinnacles of the elven cities several hundred miles away. They were distant and indistinct but he could make out the rough shape of Kor Vanaeth and knew the names and positions of several others from the map spread in front of him. Two large rocks kept the fluttering parchment from blowing away in the high wind coming off the mountains. Winter nipped at the air and a light frost rimed the battlements and glistened on the grasslands below.

'He said that gold-gathering put paid to the gilded road, to all the golden byways of the Karaz Ankor,' said Morgrim, stoking up his pipe. 'That it was dawi, not urk or grobi, that picked the great shining roads clean.'

'It's a myth.' Snorri put the spyglass away, braced his hands against the wall. Apart from the hearthguard manning the watchtowers, they were alone.

'Perhaps,' admitted Morgrim, blowing out a plume of grey-blue smoke. 'But we *have* become greedy.'

'Is it greed then that brings thirty thousand of the *kalans* to Kazad Kolzharr?'

'Some, yes. For you, cousin, I do not think so.'

'I have a score to settle with my father then, do I?'

'Do you deny it?'

Snorri turned to face him. 'Why are you here, Morg? You claim it is to watch my back, but is that all?'

Morgrim slapped the battlements with the flat of his gauntleted hand. 'You are as cold as this stone, Snorri. The last few years have hardened you. I am here because I am hoping to catch a glimpse of the dawi I once knew…' Morgrim met his gaze. 'My cousin and friend.'

For a moment, Snorri's tough, weather-beaten face softened. Since the garrisoning of the fortress at Black Fire Pass they had seen the musters of the elves, their horse guard and warriors scouting as far as they dared in dwarf territory. The pointy-ears did not believe in peace. Just as the dwarfs did, they knew that war was inevitable. It merely remained to see who would cast the first spear.

After eight years, after honouring his promise to Elmendrin and suffering the oathmaking of King Brynnoth and Thagdor, Snorri had decided it would be him. Regardless of what his father wanted, he would march on Kor Vanaeth and destroy it.

Word had reached the fastness that the High King would attempt one last act of diplomacy before committing to war. In his heart and his head, Snorri knew this would fail.

'The dawi you knew, he stands before you, cousin. But if I am to accept the mantle of High King one day, I must seize destiny for myself. I must slay the drakk of which Ranuld Silverthumb spoke. I must defeat the elgi.'

'Is there nothing I can say to keep you here behind these walls? If not for your father's wishes, what of Elmendrin?'

'My father chases a foolish dream, one that ended long ago. And as for her… She…' Snorri faltered, looking down. 'She is–'

'My prince,' uttered a voice from the other end of the wall.

To Morgrim's ears it seemed to be closer, but Drogor had

barely mounted the battlements and was striding towards them.

Like the cousins, he wore full armour, plate over mail with a thick furred cloak to ward off the cold. He wore his battle helm from Karak Zorn, the one with the saurian crest, and lifted the faceguard to speak further.

'Our runners have returned,' he said, with a small nod of acknowledgement for Morgrim who reciprocated reluctantly.

Drogor was clutching a piece of parchment and presented it to the prince. Snorri read it silently, his expression hardening with every line.

'The elgi have mustered a large force on the outskirts of Kor Vanaeth.'

'Apparently, their spies have discovered your intention to attack them and are making ready their defences,' said Drogor. 'It's possible they will ride out against the kazad, my prince.'

Snorri snapped at him, 'Do not call me that, Drogor. How many times must I tell you?'

Drogor bowed. 'Apologies, Snorri. I am your thane, you are my prince, one day to be High King. It feels dishonourable to address you any other way.'

Snorri returned to the letter.

'Rangers have been attacked on the road and a band of reckoners put to flight.' His eyes widened in shock, quickly narrowing to anger. 'Priestesses of Valaya were amongst their number.'

'What?' asked Morgrim. 'What were priestesses doing this far from the hold? It makes no sense.'

Snorri glared at his cousin. 'Eight years ago they came forth from their temple, did they not?'

'Elmendrin was not amongst them?' Morgrim betrayed more than mere concern.

Snorri gave him a wary glance before reading on.

'No, she is back at Everpeak, but they would undoubtedly be her maidens.'

Morgrim frowned, unconvinced. 'Valayan priestesses abroad on the road? It makes no sense. Let me see that letter.'

Snorri handed it over but it broke apart in his metal fist, fragmenting like ash.

'Odd,' he said. 'I've never seen parchment do that before.' He looked at it for a moment then cast it over the wall, where it was caught by the wind and borne away.

Morgrim turned to Drogor, who was waiting patiently for the prince's orders.

'Where is this runner now? I would speak with him.'

Drogor grew solemn, though his eyes remained cold and lifeless. 'He is dead, shot with elgi arrows.'

Morgrim sneered. 'I see.'

'Is there a problem?'

'Nothing that cannot be rectified.'

'It matters not,' said Snorri. 'Slaying rinns and priestesses, it cannot go unanswered any longer.' He was stern, and he spoke through a portcullis of clenched teeth. 'Gather the clans. All of them. And send word to Brynnoth and Thagdor. This time I won't be dissuaded. We march on Kor Vanaeth.'

'What about your father? He sues for peace, and any war-making that we do here could–'

'Let him!' Snorri roared. 'He's knows it's over, as well as I. Peace is dead, has been for eight years.'

'And while peace fails, what will we do?'

Snorri's face was pitiless as knapped flint, and just as unyielding.

'What we should have done years ago. Kill elgi.'

⟞ CHAPTER TWENTY-EIGHT ⟝

The Sea Gate

TOWERING CLIFFS, THRONGED with shrieking gulls and carved with the likenesses of the ancestors, loomed over Forek Grimbok and the hearthguard.

'Is that it?' he asked the armoured warrior standing next to him at the ship's prow.

'Aye,' murmured Gilias, tightening his grip on his axe haft instinctively. 'The Merman Gate, entryway into Barak Varr, the Sea Hold and realm of King Brynnoth.'

The pair of cyclopean statues were fashioned seamlessly into the rock face, depicted wearing fishscale armour and fin-crested war helms. One was female and carried a trident in her left hand; the other, male, bore an axe that he held across his chest.

'Magnificent,' breathed Forek.

Insisting they make all haste to Barak Varr, the High King had petitioned the King of the Sea Gate to both receive them and send a vessel to bear his emissary to the hold. Though dwarfs were not fond of water-borne travel, preferring solid rock as opposed to a leaky deck beneath their boots, Forek and his retinue had adjusted quickly.

Over the last eight years relations had soured between the

two holds. Brynnoth did not believe in peace, but he also did not believe in denying his king and so had acceded to Gotrek's request.

The most direct route from Everpeak to Barak Varr was Skull River, one of several large tributaries that joined the Black Gulf. The river widened as it met two shoulders of jagged rock that formed the monolithic cliffs that had glowered down on them several miles out. The sweeping crags arched over an immense gate of bronze, green with verdigris and clinging seaweed. A dwarf face, with a sea serpent coiling from its open mouth and an ocean wyrm perched atop its helmet, was emblazoned across it that split in two as the gate opened.

Either side of the gate was a tower, a garrison of dwarf quarrellers within each and a journeyman engineer to pump the crank that worked the mechanism which opened it. The reek of salt and the open sea hit them in a wave as soon as the bronze gate was breached.

Like his retinue of hearthguard, Forek looked up as they passed under the archway but saw the faces that regarded them were far from friendly.

'Why do I feel a chill in this wind all of a sudden?' he asked, determined not to flinch against intimidation.

'They are Gatekeepers,' explained Gilias, 'and not prone to warm welcomes. Barak Varr and Karaz-a-Karak are not on the best of terms at the moment.'

'King Brynnoth knows who his allies are,' Forek assured the hearthguard. 'He would not have aided us if he felt otherwise. Grudgement for Agrin Fireheart will be done, but not until the truth is known. A war would eclipse all hope of that. It would be petty and unworthy of the runelord. Brynnoth knows this.'

'You seem very sure,' said Gilias.

Mist wreathed the passage of the grubark in a white, impenetrable fog but the hearthguard rowed unerringly, one of the warriors working the tiller to keep the rudder straight and their small ship from falling foul of the banks.

'I will make certain of it upon making the shore,' said Forek. He tried not to breathe too deep of the briny air, already feeling a little nauseous with the gentle rocking of the boat.

'Here.' Gilias uncorked a flask of tarry liquid and offered it to the reckoner. 'This'll calm your stomach.'

Forek took a grateful swig, gulping back the fiery liquid and trying not to cough. He was used to 'gentler' brews, not the harsh muck enjoyed by the king's protectors.

'Tromm,' he said, nodding thanks, 'that feels better al–'

Forek stopped mid-sentence, his mouth suddenly agape. The mist had thinned and parted, revealing the majesty of the Sea Gate.

Massive columns surged upwards from dark water, decorated with immense statuary and brazier pans of burning coals as broad as a hundred shields laid edge to edge. The columns supported a vast ceiling of rock, a natural cave that served as Barak Varr's dock. The rune of *bar* – that which means 'gate', and is a potent symbol of protection – was emblazoned upon slabs of rock, towers and minarets, portcullises and keeps built into the cave wall. Tips of spear-sized quarrels could be seen poking out through arrow slits and stone throwers mounted on rotating platforms were angled towards them in a blatant threat.

Barak Varr was a hold that took its defence very seriously, and even a vessel that had encroached this far into its borders was not guaranteed continued safe passage.

Somewhere a bell was tolling, its sound solemn and echoing. A hold was still in mourning for its venerable dead, and it only made the cavernous chamber more desolate. Ordinarily it would be bristling with vessels from across the Old World: strange barques of dark-skinned merchants, the skiffs of Southland traders and even elven catamarans had all been seen at the Sea Gate before. Not so any more. Impending war had seen much of the trade dry up and now only a few dwarf vessels occupied the yawning expanse of black water.

'It's like a graveyard,' remarked one of the hearthguard, until Gilias silenced him with a look.

Forek agreed, the doleful bell ringing in the distance to announce them. His reckoning days had never brought him to Barak Varr before. Perhaps it was on account of the strong bond between it and Everpeak that this was the case. But whatever he had expected, this was not it.

As they were ushered towards a jetty, several warriors wearing scaled mail and carrying axes and crossbows met them. Their helmets were almost conical, fashioned into the simulacra of a sea dragon's snout, and had a pair of jagged fins protruding from either temple. Shields strapped to their backs were scalloped at the edges and their axe blades were flanged like a trident's teeth.

'Quite a show of force,' murmured Gilias, careful to keep his voice low.

Forek muttered, 'Once King Brynnoth has received us, all will be well. They are just wary of dawi not of their hold.'

As soon as they set foot on dry land, Forek whispered an oath of gratitude to Valaya for her deliverance and then one to Grungni for creating the earth.

Two figures not part of the throng of warriors awaited them on the flagstoned shore. As soon as Forek saw one of them he realised why there were so many warriors.

'That is High Thane Onkmarr.'

'You sound surprised,' said Gilias as they walked along the jetty to the creak of wood bending beneath the weight of so many armoured warriors.

'I am.'

The other dwarf Forek didn't know. He was dressed in black leather armour over a scruffy-looking tunic. The eyepatch he wore, together with the mattock head he had instead of a foot, marked him out as a ship's captain but the reckoner thought he looked more like a pirate.

'If Onkmarr is here then that can mean but one thing.'

'Which is?' hissed Gilias as they neared the edge of the jetty.

Forek replied in the same guarded tone, 'That King Brynnoth is not.'

HEGLAN AWOKE TO a hammering against his chamber door.

He was face down in a scrap of parchment, ink smears on his cheeks from where he had fallen asleep pressed against his still-wet scribblings, exhaustion forcing him to eschew his bed in favour of the first available place to collapse.

At first he was disorientated. This last session in the workshop had been the longest, several weeks in isolation with only stonebread and strong beer to sustain him. Dawi had survived on less, he had told himself at the outset of his labours. His avian menagerie startled him and he gasped aloud at the talons of a crag eagle bearing down from on high. Belatedly, he came to his senses, still slightly fuddled by strong drink but at least now able to make out someone calling his name.

'Heg? Open the door, brother. Heg?'

Tripping on a stuffed griffon vulture that had fallen from its perch, he stumbled to his feet and hurried over to a crank that would seal off the hidden vault where he kept his secret labours. Setting the mechanism going, he quickly gathered up the scraps of parchment he had been sleeping on, rolled them up and stuffed them in a drawer.

By the time he reached the door and opened it, the vault was shut and Nadri Gildtongue looked less than impressed.

'What are you doing, Heg?' he asked bluntly.

'I was sleeping, brother. What's your excuse for being here?'

Nadri barged his way in and began to look around.

'I haven't seen you in months. I've spoken to your guild-master,' he said, rifling through tools and sketches, drawers of cogs and nails and bolts. 'Your absence has been noted.'

'If you tell me what you're looking for perhaps I can help you find it.'

'You are doing it again, aren't you?'

'Doing what?'

'Building the airship. I am no wazzock, Heg, do not treat me as one.' Nadri rapped his knuckles against the room's back wall. 'What is behind here?'

Heglan feigned confusion, but inwardly stifled a pang of anxiety. Nadri was certainly no fool. 'It is a wall, brother. Solid rock is behind it.'

'Every other surface in this workshop is covered in designs and formulae and notes. You have papered it in parchment scribblings, Heg. Yet this wall is barren.' Nadri shook his head, his face clouded by anger. 'Don't lie to me. Show me what you're hiding.'

Heglan closed his mouth – protesting his innocence would be pointless now – and opened up the vault.

The skylight beamed weak winter sun onto the hull of a magnificent ship. It was lacquered black, fully restored and even larger and more impressive than before. Gone were the rotary sails and the sweeps, but there was more rigging and a sack that looked like a stitched animal bladder draped the deck.

'It's unfinished but an inaugural flight is close, I think.' Heglan's eyes widened, his hangover all but forgotten in his excitement. Like an artist with his latest masterwork, he relished the opportunity to show it off.

Nadri was less enthused but couldn't hide his awe.

'It is incredible, Heg. But you will be expelled from the guild for this. Strombak will see to it that you are given the Trouser Legs Ritual and kicked out.'

'When he sees what I have crafted, when he witnesses its first flight he will–'

'He doesn't care, Heg! He will expel you and further shame will be heaped on the Copperfists. First Grandfather Dammin and now you… Our father, Lodri, will never be allowed at Grungni's table. He will wander forever at Gazul's Gate.' Nadri tugged on his beard, fighting back the tears in his eyes. He rasped, his voice choking, 'Dreng tromm, brother.'

'The skryzan-harbark will fly, Nadri. I know it. And when it does our family's shame will be expunged, our seat in the Hall of Ancestors assured. Please don't tell Strombak what I am doing, not yet. I must–' He stopped, as if seeing his brother for the first time since he'd entered his workshop. 'Wait… why are you wearing your armour?'

Nadri was clad in ringmail. A helmet was tethered to his belt by its strap and there was a small round shield on his back, an axe looped by his waist.

'It's why I came to find you, brother,' he said with a hint of melancholy. 'King Brynnoth is going to war. Our kalan marches with him.'

Heglan was shaking his head, fear for his beloved brother lighting his eyes. 'No. You are a merchant, not a warrior.'

'We are all warriors when the horn blows calling us to war. The elgi are to be held to account for Agrin Fireheart's death at last.' Nadri's face darkened, his mouth becoming a hard line. 'And I shall seek vengeance for Krondi.'

'But war? When did this happen?' asked Heglan.

'It is happening now, brother. The king has already left Barak Varr and another two thousand dawi of the kalans follow in his wake.'

'But what of trade, who will bring gold into the Sea Gate if you are at war?'

'There is no trade! It ended years ago and has been drying up ever since. The only currency now is that of axes and shields, war engines to break open the elgi cities. It's why Strombak has not been to find you. He is in the forges, as you should be, fashioning weapons for our king.'

Like a hammer blow had struck him on the forehead, filling his skull with a sudden realisation, Heglan went from being stupefied to urgently casting about his workshop.

Nadri frowned. 'What are you doing now?'

Heglan was ferreting around in drawers and racks, sweeping aside tools and materials. 'Looking for my axe,' he said. 'I'm coming with you.'

Nadri went over and held him by the shoulders to keep him still.

'No, brother. You are staying here. Finish your airship. Strombak will definitely cast you out of the guild if you tell what you've been up to now. Realise grandfather's dream. It might be your last chance.'

Worry lines creased Heglan's brow. 'Why are you talking like this? A moment ago you were chastising me.'

'I changed my mind. You were right. Nothing will be the same after this,' he said, sombrely.

Heglan grew fearful as he saw the fatalism in his brother's eyes.

'You are coming back, aren't you?'

'I hope so.'

'You have to come back. Father is dead, mother too. You are my only family, Nadri.'

'And you mine, Heg.'

They embraced awkwardly, Nadri's armour unfamiliar on his body and getting in the way.

'Keep it secret, Heg,' he said.

Heglan was weeping. '*Dreng tromm*, Nadri…'

Nadri held him behind the neck, pressed his forehead to his brother's.

'*Karinunkarak*,' he murmured.

'*Karinunkarak*,' Heglan replied in a choked whisper.

It meant 'protect and endure', but words were not shields or armour.

Detaching himself from his brother's embrace, Nadri met Heglan's gaze one last time and then left the workshop.

The door slamming after him arrested Heglan from his reverie. He turned to regard the airship, a masterwork waiting for its artisan to finish it.

Seizing a hammer that he'd spilled onto the floor, he locked the door to his chamber and went to work.

ONKMARR HAD WASTED no time in getting Forek and his retinue on their way. They didn't leave the dock and certainly had not been granted admittance to the Sea Hold itself. Instead, as the high thane and regent left them, the Everpeak dwarfs were guided by the rough-looking captain to where his ship was berthed.

It was a massive vessel, engraved with runes along its hull and festooned with rows of sweeps along either flank. A vast paddle sat at the stern that could pivot back and forth like a rudder, but there were no masts, no sails to speak of. It was armoured in plates of metal, the heavy wood of its structure thick and well lacquered. Three bolt throwers, one at the prow where Valaya's effigy looked stern in her warrior aspect and two more to port and starboard, provided obvious protection but in addition to them were racks of crossbows and harpoons that Forek could see jutting up above the bulwarks from below. A crew of leather-skinned, weather-beaten dwarfs hoisted barrels and other provisions up a ramp onto the deck. They too were armed.

'A mission o' peace never looked so tooled up, eh?' the captain remarked over his shoulder as he led his passengers up another ramp. The swarthy-looking dwarf grinned, revealing several gold teeth, as he noticed Forek looking at his missing foot. 'Ah, don't let that bother ye, lad,' he said in a gravel-thick voice. 'I needs hands to steer a ship, not feet. And as you can see, I have both of those.' He patted a broad black belt, a rune axe looped on one side, spyglass on the other. The dwarf sea captain gave a shallow bow. 'Nugdrinn Hammerfoot. I'll be the zaki taking you across the Great Ocean.'

Halfway up the ramp, Forek shook the dwarf's proffered hand and felt whale grease and spit between his fingers.

'This is your ship?' he asked, for want of a better reply.

'Aye, the *Azuldal*,' he said proudly. 'Come aboard.'

Up on deck, the *Azuldal* looked even more fortified. It was a keep, just one that floated on water.

'There are no sails?' Forek asked, noticing a hooded figure sitting at the ship's forecastle. He faced in the direction of the sea, clutching an ornate staff in both hands.

'That's right, lad. Paddles, oars and solid dawi grit is how we'll make passage.' He jerked a thumb at the mysterious passenger. 'Oh, and a little rhun won't hurt us either,' he added in a conspiratorial whisper.

This must be Thorik Oakeneye, Forek supposed, the runelord who would break the veils clouding Ulthuan.

'How many times have you travelled across the Great Ocean before, Captain Hammerfoot?' Forek asked, still beguiled by the runesmith.

'Never.' He was already shouting to his crew, getting them to make ready for depature. With a creaking refrain, the paddle at the ship's stern began to turn and the long sweeps pierced the dark water as they started to pull.

'Then how do you know you can successfully navigate it?' asked Forek urgently.

Nugdrinn scratched under his patch at his missing eye.

'I don't, but that's where the adventure comes in, lad.' His good eye narrowed as he caught on. 'You look concerned.

It's not the navigating that should worry you, it's the blood-hungry creatures of the deep.' He laughed, loud and hearty, stomping towards the helm.

Forek watched him go, only vaguely aware of Gilias Thunderbrow's warriors making ready behind him. He felt a hand upon his shoulder.

It was Gilias. The hearthguard's eyes followed Nugdrinn limping up every step of the helm until he reached the ship's wheel.

'Thorik Oakeneye will guide us, but he will keep us afloat. Don't worry.'

'I'm not worried,' said Forek, unconvincingly.

Gilias laughed. 'Of course not.'

Nugdrinn was pointing at the horizon with a grubby finger.

'We're under way!' he cried, 'To the land of the elgi with all haste!' He looked down at Forek. 'You should tie yourself down, ufdi. It'll be a rough passage, I'd warrant. Ha, ha!'

'He's mad,' he hissed to Gilias.

'He'd need to be to venture where we're going.'

'Aren't you concerned?' he asked the hearthguard.

'No,' he said. 'I am more concerned with what happens if you fail.'

Forek could find no argument with that, and as the *Azuldal* pulled out of Barak Varr and drove towards the Black Gulf, he wondered what would await when they arrived on Ulthuan.

If they arrived on Ulthuan.

⤛ CHAPTER TWENTY-NINE ⤜

Hunted

HEAVY RAIN PEELED off the hood of Sevekai's cloak, teeming in rivulets of dark water that pooled at his already sodden feet. Brooding clouds overhead showed no sign of abating and an ever-present thunder promised worse weather to come.

The skull-headed rock seemed to glower down at him, presaging darker times ahead. Sevekai glared back, unimpressed.

'Hell's Head indeed,' he muttered. 'You'll need to summon more than just rain to kill me, spirit!' He cursed with all the names of the dark elf gods of the underworld. It had been days, but still no sign. 'Boredom might, however,' he admitted.

Crouched in the lee of the Hell's Head crag, there was little else to do but wait. She said she would be there and though it went against every instinct he possessed he had to trust her.

A biting wind was blowing off the mountains, chilling the air and turning the rain to sleet. Drawing his cloak tighter around his body, Sevekai tried to imagine warmer climes.

'Why are we still here?' moaned Verigoth. The grey-pallored shade looked more sullen than usual. 'Our task is finished.

The asur will soon be at war. Why must we remain?'

Sevekai didn't have the heart to tell him they would not be returning to Naggaroth any time soon, that Malekith had left them here to rot or find passage back to the frozen island for themselves. No, it wasn't a lack of heart; he just preferred the other dark elf to suffer.

'We are here because our dark lord wills it.' A raven had perched on the overhanging rock, seemingly oblivious to the rain, and cawed at the bedraggled warriors. Flitting from one settlement to the next, often sleeping on bare rock or under shadowed trees, they looked ragged. Verigoth wasn't alone in his displeasure. At least they were alive. For now. If *she* got her way, the other bitch making Sevekai's life torment, then the situation might change. 'And even this far from his court, do not think for a moment that his eye isn't ever watchful.'

In truth, though, Sevekai had begun to wonder the same thing. Not why they were still here, but rather why they were in the Old World at all. What would a war between elves and dwarfs achieve? It would not restore the druchii to glory. Not for the first time he considered his position but was wise enough to keep his misgivings hidden beneath his surface thoughts. Drutheira might be close and reading his mind. Worse still, Malekith could be listening.

The raven took flight, and Sevekai prayed to the gods of the underworld that it wasn't a Naggarothi messenger.

For the last eight years, ever since murdering the dwarf wizard or whatever he was, the shades had gone to ground. Occasionally they had resurfaced to attack a band of dwarfs or ambush a caravan. Discord needed to be nurtured if it was to flourish into something as permanent and debilitating as enmity. Sevekai had curtailed their activities deliberately. Flames had been fanned, they merely needed to watch and see where they spread. The dwarf king had shown more resilience than he had expected in resisting a declaration of war. In part, this forced the shades out of hiding, but the other mud-dwelling lords had fomented the inevitable war nicely with their bigotry and greed.

The message from Drutheira came as a surprise. He

had neither seen nor heard from her since they had been reunited in the gorge. They were evading a band of dwarf rangers – heavier patrols along the roads had made travelling more difficult – when her face had manifested in the rotting intestines of a dead raven. Perhaps the one on the rock earlier had been looking for its mate.

She had bidden Sevekai meet her at this place, and wait there until she arrived. The sending was so incongruous, so unlike her in its tone and desperation that he decided to believe the witch. Any chance to see Drutheira squirm, whatever the cause, was worth taking. And, besides, there was something more than lust which compelled him.

The others didn't chafe much. Likely they hoped she would spirit them away with sorcery. Sevekai let them believe that, even though he knew that though Drutheira was powerful she did not possess that kind of craft, even with her lackeys. Only one of the party seemed sceptical.

'You still think she will come?' asked Kaitar.

Sevekai met the cold bastard's gaze and suppressed a shudder, telling himself it was caused by the wind.

Losing Numenos at the gorge had been a blow. Now they were five, and could ill-afford to lose anyone else, but he wished bitterly there was one less of their number. Verigoth was rumoured to have a witch elf for a mother, his pale skin indicative of Hag Graef, the lightless prison city. Hreth and Latharek were twins from Har Ganeth, City of Executioners, and as hard as druchii came but even they looked ill at ease around Kaitar.

Sitting in a circle around a guttering fire that was more smoke than heat, every face was forlorn.

All except for Kaitar. He was smiling.

'I see little to be pleased about,' said Hreth, a dangerous edge to his tone.

'Perhaps he likes the rain,' suggested Latharek, smirking with his brother.

Kaitar grinned, showing perfect teeth. Ignoring the brothers, he turned to Sevekai. 'You didn't answer my question. Will the witch still come, because if not…'

Sevekai didn't look up. 'She'll be here.'

Hreth got to his feet, rain hammering against his cloak and running down the broad-bladed knife he wore at his hip. 'Where is it exactly you hail from again, Kaitar?'

Kaitar didn't look back. 'Many places, none. It doesn't really matter.'

'I think it does,' said Latharek, standing up next to his brother.

Sevekai edged back, hand slipping furtively to his sickle daggers, but otherwise content to let it play out.

'You don't want to know where I am from, Hreth,' Kaitar answered, staring into the embers of the fire which seemed to spit and flare into life.

Hreth would not be dissuaded. 'I have been to many of the dark cities but never met one such as you.'

Latharek joined in, 'Yes, you are barely druchii at all.'

Kaitar laughed, goading Hreth.

'Something amuses you?'

'Only your foolishness.' He looked up from the fire.

Sevekai licked his lips, anticipating violence. Verigoth remained still and silent.

'Sit down,' Kaitar told the brothers.

Eight years had frayed tempers, stoked discontent to the point where it was about to spill over into something more lethal. Perhaps this was how Malekith had intended to deal with his errant scouts, by having them kill each other.

'Now,' Kaitar added.

Sevekai's skin tingled and he thought he detected a slight resonance to the warrior's voice.

Hreth and Latharek sat down as ordered, as if pole-axed and struck dumb.

'That's better,' said Kaitar. 'Is that any way to behave when we have guests?' He turned to Sevekai, who couldn't stop his flesh crawling nor the itch behind his teeth. 'You were right.'

'About what?' Sevekai asked.

Kaitar pointed to the tip of a craggy rise.

'She did come.'

Drutheira had arrived with Ashniel and Malchior.

Sevekai gave Kaitar one last look before greeting the witch.

'Enter, stranger...' He gave a mock bow, masking his discomfort with absurd theatrics.

Drutheira did not appear to be impressed.

'We do not have much time,' she hissed, glancing at the brooding sky overhead. Now he saw them up close, Sevekai thought the coven looked more ragged than his own tattered followers.

'You've been prettier, my dear,' he said, betraying a mote of concern at Drutheira's appearance.

'Like a cold one sniffing blood,' she spat, seeming not to hear the gibe. Her fingers were thin, almost like bone, and her sunken cheeks reminded Sevekai of a cadaver that had yet to realise it was dead. 'It has taken all of my power to stay hidden.'

The two at her side bristled at this.

Her power?

Sevekai could almost hear their thoughts, slipping porously through their hateful eyes.

'The elf woman? I thought we had eluded her years ago.'

Drutheira rounded on him, snarling. 'She is a mage, idiot! Such creatures cannot be eluded. She has found my magical spoor, tracked me, dogged me without relent.'

'Then you must flee.'

'I *am* fleeing, my *love*,' she said, 'to you. I need you to kill her for me.'

Now Sevekai laughed. 'And her beast too, I suppose?' His face hardened. 'You reap your own harvest, Drutheira. Leaving a stain on that gorge was a mistake, one that will hound you to the edge of the Old World.'

'Do you know how many settlements I have razed to ash over the last eight years?' she asked, fashioning a coruscating orb of dark energy in her hand. 'And my wrath is far from spent.' The orb writhed as if constricted in Drutheira's grip, oily tendrils coiling and uncoiling in agony, eager to be unleashed.

Sevekai stepped back.

'This black horror will strip flesh from bone,' she promised. 'I saved your miserable life in that gorge. That dwarf would have killed you all had I not intervened. *Now*,' she said, the summoning receding into trailing smoke that left a dark scar on her open palm, 'the balance of that must be accounted.'

'What makes you think I can kill her?'

'You are not fixed in her eye. She won't see the blade until she's already dead from its poison.' She cast another glance skywards, imagining the beat of heavy wings, a shadow overhead...

Sevekai smiled.

'You *are* weak, aren't you?'

Drutheira came close, so only he could hear her.

'She has hunted me for eight years, Sevekai. I am exhausted,' she said, with a furtive glance at her predatory cohorts, but they were just as wasted. Drutheira's voice dropped to a whisper. 'She will kill me.'

Appealing to the heart of an assassin is no easy thing but despite their ostensible enmity Sevekai did not want harm to come to the sorceress.

'I know a hidden path, one that will take us south, beyond the mountains and to the coast. There is a ship waiting in dock that can take us to the Sour Sea and from there we'll make our way back.'

Drutheira dragged Sevekai close and hissed, 'I will not make it that far. She must die.' Her face darkened, blackness pooled in her sunken eyes and a shadow of a grin lifted her features. 'You have no choice.'

Sevekai threw her off.

'Another dagger in my back, Drutheira?' he snarled. 'You led her here deliberately.'

All of a sudden, the sorceress did not appear so weak or desperate.

'I'm sorry, *my love*, but our survival depends on us working together. Our dark lord has decreed it. I need the elf bitch dead. She is interfering with my plans.'

Murderous intent flashed over Sevekai's face.

'How close?'

'A day, if that. It is Malekith's will that the dragon rider dies.'

The shade shook his head, 'And here I was thinking all I had to be concerned about was the rain.'

'And one other thing,' Drutheira said, keeping her voice low as her gaze lit on Kaitar. '*That* is not a druchii.'

WITH THE COMING of the dream, she smelled smoke and heard the crackle of fire…

Cothique was burning.

Liandra ran through the streets, crying out for her mother, desperate to see her father and brothers. She was young, too young to wield a sword or spear. Not like them. They would have killed the raiders, put them to flight, but the warriors defending Cothique were all dead and only women and children remained.

A terrible clamour raked the air, and it took a few minutes for Liandra to realise the sound belonged to gulls, screaming as the air in which they flew was set aflame.

The port was ablaze, half-burned bodies face down in the water from where they'd tried to douse themselves. Quarrels protruded from their backs like spines.

Everything was haze and shadow, muffled by the flames, clouded by the smoke. Liandra coughed, bringing up a ropey phlegm that spoiled her summer dress. She was crawling before she realised she had fallen, hands and knees in the dirt and blood. It sluiced down the streets in a river.

Somewhere, she couldn't tell precisely in her dark occluded world, a horn was braying. Liandra knew that sound, just as she knew the raiders were taking flight, their black galleons brimming with slaves. Lothern had answered, their ships had come and sent fear running through the hearts of the druchii.

Reaching out, half blind with smoke, Liandra found the edge of a broken cart. She began to crawl beneath it when an iron-hard grip seized her ankle. She screamed as she was pulled, looking back through tear-streaming eyes into the face of a wraith.

Though her brothers had told her tales, she had never seen a druchii before. He was pale, his features so like and yet unlike her own; appearing sharper, as though she would cut herself on his nose or cheekbones.

She screamed again and the druchii laughed, drinking in her terror. His face was painted in cruel, angular runes that made Liandra's eyes hurt, or that might just have been the fire. She kicked wildly, connecting with the druchii's face, and he snarled in anger at her. She tried again, but he caught her ankle, twisted it hard until she thought she might pass out from the pain.

'Khaine's hells are reserved for little ones like you,' the raider hissed, drawing a curved dagger with serrated teeth along its edge.

His breath smelled of blood.

She struggled, looking around for help, but there was no one. Only fire and smoke. The warriors from Lothern would not reach her in time. Gutted on a druchii's blade or a prisoner on their foul ships, either way she was as good as dead. But Liandra was a princess of Caledor, she had a warrior's heart and fire in her veins to fuel it. She would not die without a fight.

A heavy punch to her jaw put the fight out of her and she mewled like a milksop farm girl, blacking out for a second. When she opened her eyes again, the dagger was all she could see, filling her eye line. She noticed the blade was black, or rather, stained that way.

She wept. 'Mother…'

The druchii grunted, the dagger falling from Liandra's sight, a grimace marring the raider's porcelain features. A woman stood over him, a broken spear haft clutched in her shaking hands.

'Get off her, you bastard!'

Liandra wept again, even as the druchii parried a second swipe of the spear haft and disarmed its wielder with ease. 'Mother…'

'Run!' she cried to Liandra, urging her daughter with all the swiftness of Kurnous. 'Flee, Liandra!'

Even as the druchii closed her down, seized her flailing fist and plunged the dagger deep.

Time slowed, the smoke and flame so thick Liandra could hardly breathe any more, the figures a few feet in front of her reduced to hazed silhouettes.

One crumpled and fell. It brought a word half-formed to her lips that she was unable to speak.

Mother.

The druchii turned. Something dark and vital shimmered on the edge of his blade. It dripped to the ground, as the last ounces of Liandra's innocence bled away with it.

Horns were braying.

Lothern had answered, but their call came too late for her mother.

Heedless of the danger, the druchii advanced on her. He got three steps before an arrow punctured his chest. Another pierced his throat and he gargled his last words through a fountain of blood.

Then he fell, and Liandra was alone.

The archer hadn't seen her. No one came.

She stayed there in the ruins of Cothique, surrounded by smoke at her mother's side, until the fire died and all that remained was ash.

Liandra awoke with a sudden start, awash with feverish sweat.

She breathed deep, trying to abate her trembling, soothing Vranesh who was similarly distressed. The high mountain air was crisp and cold. It chilled her, but she relished it, found it calming.

'Mother…' The word escaped her lips without her realising, and terror was subdued by a hard ball of iron that nestled in her heart.

Eight years she had been hunting. As soon as she learned of the druchii's presence in the Old World, and she felt the resonance of the Wind of Dhar in the gorge to confirm her, she had not rested. Kor Vanaeth was left to one of her father's seneschals. He was a good man, a dependable warrior, but not one in whom Liandra could confide.

Not like Imladrik.

Every since the day they parted ways, she had ached for his return. Not once had she gone back to Kor Vanaeth, preferring the cold solitude of hunting dark elves. She cared not for the imminent war. It didn't matter to her who had killed the dwarfs. None of that mattered now. She just wanted revenge.

And her prey was close.

She breathed deep of the mountain air again… and smelled smoke, heard the crackle of fire.

A tremor jerked her heart and she gasped, reliving the dream all over again. Then fire turned to ice in her veins.

She wasn't dreaming. The fire was real. Smoke carried on the swift mountain breeze.

Kor Vanaeth was burning.

⤙ CHAPTER THIRTY ⤚

A Hurled Spear

By the time the armies of Barak Varr and Zhufbar had reached the fortress at Black Fire Pass, it took thirteen days for Snorri Halfhand's throng to meet the elves in pitched battle.

It took less than three hours to defeat them and send the survivors fleeing back to their city.

Now, Kor Vanaeth was surrounded by almost forty thousand dwarfs. Like an ingot of iron clenched in the tongs, they would hammer the elves against the anvil until they broke.

On a dark heath strewn with battered shields and snapped spear hafts, a conclave of dwarf lords had gathered to decide upon their siege tactics. Frost crisped the ground underfoot, showing up spilt blood that glistened like rubies in the light snowfall. It made the earth hard and the grass crunch like shattered bone.

'We could just wait them out,' suggested King Valarik of Karak Hirn. 'Set up our pickets and let the elgi starve.' Two great eagle wings sprouted from his war helm and a suit of fine ringmail clad his slight frame. A short cape of ermine flapped in the wind, revealing the haft of his mattock slung beneath it on his back.

A susurrus of disproval emanated from the gathered lords. Valarik was youthful, his hold barely founded. It was only natural the older, venerable kings would take exception to his idea.

'They already look beaten.' There was a glint in King Hrekki Ironhandson's eye. It sparkled like the tips of his bolt throwers in the low winter sun.

A gust of cold air ghosted from Snorri's mouth as he exhaled.

'Because they are.' Like many dwarf kings, a vein of greed as thick and beguiling as any motherlode ran through Ironhandson. He licked his lips as he imagined the plunder inside the elf city that would swell his coffers.

Snorri didn't feel it. He only wanted to show his father he was wrong and that the elves were a threat in need of ousting from their lands.

Thagdor certainly thought so.

He regarded the lines of battered but defiant spearmen, the rows of dishevelled elven archers upon the wall with disdain.

Their horse guard were all dead, the silver-helmed riders smashed against a bulwark of dwarf shields. The King of Zhufbar had revelled in this, for they were his shields.

'Aye, as bloody weak and feeble as I thought. We should've done this years ago.'

Why then, thought Snorri, *do I not feel it?*

He expected satisfaction, a sense of righteous vengeance, but all that filled him was a terrible emptiness, which he could fill with neither gold or violence.

He had gathered the kings together, standing behind the serried shield walls of almost forty thousand dwarfs, to plan the assault. It only occurred to him now that the battle required little in way of strategy. The dwarfs possessed an overwhelming advantage in terms of their numbers. They could simply march on Kor Vanaeth and not stop until it was rubble under their stomping boots.

The left flank contained the bulk of Karak Varn's war engines. Ironhandson was particularly proud of them, a battery of fifty stone throwers and half that again in ballistae.

Untouched in the pitched battle, his engineers and journeymen made ready to unleash them now.

Brynnoth said nothing. He had come to the council as requested, but cared not for tactics. Like most of the clans of Barak Varr, he just wanted revenge. Dwarfs are patient creatures, but eight years had begun to seem a long time coming for Agrin Fireheart's retribution.

Snorri recognised the merchant Nadri Copperfist amongst the king's retinue. Doubtless, his place there was because he had found the runelord and desired vengeance of his own. A merchant no longer, he had left the name Gildtongue behind and become a warrior. Before it was over, Snorri suspected many more would have to do the same. Rope makers, lantern-bearers, barrel-wrights, muleskinners, gold-shapers, rock-cutters, brew-hands, all the dwarfs of the clans would set down the tools of their various trades and take up their axes in this cause.

His father had seen that. After eight years, Snorri was only just beginning to see.

'We should let the elgi surrender,' said Morgrim. His mail hauberk was chipped in places, some of the rings split and dented from elven lances. A worn shield hung over his back and a hammer, stained dark crimson, was looped in his belt. Pleading eyes regarded Snorri from beneath the mantle of his horned helmet as his cousin sought to end the fight.

Snorri held his gaze for a moment before casting it over the city. Every one of the elves had retreated behind its walls. His rangers had estimated somewhere in the region of eight thousand warriors still lived and were able to fight. Mainly spearmen and archers; the cavalry were either dead or would be no use during a siege. There were bound to be sorcerers too, but the prince was unconcerned. Both Brynnoth and Thagdor had brought their runesmiths.

'They won't surrender, cousin,' said Snorri. His burnished breastplate shone dully in the sun as if lacking some of its former lustre. It came with a winged helm that the prince kept in the crook of his arm, and had a shirt of mail beneath it. His axe was unsullied and sat upon his back in its sheath.

His iron gauntlet flexed. 'And nor would we let them. We must send a message. Elgi are not wanted in these lands. They are trespassers and interlopers, and won't be tolerated any more.'

Morgrim lowered his voice. 'You think it will end here? You've made your point, cousin. Let them go.'

He half glanced at Drogor who was standing stock still beside his cousin, eyes front.

Snorri shook his head.

'Can't do that, Morg. The elgi have enjoyed our mercy long enough. Agrin Fireheart lies eight years dead and that must be accounted for. There are entire chapters of grudges devoted to the acts of murder and sabotage perpetrated by these thagging pointy-ears. Have you forgotten Zakbar Varf?'

'That was a trading settlement, *this* is a city!' Morgrim bit his tongue, struggling to rein in his exasperation. He urged, 'Please don't do this.'

Snorri paused, betraying the slightest chink in his resolve.

Drogor's grip tightened on his axe haft, and the prince hardened again.

'It's already done,' he said, thinking about the elven corpses littering the battlefield behind them. He signalled to King Ironhandson. 'Bring it down,' he told him. 'By Grimnir, bring it all down.'

Greed lighting his eyes like a bonfire, the King of Karak Varn raised his fist.

Horns blared, drums beat, warriors clattered their shields.

'Khazuk!'

Hurled stones and flung bolts thickened the air, whistling in a murderous clamour.

The inevitable war had finally begun.

FIGHTING OUTSIDE THE gate to Kor Vanaeth was fierce.

Nadri hacked his blade into the elven wood, finding it much more unyielding than he would have first believed.

In their eagerness to kill elves, and their greed, the dwarf army had not bothered to hew down the trees for battering rams. Instead they would use their axes to cut the city gate down, for surely an elven gate would be easy to breach?

The last hour had proven the falsehood of that, but even as the arrow storm raining down on them from above claimed yet more of Grungni's sons, the gate was slowly beginning to buckle.

Wrenching his axe loose, Nadri saw and heard a crack split its length all the way to the keystone above.

'It yields!' roared King Brynnoth, shielded by his doughty hearthguard.

Within a few paces of his liege-lord, Nadri struck again, urging his clan to greater efforts. He had killed many elves in the earlier pitched battle, and saw their faces with every blow against the gate. Bloodied grimaces, terror-etched or dead-eyed, they rattled him to the core. Then he remembered Krondi, gutted like a fish, and his grip hardened to chiselled stone.

Hammer-armed dwarfs from the Sootbrow clan thumped the cracks, widening the breach with each successive blow. Miners by trade, the Sootbrows worked with steady momentum like they were at the rock face hewing ore.

'Ho, hai, ho, hai…'

Their labouring song was mesmeric. Even when one of their number was felled by an arrow and gargled his last, they did not pause or falter.

The war machines were silent. King Ironhandson had ordered an end to the barrage as soon as Prince Snorri had blown the signal to march. Nadri had been glad of it, muttering an oath to Krondi as they advanced on the city. How far away his life as a merchant seemed now. He spared a brief thought for Heg before the arrows started flying, hoping his brother was still safe in the Sea Hold.

With a sickening splintering of wood, the gate broke apart. A forest of spears glittered on the other side. Behind them, a host of angry and defiant elven faces.

Shields up, the dwarfs barged forwards. Some spears found a way through, skewering mail or splitting plate. With their shields facing elven aggression in front of them, the dwarfs were vulnerable to arrows from above. Even when over a hundred dead littered the gateway, the sons of Grungni did not relent.

Unable to hold back such a determined tide, the elf spear line buckled and the dwarfs poured in.

An elven lordling wearing shining silver scale, a feather of amethyst purple poking from the tip of his helmet, and riding a white horse, raised his sword to urge the garrison of Kor Vanaeth on. Archers mounted on the steps loosed the last of their remaining shafts into the courtyard that was clogging quickly with elven dead.

Nadri took an arrow in his shoulder before he raised his shield to block three others. Head down, seeing mainly booted feet and the skirts of elven scale mail, he swung like a blind man in a bar fight. The hard *thwack* of his axe blade hitting flesh then bone was the only sign he was still in the fight. A spear tip glanced off his helmet, setting a ringing in his ears and a dense throb in his skull. Blood pulsing, heart thundering, he lashed out and was rewarded with a half-strangled scream.

Sweat filled his nostrils, some his own, some his warrior brothers'. He heard their grunting, the muttered curses.

'*Thagging elgi!*'

'*Dreng elgi!*'

'*Uzkul, uzkul!*'

No way out of the melee, surrounded by the din of battle and dying, Nadri roared his own war cry.

'*Krondi! Dammaz a Krondi!*'

A brief cessation to the killing allowed him to look up. The elves were retreating further into the city, but their numbers and formation were scattered. Most of the archers had emptied their quivers so abandoned their bows in favour of knives.

Nadri saw a spearman brought to his knees by one of the hearthguard. Another smacked the elf around the face, his neck snapping wildly to the left before he slumped down and was still.

A second clutched the air, his spear wrenched from his grip before the hammers were upon him, silencing his screams.

Spurring his mount the lordling rode at King Brynnoth, who had demanded to lead the attack personally, uttering a battle cry to his elven gods.

The king of the Sea Hold shoulder barged the steed, thudding his armoured bulk into the beast's chest and stealing away its breath. With a shriek, its ribcage cracked; heart failing, the horse collapsed and bore its rider with it.

Brynnoth showed no mercy as he cut off the lordling's screaming head.

That was an almost an end to it.

Seeing their commander slain was enough to break the elves. Those who could, ran; those who couldn't, surrendered. Several of the pleading elves died before Prince Snorri entered the fray to call a stop to it.

Nadri stood in the middle of the carnage, breathing hard, an ache in his back and shoulder where the arrow remained.

'Get the healers to look at that,' said a voice behind him. He half turned and saw the Prince of Karaz-a-Karak. He was about to kneel when the prince stopped him.

'You've fought and bled, by Grimnir,' he said.

For Agrin Fireheart, the dwarfs of Barak Varr had been given the honour of breaking the gate, and it didn't take forty thousand to sack a city of eight. Some of the walls had collapsed, weakened by stone throwers, brought down by grapnels, but the incursions of the other dwarfs had been mild compared to the effort of the Sea Hold clans.

Prince Snorri met Nadri's gaze. There was steel there, and stone.

'No son of Grungni who has fought this day kneels to me. Go find a healer, lad. The deed here is done.'

He walked on, several of his thanes in tow.

Nadri had expected to feel satisfaction, a sense of closure, even relief. He felt none of these things. Looking around at the corpses, the greedy looting that followed, he found he felt nothing at all.

A WARRIOR OF the hearthguard hurried over, his heavy armour clanking. He'd run a good distance, heaving and gasping in his suit of plate and mail, lifting his visored helm to speak.

'My prince.'

Snorri took the proffered spyglass, nodding thanks,

before aiming the device at the sky. The lens was grimy, smeared by dirt and smoke. Snorri had to rub it with his thumb to clear it, and tried not to rush.

'What do you see?' asked Drogor, sidling up beside him.

The pair of them were beyond the borders of the city, which was still burning. Once the brief siege was over, Snorri had returned to the heath where he could plot his next move. He'd had a map in his hand, his eye on the road to Tor Alessi, when the hearthguard had interrupted.

'It's large, moving quickly and against the wind,' he told Drogor. He peered for longer, squinting for a sharper look. Then he put down the spyglass and yelled to one of the Karak Varn engineers. 'Bolt throwers!'

The dwarfs followed the prince's pointing finger, the master surveying the sky with a spyglass of his own. 'Drakk!' he bellowed to his kinsmen, prompting frantic scurrying as spear-tipped shafts were loaded into cradles, windlass cranks turned and sighters levelled.

'Did he say "drakk"?' asked Morgrim, joining them. Behind him, the dwarfs of Karak Varn had begun loading carts and wagons to ferry their plunder back to the hold. King Ironhandson's booming laughter overwhelmed the crackle of the inferno gutting the city as he saw his treasure hoard swelling.

Brynnoth and his warriors had come together, apart from the rest of the army. Heads bowed, listening to the sonorous tones of their king, they were holding a vigil for Agrin Fireheart.

'None other,' uttered Snorri, his voice full of loathing. 'I *hate* drakkal.'

Morgrim squinted but couldn't make out the beast or its rider clearly enough. It was a dark shape, sweeping between clouds of smoke.

'It could be Prince Imladrik.'

Snorri turned on him. 'Your pet elgi?'

'He is a friend to the dawi, and to me.'

'All elgi became enemies as soon as we crushed that army.' Drogor thumbed over his shoulder where the shattered horse guard still lay bleeding and broken. Most were probably dead by now. 'Do you think he'll still clasp your hand in a warrior's grip when he sees this?'

Morgrim ignored him, looking to his cousin.

'We cannot loose.'

Snorri clenched his teeth, considering Morgrim's request, but in the end had to shake his head.

'Can't risk it. That drakk will burn our camp to cinders, cousin.'

'We are at war now,' Drogor reminded them. 'Our stone was cast and more will be needed.'

Morgrim bit his tongue. He hoped it wasn't Imladrik. Not since the brodunk had he seen the elf prince, and despite the discord between their peoples, he still regarded him as a friend. He warranted that friendship would be tested if Imladrik saw what had transpired at Kor Vanaeth.

The low rumble of cracking stone presaged the collapse of the gatehouse, leaving the entire city razed and brought to rubble. A cheer rose up from the dwarfs of Zhufbar who were presiding over the demolition. Morgrim tried hard not to despise them for it.

Bolt throwers cranked to the highest possible elevation, the master of engineers looked over expectantly at the prince.

'The drakk!' bellowed one of the engineers, his crew trembling with fear at the sight of the monster.

A bestial shriek, chasm deep and full of hatred, echoed across the sky. It was a challenge. If the dragon rider was Imladrik, he had seen the carnage by now and had chosen to attack. Morgrim unslung his hammer, the runes flaring bright across its head.

Snorri ran out into the open ground, snarling to match the beast.

'Hold fast, let it come!' He swung up his axe, brandishing it at the sky and the winged shadow rapidly closing. 'Face me!' he roared. 'I am the *dreng drakk*. Taste this steel, for it will cleave you unto death!'

Morgrim ran after him, grabbing Snorri's arm. 'What are you doing?'

'You wanted me to hold off the bolt throwers, that is what I am doing.'

'Don't be an idiot.'

Snorri glanced at Morgrim over his shoulder. 'Still want to shake hands with the elgi?'

He looked back at Drogor, but the Karak Zorn dwarf hadn't moved and was watching the sky. Morgrim scowled before standing at his cousin's side.

'Get back,' Snorri warned. 'I don't need your arm in this fight.'

Morgrim was resolute. 'I am your cousin, blood is blood. Here I will stand.'

'Move! It comes for me.' His gaze flicked between his cousin and the growing shadow in the sky. The beat of heavy wings resolved above the wind.

'Then give the order to loose,' said Morgrim. 'That beast will burn us where we stand, unless you plan on slaying it with a single throw of your axe.'

Snorri looked like he was considering it.

'Don't be a stubborn fool. I don't want to die here.'

Something redolent of ash and sulphur tainted the breeze.

'Dragon's breath.' Morgrim readied his shield, knowing it was too late to retreat now.

So too did Snorri, but the prince had long embraced his fate.

'Let it come!' he shouted, hefting his battle axe. 'I'll kill it!'

The dragon dived, scales shimmering like fire in the sun. Like a red blade ripping through a bank of snow-shawled cloud, it angled towards the prince.

Shouts were coming from other parts of the field as more and more dwarfs heard and saw the beast.

A roar like a discordant bell pealed out of the heavens as dragon and rider cried in unison.

King Ironhandson was being barrelled away from danger by his warriors when he jabbed a finger towards the sky.

'Loose!' he cried. 'Bring the monster down!'

Some dwarfs hid behind their shields, others scurried behind carts and wagons. A few drew their weapons and rushed to the prince's side.

Fumbling their war machines, the engineers of Karak Varn unleashed a volley but by then the dragon had pulled out of its dive and climbed for higher skies. Every shaft went wide of the target.

Snorri raged.

'No! Come back,' he roared. 'Come back and face me, beast!'

'It's gone, cousin,' said Morgrim, pulling Snorri back.

'I could have killed it,' he spat, 'and fulfilled my destiny.'

'You will,' said Drogor, his eyes on the sky following the departing figure of the dragon. His voice was calming, and the two cousins climbed down from their heightened emotions at once. Both regarded the Karak Zorn dwarf as he turned his gaze on them.

'Not yet, but soon my prince. Now, we must march.'

Snorri shook his head as if coming out of a daze.

'Yes…' he murmured, blinking twice in close succession. 'Gather the kalans, sound the horn. We march for Tor Alessi.'

TEARS STREAMED DOWN Liandra's face, and Vranesh wailed in empathic anguish.

Kor Vanaeth was gone, sundered to ruins, and Fendaril was surely dead. She had failed her people, obsessing over vengeance and a desire to punish all druchii for what they had done. Her father knew she was volatile. Only now did she realise why Lord Athinol had sent her to the Old World. Soaring into the high skies, she welcomed the loneliness and the chill in her bones. It numbed her from feeling.

She had seen an army outside her city. Others would come, compelled by greed. Though her desire to return and take out her anger on the dwarfs was strong, she resisted. The other cities would need to be warned.

Tor Alessi was the greatest of them, so she would go there first.

Urging Vranesh, she tried to push the images of Kor Vanaeth from her mind but they burned, just as the city had burned, and would not fade.

➤➤ CHAPTER THIRTY-ONE ➤

A Shaming

THEY WERE UGLY creatures, the king decided.

Bulbous noses, ruddy cheeks, their jutting foreheads and brutish feet. Every cobble-booted step as they walked down the long aisle towards the throne put his teeth on edge. And the smell... Caledor held a pomander up to his nose to smother the worst of it. Sadly, it could not hide the dirt or hair of the beasts.

Caledor could easily believe they lived in holes in the ground.

So incongruous in his pristine hall, amongst the fluted archways and pale stone. The throne room of the palace at Lothern was so smooth and perfect. These *dwarfs* – even the name was lumpen – were just... gnarled.

He leaned over in his throne.

'They seem humbled,' he remarked, considering the sober expression of the one in front. Like the rest, he had a long plaited beard which was no doubt crawling with lice and other vermin. 'Do they seem humbled to you, brother?'

Imladrik was standing beside the throne, one hand on the hilt of Ifulvin, the other behind his armoured back.

Though he wasn't wearing a helmet, his face was hard as steel as if masked by one.

'They look proud to me. Defiant.'

Caledor shook his head. He wore robes, white as swan feather with a gold trim, and reclined like a dilettante. No effort had been made to adopt the mantle of the warrior king. In fact, since the dwarf vessel had found its way into the harbour of Lothern, little effort had been made at all.

Ushered from the city to the Phoenix King's court, few words beyond those which were necessary had been exchanged. A cohort of spearmen had shadowed the dwarf ambassador and his small retinue, the rest of the dwarfs staying behind with their crude-looking ship.

Word had come from the High King, brought by eagle riders, that he wished to parley. Amused, Caledor had granted his request. Less than two weeks later, the dwarfs had arrived. A fast crossing across the Great Ocean. Apparently, they had navigated its many perils through the efforts of their veteran captain and a dwarf wizard of some description. His mages had dismissed the feat as hedge magic, or some baser sorcery, but the fact remained that they had penetrated the veils and reached Ulthuan as swiftly as any elf vessel.

'I think they looked humbled,' Caledor reasserted, 'even grovelling.' He reached for his goblet, supping deeply and regarding the approaching dwarfs over its gilded rim.

There were six in total. Five were warriors, armed and armoured despite Imladrik's protests to the contrary, but one carried no weapon and wore a tunic and cloak. Obviously, this was their ambassador. He clutched a letter in his grubby little hands.

As the dwarf delegation came to within ten feet of the throne, Imladrik raised his hand and a line of spearmen stepped between them.

'That's far enough,' he said.

Caledor waved him down.

'Nonsense!' he cried. 'Let them come closer. Is this any way to treat guests of our court?'

If the dwarfs understood his mocking tone, none of them showed it.

Pausing in his theatre for a moment, Caledor looked to Hulviar who was standing on the opposite side to Imladrik.

'They *can* understand us, can't they, Hulviar?' he muttered.

'My lord,' one of the dwarfs spoke up.

The ambassador stepped forwards as the line of spearmen parted. He bowed.

'I can speak elven, if only rudimentarily.'

Caledor snorted, laughed. His eyebrows arched incredulously.

'Then you are a clever pig, aren't you?'

The ambassador became indignant. 'I am no pig, my lord.'

'You dig holes in mud where you then live, and protest you are not swine?' Caledor smiled haughtily. 'Intriguing. What do you make of my court?' he asked, gesturing expansively to the columns of white marble decorated with statues of griffons rampant, brooding dragons and majestic eagles. Banners and tapestries hung along the walls, which were punctuated by fist-sized rubies and sapphires. It was austere, but it was also magnificent.

'A fine antechamber, my lord.'

A nerve trembled in Caledor's cheek, the king unable to tell if the dwarf was now mocking him.

'Is your sty so much grander then?'

'I am no pig,' the ambassador repeated. 'I am Forek Grimbok, dawi of Karaz-a-Karak and representative of the High King.' He brandished the letter. 'And I bring his terms in this missive.'

Caledor arched an eyebrow, half distracted by drinking his wine. He drained the goblet and gestured to a nearby servant to bring another.

'Terms?' he said, focusing his full attention back on the dwarf.

'Yes,' said the ambassador. 'For peace. That is why we are here. That is why we have travelled across the Great Ocean from the Old World.'

Caledor smiled, nodded. '*Peace*, is it? Where was this

peace when Kor Vanaeth was attacked? Does your *king* have an answer for that in his letter?'

The ambassador struggled to hide his surprise. News about Kor Vanaeth had arrived only that morning, sent by Liandra Athinol, the city's custodian.

'It does not,' admitted the dwarf. 'Nor have I heard of such an attack.'

'Burned to the very stone,' said the king, dangerously.

Some of the other dwarfs shifted uncomfortably at the obvious change in mood. Several of their hands strayed to the hilts of their axes.

Imladrik hissed through clenched teeth, 'You should have let me disarm them.'

'Don't be silly, brother,' Caledor admonished. 'Forek, here... that is your name, isn't it? Yes, that's what you said. Forek, here, has said he knew nothing about it. Nor, apparently, did his king. It seems his subjects are roaming his lands killing and sacking cities according to whim. Is that about right, Forek?'

The ambassador's jaw hardened. He eyed the spearmen either side of them, caught the gaze of another dwarf who merely shook his head.

'I have said I know nothing of that.' He showed the letter again. 'Again I say, here are my High King's terms.'

Caledor leaned back in his throne.

'*High* king? Seems an odd turn of phrase for such a diminutive race.'

'He is lord of the Karaz Ankor, greatest dawi of the realm!'

'Yes, yes, I understand.' Caledor waved away the impassioned protests of the ambassador. 'Well then, you had better read these terms before more cities are put to the torch, hadn't you?'

The ambassador looked momentarily confused, but then cleared his throat and was about to read when Imladrik stepped from the throne's dais and took the letter.

'Tromm,' he muttered under his breath with a nod to the dwarf, who replied in the same way.

He glared at Caledor, who seemed disinterested but there was a glint of something unpleasant in his eye, an idea forming that Imladrik hoped would not come to fruition.

The Master of Dragons read swiftly. His expression darkened further when he was done.

'Well then,' asked Caledor, 'what are the dwarf king's terms?'

Imladrik met his gaze, knowing the response before it was given.

'He asks for recompense and apology for the hostilities directed at his people. Furthermore, he demands a cessation to all further violence against the dwarfs.'

'A long letter for such a short list of terms,' said Caledor.

'There is more, which you would not be interested in, my king.'

'You are right about that, brother. The griping and posturing of these mud-dwellers is not my concern.'

He nodded to Hulviar.

'Seize them!' snarled the seneschal.

Twenty spearmen levelled their weapons at the dwarfs, but the warriors were ready with axes drawn and smashed several of the tips aside.

One dwarf was pierced in the back and side before he could swing. Another was brought to heel with three points at his neck. A third was pinioned in the leg and couldn't move. A fourth was similarly trapped. The fifth, their leader, rolled beneath the jabbing spears and came up to bury his axe in an elf's shield. The blow split it in two, breaking the elf's arm and drawing blood.

The ambassador cried out, 'Gilias!' as the dwarf advanced on another spearman, barging into him and bearing the elf down.

'They mean to kill us!' cried Gilias.

Caledor was up and out of his throne in an eyeblink. His sword, by his side until that moment, was now drawn and sunk halfway up the long blade into Gilias's chest.

The dwarf grunted once, unable to comprehend what had happened at first, then he spat a stream of blood and collapsed.

Caledor turned to his spearmen, who had completely subdued the dwarfs.

'Hold them,' he said.

They were chewing and tugging their beards, moaning in their crude language and glaring first at the King and then at their fallen kinsman, his life pooling beneath him.

'Thagi!' shouted the ambassador. He'd balled his fists but with a spear tip at his neck was powerless to do anything.

Caledor rounded on him.

'Brother, wait...' Imladrik tried to intercede but the king pushed him aside.

'You burn my cities,' he said to the dwarf, 'and come here expecting apology and recompense? I do not give apologies, *pig*, I grant pleas. You and your kind are worthy of neither.'

'Let us go,' the ambassador warned. 'And allow us to bear Gilias Thunderbrow's body back to his kalan, you thagging pointy-eared bastard.'

Sneering, Caledor looked Forek up and down. He reached out to seize his beard, pulled it hard until the dwarf ambassador winced.

'You are an uncouth creature,' he told him, smiling cruelly.

'I cannot be a party to this,' said Imladrik, shaking his head, and went to leave before his brother's command rooted him to the spot.

'You'll stay and witness this,' he said. 'I want you to see what your lassitude has bred in these pigs.'

Imldrik glowered, but he obeyed.

'Let us go,' said Forek. 'What are you going to do?' There was fear in his voice that warred with the anger.

Caledor released the fistful of hair in his grasp.

'You know, I am not ignorant of your ways,' he said, backing off.

Hulviar had drawn a long dagger from his belt. So had several of the spearmen who were otherwise unencumbered by pinning down the dwarfs.

'I understand you place great importance in your beards, is that right?'

'Brother, no,' Imladrik warned.

'Stand fast!' snapped Caledor, whirling around to glare at him before returning his attention to the dwarfs.

Forek glowered, tears of rage welling in his eyes.

His voice was barely above a whisper as he pleaded, 'Do not do this. I beg of you.'

'Now, he pleads. Now, he begs,' said Caledor. 'Too late, pig. My brother was right. You are proud and defiant.' He raised his finger as if finding the answer to a question that had so far eluded him. 'But I know how to humble you.'

'Please…'

'Caledor…' Imladrik warned him again.

'Silence, brother. I am your king, now do as bidden.'

'Please,' said Forek. 'Dreng tromm, it is our legacy, our ancestry. It will bring great shame on my clan, on all our clans.'

Caledor's eyes were cold and pitiless as the stone of his hall as he regarded the ambassador.

'Shave them. Every lice-infested inch.'

Hulviar and the other elves that had drawn their daggers came forwards.

The dwarfs struggled, but were held by the spearmen.

'Dreng tromm, dreng tromm,' wailed the ambassador, and he and his retinue broke out in a raft of curses in their native tongue.

Caledor returned to his throne to watch.

The elves were not kind in their ministrations. Skin was cut, punches thrown and blood shed on the pristine white of the Phoenix Court.

The dwarfs fought, they gnawed and kicked and scratched, but to no avail. The elves held them and did not let them up until every bruised and savaged inch of their faces was shorn.

Throughout the shaming, Caledor looked on impassively.

'See, brother,' he said, watching the dwarfs squirm and quail, 'I said they were humbled.'

He turned to Imladrik, but the Master of Dragons was already walking away.

◄ CHAPTER THIRTY-TWO ►

The Runes Fail

In the deeps below Everpeak the clang of hammer hitting anvil resounded. For the last eight years and more it had done so with barely more than a moment's respite.

Morek spoke the rites with sonorous solemnity, broke the karadurak, tempered the star-metal and from it fashioned such artifice as only happened once in a generation.

Hissing vapour rushed from the barrel. A gromril blade, its runes refulgent in the forge flame, came forth from its raging depths.

'*Drengudrakk,*' he intoned, naming the weapon clutched in his gauntleted hand.

Ranuld Silverthumb, looking on from the shadows, merely nodded.

'Tromm, Morek,' he uttered, 'and so the rhun is struck and the rite spoken. Metal has come from fire and water, bound by the rituals of earth and air. All the four elements are bound within, trapped by meteoric iron sent from the vaults of heaven.'

Morek looked exhausted, lathered in sweat and soot, his chest, face and fingers burned. But he was exultant.

Bowing his head, Ranuld told him, 'You are now a true master of the rhun.'

A grimace stole upon the runelord's face and he clutched his shoulder suddenly, teeth clenched tight in his mouth.

'Master!' Morek went to him at once, the blade left upon the anvil, but Ranuld stopped him with his upraised palm.

'No,' he rasped, his anguish almost palpable. 'Set it properly. Do it!'

Morek was caught by indecision. He looked once to the blade and then to his master, who was doubled up in pain.

He was by Ranuld's side a moment later, helping the venerable dwarf to his seat in the forge.

'Pipeweed…' he gasped, pointing fervouredly at a small stone box resting on a shelf.

Morek left him to retrieve the box.

Hands shaking, Ranuld opened it, took the pipe and the weed from within, stoked the cradle and lit it.

After a few draughts, his hands steadied, the pain eased and he breathed again.

His eyes were watering, from the seizure or something else, Morek could not tell. He regarded his apprentice with a crestfallen expression, shaking his head.

'What is it, master? Are you–'

'Wazzock!' snapped the runelord. 'Look at that,' he said. 'Look!'

The rune axe upon the anvil had a tiny fissure running through the metal. It was cracked, ruined.

'The magic was not properly bound,' Ranuld told him. Struggling but refusing any help, the runelord got to his feet and shuffled off. 'You should have left me. The rhun is all that matters. Legacy is all I have left to give.' He turned, snarling, 'Let me die next time, and save your worthless concern.'

He tromped from the forge, headed for the deeper vault where Morek was forbidden.

'Not ready,' he chuntered to himself beneath his breath. 'Not nearly ready.' Slowly shaking his head, he disappeared into the soot and smoke. Before he was lost to the darkness completely, his voice rang out, 'Again, do it again.'

Morek slumped to his haunches, regarding the broken metal on the anvil.

Taking up his tongs, he gripped the sundered blade and returned it to the fire.

SPEAKING THROUGH THE magic of rune stones was not so easy. Ranuld leaned heavily on his staff, standing before the dokbar, and saw little of Thorik Oakeneye. It was as if some great arachnarok, like the beasts that once roamed the deeps, had spun its silken threads across the shield's surface and obscured it from sight. As if he were trapped at the bottom of a long well, Thorik's voice was muffled and echoed. As Ranuld listened, his expression clouded.

Thorik spoke of a 'great shaming', of 'misdeeds' and 'foulness beyond countenance'.

Throughout his report, which must have taken a great deal of strength to send, Ranuld tugged his beard, muttering, 'Dreng tromm, dreng tromm…'

Perfidy beyond reckoning had been done.

When Thorik was finished, Ranuld looked his fellow runelord in the eye.

'The conclave must gather at Karaz-a-Karak.'

Thorik nodded.

'As soon as I reach the Sea Hold, I will make all haste.'

'War has come, unleashed by the arrogance of youth,' Ranuld said. 'The gronti-duraz must walk. Together we will wake them from slumber.'

'Tromm, my lord.'

'Tromm,' uttered Ranuld, bowing his head as Thorik faded and the dokbar returned to silver once again.

Regarding the silent ranks of stone golems, Ranuld prayed to Grungni that they would listen.

⫷ CHAPTER THIRTY-THREE ⫸

Mustering the Throng

'STAND ASIDE!'

Rundin's voice was laced with threat, but the three gold-masters did not yield.

'King Grum has insisted he not be disturbed,' protested one.

'War has come to the Karaz Ankor,' said Rundin. 'All dawi must stand and fight, including the skarrens.'

'Edicts of the mountains do not bind the hills,' said a second.

'I am the king's protector,' declared Rundin, shoving aside the dwarfs, who were wise enough not to resist.

'He is alone, what does he need protecting from?' asked another.

Rundin threw open the doors to the counting house, sparing the goldmasters a final scathing glance.

'Himself,' he answered, stepping inside.

The counting house was dark, even the lamps had been doused, and it stank of sweat. Another stench accompanied it, something acerbic that stung the nostrils.

Rundin's nose wrinkled when he identified what the smell was.

'Grungni's oath…' he muttered, realising just how far his king had fallen.

Skarnag Grum was crouched naked before a candle flame, surrounded by gold. He almost bathed in it, watching the coins trickle from his grasp, delighting in the way they flashed as they caught the light.

'*Gorl* is *galaz* is *gorlm* and *bryn*…'

In Khazalid there were over four hundred different words and expressions for gold. Grum was reciting every single one in a fevered cantrip.

'…is *konk* is *ril* and *frorl* and *kurz*…'

'Valaya's mercy,' Rundin breathed, stepping into the corona of light cast by the candle. 'What has become of you, my noble King Grum?'

At the mention of his name, the king of the hill dwarfs looked up with rheumy, manic eyes.

'Run-din.' His mouth struggled to form the word, drooling saliva.

Holding back his anguish, Rundin knelt beside the king.

'Yes, my liege,' he said, cradling his cheek like a father to a beardling. 'It is me.'

Capricious as winter snow, Skarnag Grum recoiled from his protector, his face a mask of accusation.

'Why are you here?' he snapped, gathering his gold to him, spilling piles of it and snatching at the errant coins. 'You want my gold, don't you? You want it!'

Rundin stood up, shaking his head.

'No, my liege,' he said calmly. 'But you must leave this place. Come with me now.'

Skarnag's eyes narrowed. 'So you can slip in when I'm absent. You have the look of a *skaz* about you, Rundin.' He stood, a filthy loincloth the only scrap of clothing to preserve a shred of dignity. 'My protector turned skaz,' he said, jabbing a finger, 'coveting my gold from afar, waiting for his chance to steal it! Is that it? Eh? Eh!'

Rundin did not want to see any more. He turned around, the king cursing his every step until he sank back down amidst his hoard.

Wiping the tears from his eyes, Rundin paused as he

reached the door. Skarnag Grum was still muttering,

'And *renk* is *glam* and *hnon* is *geln* and *bruz*…'

The goldmasters were waiting for him on the other side, their faces caught between fear and admonishment.

'There will be consequences for what you did,' said one.

'Defiance of the king is an act worthy of grudgement,' said another.

Rundin did not meet their eyes. Such wretched dwarfs who had so utterly failed their king were unworthy of his attention.

'Whatever that dawi was in there,' he said, leaving the goldmasters in his wake, 'he is not our king.'

Beyond the Great Hall, which led from the counting house, a long gallery was thronged with hill dwarfs. News had travelled fast of King Gotrek Starbreaker's declaration of war. Clans were amassing, unsure what to do, waiting for the orders of their king. Orders that Rundin knew would not come.

'Kerrik Sternhawk!' he bellowed at one idle-looking warrior. 'Follow me.'

The dwarf obeyed at once. He was fresh-faced with barely a growth of beard, a youth but one that Rundin knew he could trust.

'Thane Rundin?' asked the beardling, falling into step with the king's protector.

'You are the Kro's fastest runner,' he said. 'I need you to convey a message of the utmost importance and secrecy. Can you do that?'

Kerrik looked concerned and confused as they left the gallery and walked out into the light, but nodded immediately.

'Good,' said Rundin. 'Relate this exactly as spoken…'

TRACING HIS FINGER across a narrow line on the map, Snorri sucked his teeth.

'Elgi will be thronging the roads,' he said.

'And if the last army we fought is any gauge, the numbers will be greater,' Morgrim suggested.

'They are bloody greater the closer we get to Tor-chuffing-Alessi,' snapped Thagdor, finding the elf words difficult to pronounce.

Since they were not dwarf holds, they had not bothered to name the elf cities in Khazalid. It had seemed unimportant.

Since Kor Vanaeth they had met the elves in battle three more times. On each occasion the dwarfs had been victorious, but on each occasion they had taken losses.

During the last engagement, a band of swift, bow-armed riders had destroyed several of the Karak Varn war machines. In another, over two hundred clansmen had died to the combined sorcery of three elven mages.

The rearguard, made up of clans from the Sea Hold, had been harried for over six days during the last march. Eighteen warriors lay dead as a result. Despite the best efforts of their rangers, the dwarfs could not bring the perpetrators to heel.

Arrows were the worst – the elves possessed uncanny accuracy. Digging graves for dwarfs slain by arrows had delayed Snorri's army by several days already.

Snorri turned to King Brynnoth, who had promised further reinforcements from Barak Varr.

'Any news from your hold, my king?'

'Some,' he said, chewing on a thigh bone he had divested of the meat several minutes ago. 'Four wagons bearing arms and armour were lost whilst crossing the Vaults, a grudge against Dammin Cloud-eye for his ineptitude,' he grumbled. 'Another message speaks of foraging in the forest for wood and provisions when the throng was attacked.'

'Attacked?' asked Morgrim. 'We are close to the forest, our route might take us into the neighbouring Grey Mountains.'

Brynnoth's face reddened. 'Said it was haunted by unquiet spirits. Trees came alive, they reckon.'

'I have heard similar tales from our cousins of Karak Norn,' uttered Valarik fearfully, making the protective sigil of Valaya.

Snorri frowned, unconvinced. Thagdor had to stifle a laugh.

'Who leads this throng?' asked the prince.

'Ungrim Shaftcleaver,' said Brynnoth. 'A trusted thane of my hold, or so I thought.'

'Perhaps he was addled by the sun?' suggested Drogor. 'I have seen such things happen before in the Southlands.'

'In winter?' said Thagdor, incredulous.

Snorri exhaled ruefully. 'It doesn't matter. Tell Shaft-cleaver to get his warriors here as quickly as he can. We are now thirty thousand dawi, just over, and there's still a long way to go to the elgi city.'

'Which route do we take then, cousin?' asked Morgrim. 'The passes through the mountains, risking the wrath of the Fey Forest?' He glared at Thagdor, who stopped chuckling to offer an apology, before carrying on, 'Or march down the Brundin Road and walk right up to their gates?'

'I'll happily ruddy knock at their doors,' boasted Thagdor.

'Aye,' agreed Ironhandson, who was still sore over the wrecking of his war engines. 'Let them see us coming. Likely the pointy-ears will soil themselves first and then flee.'

Snorri doubted that. The elves were not as soft-skinned and callow-hearted as any of the dwarfs had believed.

Crouched over the map, his lords arrayed around him, he found he was at an impasse. Though he would never admit it, he had given little thought to what might happen after Kor Vanaeth. So far, he had simply marched onwards, headed for Tor Alessi and fighting whatever stood in his way. Now he had three kings at his behest, as well as their armies. Thirty thousand of his kinsmen were relying on his judgement and leadership. How Snorri wished his father was there at that moment, and felt a prick of regret at their parting and his actions since.

'Which is it to be then, lad?' asked Thagdor, stabbing at the map with his finger. 'Road or mountain pass?'

Snorri rubbed his beard. Both ways were perilous, and so far no rangers had returned from their scouting to offer any idea of the sort of numbers the dwarfs faced at Tor Alessi. It was their largest settlement, but Kor Vanaeth had fallen easily enough. Surely, this Tor Alessi would capitulate in similar fashion.

'Cousin,' muttered Morgrim, 'you must make a decision.'

Snorri answered through clenched teeth, 'I am thinking.' He had settled on a course and was about to tell his generals when a shout came from deeper in the camp. Through the parting throngs, there hurried a beardling, a runner.

'Prince Snorri,' he gasped, struggling for breath. The youth kneeled until Snorri told him to get up and spit out whatever he had come to tell him. 'Rangers, my liege,' said the youth, 'from Karaz-a-Karak.'

At some instinctive sign Snorri looked up over the runner's shoulder and beheld a face he hadn't seen for some time. Despite the obvious tension associated with the ranger's arrival, he smiled.

'Tromm, Furgil.'

SUPPING DEEP OF the black beer in his tankard, Furgil smacked his lips and sighed.

'Been a while since I had the taste of proper ale on my tongue,' he said. 'Grog has been all we had to sustain us for the last two weeks.'

The pathfinder had arrived in camp with nineteen other rangers, all well-worn and travel-weary but clearly having seen little actual battle. Apparently, they had skirmished with orcs and goblins of the mountains, even seen a band of elven riders in the distance, but little else. Wisely, their enemies were moving away from the dwarf holds of the Worlds Edge. Should they not, they would be trampled by a shield wall of some fifty thousand dwarfs or more. Warriors were amassing; the High King had called the clans and declared war.

WHEN HE HAD heard of the ambassador's shaming, he and his guardians, Snorri had spat numerous oaths of vengeance. Grimbok was no friend to him, but he was a dwarf and no son of Grungni should endure such mistreatment. When his apoplexy had passed, he fell into a deep introspection, chewing at his beard as his father might have done in a similar situation.

Snorri reclined on a leather-backed throne sitting in the lee of his tent. A hearthguard stood nearby, eyes fixed on the horizon line that presaged storm. Grey, black clouds streaked low and fast, swelling with each passing moment and filling the sky with an endless gloom.

'A wretched day to march,' said the prince, drawing on his pipe. He was fully armoured, only his war helm resting against the leg of his throne, and shifted uncomfortably in his full panoply of battle. 'I would prefer a steam bath and the attention of a buxom rinn.'

'Wouldn't we all,' remarked Furgil, taking another pull of the black beer and leaving the foam to evaporate on his beard. 'Except the bath, of course. An annual *dunkin* is just fine for me, my prince.'

'Am I still your prince?' Snorri asked curtly. 'You have brought message of my father, his intention to make war, but said nothing of his mood.'

The tent was pitched on a rugged hillock that offered a decent view of the encampment. With his back to his lord, Furgil swept his gaze across the numerous snapping pennants, clan icons and banners that were mounted on the army's tents. Dwarfs were massed outside them, some sparring, others merely sitting. They encircled fires, clutching tankards like he was, smoking or muttering. Some recounted grudges, others sang songs or bemoaned the weather and the air. Dwarfs were not so fond of air, at least not that which smelled of grass and river and bird. They longed for heat, for ash and smoke, for the reek of the deep earth.

There were a host of machineries, mostly under tarp but some being tended by engineers and their journeymen. He saw ballistae and catapults of varying size and girth. Many bore the rune of Karak Varn.

'You have gathered quite the host,' said Furgil, turning to face Snorri at last, 'and, yes, you are still my prince and always shall be.' He bowed his head, low in respect and fealty. 'Your father is angry,' he said, 'and asks me to bid you wait for his army to reach you before marching further.'

Snorri scowled. 'I will not be cowed by him, Furgil. When you return, you must tell him that. This–' he gestured to the throng of dwarfs below, '–is *my* army. He may have declared war but it is I who have waged it first.'

'As you wish, my prince. I merely convey the message.'

Snorri's scowl turned into a questioning frown, and he leaned forwards. 'Have all the holds mustered?'

Furgil nodded, draining his tankard before answering. 'Aye. As well as the clans of the capital, your father the High King has Karak Drazh and the mining clans of Gunbad and Silverspear with his banner. Even Varnuf of the Eight Peaks marches, along with the holds of the south. North, there's King Grundin and a contingent from Karak Ungor who have already suffered from elgin perfidy.'

Snorri raised an eyebrow in query.

'Bagrik, their king, was slain by treachery,' Furgil explained. 'The length and breadth of the Worlds Edge, even the Vaults, the Grey and the Black, are bound to this war.'

'Not all the realms of the dawi, though,' said Snorri, his eyes never leaving the ranger who lowered his gaze in shame.

'No, not all. Not yet.'

'You know something my father and I do not?'

'Only hope, my prince. Hope in an old friend to do what is right. That is all.'

Snorri laughed. 'I expected my father to be less understanding.'

'Oh, make no mistake, my prince, grudges against Thagdor, Brynnoth and Valarik have been writ. Retribution for their transgression will be taken in wergeld or actual blood, the Starbreaker has avowed it, but not until the war is done.'

'They best hope it claims them, then,' muttered Snorri, knowing well his father's wrath.

Furgril merely nodded.

'Tromm for the beer, but I should be on my way.'

Snorri didn't answer immediately. His mind was elsewhere, back during his carefree days of adventuring with Morgrim in the lower deeps. He glanced down into the encampment, knowing his cousin was somewhere below, preparing for the march. It would have to wait, Snorri decided.

'Tell my father we will hold here for a week but no more. If his throng hasn't reached us by then we will have to march.'

'I'll tell him, my prince.'

Furgil was already on his way, signalling to his rangers who waited silently for him below, when Snorri called out to him.

'You are a loyal servant of the Karaz Ankor, Furgil. It's a pity your countrymen are not like you.'

Furgil paused but didn't answer. He left as quietly as he'd arrived, headed east to the host of the High King.

'Summon my war council,' Snorri said to the hearthguard once Furgil had gone.

◄ CHAPTER THIRTY-FOUR ►

War of the Beard

'THAT IS WHAT they are calling it, my king.'

'Even for elgi that is bold,' said Gotrek. 'They mock us with the very name of this conflict.'

Thurbad didn't disagree, so just nodded.

After a short rest in the Mootlands of the half-folk, the army of Karaz-a-Karak and its vassal lords was preparing to move on. Furgil had recently returned bringing news of the prince's intention to wait for his father. A week was not long, however, and winter ground made for a difficult march, even for dwarfs. Time could not be wasted if they were to meet Snorri's deadline.

Gotrek cast a mantle of red velvet, trimmed with eagle feathers, over his shoulders. Thurbad attached the pauldron pins, then tightened the clasps of the king's gromril armour so it hugged his waist.

He groaned. 'Been too long vacillating in my throne room,' said Gotrek. 'Must have gotten fat.'

'Winter padding, my king.'

Gotrek smirked at the hearthguard, who hadn't even paused to acknowledge his joke.

'Aye, something like that.'

He would have preferred a hold hall, a roaring hearth at his back as he donned his armour, but out on campaign a tent would have to suffice. Gotrek scowled at its weakness, wishing for solid stone above and about him. The wars with the greenskins and the monsters of the Ungdrin were vicious affairs, cramped, brutal and close up, but at least they were beneath ground. Sky and forest were not to the High King's liking, and made him uneasy.

'Should I have marched before now, Thurbad?' he asked candidly.

Now the hearthguard paused, halfway to buckling a leather weapons belt.

'You may speak your mind,' Gotrek told him. 'Have no fear of grudgement.'

Thurbad looked the High King in the eye. 'No, my king. You did what was necessary to protect the Karaz Ankor. A calm head should always prevail over a rash one, or so my father always said.'

'Then he was a wise dawi, your father.'

'Tromm, he was.'

'It would have spared Grimbok his fate, your hearthguard too and the life of Gilias Thunderbrow, if I had thrown in with my son and marched.'

'He is in the Hall of the Ancestors now,' said Thurbad. 'I could wish no more for him than that. As for the others...' He looked away for a moment, and Gotrek knew he was picturing the wretched dwarfs, their beards shorn, their ancestry taken from them. Even in death, their shame would cling to them like a miasma, bound forever to Gazul's Gate through which the unquiet could not pass.

Gotrek put his hand on the hearthguard's shoulder.

'We will avenge them.'

Thurbad nodded, buckled the High King's belt and stepped back.

'You are klad, my king,' he said, handing Gotrek his axe.

'To think,' said Gotrek as he took the weapon in his hands, 'we were once allies.' He ran his thumb over the blade, drawing a ruby of blood that ran all the way along the axe's gromril edge.

'Will you punish him, my king?'

'Snorri did what he thought was right. He predicted war and war we have got, sacking the elgi settlement didn't cause that. It was already done when our kin died on the road and Agrin Fireheart lost his life. But, yes,' added the High King, 'I will punish him.'

Over fifty thousand amassed in the army of the High King. More were coming from the north and south but would not reach them in time. It wouldn't matter. Gotrek was resolved to meet up with his son and march on Tor Alessi until its walls were down and its people ash on the breeze.

'War of the Beard,' he snorted, suppressing a sneer. 'They are owed, Thurbad. The scales are unbalanced and I mean to redress them with death. It is a different conflict we shall bring to the elgi, not of beards, but a War of Vengeance.'

THE KINGS OF Kagaz Thar and Kazad Mingol looked around furtively.

Even surrounded by their warriors, shrouded in the gloom of the shaded glade in the forests beyond Kazad Kro, they looked uncomfortable and slightly afraid.

'Why have you brought us here, beardling?' King Kruk asked of Kerrik Sternhawk.

The liege-lord of Kagaz Thar was dressed in a leather cloak fashioned to look like overlapping leaves. His armour was rough and rugged like tree bark and he wore muddy kohl around his deep-set eyes. An unkempt beard framed an angular face with bushy eyebrows and a flat knot for a nose. Gnarled as oak, bitter as a winter storm, King Kruk was far from happy at being summoned by Skarnag Grum. 'The High King doesn't venture from the Kro. Ever. What is the meaning of this?'

'Aye,' agreed King Orrik. He'd looped his thumbs beneath his belt and rocked back on his heels as he eyed the arboreal gloom nervously. 'In times of war, we should hole up behind walls, shut our tower doors and gates until this wind of conflict passes by.'

The King of Kazad Mingol wore a tall helm that resembled the towering keep from which his hold hall took its name. His beard was long, bound by clasps of iron, and his moustaches curled in blond loops beneath his nose. His teeth seldom parted when he spoke, a portcullis ever shut, his mouth a tight line that rarely broke a smile. Lamellar armour clad his body, and one of his warriors hefted a large shield that bore the emblem of his hold, a tower fort impervious to attack.

'Please,' uttered Kerrik, who could not be further out of his depth if he were swimming the length of the Black Water in full armour, 'all will be explained soon.'

'Three hours we have been here already!' snapped Orrik, glowering at the youth. 'When do you expect *soon* to be?'

'I…' Kerrik looked around but could find no sign or suggestion of his lord. 'I don't know.'

'This is a lot of *krut*,' said Kruk, gesturing to his warriors. 'I have waited long enough.'

'You're leaving?' asked Orrik, his indignation vanishing. 'But what of Grum? You would defy his summons?'

King Kruk paused, as did his warriors. Grum was a fearsome and brutal king. Neither Kruk nor Orrik wanted to incur his wrath, but waiting in the forest for something that might never happen could be just as deadly to their health.

'It does not sound like Grum to me. Why would he leave his counting house, the warmth of his hall to meet us out here?' He leaned in close, hissing. 'There might be elgi, or the Starbreaker's warriors. And I wish for neither an arrow in the back nor to be pressed into the mountain king's horde.'

Orrik nodded, seeing the sense in that.

Both were set to leave when a voice rang out of the shadows.

'Hold,' it said, as Rundin stepped into the light.

'Ravenhelm?' asked Kruk, turning.

Orrik eyed him shrewdly. 'The High King's champion. What are you doing here?'

'Looking for some skarren backbone, but seeing little,' he snapped. 'This beardling has more courage.'

Kruk snarled. 'Be careful, king's thane,' he said, gesturing to his warriors.

One hefted his axe until he heard the tautening string of a crossbow.

Orrik looked around. Over twenty of Rundin's rangers surrounded them, though they had yet to take aim. Silent as shadows, they had crept up on the dwarf host without being noticed.

'I brought them so you would listen,' said Rundin.

Grumbling, both kings turned around and settled in to hear what the champion had to say.

'I'm not here on Grum's behalf,' Rundin began.

'Then whose are you here on?' Kruk's eyes narrowed.

'Our people's, the skarrenawi.'

'You mean your own,' said Kruk. 'What are you brewing, king's thane?'

'He speaks of betrayal, dressed in the cloak of patriotism,' spat Orrik, hawking up a fat gob of phlegm at the champion's feet.

'Aye,' said Rundin, advancing on the two liege-lords until they were almost nose to nose. 'I do. But not of mine, of our High King's.'

'Thagging traitor!' Kruk made to move, slipping his hand around the haft of his axe, but Rundin put him down with a swift punch. Now the rangers brought up their crossbows, keeping King Kruk's warriors in check.

'I am sorry, my king,' said Rundin, 'but I need you to listen.' He glared at Orrik who was just releasing the grip of his hammer, adding, '*Both* of you.'

Kruk was rubbing his jaw but got to his feet unaided. Begrudgingly, he conceded.

'Go on then, speak your piece.'

Rundin nodded and stepped back, adopting a less threatening posture.

'Our liege-lord is mad. His mind is lost to the yellow fever.'

Orrik was shaking his head, incredulous. 'What do you mean, "lost"?'

Rundin rounded on him. '*Gorl* and *galaz* and *bryn*. Gold, King Orrik. Skarnag Grum had succumbed to the gold lust. He drools in his counting house, oblivious to his kingdom and his people. I entered in search of counsel and found not a king, but a zaki in his place.'

'Grum has always been covetous, but the fever?' said Kruk. 'I can't believe that.'

'Come and see it for yourselves if you must,' said Rundin.

Orrik sniffed with mild contempt. 'Even if he has succumbed to the fever, what care is it of ours?'

'Our High King is lost, and one of you must take his place.'

The glint of pride shimmered in the eyes of both kings as they weighed up the possibilities. That pride vanished with the champion's next words.

'To lead us into the war.'

'Out of the question!' Kruk was already leaving. He glared at the nearest ranger, daring him to shoot.

Orrik squared up to Rundin. He was taller than most dwarfs, even the champion, but the extra foot he had on him didn't make Rundin balk.

'You're a fool, Ravenhelm. Why would we go to war when we can batten our hatches and seal our gates? We'll weather this storm. It'll blow itself out soon enough.'

'It won't,' Rundin told him. 'You think the elgi will yield? Did you not hear what their king did to our ambassadors? He shaved them, sheared the hair from their faces like they were hruk. If that is his reaction to a banner of peace, what do you think he'll do to a host of dawi under the banner of war?'

Now surrounded by his warriors, Kruk looked over his shoulder. 'The Starbreaker will crush them, send them back across the sea. Why should we get involved?'

'Because we are dawi by any other name!' Rundin declared. 'Our blood runs the same as the mountain clans. We should take up arms, honour them with our pledge of allegiance.'

'For what?' asked Orrik, backing down when he realised Rundin couldn't be intimidated by his size. 'So our throngs can dwindle in the war, so our hold halls can ring empty, their coffers depleting as they're spent on armour and blades? There is no profit in war, not for us, not this way. It is Gotrek at whom the elgi have taken umbrage. Let him fight them.'

'Don't you think that the war will come to us?' Rundin asked of Orrik's back, the other king now departing too. 'I cannot muster the warriors of Kazad Kro or the rest of the skarrens without your help. With it, we can join with Gotrek, end this war quickly. I know it!'

Neither Kruk nor Orrik answered. They were leaving and the rangers would not stop them. No hill dwarf would draw on another, not without grudge.

'It will come to us,' Rundin called after them. 'Not this day perhaps, maybe not for a decade or more, but war will rage and come to our gates. Alone we will perish, but together we have a chance.'

'Go back to the Kro, Rundin of the Ravenhelm,' Orrik replied, slowly disappearing into the wooded darkness. Kruk was already long gone. 'And serve your king as you pledged oath to do so.'

Rundin seethed. His teeth were clenched, his fists tight as his knuckles cracked impotently. 'I serve my people,' he said to the air and the shadows.

'What shall we do, my lord?' Kerrik Sternhawk was at his side, wringing his hands fearfully.

'Go back,' said Rundin. 'There is nothing else *to* do.' He met the beardling's gaze. 'Speak to no one of this.'

'I won't, my lord.'

'I have to convince them, Kerrik, that this is right.'

'What if you can't, my lord?'

'Then we'll all be doomed, lad. Every thagging one of us.'

THE ROWS OF dwarfs marching from the flank of the mountain seemed endless.

Soaring high above a thin layer of cloud on the back of Vranesh, Liandra had never seen so many of the mud-dwellers in one place.

Since the sacking of Kor Vanaeth and her arrival at Tor Alessi, she had learned King Caledor had insulted them. Some grievous slight had made their oafish chieftain decide upon war. Liandra relished the opportunity to wet her blade on the dwarfs, mete out her revenge for what they did to her city.

She was tempted to fly lower, harass the dwarf army's flanks and rearguard, spit flame over their war machines, but decided against it. A lucky shot from one of their ballistae could shear Vranesh's wing easily enough, and there were many in the wagon train that followed the armoured dwarf hordes. Doubtless, many more would be marching under the earth, along roads lost to darkness and filth. Perhaps the elves could flood the tunnels and drown a great many mud-dwellers before they even reached Tor Alessi. She decided to suggest it to Prince Arlyr upon her return.

It would almost be worth losing her quarry to see that. The dark elf had been close, the one from the gorge that had left its spoor and eluded her for eight years. In her mind, Liandra had transformed the creature into a spectre of the one that had killed her mother on the burning shores of Cothique. Though the perpetrator of her mother's murder was dead, this spectre represented everything Liandra hated about the dark elves. After the dwarfs had been defeated at Tor Alessi's gates, an outcome of which she was certain, she would resume her hunt.

Dark elf, dwarf, it didn't matter to Liandra. Imladrik was right, she *was* a supremacist, utterly convinced of the asur's superiority over all sentient races. Crushing the dwarfs in the Old World was the first step towards dominion. Then, with a strong and thriving colony on the mainland, the high elves could turn their attention to Naggaroth and the overthrow of Malekith.

Having seen all she needed to, Liandra turned Vranesh about and headed back towards Tor Alessi. In her head, she saw the flames renewed, first at Cothique then Kor Vanaeth. She had seen something else too, a third vision framed in fire, but had banished that one from her thoughts with a shudder. Steel returned quickly, hardening her heart, strengthening her arm and conviction.

'All of them will burn,' she whispered to Vranesh.

The beast growled, low and threatening, its voice lost on the wind.

SEVERAL DAYS HAD passed since their close encounter with the dragon rider. Drutheira had no idea why they had been spared, but she had no intention of wasting her reprieve either. She sat cross-legged in front of a pyre of blood-slicked skulls, hunkered beneath the half-broken roof of a ruined outhouse. It had been a trading post before the dwarfs had razed it. There were no bodies, but the raiders-turned-fugitives had discovered several graves buried in the hard earth.

Behind her, Malchior and Ashniel were flensing the skin and meat off the elf riders Sevekai and his warriors had killed. The small band of reavers had been utterly unprepared for the assassins and died without any fight. Their headless corpses would be left to rot, sustenance for the carrion flock already circling overhead.

She was weak. They all were, and she needed the knives and quarrels of the shades for the communion of blood with her dark lord.

Crimson smoke was already coiling from the piled skulls when she summoned the other sorcerers.

'Come forth, make the circle,' she hissed, her limbs trembling.

Both her fellow coven members looked gaunt and wasted. Their efforts to hide from the dragon rider had been taxing in the extreme. Malchior was weary, but Ashniel managed to make daggers with her gaze.

'Sit. Now,' Drutheira commanded.

Once the circle was made, she began to incant the rites. Red vapour coalesced into something more corporeal and Drutheira felt the chill of Naggaroth knife into her through her robes. She wrapped her cloak tighter, speaking the words of communion faster and faster, Malchior and Ashniel echoing every syllable.

A face half-materialised in the crimson fog but then collapsed as swiftly as it formed.

'No…' Drutheira barely had breath to voice her anguish.

Communion had failed, or rather it was *made* to fail.

She sagged, head slumping into her lap, and wept.

'What is it?' hissed Ashniel, fear and anger warring for supremacy on her face.

Malchior could only stare at the dissipating smoke, caught

on the breeze and borne away to nothing. Four blood-slick skulls stared back, grinning.

Drutheira didn't answer. She rose wearily, leaving her cohorts in the ruined outhouse. Snow was falling, peeling off the mountains. It shawled her dark cloak in a fur of ice as she crossed the open, heading towards a shattered building that had once been a stables. Frost crusted her robe where she'd been sat on the ground.

Sevekai was inside, making a fire.

'More riders are coming, my dear,' he said without looking up as the sorceress approached.

The other shades were absent, keeping watch at the edges of the settlement. No more than one night at a time, then they had to move on.

'Hunting us, hunting for them–' he nodded towards the headless corpses of the reavers, '–it doesn't matter. We have to leave soon.'

'Leave?' said Drutheira. 'I can barely walk.'

Sevekai looked up at her.

'Then you'll be captured, and likely killed. The asur have our scent, and war or not they are coming.'

Drutheira stared for a moment, her eyes dead and cold.

'Malekith has abandoned us,' she said simply. 'We are alone, Sevekai.'

Sevekai returned to his fire, coaxing the embers to greater vigour. 'We have always been alone.'

'How long can we stay here?'

'A night, no more than that.'

'I once had a tower, a manse and slaves to do my bidding,' she muttered bitterly.

'I thought *I* was your slave.'

There was a glint in Sevekai's eye that Drutheira didn't care for, but she didn't rise to his goading.

'You said you had a ship,' she said instead, 'south across the mountains at the Sour Sea?'

'There's no way we're going south now, too many dwarfs march that way.'

'How can you possibly know that?'

'Because I skulk in shadows and listen. Armies of dwarfs

move north and south towards Tor Alessi.'

'Then what do you suggest? You are the scout, guide us!' she snapped.

'We lay low, find a way to restore your strength and that of your lackeys.' He looked up again, a question in his eyes. 'I suppose you lack the craft to open up a gate right back into Naggaroth, yes?'

Drutheira scowled.

Shrugging Sevekai said, 'Thought so,' and prodded the fire with a shaft of broken roof beam. Then out of nothing he asked, 'What did you mean in the valley, when the dragon rider was close?'

'About what?' Despite herself, Drutheira came down to sit next to him, warming her hands on the fire.

'Kaitar. You said he was not druchii.'

Ever since their reunion, Drutheira and the other sorcerers had kept their distance from the enigmatic shade. He seemed to prefer that too, often scouting ahead, sometimes gone for more than a day at a time.

'He feels... empty, I suppose. Like a vessel of flesh into which something has crept and spread itself out.'

'That is meaningless,' said Sevekai.

'Perhaps, but I can explain it in no other way.'

The shade considered that for a moment before saying, 'I'll admit he has caused me some disquiet. At first I thought he was an assassin, a true servant of Khaine, taken on Death Night and inveigled into my ranks to kill us when our mission was done with.'

'And that has changed?'

'No. I still think he means to kill us, which is why I need your help to kill him first.'

Malice and desire contorted Drutheira's face, and Sevekai revelled in both expressions. Embers thought long extinguished rekindled and flared.

'Kill the shade and the rider,' she purred, creeping closer, her hand straying onto Sevekai's thigh, then further...

'Kill them all,' he murmured, pulling her down and into his embrace.

◄ CHAPTER THIRTY-FIVE ►

Against the Glittering Host

SNORRI'S FEET WERE aching. Even in his boots, robust as they were and made from dwarf leather, the frost-bitten ground had taken a toll. Declining the offer of a palanquin, a throne and bearers to carry him, the prince had joined the ranks at the head of the army. Better they see him that way, as one of them, a dwarf warrior first and a prince second.

'I thought marching in winter was only something mad or desperate generals did?' groaned Morgrim, whose bunions were the size of chestnuts. He and several hearthguard from Everpeak protected the prince's right flank and strode in lockstep with him.

'Who's to say I am not one or both?' Snorri replied. 'Although, if anyone asks I'll say you convinced me do it.'

They shared a fraternal grin, something that had been lacking in their relationship of late but had oddly warmed with the onset of winter.

'We are close, Snorri,' uttered Drogor, on the prince's left amongst a second cadre of hearthguard. Now a thane with holdings in Everpeak come the end of the war, Drogor also carried the army standard after the prince's last bearer was slain by an elven scout during a previous skirmish. It was

409

little more than a raid, the enemy gauging their numbers, but Bron had lost his life as he sounded the alarm.

So many had died already in similar meaningless circumstances. Snorri kept his thoughts on the matter to himself; not even Morgrim or Drogor would know them. It would hurt morale if his kith and kin thought his resolve was wavering.

'Signal a halt,' ordered the prince, and Drogor raised the banner.

Horns blared across the marching ranks, which stopped immediately to the clattering discord of settling shields, armour and weapons. Some of the mules brayed before their skinners quietened them with soothing words. The creaking wheels of wagons, carrying provisions, quarrels, spare shields and helms, were the last sound to abate. Some of the larger beasts towed machineries and these were marshalled by engineers and their crew, smothered in tarps for now but ready to be deployed at the prince's command.

Looking back over his shoulder, beyond the hulking hearthguard, Snorri saw sappers, warriors from over fifty different clans, grey-haired longbeards, quarrellers and rangers, the heavily armoured cohorts of ironbreakers and the dour faces of runesmiths. This was a mustering of some potency, one that would tear down the walls of Tor Alessi with or without his father's help.

True to his word, Snorri waited seven days for the army of the High King to arrive. But his father was late and the prince's patience at an end. The reinforcements from Barak Varr had also failed to materialise, so with just over thirty thousand dwarfs at his banner, he had marched.

On the fifth day, a band of rangers had returned from scouting. Their leader, Kundi Firebeard, had said the elves numbered in the region of ten thousand, including cavalry.

'Heh, what use are horses during a siege?' Drogor had asked.

'I have seen riders charge from a gate to sack machineries, kill their crews,' Morgrim had replied. 'We shouldn't underestimate the elgi knights.'

'It doesn't matter,' Snorri had told them both, 'we are

committed to this now. Riders or not, Tor Alessi will fall.'

In the end the prince had chosen the Brundin road, the stories of monstrous trees coming to life and hellish sprites, however far-fetched, enough to dissuade him from taking the mountains. Expecting resistance, the dwarf throng had marched in a tight column with rangers roaming its flanks and rear. They need not have bothered. No elven war host stood in their way. No scouts harried their advance this time. The dwarfs had been allowed to march on Tor Alessi unimpeded.

Several times since they had set out, Morgrim had voiced concern that their haste would mean the High King's army was that little bit farther away.

Snorri had dismissed his cousin's misgivings, stating that thirty thousand dwarfs were more than enough to crack open one elven citadel.

That conviction had not changed.

'Twenty of the hearthguard with me,' said Snorri, gesturing to the last rise. Over that and they would see the port city and its defences relatively close up for the first time. 'You too, cousin.'

Led by the prince the dwarfs climbed up the boulder-strewn ridge, descending to their bellies as they neared the summit in case elven spotters were watching the approach and had ready quarrels to hand.

Snorri was the first to reach the top and peer over the edge.

The city was distant, still another hour's march away, and the dwarf army would be revealed long before they reached it. Bigger than Snorri first imagined, Tor Alessi was erected around a port and used most of the coastline in its defences. Aside from rugged, impenetrable cliffs facing out towards the sea, high walls surrounded a core of inner buildings and there were three large gatehouses. Elven devices, the eagle, dragon rampant and the rising phoenix, were emblazoned on each. Snorri counted three massive towers amongst lesser minarets and minor citadels. There was a large keep, appended in part to the port, and this was protected by a second defensive wall with only one gate.

Impressive as it was, what surrounded the elven city surprised the dwarf prince more.

'I did not know it was at the centre of a lake,' said Morgrim, as if speaking Snorri's thoughts aloud.

Snorri reached for a spyglass offered by one of his hearthguard and peered down the lens.

'It's no lake…' he breathed after a few seconds. Putting down the spyglass, he licked his lips to moisten the sudden dryness. 'It's an army.'

An undulating ribbon of almost endless silver surrounded the outskirts of Tor Alessi, a vast host of elves that glittered in the winter sun. Pennons attached to the lances of knights whipped around on the breeze coming down off the ridge and numerous ranks of spearmen stood in ready formation with rows of archers to their rear.

'Grungni's hairy arse…' muttered one of the hearthguard.

Morgrim ignored him, pointing to the elven right flank. 'There,' he said, 'machineries.'

Snorri had seen them during the brodunk, elven chariots drawn by horses. There were at least a hundred in a close-knit squadron, scythed wheels catching the light and shimmering like star-fire.

He cast his gaze skywards and felt suddenly foolish for their attempts at subterfuge. Circling above were flocks of birds. Not like the screech hawks, talon owls or griffon vultures of the peaks, these were giant eagles with claws and beaks like blades.

Snorri lowered the spyglass for the second time.

'Looks like they're expecting us,' he said to the others.

'It explains why the road became suddenly empty,' said Morgrim.

'Because they were all here.'

Snorri got to his feet, seeing no point in stealth any more. 'I am no engineer, but a sight more than ten thousand wouldn't you say, cousin?'

Morgrim nodded slowly, taking in the glittering host in all its shining glory.

'What do you want to do?'

The prince sniffed disdainfully, hiking up his belt.

'First I want to punish Kundi Firebeard for his abject stupidity, then I want to march down there and kill some thagging elgi.'

IT WASN'T LIKE Kor Vanaeth and the clash for the gate. Nadri had never fought in open pitched battle before. Before the short siege at the elven city, he had never donned axe and shield in anything more than a skirmish. Unlike Krondi had been, he wasn't a campaigner or a soldier; though he knew his axecraft as all clansmen did, he was a merchant. With war unleashed upon the land, Nadri had exchanged gold for blood as his currency.

It was proving a difficult trade.

Two dwarf war hosts had descended the ridge into the teeth of the elven hordes. His liege-lord King Brynnoth led one, his cup of vengeance not even half full from Agrin Fireheart's untimely death. The other was led by Valarik of Karak Hirn, though Nadri did not know him except by sight.

Arrows met them at first, a heavy rain of steel-fanged death that reaped a lesser tally than the pointy-ears had hoped. Dwarfs knew defence as well as attack, and their formations were peerless. Locking shields front, back, to the flanks and above, several large cohorts had weathered the arrow storm with almost no casualties. But for the uncanny accuracy of the elven archers, no dwarf blood would have been spilled at all.

Dismayed at such resilience, the elven lordlings had called for their cavalry. Clarion horns, shrilling much higher than the pipes of Barak Varr, had signalled the charge. The earth shook with the pounding of the knightly horse, and had made Nadri's teeth chatter.

Even in the third rank, behind kith and kin he had known most of his life, he felt the impact of elven lance. It tore into them despite their organised shield wall, raked a great ragged cleft, and left them bleeding. With dogged tenacity, the dwarfs had closed, holding though the urge to run was strong.

Now they were locked with the high-helmed elven knights, matching axe and hammer to longsword.

Sweeping out his arm, Nadri felt more than saw his axe cleave horseflesh. The beast whinnied, its caparison shedding against his well-honed blade. It cut the saddle belt too, plunging the rider into the mass where he slashed wildly for a few moments before he was lost beneath a hail of hammer blows.

Something smacked into his shoulder, and he was about to strike when he realised it was Yodri, a fellow clanner. The old dwarf risked a gap-toothed grin when he saw Nadri's face. The merchant smiled back, grim rather than humorous, before Yodri's expression slackened, the longsword through his neck puncturing his good mood. The blade withdrew with a meaty *schluk!* before it struck down on Nadri, who had enough about him to raise his shield. A thick dent appeared on the underside next to where he'd pressed his cheek. A third blow took a chip of the shield's edge, allowing a narrow aperture through which to see his attacker.

Cold fury lit the knight's face, a snarl growing on his lips with every determined blow. He swung again, Nadri unable to manage any reply, tearing the shield from the dwarf's agonised grasp. Rearing horse hooves put Nadri on his back and he half expected to be ground into paste by them before a heavy shaft punched the beast's flank and sent it and rider sprawling.

'Grimnir's balls, it's a good job them thaggers from the Varn are accurate!' said one of the Copperfist clan that Nadri couldn't place at first.

It was Werigg Gunnson, an old friend of his father's.

Nadri looked to where Werigg was pointing. King Ironhandson's engineers were loosing their ballistae, and the bolt throwers were exacting a heavy price from the knights, whose armour meant little against the thick arrow shafts.

Overhead, there came the heavy *whomp* of stone throwers loosing their cargo. The dwarfs of Karak Varn were neglecting the walls in favour of punishing the stranded cavalry. Through the melee, where the press of bodies and the thicket of limbs had thinned, he saw a swathe of dwarf dead, cut up by the chariots. Here the stone throwers struck next, rewarded for their efforts as one of the elven machineries exploded in a storm of wood, bone and flesh. Blood slicked the flung rock, painting it in a greasy line as it rolled to a halt.

'Either that or the blind buggers are just lucky, eh?' Nadri felt rough hands drag him to his feet and saw a grizzled-looking dwarf facing him. 'Up yer get, lad. More killing to be done.'

Still dazed, Nadri grabbed a shield, not caring if it was his own, and saw the knights had broken off their attack and were retreating towards the city gates. A host of spearmen, out of range of the war machines and thus far unscathed, parted to let them through. Then they closed ranks and lowered their pikes at the badly bloodied dwarfs.

'See,' said the old-timer, hawking up a gob of pipeweed he'd been chewing. 'Plenty more.'

Nadri eyed the determined elven phalanx even as the dwarfs drew back into formation, raising shields as the arrow storm began anew, and groaned.

HIS RETINUE OF hearthguard just below, Snorri surveyed the battle from a grassy tor through the spyglass. This was but an opening skirmish and though he had wanted badly to lead it, knew his place as army general was here.

Brynnoth was ever wrathful and had insisted on leading the first attack. Though brave, the clans of Barak Varr were being hammered by the elves. During the skirmish, arrows had killed a great many dwarfs and left countless more for the ministrations of the priestesses of Valaya. Even as the battle raged, the dour warrior maidens roamed the field, dragging back the wounded or silencing those beyond help. Since the initial charge and subsequent breaking of the high-helmed cavalry, the dwarf front line had advanced considerably. Met by a thick wall of heavy-armoured spearmen, their march had now halted. Though difficult to ascertain through the spyglass, it looked like the two forces were at an impasse. From a brutal opening skirmish with a splintered cavalry force, the dwarfs now faced a determined grind.

Snorri smiled despite the grimness of the vista. Dwarfs knew how to fight battles of attrition. Even with their spears and high shields, the elves would soon learn the folly of these tactics. Unwilling to loose directly into the fighting ranks, the elven archers unleashed volleys of arrows in the air and the prince of Everpeak watched their deadly trajectory until they fell amongst the rear ranks. Pushing hard against the backs of their fellow clanners in order to roll the elven line, many dwarfs had their shields front and were struck down. Several ranks lay dead before a proper defence stalled further casualties. Quarrellers attempted to reply in kind, but the dwarf crossbowmen had neither the range nor the accuracy to be effective.

Panning the lens across the melee Snorri found Brynnoth, or at least several of his royal hearthguard, the Sea Wardens, battling furiously in the centre. The king would be amongst them, at their heart, and strong as he was the elves were showing no signs of capitulation. Several large cohorts, including those from Everpeak, were ready as reinforcement. With almost a third of his army committed already, Snorri was reluctant to feed any more into the grind.

He considered employing the war machines to thin the elven ranks, but the proximity of dwarf warriors made it too risky. Without the need to punish the knights, they were standing dormant so Snorri gave the signal for them to be brought forwards and batter the walls instead.

A drum beat was followed by the raising of banners down the line until the message from the prince was conveyed to Ironhandson and his throwers. A few moments later and a cascade of bolts and boulders assailed Tor Alessi's walls.

Snorri followed their descent through the spyglass, grumbling in dismay as an arc of lightning tore one stone from the sky, disintegrating the missile in a shower of debris. Several more went the same way as the elves revealed their mages, casting fire and ice from their fingertips to blunt the dwarf barrage. A few missiles struck but the damage they caused was negligible to a city that size. Bolts from the ballistae were snatched out of the very air by flocks of the great eagles, the massive birds of prey snapping them in their vice-like claws before diving down onto the machineries themselves.

Engulfed by a swarm of flapping feathers and flashing silver beaks, dozens of dwarf crewmen and engineers lay dead before Ironhandson restored order with his rangers and saw the beasts off.

'It is harder than I thought,' Snorri confessed under his breath.

'We knew the elgi were tough, cousin, but we are tougher,' Morgrim reassured him.

'Do you think this is their entire force?'

Morgrim frowned, watching the battle from afar without the benefit of the spyglass, and shook his head.

'The city will harbour a second army, I am sure.'

'We have to crack the gates anyway,' suggested Drogor, his grip tight on the banner where it snapped in the breeze. 'A stern push would sweep this force away and let us bring the fight to the walls.'

'Lay siege?' asked Snorri, looking askance at the Karak Zorn dwarf.

'No, forge a hammer and break down the gates. Once inside the elgi's resolve will waver.'

Snorri rubbed his bearded chin. The entire throng on the field was engaged. Two thick lines of infantry cut and hewed at one another with neither willing to yield. The arrows levelled the scales for the elves, preventing the dwarf line from a concerted push, but the clans were gaining ground on the walls.

'It's not a bad idea.'

Morgrim disagreed. 'Patience is more prudent, Snorri. We grind the elves down, then retreat to our lines and lay siege.'

'I want this over quickly. No elgi rabble is going to defy me.'

Drogor said, 'Perhaps Morgrim is right. Hurt the elgi at the gates, sound a retreat and surround them.'

Morgrim was nodding, surprised that his old friend was agreeing with him.

'Besides,' added Drogor. 'It's likely your father will have

arrived by then with the army from Karaz-a-Karak. There would be no shame in leaning on his larger throng.'

His mood souring swiftly, Morgrim tried to intercede. 'That is not what I meant, cousin–'

'Enough!' The spyglass snapped shut, revealing the anger-reddened features of the prince. 'I will not have my father come here and see this place intact. It will be rubble by the time he reaches the field.' Snorri donned his war helm, the feathered wings fluttering in the breeze. He spoke at Morgrim, glaring around the nose guard. 'I'm ordering the reinforcements in. Sound the clarion. I'll lead them myself.'

SHIELD FORWARDS, SHOULDER locked, Nadri was pinned. He found himself in the third rank of the Copperfists, pushing hard against the wall of elven spears. In such tight confines, there was no room for axe work, save for those chopping frantically at the front. Several dwarfs had already fallen to spear thrusts, their anger blunted on high shields over which almond-shaped eyes glared with contempt.

Unlike the fight against the knights, which was a maddened frenzy of plunging lances and flailing horses as the cavalry sought to rip the dwarfs open, this was a strength-sapping grind. Heave and push. Heave and push. Dwarf and elf shoved against one another, pressing with all the weight of their formations until one bent and broke.

So far, the contest was evenly matched.

Impossible to tell for sure, but Nadri felt like it was the same across the line. One shield wall had met another, though the elven forest of spears was making hard work of it for the dwarfs. As warriors died on both sides, those behind filled their place. From the front rank, which was brutal even from his position two rows behind, Nadri heard a grunt. Another dwarf had fallen, arterial crimson jetting from his neck and blinding the one behind him who also died to a quick thrust from the white-haired champion leading the cohort of spears.

Suddenly and without realising, Nadri was at the front. A jabbing spear was turned aside by an instinctive parry with his axe haft. A sword blow fell against his shield and stung his shoulder with the impact. He roared, invoking Grungni and Grimnir, thrashed out with his axe. Scale mail parted, shearing off like autumn leaves, and a spearman crumpled trying to hold in his guts. As another warrior took the elf's place, the champion was pushed closer. His sword flashed, an eldritch blade that bore glowing elven runes of power.

Nadri met the attack with his shield and his defence was almost cloven in half.

Spitting some curse in elvish, the white-haired champion swung again. This time Nadri ducked and the rune sword shaved off the sea dragon device on his helmet.

Like his kin, the elf was dressed in blue-grey robes, his armour like polished azure, only metal and much more unyielding. He wore a conical helm, a star-pattern emblazoned on its nose guard, with a shock of horsehair protruding from the tip.

'Uzkul elgi!'

A shout came from further down the line, a few places to Nadri's right. Whilst the other dwarfs fought, their champion, Vrekki Helbeard, stepped forwards. He was pointing at the white-haired elf with the spiked tip of his mattock. The weapon was dark with blood.

Nadri felt a hand grip his shoulder and then heard the gravel voice of Werigg Gunnson in his ear.

'Let him through, lad,' he said. 'Helbeard challenges the elgi.'

'How, in this?' asked Nadri, fending off another thrust that nearly took off his ear.

As the challenge was met, the pressure on the dwarfs leavened. Vrekki shouldered up the line and was standing alongside Nadri, the elf champion facing him.

The fighting hadn't ceased, it merely allowed for the passage of the two warriors so they might meet in combat. No order was given to let through, it was merely *understood*. Vrekki threw the first blow, taking a chunk from the elf's shield, and the crushing pressure of the grind returned in earnest.

Through the frenzy, Nadri caught slashes of their duel, although to refer to it thus would not be accurate. Vrekki fought two-handed, using the thick haft of his mattock to parry. Like the elf, he had runes too, and they flashed along the shaft of his weapon and the talisman he wore around his neck.

To Nadri it seemed like many minutes but it was over in seconds.

Vrekki battered the white-haired champion hard, hurling blow upon blow against his shield. It looked like he was winning, until having soaked up all the punishment he was willing to, the elf thrust from beneath the guard of his shield and pierced poor Vrekki's heart. The champion died instantly, his mouth formed into an inchoate curse.

With their thane's death, Nadri felt the Copperfists falter. A ripple, almost impossible to discern, fed down their ranks. The elves felt it too and pushed. Two spears came Nadri's way at once. He parried one, but the other pierced his chest, just below the shoulder, and he cried out. The white-haired champion had discarded his shield and fought only with his sword. Pinioned and in agony, Nadri was an easy kill. But before the deathblow came, he flung his axe. It turned one and a half times in the air then embedded itself in the elf's face, splitting his nose in two and carving into his skull like an egg.

He fell, brutally, and the momentum shifted again.

There was a cheer of 'Khazuk!' of which Nadri was only vaguely aware, before the push came again. It pressed him into the spear that was pinning him and he roared in pain and anger. Unarmed, there was little he could do but hold up his shield and pray to Valaya it would be enough. At either side, though he couldn't move to look properly, he felt his fellow clanners hacking with their blades.

'Take it, lad!' Werigg bellowed from behind, a hammer slipped into Nadri's grasp which he used to smash the spear haft jutting from his chest. The immense pressure of the other dwarf's considerable bulk levelled against his back followed swiftly after as Werigg got his head down and pushed.

The elves were reeling, on their heels and close to capitulation. Like a ship, the dwarfs its starboard, the elves port,

the line pitched and yawed as both sides fought for supremacy. More tenacious than they had any right to be, the elves
held on.

'Khazuk!' the Copperfists yelled, but still could find no
breach in their enemy's resolve.

A foot... two... then three, the dwarfs gained ground by
bloody increments but the elves would not yield.

Amazed he was still alive, Nadri forgot the pain from
his chest and bludgeoned spearmen with his borrowed
hammer.

'Uzkul!' he cried as a splash of crimson lined his face like
a baptism, echoing Vrekki, honouring the thane's sacrifice.
It was madness, a terrible churn of bodies and blades without end. He wondered briefly if the halls of Grimnir were
steeped in such carnage.

A horn rang out, so deep and sonorous as to only be
dwarfen, dragging Nadri from his dark reverie.

THE ELF LINE trembled, just the lightest tremor at first but
then building to a destructive quake. Like a tree hewn at
the root and felled by its own weight, the spearmen buckled. It was as if they bent at the middle and were funnelling
into the hole where Snorri had forced his wedge of gromril.

Hearthguard were tough, implacable warriors and Snorri
had rammed a cohort of a hundred right down the throat
of the elven infantry. To see them broken so utterly by the
prince's charge stirred Morgrim's blood, but it was also
reckless.

'You did this,' he said, a grimace revealing his displeasure.

'I did nothing but agree with you, old friend,' said Drogor
with a plaintive tone, though his eyes flashed eagerly to see
such carnage wrought upon the elves.

'He has overstretched and left himself vulnerable.'

Drogor appeared nonplussed, gesturing to the elf ranks.

'The elgi are in flight, I can see no danger. Your cousin
has done what Brynnoth could not, and broken their ranks.'

'Aye,' snapped Morgrim, 'and he will not stop until he's
reached the walls and torn apart the gate. That, or until he's
dead. You goaded him.' He was nodding, a distasteful sneer

on his face. 'You drew him into this fight by mentioning his father.' Morgrim turned to the other dwarf, the rows of silent hearthguard Snorri had left behind unmoving like statues behind them. 'Why?'

'Snorri, our prince, will do what he wants. It was he who brought an army to these gates, who forged the will of no less than four kings into a throng capable of challenging the elgi in their greatest citadel. Do you really think I, a lowly treasure hunter from the Southlands, could do *anything* to affect the mind of a dwarf capable of that?'

Morgrim snarled, turning away.

'Signal Thagdor's clans. I want Zhufbar prepared to march in support of the prince.'

Drogor didn't react. His face was set as stone as he lifted the banner.

THE ELVES WERE running, but to Snorri's annoyance their flight was not a rout.

Shields as one, spears to the fore, the elves retreated in good order. At the head of the hearthguard, Snorri battered at them. He carried no shield, and instead wielded an axe in either hand.

Hacking away a desperate lunge with the short haft of his hand axe, he buried his rune axe in the attacking elf's torso. Silver scale and blood shed from the warrior like he was a gutted fish. Snorri whirled, cleaving the forearm of another, splitting apart his shield. A stomp forwards with a heavy boot and he cut the groin of a third elf, bifurcating the spearman all the way to the sternum. A shoulder barge put down a fourth before the prince took a shield smash to the face, which he shrugged off with typical dwarf resilience.

'Harder than that, you kruti-eaters,' he spat, hewing down another.

For all the carnage he wreaked, him *and* his hearthguard who were just as merciless, the elves maintained their ordered retreat.

'Stand and fight, thagging cowards!' Snorri raged at the disappearing spearmen, who were edging closer and closer to the wall and the gate.

Within a hundred feet of the defences, the archers took aim again and loosed. With the measured retreat of the spearmen, gaps had begun to appear in the fighting. It was no longer a tightly packed melee with heaving, pushing ranks; rather a patch of open killing ground had materialised between the two forces that was thronged with the dead and dying.

A shaft struck Snorri in his shoulder guard but he ignored it, ignored that the tip had pierced metal and meat. One of the hearthguard took an arrow in the neck, an impossible shot between helm and gorget, and died gurgling his own blood.

Seconds after the first arrow, another shaft hit the prince in the thigh. He cursed once, snapped it and drove on.

'Into them,' he bellowed. 'By Grimnir's wrath, we'll overrun the gates!'

A cheer rang out from the nearby clans, but the hearthguard were stoic in silence, determinedly sticking to their task.

The elven shield wall returned, spears levelled like spikes. At some unseen signal they stopped falling back and solidified again, hoping to bulwark the dwarfs against a cliff face of high shields.

Charging, impelled by their prince, the dwarfs hit it hard. Several warriors, not expecting the sudden shift, were impaled and the brutal melee renewed. As elf and dwarf clashed at close quarters, jabbing, hacking, cleaving, the arrow storm continued unabated. Hearthguard warriors lifted their shields to protect the prince, whilst the pushing back ranks were pinioned. Like an anvil the dwarf line had come together, some three thousand warriors of the clans and brotherhoods, fighting shoulder to shoulder against a thin, glittering line of elves. Attrition was simply the reality of war for dwarfs, they weathered it well, used it to break the most determined and numerous of foes. Here against elven skill and discipline that strategy was being sorely tested.

Caught between the will of the spears and the volleys of the archers, the dwarfs were taking a beating.

Snorri tried to change that single-handed. He ploughed

into the enemy ranks, splitting them down the middle. A champion, some elven lordling with a shimmering spear and armour of gilded metal, went to impede him. The prince cut him down like he was a common soldier.

Elves recoiled from the vengeful prince. Dwarfs followed him, King Brynnoth leading a determined charge of his own, Valarik too. Like a swelling tide, the sons of Grungni puffed up their chests and became the hammer.

Such discipline the elves possessed, not like the ragged tribes of the greenskins or the feral beasts of the dark wood, but even their resolve was buckling in the face of the dwarf onslaught. And just as it felt as if they were about to break for the last time and surrender the field, white mantlets decorated to look like overlapping swan feathers tilted to reveal the deadly reason why the elves had drawn their enemy on.

Bolt throwers, rank upon rank of them, but not like the dwarf machineries for these racked a quartet of bolts at a time, unleashed a devastating salvo.

'Mercy of Valaya…' Snorri breathed, as the spear-thick arrows descended.

HORNS WERE BLOWING. Nadri heard them above the whipping report of the elven bolt throwers raining down death upon them. Despite the terrible barrage, the Copperfists continued to advance. As they closed on the wall, barely twenty feet away and almost beyond the minimal range of the elven reapers, Nadri saw the gate open into Tor Alessi. There were more warriors within, hard-faced veterans wearing long skirts of mail, adorned with jewelled breastplates and carrying immense two-handed swords.

The spearmen retreated into the relatively narrow aperture, walking backwards unerringly, spears outstretched as they condensed their long shield wall into a tight square of blades angled in every direction.

Without the bolt throwers to skewer them relentlessly, Nadri felt a tremor of relief through the ranks, but it was short lived. Murder holes opened in the walls above, manned by pairs of archers who had fallen back into the city before the spearmen. The storm returned, thickening the air with hundreds of feathered shafts.

Nadri's shield sprouted more than a dozen arrows in a few seconds.

The hand-to-hand fighting had all but ceased, the spearmen retreating faster than the dwarfs could keep pace and the archers making them pay for every step.

A flash of light and the stink of burned flesh heralded a magical attack. Turning their efforts from destroying the deadly cargo of the siege engines, the elven mages had their eyes fixed on the advancing dwarfs.

From nearby came chanting, a doleful, sombre refrain that fizzled out a second lightning arc before it could strike. Incandescent serpents of amethyst, spears of luminescent jade, the enchanted manifestation of dragon-kind spitting crimson flame, came at the dwarfs in a sorcerous hail that the runesmiths were hard pressed to repel.

Nadri grit his teeth, barely fighting, merely marching against the attack. He felt the hairs on the back of his neck spike, tasted copper in his mouth and smelled the reek of brimstone in his scorched nostrils. The dwarfs resisted, calling upon their natural resilience to harmful magic, channelled it back to the earth, back to rock where it would be safe and dormant.

The king's banner was aloft; he saw it above the throng, flapping defiantly. It was an order to charge, to run at the gates and bring them down while the elves were in retreat, but the arrow storm was unrelentingly heavy. A pity Werigg had no words of encouragement, but Nadri felt the old solider at his back, his hand on his shoulder if not gripping quite so tight now the battle pressure had lessened.

They got another foot before a second horn was sounded, followed by the beat of drums. The banner dipped, away from the gates. A signal to retreat.

Nadri couldn't decide if he felt indignant or relieved. They had bled so much to reach this far and gain so little. The bellowed command from one of the thanes further down the line confirmed it.

'Retreat!'

Nadri was confused. He had always believed there was no word for 'back', 'give up', in Khazalid. Seemed he was wrong, they all were.

'That's it,' he called over his shoulder. 'Werigg, we lived, we–'

The old soldier's glassy eyes staring back unblinking supplanted Nadri's relief with grief. Werigg's hand was still upon his back, seized with enough rigor to keep it there, his body pressed into the throng unable to fall. A dark patch blotted his armour, running stickily over the mail. A spear tip was lodged in the middle of it, broken off at the end. Nadri remembered the one in his chest, the second one he'd deflected, unknowingly, into Werigg's gut. A mortal wound. As the dwarfs peeled away and the throng parted, Werigg fell and Nadri wasn't able to catch him or carry him. Borne away by the urgency of the crowd, he couldn't stop and the old soldier was lost from his sight.

SNORRI CURSED, HE cursed in as many foul ways as he knew, spitting and raging as the retreat was sounded. He turned briefly, looking over his shoulder to see the throng from Zhufbar heading back to the encampment at the edge of the battlefield. He also saw Morgrim, arms folded after issuing the command.

Cursing again, Snorri flung his hand axe in a final defiant gesture and it stuck in the thick wood of the elven gate like a promise.

We'll be back, it said, *the killing isn't done, we are not done. Battle has only just begun.*

He seethed, marking the face of each and every elf that looked down on him with haughty disdain from the city walls.

'Khazuk,' he screamed in promise. 'Khazuk!'

But the elves didn't understand, nor did they care.

◄ CHAPTER THIRTY-SIX ►

Preparing to Lay Siege

ONCE THE WITHDRAWAL from outside the city began the hail of arrows ceased, the elven reapers returned behind their mantlets and the mages to their towers. It was not a benevolent act towards a respected foe; it was a pragmatic one. The elves were not so foolish as to believe they had won. They knew enough of dwarfs to realise they would come again. Arrows were finite, so too the strength of a wizard. Both needed conserving if they were to hold the city.

From inside his tent looking out onto the field, Snorri glowered. He chewed his beard and muttered, trying to excise his feeling of impotence with the clenching and unclenching of his fists.

A young priestess was tending the wound in his shoulder, packing it with warm healing clay, but he ignored her. Since the retreat, he had spoken to no one.

Morgrim approached, invading the prince's solitude. Over an hour had passed since Snorri had glared at him upon the army's disappointing return, and as the injured were patched up and armour mended by the forges he decided it was time to confront his cousin.

The foulness of his mood was etched across the prince's

face. 'Don't you understand what "do not disturb" means?' he grumbled.

'Aye, and I understand what would have happened had you fought on,' Morgrim replied curtly, surprising Snorri with his choler. 'Eight hundred and sixty-three dead, the reckoners are still tallying the injured. What were you going to do if you had reached the walls, climb them with your axe or hack open the gate?'

'If needs be, by Grungni. I'll make those elgi pay.'

'What price do you think they owe you, cousin? Was the *rhunki* lord a friend of yours, was he known to you or even of your hold? We all mourn for Agrin Fireheart but this goes beyond that.'

Snorri leaned forwards, fighting back the pain as he felt his injuries anew and scowling at the priestess who scowled back.

'It was an affront to all dawi, what they did. Slaying a rhunki of such venerability...' He shook his head, rueful. 'My father should have declared war there and then.'

'And now we come to the root of it,' said Morgrim, folding his arms.

'Meaning?' asked Snorri, sitting back before the priestess clubbed him.

'Your father, the High King.'

Snorri's expression darkened and he dismissed the dwarf maiden trying to tend to him with a curt word. She glared but relented. 'What is it with these Valayan rinns?' he griped.

Morgrim went on. 'Ever since you heard that prophecy in the ruins of Karak Krum, you have railed even harder against him. You made this cause your own, this war, to slight the High King, declare grudgement if I am wrong.'

Snorri seethed, fists balled, and looked like he might spring from his throne and knock his cousin onto his back. Anyone else but Morgrim and he would have raised fists, but after a minute he climbed down from his anger.

'He who will slay the drakk, he who will be king, those were his words. Am I still to believe them, cousin?'

Like heat from the cooling forge, Morgrim's ire dispersed in the face of Snorri's humility. 'You are prince of

Karaz-a-Karak, heir to the Throne of Power and the Karaz Ankor. Your destiny is great as are you, cousin. Don't let this feud with your father get in the way of that. Embrace him again. Show him you are the High King's regent he needs you to be.'

Holding Morgrim's gaze, Snorri slowly nodded and then looked across to the killing field where a host of broken shields, shattered helms and axe hafts remained. Both sides had allowed the other clemency to remove their dead but the earth was soaked with blood that would not be so easy to excise. And amidst all of this carnage, Tor Alessi still stood like a defiant rock in the storm.

'They are harder than they look,' Snorri conceded.

'Aye,' Morgrim agreed, following the prince's eye.

'Gather the other kings,' said Snorri. 'We need a different strategy.'

'Such as?'

'What we should have done when we first got here. Lay siege.'

THE PRINCE'S DECISION was met with unanimous approval. Even King Brynnoth, whose eagerness to kill elves hadn't lessened much since Kor Vanaeth, was in agreement. The dwarfs would do what they did best; they would wait.

For the rest of the day, whilst blacksmiths repaired armour and weapons, healers tended and the victuallers and brewmasters kept the army fed, bands of rangers ventured into the nearby forests. They returned with cartloads of wood and at once the dwarf engineers and craftsmen began to fashion battering rams and siege towers. Raw iron had been brought from the holds for just such a purpose and once they were done with arming the clans, the blacksmiths began labouring to reinforce the wooden siege engines. Stout ladders were made too, along with broad, metal-banded pavises and mantlets for the quarrellers.

Every dwarf in the throng had a trade and every dwarf was put to the task. Unlike most armies who possessed dedicated labour gangs to achieve such a feat, barring the warrior brotherhoods dwarfs could call upon their entire host and so the engines went up quickly. From their tents and around the flickering glow of cook fires came the sound of deathsong, sombre on the breeze. For their enemies or themselves, the sons of Grungni accepted either.

It put Nadri in a grimmer mood than in the aftermath of the battle. He hadn't seen Werigg amongst the dead, and barely knew the old warrior anyway. Yet it burdened him, especially the callousness of his death. Seeking to stymie his grief, Nadri had looked to other tasks to occupy his mind. His father, Lodri, was a miner and lodewarden. He knew rock and metal, and had passed some of that knowledge on to his sons. The ex-merchant, a trade to which he doubted he would ever return, was hammering the roof of a battering ram when a voice intruded on his thoughts.

'Stout work.'

Nadri kept labouring, carefully beating the plates with a mallet and then using a hammer to drive in the iron nails that secured to its frame.

'I said stout work.'

Looking up, Nadri reddened at once when he saw it was Prince Snorri Lunngrin addressing him, his retainers and bodyguards close by.

'It'll need to be to turn those elgi arrows, but thank you, my liege.'

'I saw you at Kor Vanaeth, didn't I?'

'You have a sharp eye, my liege. Yes, I fought at the gate.'

Snorri seemed to appraise him. 'You're not a warrior, though.'

'No, my liege. I am a merchant but took up az and klad to fight the elgi for my king.'

'And you shall be remembered for it. What's your name, dawi?'

'Nadri Lodrison, my liege. Of the Copperfist clan.'

'Tell me, Nadri, do you have any kin, a rinn or beardlings back at the Sea Hold?'

'A brother only, my liege. Heglan. My father died during the urk purges of your father, Gotrek Starbreaker the High King.'

At mention of the name, the prince visibly stiffened.

'He does not fight, your brother?'

'He's an engineer, my liege, fashioning war machines for the army of Barak Varr.'

That was a lie as far as Nadri knew but he saw no reason to reveal that Heg was trying to build a flying ship. Unless the master of engineers had discovered his workshop and then he might be toiling in the mines instead. A sudden pang of regret tightened Nadri's stomach at the thought of his brother, but he was glad too, glad Heg didn't have to endure all of this. At least not yet. 'And I would dearly like to see him again,' he added in a murmur.

Snorri nodded, genuinely moved by such fraternity. 'You will, Nadri. The elgi will break against our siegecraft and the war will be over. Grungni wills it, Grimnir demands it and Valaya will protect us throughout.'

'Tromm, my liege.' Nadri bowed his head, whilst the prince echoed him and continued on his tour of the siege works.

'I just hope I am alive to see it,' he whispered when the prince was gone, and returned to his hammering.

'IT WAS A good idea to tour the ranks,' Morgrim muttered in Snorri's ear.

'Aye, there's not only pride that needs salving after a beating like that.'

The dwarfs were passing through a throng of blacksmiths' tents, and the air was pleasingly redolent of ash and smoke. The ring of metal against anvil was soothing and brought with it a small measure of home.

Only Drogor seemed unmoved. 'Were we beaten, though?' he asked. 'I see dead elgi littering the outskirts of the city, not just dawi.'

Morgrim grew belligerent. 'We *were* bloodied, kinsman. Badly.'

The three were accompanied by one of the hearthguard, a flame-haired brute called Khazagrim, who bristled as he remembered the battle. Otherwise, he was silent and only present to protect the prince against elven assassins, should any try to kill him.

'It didn't look like defeat to me,' said Drogor.

'I didn't say we were defeated. I–'

'Enough bickering,' Snorri sighed. 'The elgi city stands, and we must find a way to bring it down. Simple as.'

They left the forging tents and came upon the edge of the camp where the war machines were covered under tarp and chained down. It was an impressive battery of machineries. Heavy stones lay piled in stout buckets, thick bolts were lashed together with rope and racked in spear-tipped bunches. Runes and oaths of vengeance were engraved upon every one. They were grudge throwers now, carven with dwarfen vitriol. Enough to bring down a city, or so they all hoped. A small group of warriors guarded the engines and bowed low to the prince and his entourage as they passed by.

'Three towers, high walls, a keep and a well equipped garrison, it's not exactly an urk hut is it now,' Morgrim chafed, once they were out of earshot. 'We need to pummel it, soften the elgi until they're ready to break, then assault. Tunnellers too. I'd suggest three.'

'Thom, Grik and Ari,' said Snorri, naming the three tunnels. 'Clan miners are already setting to the task, the Sootbacks, Blackbrows, Stonefingers and Copperfists.'

'How soon until they're fully excavated?' asked Morgrim.

'Several days.'

'Our siege works will be ready for a first assault within the hour,' said Drogor. 'We could have the walls down by nightfall if we push hard. Tunnels would finish them off.'

The glint in Snorri's eye as he ran a hand over the carriage of one of Ironhandson's stone throwers suggested he liked that idea, but Morgrim was quick to dispel it.

'We should rest and attack at the dawn, wait until the tunnels are more advanced,' he said.

'A night attack would terrify the elgi,' Drogor countered.

'Having seen their discipline, I doubt that. In any case, our forces are spent and would do well to rest.' Morgrim tried to keep the argument from his tone.

'We'll bombard them instead,' Snorri declared, slapping the stone thrower's frame with the flat of his hand. He turned to Drogor. 'Have the king of the Varn bring his war machines up and assail the walls. No sleep for the elgi this night,' he grinned.

Drogor bowed and went immediately to find Ironhand-son. Like many of the kings he had retired to his royal quarters until needed.

'Hrekki won't be pleased at being disturbed,' muttered Morgrim. 'He'll be on his fifth or sixth firkin by now.'

Snorri was dismissive. 'Let him moan,' he said. 'Not all dawi of royal blood have gone to their beds for the night.'

The cousins had reached the edge of the camp and Snorri mounted a rocky hillock so he could gesture to the distant, brooding figure of Brynnoth.

The king of the Sea Hold was crouched down, a plume of pipeweed smoke escaping from his lips that trailed a vapor-ous purple bruise across the twilit sky. The silhouette of his ocean drake helm sat beside him, a predatory companion. Though he had borne the brunt of the fighting, he had yet to remove his armour or accept healing of any kind.

'He is marred by this,' Snorri observed, striking up his own pipe.

'Do you think any of us will not be by the time this is over, cousin?'

Snorri had no answer, contemplating as he smoked.

'How's the hand?' Morgrim asked after a short-lived silence.

'Hurts like a bastard.' What Sorri's reply lacked in elo-quence, it more than made up in its directness.

'I watched you fight. Never seen you better, cousin.'

'Even with a gammy hand – ha!'

Snorri looked askance at his cousin, but Morgrim was in no mood for jests.

'You *want* to kill the elgi, don't you? It's like you hate them, Snorri, and don't care what you have to do to vent the anger that comes with it.'

Again, Snorri fell to silence.

'Keep at it and it'll kill you, cousin. That's why I pulled the throng back. It was the only way to get you to stop.'

The alarum bell pealing out across the camp interrupted

them. All three dwarfs drew their weapons. Even Brynnoth was up.

'Elgi?' the king of the Sea Hold called.

'Could be an attack?' suggested Morgrim, put in mind of an elven sortie from the gates.

Snorri shook his head at them both. 'Our look-outs would have seen it before it got this close, that's the camp alarum.'

They ran down off the hillock and back through the entrenched war machines. From deeper in the camp there came the sound of further commotion. A horn was braying and there was the beat of distant drums tattooing a marching song.

'Not elgi,' breathed Snorri, his face thunderous.

Morgrim espied banners, waving to and fro above the throngs. They bore the red and blue of the royal house of Everpeak.

'The High King,' he said.

Snorri was already scowling. 'My father is here.'

THE WAR MACHINES from Karak Varn had been brought forwards and were loosing their deadly cargo by the time the High King's royal tent was up and Gotrek seated upon his Throne of Power. A single dwarf was granted audience with him, but the meeting was far from cordial.

In the half-light of the tent, Snorri returned the fierce glare of his father with one of equal reproach.

'I did what I did for the Karaz Ankor, and would do it again,' he pledged.

Supping on his pipe, Gotrek merely glowered.

The High King's tent was festooned with banners and statues of the ancestor gods. All three were represented in chiselled stone, each a shrine of worship for when Gotrek wanted to make his oaths. They were shrouded, smoke clouding the room in a dense fug, drowning out the light from hanging braziers and lanterns. A thick carpet of rough crimson material, trimmed with gold, led up to the High King's seat. Even though he wasn't yet clad in his battle armour and instead wore a travelling cloak of tanned elk hide over tunic and hose, he still cut an imposing figure. A simple mitre with a ruby at its centre sufficed in place of his crown, but Gotrek's rune axe was nearby, sitting in its iron cradle, shimmering dully in the gloom.

'Have you nothing to say to me, father?' Snorri had expected wrath, reproach, even censure. The silence was maddening. He snorted angrily, 'I have a war to fight,' and was turning when Gotrek spoke at last.

'A little profligate, my son,' uttered the High King in a rumbling cadence, 'to loose the mangonels and onagers so indiscriminately.'

Biting his tongue, Snorri faced him again but wouldn't be baited.

'The elgi will not rest during the barrage. Come the dawn, when we attack, they'll be tired. Weaker.'

'Hmmm…' The High King grumbled into his beard, then let the silence linger.

It was the Ancient who had once said, '*In talks or negotiation of any kind, only speak when necessary and let silence be your greatest weapon. For in quietude your opponent's tongue will reveal more than he wishes in seeking to fill it.*'

Snorri knew the tactic, but spoke anyway.

'Are *they* strictly necessary, father?' He gestured to a small cadre of warriors at the side of the High King. At first, the prince had thought them to be hearthguard. Certainly, they wore the armour and trappings of these veterans. But even Thurbad amongst their ranks, the High King's ever-present shadow, was not enough to persuade Snorri that these were not singular dwarfs of a different order.

There were seven in total, clad in gromril plate, wearing war helms with full-face masks and a mailed smock that went from armoured chin to chest, draped over the gorget like a beard of chain. No skin was visible on a single one, and for a moment the prince wondered if they were truly alive at all or some runic golems brought to life by Ranuld Silverthumb.

In the end, the High King revealed nothing and merely dismissed them with a nod.

Thurbad led the warriors out of the tent, and father and son were alone.

'Attacking Tor Alessi alone was an unwise move,' Gotrek uttered flatly.

Snorri bristled but held his temper again. 'You were late.'

The High King made no such concession and bellowed, 'And you are reckless! Starting a war without any thought to the consequences. Rushing in like a fool. You are a bear-dling playing at being a king, and I will have you kneel before me as your liege-lord.' He sat up in his throne. 'Do it now, or I'll put you down myself.'

Snorri thought about protesting but saw the wisdom in bowing to his father and his king.

'I acted for the benefit of the Karaz–'

'No! You acted for your own self-interest, Snorri. You attacked a city, destroyed it, and threw us into war.'

Snorri glared, unprepared to capitulate completely. 'War was inevitable, father. I merely struck first.'

'I forbade you.' Gotrek was on his feet, two steps down from his throne. 'And you mustered an army. And you played on Brynnoth's grief, drew him and three other kings into this.' He shook his head, snarled. 'I daresay Thagdor and the rest were easily convinced.'

'They saw as I did.'

'And they'll be punished for that. Grudges laid down in blood.' Taking a long pull of black beer, Gotrek exhaled an exasperated breath. He sat back down again, wiped his beard. 'By seeking to unite the clans, you have divided us.'

Snorri frowned, confused. 'But now you've declared war, the dawi are one.'

'Because of you, I have to sanction four of my vassal lords. If you were not my son, I would have killed you for such a transgression.'

Snorri got to his feet, and the High King roared.

'Don't defy me further. Kneel down!'

'I will not, father!' He thumped his chest. 'I regret nothing. Nothing! You've grown old sitting in that chair. Peace has softened you, made you weak. We've already been invaded, our holds and borders both. The skarrens flourish, their king mocks you, and we ignore it. I was wrong about the war, about it being inevitable. We were already *at* war, a war of wills. Ours versus the elgin's…' Snorri's tone became pleading, 'and we were losing, father.'

The prince let his arms drop to his sides. He lifted his chin, pulling aside his beard to expose his neck.

'So, do as you will. But I didn't divide the holds or the clans. You did, when you put the crown of Karaz upon your head and did nothing. Kill me, if the *Dammaz Kron* demands it.'

Gotrek's fists were clenched like anvils, his chest heaved like a battering ram. Wrath like the heart of Karag Vlak boiled within him.

'I cannot,' he growled through a shield wall of teeth.

'Come, do it! If that is your will, but promise me you'll destroy these elgi and drive them from the Old World.'

'I cannot!' he snapped, standing.

Snorri took three paces until he was before his father at the foot of the Throne of Power.

'Why, father? Mete out your retribution.'

'I cannot,' he hissed.

'Why?'

'Because I cannot lose my only son!' The anger died as quickly as it had erupted and the High King sagged, his face a fractured mask of weariness and remembered pain. 'Your mother, my queen, is dead, and when she passed half my heart went with her, dreng tromm.'

Releasing a shuddering breath, Gotrek gripped Snorri's shoulder. Tears glistened in his eyes. The High King's voice came out in a rasp.

'I am afraid. This war will destroy us if we let it. I fear it will destroy you too…'

'Father…'

They embraced, and the bad blood between them drained away.

'I'm sorry, father. I should not have defied you. Dreng tromm, I should not–'

'Enough, Snorri.' Gotrek held Snorri's face in his hands. He clasped his neck, bringing their heads together, and closed his eyes. 'It doesn't matter now. I have been a poor father. I tried to teach you, but was over harsh. I can see that now. I am an old fool, who almost forgot he had a son.' He pulled back, meeting Snorri's gaze. 'We will break the elgi together, and take back the Old World.'

Snorri nodded, wiping away tears with the back of his hand.

'Now,' said the High King, 'tell me of the siege preparations. We have a city to sack.'

⊰ CHAPTER THIRTY-SEVEN ⊱

The First Siege of Tor Alessi

FOR SIX DAYS, Liandra's morning had begun the same.

Clanking armour as the wearers stomped in unison, the stink of their bodies potent on the breeze, the reek of their dirty cook fires, their furnaces, the soot and ash that seemed to paste the very air, make it thick and greasy. Worst of all were their voices, the crude, guttural bellowing, the flatulent chorus as they rose from their pits, the holes they had dug or the tents they had staved for sleeping in.

'Khazuk!'

She knew this word, the one they were bleating now, together and in anger. It put her teeth on edge, made her want to unsheathe her sword and begin killing. Liandra did not speak Dwarfish, she found the language base and flat like much of what the mud-dwellers built, but she knew a call to battle and death when she heard it.

Every morning it was like this and every morning, and deep into the night she had endured it. Now, at last, she would get a chance to do something about it.

In a high vault of the Dragon Tower, she looked out onto the battlefield beyond the walls of Tor Alessi at the dwarf host. They marched in thick phalanxes, shields together, axes held upright like stunted ugly statues.

Stout-looking siege towers rolled between the squares of armoured warriors. On a ridge line far behind the advancing army she saw their bulky war engines, strings tautened, ready to loose. Several carried score marks, the deep gouges of eagle claws. There were fewer now than the dwarfs began with, but still a great many remained. A thick line of crossbows sat in front of the machineries, a little farther down the incline, taking shelter amongst scattered rocks.

It would not avail them, elven eyes could see and kill a dwarf hiding in rock easily enough.

And they were digging. How like the mud-dwellers to burrow underground like small-eyed vermin. Like the rocks, there was an answer to that too. She had spoken with Caeris Starweaver and knew of his plan to sunder the tunnels with the dwarfs still in them. Liandra sneered; they were persistent creatures, seemingly content to batter at Tor Alessi's walls until they broke. Given time, under such constant pressure, they probably would, but then she knew what was coming across the sea and what would happen when it arrived.

She looked towards their own forces and saw the disciplined ranks of spearmen arrayed on the wall. Behind them and below were ranks of archers, their spotters in position between the spearmen to guide their arrows. Several mages had joined the warriors on the battlements and there were small cohorts of Lothern axemen between the spears too. For doubtless, the dwarfs would try to climb again and a heavy blade severs rope more easily than a spear tip.

Some of the refugees from Kor Vanaeth, a pitiful number, swelled the elven host. They were positioned at one of the gates. From the disposition of their forces, the dwarfs looked to be assaulting all three at once. It had taken much resolve not to take flight on Vranesh's back before now and burn a ragged hole in the mud-dwellers' ranks, but that would not win the battle. She needed to choose her fights more carefully than that.

'Princess Athinol…' One of Prince Arlyr's retainers was waiting for her in the tower's portal. He cast a fearful glance into the stygian dark of the vast tower at the hulking presence spewing sulphurous ash into the chamber.

Arlyr was commander of the Silver Helm Knights and like all young lordlings, he was impatient to sally forth, but required a distraction.

Liandra had decided to be much more than that.

'Tell him I am almost ready,' she said, donning her war helm and turning from the battlefield. It wouldn't be long before she'd see it again, this time on leather wings and spitting fire.

DULL THUNDER RUMBLED from above, shaking the roots of Ari and spilling earth on the miners. They were close, almost to the wall. Six days of hard toil had almost come to fruition.

Nadri wiped a clod from his brow, spitting out the dirt before hacking down with his pick. It was tough work, but preferable to the battlefield. A muffled clamour was all that reached them from above, and even that was barely audible through the digging song and the thud of sundered earth.

'Ho-hai, ho-hai...' Nadri joined in with the sonorous refrain, reminded of the attack on Kor Vanaeth's gate. Rise and fall, rise and fall, his pickaxe was almost pendulous. The diggers cut the rock, the gatherers took it away in barrels to shore up the foundations. Runners brought stone flasks of tar-thick beer. Used to the finer ales, Nadri found the brew caustic but at least it was fortifying. Every miner took a pull and their spirits and strength were renewed. They cut by lantern light, the lamps hooked on spikes rammed into the tunnel walls with every foot the dwarfs dug out. Just a few more and they would breach.

Behind the miners were a wedge of the heaviest-armoured warriors Nadri had ever seen. He had heard tales of the ironbreakers, the dwarfs that guarded the old tunnels and forgotten caves of the Ungdrin road, but had never seen one face to face. Up close, they were imposing and seemingly massive. Hulking gromril war plate layered their bodies and their beards were black as coal, thick and wiry. Hard, granite-edged eyes glinted behind their half-masked helms, waiting for the moment when the digging was done and the fighting would begin.

Rest over, Nadri gave the flask back to the runner with nodded thanks, and returned to the rock face.

Soon, very soon now.

THE IRON RAMP slammed down into the breach with enough force to knock the defenders onto their backs.

The dwarfs raised shields immediately as they were met by an arrow storm.

Morgrim roared as if his voicing his defiance could turn the shafts aside, and ploughed forwards.

'Uzkul!'

The reply came as a roar of affirmation from Morgrim's warriors, who surged alongside their thane into a host of elven spears.

It was the third assault in six days. The dwarfs had used probing attacks after the night bombardment, picking at weak points, gauging the strength of the defences and defenders. The east gate was deemed the most likely point of breach, it was the most distant of the routes into the city and therefore less well fortified. For the last three days, Gotrek Starbreaker had amassed forces in the east, concealed by trenchworks. Stray barrages from the stone throwers had weakened the gate house around the towers. Great clay pots of pitch were being readied to weaken it further.

Morgrim took the north wall, volunteering to lead a cohort in one of the siege towers and onto the very battlements of Tor Alessi. It was to be a hard push – the High King wanted the elves to think this was the main point of assault. Morgrim was happy to oblige.

Half-sundered by their war machines, chunks of battlement broke away as the dwarfs tramped over it. One poor soul lost his footing and fell to his death many feet below. No one in the front ranks watched him but a grudgekeeper in the rearguard called out the dwarf's name to ensure he would be remembered.

'Uzkul!' Morgrim yelled again, bludgeoning a spearman's

skull as he fended off another with his shield. He drew one elf in, butting him hard across the nose and splitting his face apart. Another dwarf finished the spearman when he dropped his guard, recoiling in pain.

An axe blade dug into his weapon's haft and Morgrim shook it free, snarling. He kicked out, snapping the elf's shin with a hobnailed boot, before burying his hammer head into the warrior's neck. Blood fountained up in a ragged arc, painting a clutch of spearmen who pressed on despite their disgust.

Morgrim smashed one in the shoulder with his shield and took a spear in the thigh for his trouble. Smacking it away before the wielder could thrust, he incapacitated the second elf with a low blow to the groin. The backhand took a third spearman in the torso. A dwarf warrior next to him fell in the same moment before one of his fellow clansmen stepped in to take his place.

Somewhere in the frenzy, Morgrim and his warriors gained the battlements. Elves came at them from either side, wielding spears and silver swords. The small knot of dwarfs, desperately trying to expand outwards and establish a foothold, was quickly corralled.

Barely before Morgrim had Tor Alessi stone under his feet, a fair-haired captain carrying a jewelled axe and a small shield hit him hard. Daggers of pain flared in his shoulder but the runes on the dwarf's armour held against the elf magic and Morgrim kept his arm. He replied with an overhand swing, denting the elf's shield before uppercutting with his own. Spitting blood, the elf's chin came up and Morgrim barged into him, barrelling the captain over the battlements and to his death. It only seemed to galvanise the other elves further.

The dwarfs gained maybe three feet. It was tough going. Arrows whistled in at them from below, piercing eyes and necks, studding torsos like spines. Out the corner of his eye, Morgrim saw Brungni spin like a nail, three white shafts embedded in his back. The inner side of the wall was open, and a yawning gap stretched into a courtyard below. It left the dwarfs dangerously exposed, a fact Brungni learned to his cost. In his death throes he handed off the banner to Tarni Engulfson before falling into a riot of elven spears below.

'Don't drop that,' Morgrim warned.

The young dwarf nodded, clutching grimly to the banner pole.

A hastily-erected line of shields protected the battling dwarfs from the worst of the elven volleys but it made fighting to the front and rear more difficult.

Farther down the wall, Morgrim saw another siege tower reach the battlements. A plume of flame fashioned into an effigy of a great eagle engulfed it before the ramp was even released, burning the dwarfs within. Cracking wood, the sound of splitting timbers raked the air as the tower collapsed in on itself, killing those warriors waiting on the platforms below. It tumbled slowly like a felled oak and was lost from Morgrim's sight.

There would be no reinforcement on the wall, not yet.

He lifted his rune hammer to rally the spirits of his warriors. By now it was a familiar cry.

'Uzkul!'

Death.

GOTREK WATCHED THE battle from atop his Throne of Power.

Below, his bearers were unyielding, their strength unfailing. It needed to be; throne and king were a heavy burden in more ways than one.

Several of the siege towers had reached the ramparts of the north wall and two of the gates were under assault with battering rams and grappling hooks. A sortie of elven horse riders had stalled the third assault, Thagdor's longbeards currently waging a contest of attrition with the high-helmed knights.

Gotrek would have bet his entire treasure hoard on the victors of that fight, but it was hard to smile when the elves were making them pay so dearly for every foot.

From the east flank, quarrellers maintained a regular barrage from behind their mantlets. Behind them on a grassy ridge, the war machines continued to loose with devastating effect. Several sections of the wall were broken and split, but not enough to force a breach. They needed the tunnels to undermine them, bring the foundations crashing down into a pool of fire as the dwarfs burned the elven stone to ash.

Zonzharr was potent dwarf alchemy that could reduce even the stoutest rock to blackened dust. The miners had pots of the stuff, hauled into the tunnels by pack mules, ready to be rolled down to the rock face when the digging was done.

Overhead the sky darkened as the elven mages practised their foul art. Summoned fire blazed into one of the siege towers, burning it to a scorched stump. A second conflagration followed but dispersed against the solemn chanting of the runesmiths.

Most of the elder lords of the rune had not joined their kings in battle. Mysteriously, they were nowhere to be found, some having left their holds for places unknown. Gotrek knew better than to question it. Ranuld Silverthumb had been runelord of Everpeak for as long as he could remember, from before even his father Gurni had reigned. The servants of Thungi had their own ways the High King could only guess at. If the ancient lords were absent, it was for good reason.

It did not mean the dwarfs were without magic of their own, however.

'There is one more weapon in my arsenal,' said Hrekki Ironhandson whom Gotrek had joined on the hillside not far from the war machines.

'Summon it and its keeper,' said the High King. His eyes never left the battlefield, for somewhere in the chaos was his only son.

SNORRI FOUGHT AT the east gate under a mantle of iron. The stout shaft of a battering ram swung between his cohort of warriors, smacking fat splinters from the wood.

'We'll make a dirty mess of their door,' he promised, shouting to be heard, 'and then we'll make a mess of them. Khazuk!'

'Khazuk!' chimed the warriors together, heaving the ram back for another blow. The end was fashioned into the simulacrum of an ancestor head, Grimnir, his beard wrought into spikes. It gored deep, tearing at the gate.

Boiling oil, alchemical fire, swathes of arrows all fell upon Snorri's warriors but they didn't even flinch. These were hearthguard, king's men, and they would not shirk from the deadliest of battles. Either the gate would fall or they would.

A prickling sensation in Snorri's beard made him look up. The view was narrow, and the prince caught snatches through the slits between the tiles in the roof.

'Spellcrafter,' he growled.

Above, an elven mage was conjuring. She wore a pale robe, emblazoned with stars, and a moon-shaped circlet sat upon her brow. But it was the crackling staff to which Snorri's eye was drawn, and the tempest waxing around it.

'Spellcrafter!' he roared this time, inciting a dour chorus as the dwarfs invoked earth, stone and metal to retard the harmful magicks.

A hundred dwarfs clamouring at the east gate chanted in unison. It began slowly but grew into an almost palpable wall of defiance. A hundred became two hundred, then three hundred until all the warriors assaulting the east gate were united in purpose.

But elven sorcery came from the Old Ones, it was High magic and could not so easily be undone. Eldritch winds were already clawing at the heathguard, tugging at their limbs, buffeting them into their fellow dwarfs. The chant faltered. Rain lashed down, sharp as knives, impelled by the gale. The slashing deluge turned the ground beneath the dwarfs' feet to sludge. Several warriors were fouled in it, some even to their necks. Easy prey for the archers whose arrows flew with storm force, piercing armour like it was parchment.

Despite his best efforts, Snorri could feel his body sinking into the mire. Hail stung his face, opening a cut on his cheek. He reached out, letting his hand axe hang by the thong on his wrist, hauling a hearthguard to his feet.

'Up, brother,' he growled. 'Stone and steel.'

'Stone and steel, my prince,' the breathless hearthguard replied.

Snorri turned, and roared to the others, 'Heads down and heave!'

One warrior was blown free of the ram's protective mantle. The elven archers seized upon him, pinioning the dwarf with a dozen arrows before he could so much as raise his shield. Another, sunk almost to the waist, was left behind and fought defiantly until a shaft took him in the neck and he spat his last.

'Thagging bast–' Snorri began, but the tempest had them now.

Rivets fixing the mantle to the ram frame were loosening. A flap of metal swung up briefly before clamping down again. In those few seconds, four hearthguard warriors lay dead with arrows jutting from their bodies.

Wrenching his boots free of the mud, Snorri stepped up to take the place of one. Clutching the iron handle of the ram, he pulled it back.

The hefty wooden log lurched, swinging wildly in the gale. Its violent backswing almost pushed the prince out from the mantle. The wind was rising, building into a fist of elemental force that would punch the roof of the battering ram clean off.

Drowned in mud or condemned to death by elven arrows, neither was a favourable ending worthy of song. The gate was weakening, Snorri could hear it even above the storm in the protestations of the wood. A few more solid hits and it would buckle. But only if there was time before the battering ram was torn apart.

Behind them to the south, distant thunder was booming.

Snorri groaned under his breath, 'What now?' before he realised it had come from the dwarf ranks.

Lightning sheared through the storm dark a moment later. It struck the elven battlements, a second arcing bolt spearing the elven mage. Her death scream echoed loudly before her scorched body crumpled and the tempest lifted.

Snorri tried not to be relieved. There was no time for it. A minor reprieve, nothing more. The real fight lurked behind the gate, and he planned to smash it wide open.

'Khazuk!'

Twenty hearthguard heaved and the ram swung back.

Grimnir snarled and the angry god swung forwards, baring his teeth.

But the east gate held.

FUNDRINN STORMHAND CALLED the lightning back. He was standing on an Anvil of Doom, feet braced apart. Great runes of power crackled and flashed across the anvil's pellucid silver surface, and the storm lived briefly in the runesmith's eyes, in the rivulets of magic coursing through his jagged red beard before earthing harmlessly.

But as soon as the storm lightning had faded, Fundrinn was calling fresh elemental power into being. It began as a mote of flame in his outstretched palm but as he spoke the rune rites the fire grew until the runesmith could no longer hold it and was forced to set the conflagration loose. What began as a flaming wind swelled into a tidal wave of burning vengeance, a score of spectral dwarf faces snarling and biting at its fiery crest.

Fundrinn cried out, '*Zharrum!*', coaxing and shaping the raging inferno with sweeping arcs of his runestaff. '*Zharrum un uzkul a elgi!*'

Across the battlefield, a second voice bellowed. It spoke unto the deep earth, making oaths of the great ancestors. One of the anvils of Zhufbar rolled forwards, impelled by the will of its keeper Gorik Stonebeard, and joined the magical convocation. He had no staff, but carried a rune hammer. As he smacked the hammer head down upon the anvil, the deep earth answered and a rippling tremor shuddered from beneath him.

'*Duraz um uzkul a elgi!*'

The tremor rolled outwards at the invocation, building in ferocity, splitting the ground underfoot.

The lords of Karak Varn and Zhufbar crafted in perfect magical concert, unleashing hellfire and earthquakes against the elven host.

Gotrek felt their power through his beard, in his finger-tips, along his teeth, and grinned.

'Burn them, bring them down!'

LIANDRA WAS BARELY in the saddle when the quake hit. Dust and grit spilled from the vaulted ceiling of the Dragon Tower, shaking its walls violently.

'Vranesh!' she urged and the beast tore up into the vaults, head down, smashing through the roof. There was no time to guide the dragon through the narrow aperture of the tower. The small minaret that served as Vranesh's rookery was collapsing. Mere appendage to the grand tower itself, it would still have buried dragon and rider.

Exploding from the shattered tower, Vranesh exulted and Liandra with him as he tore into the sky. Empathic joy rippled through the elf's body, and she embraced a thrill of violent intent as she beheld the dwarfs below.

'*Higher, higher…*' she coaxed, guiding Vranesh into the ice cold skies, daggering through cloud until they were lost from sight. There they roamed, Vranesh trailing tendrils of smoke from his maw in hungry anticipation.

In the solitude high above Tor Alessi, Liandra's thoughts returned to Imladrik. She remembered their last conversation in the gorge, the widening gulf she felt growing between them, and wondered where he was now and if he had thought of her since then. For a moment, the iron grip she had on her lance loosened and she considered that vengeance would not be an adequate substitute for her grief. Then she thought of Kor Vanaeth and her people, dying at the hands of the cruel dwarfs, and her resolve became a thing of unyielding ice.

Liandra leaned over in her saddle, roving the enemy army with her eyes for a target.

'There,' she hissed. 'Dive, Vranesh!'

SILVER LIGHTNING BREACHED the cold winter cloud as a beast of old myth fell upon the war machines.

Gotrek had barely ordered his bearers forwards before the dragon had torn up three engines and devoured their crew.

Snapping wood, torn metal and shouting dwarfs merged into one discordant sound. Screwing up his courage, a thane of the Varn rushed at the beast with his rune axe trailing fire, but was dispatched by a lance strike through the heart before he'd done much more than heft the blade.

An elf maid, armoured in dragon scale. She gutted three more dwarfs before her eyes met with the High King's. Bolt throwers further down the line of war engines were already turning as the elf's beast started in on the quarrellers. It led with its forelegs, gouging a deep, ruddy furrow in the dwarfs' ranks, their hand axes and crossbow bolts unable to penetrate its dragonscale.

Gotrek snarled at the nearest ballista crew, knowing he wouldn't reach the elf dragon rider in time to save the quarrellers from being devoured by her mount. 'Shoot that elgi bitch!'

Its strong pinions flexing, the dragon took flight with its rider as the first of the iron shafts flew, cutting air. She dodged a second volley too, the beast snapping one in midflight before it turned to spew fire.

Heat ten times more potent than a forge furnace washed over Gotrek and his charges, but the magic of the Throne of Power kept them safe. Singed but alive, he glowered through a wall of flickering haze at the fleeing beast and its rider.

'Crozzled my bloody beard,' he growled. 'Drakk,' he said as the fire died, now just a a blackened ring on the hillside. 'I hate drakk.' He rapped on the arm of his throne with a ringed fist. 'Forward. We make for the east gate. Furgil and the others best be ready. Thurbad,' said Gotrek, looking down to his captain of the hearthguard and the seven iron-bearded warriors that accompanied him. 'Gather fifty warriors, including the steelbeards. You're with me. Leave the rest.'

'But you'll be open to attack, my king.'

'Aye,' said Gotrek, eyeing the dragon as it dived down to spew more fire, 'and if we're lucky, she'll take the bait.'

ON THE NORTH wall the fighting had grown fiercer. Elf and dwarf lay dead and dying upon the battlements, gutted and staved in, broken and cleaved. Two great civilisations were destroying one another, yet no one cared to notice.

Morgrim's hammer felt heavy as he bludgeoned but not from the heft of the weapon, he could wield it all day and night if needed. It was the blood upon it, the slaughter that weighed the dwarf down.

A screech that resonated across the sky, tearing it open, shook Morgrim from his reverie. An upper tower had collapsed and something leathern and terrible had shot out from it like a battering ram.

'Drakk!'

His warriors cried out and balked when they saw the dragon smash through the tower roof. Pieces of stone, shattered chips of tile cascaded onto them but were a paltry shower compared to the deluge that slammed down into the elves amassing in the courtyard. Fixed on the beast, the dwarfs barely paid any heed. One abandoned all thoughts of defence altogether and found a spear in his gut for his trouble. Another jumped off the battlements, mind crushed by fear. Dwarfs were a hardy race, and their history with dragons was long and bloody, but such primordial beasts were terrifying even for the sons of Grungni.

Morgrim marshalled his courage, still fighting hard with an eye on the sky as the beast wheeled above. 'Hold fast!' he yelled at the clanners. 'Stone and steel!'

Gritting their teeth, the rest of the dwarfs gripped their axe hafts and fought on.

Through maddened slashes of the battle, Morgrim saw the dragon savage the war engines before turning its wrath onto the High King. His heart quickened for a moment when his liege-lord was engulfed by flame but then returned to normal when he saw the High King was unscathed.

Soaring skywards, the beast pulled out of bow range before coming down hard on the tunnellers. Dragon fire stitched across their ranks, igniting the pots of zonzharr and pushing a ferocious inferno down Grik's gullet. Morgrim was forced away before he could see more, but the image of burning dwarfs staggering from the tunnel mouth was etched into his mind.

With the wrenching of stone Grik collapsed, releasing a pall of dust and trapping the survivors inside with the fire.

BELOW THE WESTERN gatehouse, Nadri toiled at the face of Ari. Strong elven foundations were making the last few feet hard, but it meant they were close. Hacking with their picks and shovels, the miners had carved out a subterranean cavern that was wide enough to admit a small army. With over four hundred ironbreakers waiting silently in the wings, it needed to be.

They were led by one of the Everpeak thanes, a foreign-looking dwarf whom Nadri had seen with the prince on several occasions and so assumed was part of his inner circle. Unlike the ironbreakers, his armour was light and of a strange design, depicting effigies of creatures Nadri wasn't familiar with. The thane seemed to be waiting for something, as though he knew they were about to breach.

A lodewarden called the sappers back. The time for digging was over, fire would do the rest. Lighting the zonzharr, the miners at the end of the tunnel retreated and took shelter behind barriers of wutroth. With a grunt, three dwarfs from the Copperfist clan rolled the great clay urn of the zonzharr down the tunnel. When it smashed against the end it immolated the base of the gatehouse wall in a flare of angry crimson fire. A cheer went up as the foundation rock broke apart, dumping earth and flagstones into the gap the miners had hewn with their pickaxes.

'Khazuk!' The chant resonated through the ironbreakers' closed helms as they rushed through the breach, led by the thane.

Nadri and the other sappers stood aside to let the cavalcade of armoured bodies through.

Jorgin Blackfinger, lodewarden of Barak Varr, climbed onto a boulder so he could be seen and heard by all the clans.

'Ready for another tough chuffing slog, lads?'

Nadri bellowed with his fellow clanners. 'Ho-hai!'

Nearly two hundred miners followed behind the

ironbreakers, brandishing picks and shovels. The light streaming through the breach was hazy, thick with grey dust, but the clash of blades was clear enough.

The elves had lost their gatehouse, a part of it at least, but their warriors were ready and willing to defend the breach. And above the carnage of the battle, a sound, deep and resonant… A primordial roar.

SNORRI HEARD THE dragon rather than saw it. Enclosed beneath the mantle of the battering ram, it was hard to see much of anything other than the back of the dwarf in front and the shoulder of the one to your side.

Words spoken what seemed like an age ago returned to the young prince, plucking at his pride.

Dawi barazen ek dreng drakk, un riknu.

A dragon slayer, one destined to become king.

Snorri felt the pull of destiny. It was slipping through his grasp.

He tried to turn, find the beast through the slit of vision afforded to him beneath the mantle, but it was impossible. The ram was moving under its own momentum, him with it. Apparently, fate was too. All he caught was snatches of sky, of armoured dwarfs embattled.

The beast cried out again, a rush of flame spat from its maw easy to discern even above the din of the assault. Burning flesh resolved on the breeze.

Trapped in the throng, battering at the east gate, Snorri railed.

But there was nothing he could do.

And then, like a magma flow breaching through the crust, the gate cracked apart and the dwarfs flooded forwards. Snorri went with them, hurled along by furious momentum. Behind him, he heard the shouts of other warriors joining the fray.

THE GOAD WAS obvious. Liandra saw it as clearly as the lance in her armoured grip. She imagined ramming it through the old dwarf king's heart, the one who lorded over the others on his throne of dirty gold. She would make him suffer, but would have to do it soon. Fires caused by the mud-dwellers' crude magic lit Tor Alessi like lanterns honouring some perverse celebration. For all that she burned, the dwarfs could visit it upon the elves threefold. She needed to redress the balance and was about to rein Vranesh into a sharp dive when the west gatehouse collapsed.

Like armoured ants, dwarfs scurried from below and attacked her kinsmen. She watched an entire cohort of spearmen, injured and confused from the destruction, wiped out by the mud-dwellers in seconds. More were coming, spilling up from the earth like a contagion, a spouting geyser of filth running amok across Tor Alessi's west quarter.

Liandra hesitated, torn by indecision. She wanted the dwarf king, to gut him like a wild boar on her spear. But the defenders at the west gatehouse were failing. They needed time to restore order, something to regain some momentum.

Spitting a curse, Liandra turned away from the king and went to the aid of her dying kin.

AFTER A WELTER of colourful swearing, Gotrek gave up on the dragon rider and ordered the host of Everpeak to march. Reacting to the gatehouse collapse, elven reserves stationed behind the city walls were swarming to the west quarter to try and staunch the dwarf incursion. Gotrek gave them just long enough to become entangled in the fight there before he nodded to his horn bearers to herald a second assault.

The east gate was breached, but the throng there led by Snorri hadn't penetrated far. That was about to change. As the deep, ululating clarion call boomed out dwarf forces hiding amongst the rocks came forth, led by Furgil. The pathfinder had done well to conceal an entire host. Combined with Snorri's clans and the throng of the High King, it was an army large enough to overrun the entire eastern wall let alone its gate.

Gotrek despaired at the thought of it. They had gone from peace… to *this*.

'So arrogant…'

'My king?' asked Thurbad, as the rest of the throng joined

them in serried ranks to begin the march. 'You mean the elgi?'

'No, Thurbad,' Gotrek replied. 'I mean us.'

His raised his axe and the dwarfs marched on the east gate.

THROUGH A FOG of dust and spilling rock, Nadri clambered out of the breach and up to the surface.

Ironbreakers were already fighting as well as several cohorts of clan warriors led by King Valarik. Seeing the imminent destruction of the wall and gatehouse, the lord of Karak Hirn had urged his throng towards it. The elves were quick to counter, and by the time most of the miners were shoulder to shoulder with their kith and kin, the fighting around the breach was ferocious.

Nadri was still blinking the grit out of his eyes, adjusting to the light, when a shadow roared overhead. Though he didn't see it, the very presence of the thing above filled his gut with ice and made his limbs leaden. The reek of sulphur wafted over him, burning his nostrils, and he heard the crackle of what sounded like a furnace being stoked only much louder, much deeper.

Someone shouted; he couldn't make out the exact word, but it sounded like a warning. Then a heavy weight smacked into him, bore him down until day became night and Nadri tasted hot armour on his tongue a moment later. Something was burning. There were screams, smoke, the stench of scorched meat, but it wasn't boar or elk. It was dwarf. The roar came again, resounded across the breach.

A gruff voice told him, 'Stay down, until the monster has passed.'

Blood flecked Nadri's cheek. It was warm and wet. After a few seconds hunkered in the dark, he realised it belonged to one of the ironbreakers shielding him. He went to move, trying to find the injured warrior, but the gruff voice spoke again.

'Hradi's dead. Stay down.'

Shouting this time, heard through a press of armoured bodies that were slowly crushing him. Nadri couldn't breathe. Terrified, he'd been holding his breath and only now realised that he couldn't draw more into his lungs. He also couldn't speak to let his saviours know they were killing him.

More shouting and the screech of something old and primordial. It was above him, squatting on the rubble. Nadri could almost see it. He caught a glimpse of scale, a tooth, a baleful yellow eye.

Shadows lingered at the edge of his sight, growing deeper as he crept closer to oblivion. Singing, he heard. It sounded distant and at odds with the battlefield. He tasted beer, rich and dark, and smelled the succulent aroma of roasting pork. 'Heg...' It was all he could think of to say, though he wasn't sure whether the name had actually passed his lips or he had merely imagined speaking. Either way, it was the last word of a wraith, Gazul beckoning him towards the gate, darkness closing in all around...

IT WAS LIKE an anvil being lifted off his back. When he came to, the pressure was gone and Nadri heaved a long, painful breath into his gut. Hours must have passed; the sky above, what little he could see through the smoke, was darkening. He saw the suggestion of walls, a ruined tower, and remembered he had fallen on the battlefield inside the elven city. It took almost a minute before he got up, and even then he only sat. He'd lost his pickaxe. A host of dead ironbreakers surrounded him, cooked in their armour. Their champion's face was etched with a grimace. They had protected him, in life and death. Deeper into the west quarter of the city, not that far from the breach, a battle was ongoing. Nadri heard shouts to the east, too, and the clash of arms at the northern gate that still held.

His dead saviours weren't alone. Nadri saw a dwarf he recognised, despite the horrendous burns. Exotic-looking armour was half-melted to his face. A veneer of soot clad his body like chainmail. Tendrils of smoke spiralled from his mouth. The rest of the brotherhood had advanced deeper into the breach, the miners too. Nadri and the others had been left for dead, except he was a sole survivor.

'Heg…' This time he knew the word was spoken aloud, and felt tears fill his eyes at his miraculous escape. Even surrounded by death, for the first time Nadri believed he might see his brother again. He was rising, pushing himself up on pain-weary limbs, when something nearby moved.

It coughed, or at least it sounded like a cough but such a thing wasn't possible. Then he saw the soot, flaking away like a second skin, the flesh beneath pristine and untouched by flame. Nadri gaped and would've grabbed for his weapon but the pickaxe was gone, lost in the chaos, and he was too paralysed to reach down for an ironbreaker's axe. Most were fused to their gauntlets anyway.

'Valaya,' he breathed, staggering backwards from the thing that also lived. 'What are you?'

White teeth arched into a pitiless smile and a voice that was several but really no voice at all said, 'Nothing you would understand, little dwarf.'

DUSK WAS PAINTING the horizon, creeping towards the battle-field with soot black fingers. They had held the breach for several hours, drawing the elves away for an attack on the east gate that had yet to breach much farther than its outer defences. Nightfall was approaching rapidly and with it the end of the sixth day and the third assault.

For all that they pushed and pressured, the dwarfs could not sack the city – though it burned badly, there were fires everywhere and even the dragon rider had been put to flight when the heavy ballistae from the Varn had pierced its wings and sent it fleeing.

Snorri raged. For every elf he cut down another took its place, two more ready after that and then three, four. It was endless. And these foes were not like greenskins or the beasts of the forest, or the terrors of the deep places or the high mountains; they were disciplined, determined and utterly convinced of the righteousness of their cause.

Only one thing gave the young prince heart as he heard his father's war horn sounding the retreat – the elves were wearying. Only a dwarf could match another dwarf in a war of attrition. Dwarfs were stubborn to the point of self destruction. Entire clans had wiped themselves out in proving that point to a rival or out of grudgement. Elves were strong, there could be no denying that now – only a fool would, and Snorri was no fool – but they were not dwarfs, and in the end that would prove their undoing.

So as the throngs departed, leaving the ragged breach in their wake and the elves to contemplate how they might secure it before the dawn's next attack, Snorri was smiling.

And what was more, the dragon still lived.

FOR NOW, THE battle was over and Morgrim toured the field of the dead with shovel and pickaxe. As before, the elves granted the dwarfs clemency to tend to their injured and dead, and the dwarfs reciprocated. But even with this tenuous agreement, Morgrim eyed the silent ranks lining the walls of Tor Alessi with something that approached trepidation.

His attention returned to the battlefield as an elf apothecary passed close by to him. Morgrim gave her little heed, but noticed there was no malice in her eyes, just a desire to ease suffering. Considering the dwarfs' own healers, he wondered just how different they really were to one another when blades and pride weren't getting in the way.

Shrouded in cloaks of deep purple, a silver rune emblazoned on the back, were the priestesses of Valaya. They roved in pairs, administering healing where they could and mercy where they could not. Morgrim thought it was the least he could do to help bury those beyond help. Though the ground was hard from the winter frost, despite the heat from the dwarf forges softening the earth, it was purifying work. There was rejuvenation in good, honest, toil, even though it was grave digging. To wield an axe for something other than bloodletting came surprisingly welcome to him.

A veritable sea of carnage stretched out in front of Morgrim. Acres of land were littered with broken shields; notched blades and spear tips; the sundered links of chainmail, rust red and still sticky; split pieces of elven scale, blackened by fire; shattered war helms with severed horns or their horsehair plumes aggressively parted; and the bodies of course, there were a great many bodies. One stood out above the others, which in itself was remarkable.

Despite the dead dwarf's expression, Morgrim recognised him. It was the miner Snorri had spoken to before they had laid siege, Copperhand or Copperfinger. Copper something, anyway.

The poor bastard, like so many others, had given his life for hearth and hold. But unlike the remains of his kinsmen, this dwarf was unscathed. There were cuts and bruises, some of which were likely from digging, for he had the trappings of a tunneller. No killing blow that was obvious, though. It was his face that drew Morgrim to the dead dwarf's side. Etched in such utter terror and disbelief. Fear had stopped the dwarf's heart; he clutched his chest in rigor mortis as if it might have burst had he not.

'Dreng tromm…' breathed Morgrim, gripping a talisman that hung around his neck.

'I've seen others who died with fear on their faces,' said a female voice.

Morgrim turned, half-crouched by the deceased, and saw Elmendrin.

'Tromm, rinnki.' He bowed his head.

'Always so respectful, Morgrim Bargrum,' she said, returning the gesture. 'What is it the warriors call you? Ironbeard? Grungni-heart would be more appropriate.'

Unused to flattery, Morgrim reddened. He gestured to the corpse.

'You see something different in this one?' he asked.

'Yes, he is dead *from* fear itself. But it's as though something just reached in and crushed the beating heart in his chest.'

'My reckoning was not quite so exact, but this dwarf's death is unique.' He looked out over the killing field. Other grave diggers had joined him, together with the priestess. Morgrim even thought he saw Drogor. The dwarf from Karak Zorn was brushing soot from his shoulders, having doubtless had a near miss when the dragon had burned the attackers at the west wall. Not many survived that assault. Indeed, Morgrim was surrounded by some of its victims as a dozen eagle-eyed elven archers kept a bead on him from the ruined battlements not ten feet away.

'He can't be buried here,' Morgrim decided, hoisting the dwarf onto his back.

Elmendrin helped him.

'King Brynnoth's tent is not that far,' she said. 'His grudge-keeper has been busy naming the dead all evening. Looks like a long night ahead of us.'

At the edge of the dwarf encampment, rites for the dead could be heard being intoned by the priests of Gazul. Morgrim had seen the solemn service many times before during battle, when tombs could not be built nor bodies returned to their holds. Instead, the dwarfs would bury them in the earth according to their clans. Shoulder to shoulder they would meet Grungni as warriors, the honourable dead. Barrows of earth would shroud them, dug by the surviving clans as Gazul's priests uttered benedictions and incantations of warding. Every dwarf war caravan carried tombstones and these rune-etched slabs would be placed upon the mounds of earth where the fallen were buried. If the ground proved too hard to dig or the army fought on solid rock or tainted earth then the dead would be burned instead and their ashes brought back in stone pots for later interment. These too were carried by Gazul's priests on sombre-looking black carts. So did the dwarfs attend to their dead, even when far from hearth and hold.

'Does Snorri know you're here?' Morgrim asked, as they started walking. A dozen bowstrings creaked at the dwarfs' departure.

Elmendrin looked down at the ground. 'No. And it must stay that way.'

'I doubt your presence will be a secret for long.'

'Perhaps, but for now I want to do my work, fulfil my oaths to Valaya. Besides,' she said, 'Snorri has more important things to worry about than me.'

'I think he would argue that.'

'Which is precisely why I must go unnoticed by the prince.' She allowed a brief pause, then looked up at Morgrim. 'The war has changed him, hasn't it?'

'All of us are changed by it, and will continue to be.'

'Not like that, I mean,' said Elmendrin.

Morgrim regarded her curiously.

She answered, 'It's made him better, somehow. As if he was forged for it.'

There was a sadness in Morgrim's eyes when he replied. 'I think that perhaps he was, that all his petulance and discontent stemmed from a desire to fulfil that for which he was made.'

'I thought so,' said Elmendrin, moving off to help one of her sisters. 'Do one thing for me, Morgrim Bargrum.'

'Name it,' he called out to her.

'Try to stop Snorri from getting himself killed.'

He didn't answer straight away, watching Elmendrin disappear back in to the mass of dead and dying. There were tears in his eyes when he did.

'I will.'

⤙ CHAPTER THIRTY-EIGHT ⤚

The Fleet From Across the Sea

THE ELF WAS painted head to toe in filth. His silver armour was muddied, his cloak torn and smeared in dung, his alabaster skin grimy and dark with a peasant's tan. Dirty white hair framed a narrow face, pinched with anger.

'Doesn't look happy, does he?' Snorri jerked his thumb at the dishevelled noble behind the cage.

'Would you be, if you were boarding with the mules?' King Thagdor laughed, loudly and raucously, until the High King approached, dousing the northerner's mirth.

'His name is Prince Arlyr, of Etaine.' Gotrek struggled with both foreign words, but spoke them anyway before turning his glare from Thagdor to the elf. 'And apparently he has nothing to say beyond that.'

'Why are we gathered here?' asked Brynnoth. 'Surely your tent would have provided better accommodation.'

They were standing next to the mule pen at the rear of the encampment, near its edge. Skinners were hustling the beasts in and out of the cages to haul machineries or cart raw metal for the new rams, but none cast an eye towards the kings.

Several bedraggled-looking elves, stripped of their

weapons and armour, walked alongside one train. They were Arlyr's warriors, put to use gathering firewood for the furnaces and watched keenly by Furgil's rangers.

The same question as asked by the king of the Sea Hold lingered in Valarik's eyes too, though the lord of the Horn Hold had not the courage to speak it. All of the kings, barring Brynnoth whose desire for vengeance still blazed hotter than his shame at defying the High King, felt chastened just to be in Gotrek's presence. The High King's ire was volcanic but kept dormant for now. None of the liege-lords wanted to be there when it erupted, and so conducted themselves as if that possibility was imminent at any time and by treading gingerly they could abate it.

Last of the kings was Hrekki Ironhandson. The lord of the Varn was slow to arrive, having trekked across from the opposite end of the field where his war machines and much of his army was mustered. He nodded to the other lords, and only once he was within the circle of kings did Gotrek continue.

'Quicker to say it here, and I want to look into this one's eyes when I do.' His attention returned to their elf prisoner, who glowered back at him.

'To say what, father?' asked Snorri.

Not since the assault on the sixth day had the dwarfs enjoyed the same level of success in breaching the elven city. Tor Alessi had abandoned its outer wall and retreated, closing its ranks further, repositioning its bolt throwers, mustering even more archers.

Even buoyed by their apparent success, the dwarfs had been unable to penetrate any further. The rubble made it impossible to bring in siege towers and excavation teams were quickly pinioned by arrows as soon as they tried to clear the ground. The elves had left pockets of murderous scouts in shadowed alcoves and secret chambers that ambushed the dwarf attackers, foiling assaults before they could begin.

Tor Alessi had shrunk, and like a trap closing around the elves inside, it had armoured them.

Snorri didn't understand the tactic. Yes, it retarded the

dwarfs' efforts, but they had already established that winning a war of attrition was playing into their hands. What did the elves have to gain from waiting and pulling in their necks, besides a slow death?

When the young prince got his answer, it was not to his liking.

'We must retreat,' said Gotrek flatly.

'Do what?' asked Thagdor, incredulous.

Snorri was speechless.

Brynnoth fought down a belligerent snarl. Of all the kings, he had seen the most battle and bore the wounds to prove it. None present had greater right to question the High King's reasoning than Brynnoth, but the lord of the Sea Hold stayed silent.

'Elgi have been sighted coming across the sea in a great fleet.' Gotrek eyed the elven noble and saw everything he needed in the lordling's supercilious expression to know what his scouts had told him was true, that it wasn't some trick or glamour, that the elves were trying to keep them embattled until reinforcements could arrive. 'Could be two hundred ships, maybe more. Drakk too, eagles and magelings. A war host that puts even this city's sizeable garrison to shame. That's right, isn't it, elgi?'

Prince Arlyr glared, and spat something in his native tongue before flashing a condescending smile.

'I think he's trying to mock you, Gotrek,' observed Thagdor.

Gotrek smiled back. 'Yet he's the one covered in donkey shit.'

'Caught between the city and the arriving army, we would be hard pressed,' admitted Snorri, seeing the sense in what his father was saying but inwardly chafing at the need to retreat. 'How close is the fleet?'

Gotrek turned his gaze from the elf to look at his son. 'Furgil says they're close enough that some of the machineries will need to be left behind if we're to make good our escape.'

'Grimnir's balls, those engines are not cheap,' moaned Ironhandson. 'I'll lose a fortune if we leave them.'

'You'll do it and be glad that I don't further balance your accounts, Hrekki,' snapped Gotrek, referring to the king's existing debt in the great book of grudges.

Knowing what was best for him, Ironhandson backed down.

Thagdor balled his fists against his hips and sighed. 'Bugger me. They're right sneaky, them elgi bastards.'

'Aye,' Gotrek agreed. 'Tor Alessi is their anvil, the fleet their hammer. We'd be crushed.'

Snorri was scowling. 'This is wrong. Escape? We're running? From *them*?' He jabbed a finger at Prince Arlyr, who appeared to be enjoying the debate more than the dwarfs. 'The wall is breached in at least two places and there are fires that will last well beyond morning.'

'Aye,' said Gotrek, 'and for fourteen days we've knocked on their door and for fourteen days been repelled. Can anyone here think of a fastness the dawi could not crack in two weeks of hammer?'

None could.

'But, father...'

'But nothing,' Gotrek began, harshly at first, but softened quickly. 'I feel your frustration, but this isn't over. We were naive to think the elgi could be so easily broken. They obviously want to stay here very badly. We'll need to beat that out of them, but all meat must be tenderised before it's cooked and eaten. Just so happens that elgi is a little tougher to chew than we thought.'

'So that's it then?' said Snorri. 'What about Varnuf and Grundin, Aflegard and the rest of them?'

Valarik looked down at this boots.

Ironhandson shook his head.

'I've sent runners north and south,' Gotrek told them, 'but so far none have returned bearing word of the other kings. We cannot rely on them for reinforcement.'

'So we're going back to the mountains?' Brynnoth didn't sound pleased.

Gotrek nodded. 'To gauge the elgi's strength, and their keenness for a fight. Admit it or not, we've underestimated this enemy, and are already counting that cost. War won't be over in a single siege.' He turned to his son. 'How many did your cousin say we'd lost thus far?'

Snorri's face darkened. 'Close to three thousand dawi, father.'

'Dreng tromm…' breathed Valarik, whilst the other kings except for Brynnoth shook their heads at the thought.

'We return to the holds,' Gotrek told them all, 'and make strategy for a long war. This is far from over. It has barely begun.'

'And what about little lord dung boots over there?' asked Thagdor, gesturing to Prince Arlyr.

Gotrek fixed the elf with a cold stare that robbed the lordling of all his defiance.

'Oh, I can think of something.'

LIANDRA WAS KNELT by Vranesh, tending to the dragon's wounds in one of Tor Alessi's ruined courtyards, when the dwarfs' message came sailing over the wall. It landed with a wet *splut!*, rolling awkwardly until it came to a halt by a spearman's boot. The elf looked down at the severed head of Prince Arlyr and was promptly sick. To see such a noble lord so brutally abused had turned the young warrior's stomach.

Horns rang out, summoning the garrison commander, Lord Impirilion.

When Arlyr's body was flung over the walls next, engraved in vengeful dwarf script, Liandra could not have been less surprised.

'They are leaving,' she told one of Lord Impirilion's retainers.

'How do you know?'

She laughed humourlessly, pointing at the headless corpse. 'What do you think that is?'

The retainer looked nonplussed at the body.

'It's a parting gift,' she told him, getting to her feet. 'Can you fly, my beast?' she asked the dragon.

Vranesh growled in affirmation.

'Where are you going?' asked the retainer. 'What about Lord Impirilion?'

'I have no business with the garrison commander, and you have no need of me here now the fleet has arrived. I will return to Kor Vanaeth. There are still people who are living like wretches in its ruins.' She swung into the saddle. 'This is not over. Far from it, and we need every bastion if we are to defeat the dwarfs on their own soil. Rest assured, this is but a taste of the war to come,' she said, a flash of excitement in her eyes as she took to the skies.

For now, fighting the dwarfs took precedence over her other concerns. Liandra's prey would have to wait, the druchii would have to wait, but not too long.

◄ CHAPTER THIRTY-NINE ►

Two Decades of War

THE FOOTHILLS NORTH-EAST of Kazad Kro were swathed in darkness. It wouldn't last; a pale sunrise was already breaching the horizon, smearing it in washed-out yellow. In less than an hour it would be vibrant and ochre, blazing like the summer. Light would paint the land, revealing the ruination, the barrows and the churned earth of over twenty years' worth of battles.

Rundin had played no part in any of them. He had trekked from his city, walking over forty miles to reach this place, which was little more than a clearing of scattered rocks.

'Took your time,' said a familiar voice, the speaker squatting on one of the collapsed menhirs surrounding Rundin.

'Just because we are not at war doesn't mean I have no other duties to attend to, brother.'

Furgil smiled, jumping down from his rocky plinth, and went over to Rundin.

The two dwarfs embraced, clapping one another on the back with genuine bonhomie. Two decades was not so long to a dwarf, but their reunion was heartfelt.

'Good to see you, Rundin.'

'And you, Furgil. How fares the King of Everpeak?'

'Troubled, as he has been for the last twenty years or more. The third siege has failed, Tor Alessi yet stands and other cities are mustering greater and greater armies of elgi. Reinforcements would be generously received, I am sure.'

At this remark, Rundin averted his gaze to the stone circle.

'And I would grant them, had I the power to.'

Furgil grunted at that, suggesting Rundin already did, but chose not to press. Instead he asked, 'And what of the skarrens, my former kinsmen?'

'Trade has come back, after a fashion. Not with the elgi, of course, but dawi from the Vaults and the Black Mountains. They bring talk as well as trade,' he ventured.

'Such as?' Furgil was typically guarded, and Rundin faced him again to gauge his humour.

'That the south is embattled, and that Gotrek is reluctant to bring full force of arms to bear against the elgi.'

'He is wise, our king. All-out war would destroy our race, as it would theirs. Hope still remains that some agreement can be reached, or that the elgi will lose heart and give up.'

'I also hear their king has no intention of leaving the Old World, that he is as arrogant an elgi as one could possibly be.'

'You hear much, old friend.'

'That sounded almost like an accusation, Furgil.'

The pathfinder shook his head. 'Not at all, but I'm surprised at your keen interest in the war, given the skarrens' abstention from it.'

'Not my choice.'

Furgil lit his pipe, allowing the silence to stretch before asking, 'How many from the hill clans are there now? Eighty thousand, more?'

'Is that why you're here, why you requested we meet? Does Gotrek want the skarrenawi for his throngs?'

'You know he does,' said Furgil. 'I just wanted to see if you did.'

'And do I?'

Furgril didn't answer, but asked another question instead. 'He still mad, is he? Your "High King", the Grum?'

Rundin's face darkened, first with anger then shame

when he realised he had no rebuttal. His voice lowered to just above a whisper, as if to speak louder would somehow heap further disgrace upon the truth.

'Lucidity comes and goes with the fever, but he's locked in the counting house most days now. I think the gold-masters are puppeting him, but there's little I can do about that unless Kruk and Orrik change their minds. And for over twenty years they've shown no sign of doing so. Both are saying the war is over.'

Furgil scoffed, watching the first rays of dawn spear across the lowlands and slowly scrape against the mountainside. "Tis far from over. I know longbeards that've slept for more than twenty years. This is nothing. High King Gotrek is mustering again, so are all the kings. You'd do well to join us. Don't think the elgi will know the difference between dawi and skarren when their armies come calling, and don't expect protection from your kith and kin in the mountains if you're not prepared to take up az un klad.'

Rundin bared his teeth. 'I don't like threats, Furgil, especially from those whom I consider friends.'

'It's no threat, it's a fact.' The pathfinder's defiance lessened, the edge to his words dulled. 'Go back to Kruk and Orrik, convince them that this is the right thing to do. Please, Rundin.'

Rundin didn't answer, he just watched Furgil go and wondered what he would have to do to get his people out from under the yoke of Skarnag Grum.

IN THE GREAT Hall a huge map of cured troll hide described the entire realm of the dwarfs and was laid out on an octagonal table of dark wutroth. It had turned from a throne room into a chamber devoted to war. Around the map, several kings and thanes of the Karaz Ankor were discussing strategy.

'And there is still nothing from the south, I take it?' Thagdor looked almost smug, despite the scar he now wore on his face. 'Bloody soft.'

'King Hrallson is besieged, you northern oaf,' snapped Brugandar. The King of Karak Drazh was the only one of the liege-lords south of Everpeak that had made the rinn-kaz. He was a severe-looking character, with a wiry beard the colour of iron and a face just as unyielding. Drazh was known as the 'Black Hold' on account of its munificent mines and quarries. Coal was its principal export, but it also yielded much in the way of metal ore. In fact, Brugandar looked more like a miner than he did a king, just with all the bearing and confidence of one.

His declarative insult incited a raft of angered murmuring from some of the kings. All knew the elves had made solid inroads to the south. Varnuf of the Eight Peaks had done well to keep them at bay for this long but even his vast armies were not inexhaustible.

Finding only fools amongst the northern kings, Brugandar turned to the head of the table and the High King. His tone changed abruptly to one of the utmost respect. Although he had not personally fought in the first siege of Tor Alessi, he had lent many warriors to the cause.

'Liege-lord,' he intoned, 'what about Karak Kadrin? Can we expect much from King Grundin and his throngs?'

Elbows leaning on the edge of the map, Gotrek looked over his steepled fingers at the many flags and icons representing elf and dwarf armies, as well as their bastions and holdfasts. There were a great deal on both sides, and the sight of this aged him further than the last two decades had. A war without end was the very thing he had fought so hard to avert, and now here they were.

'Musters in the north must continue without interruption,' he said. 'And as requests to the mines at Silverspear and Gunbad have gone unanswered, I can only assume those greedy bastards have decided that digging is preferable to fighting. We are alone in this.'

'Three times we've marched on those walls,' said Valarik, 'and three times we've failed to take the city. What else can we throw at it?' The king of the Horn Hold had grown older too, but with experience and wisdom. For its part in the conflict thus far, Karak Hirn and its king had earned great respect amongst the lords of the Worlds Edge.

'Dawi bloody grit and chuffing determination is what!'

said Thagdor, thumping the table. 'They'll yield, they have to at some point.'

Ironhandson was unmoved by the King of Zhufbar's typically demonstrative outburst and stroked his beard thoughtfully. 'What of the garrison at Black Fire? Does your son bring any news, High King?'

Gotrek raised his eyebrows, arrested from whatever dark reverie had claimed him for the last few minutes. Snorri was not at the rinnkaz. Upon the third defeat at the gates of Tor Alessi, he had gone back to the fortress at Black Fire Pass, Kazad Kolzharr, to act as his father's eyes and ears beyond the mountains.

It had been weeks since his last runner to Everpeak.

The High King was about to speak when Thurbad entered the war chamber and every pair of eyes within it turned to alight upon him.

'Lords,' he addressed the assembly, before approaching Gotrek. 'A message from the Kolzharr, my king.' Thurbad handed over a piece of slate the size of his fist.

'As if Valaya's own hand had a part in it,' said Ironhandson, marvelling at his own apparent prescience.

Gotrek ignored him and took the slate.

Silence fell in the Great Hall as everyone present watched the High King read.

'"Our rangers bring word that the king of the elgi has been sighted,"' Gotrek began aloud. '"Tired of impasse, he has taken to the field at Angaz Baragdum with a sizeable army. I shall meet him and give battle."'

Gotrek put the slate down, still staring at the Khazalid engraved upon it.

In the end, Thagdor broke the silence.

'Well this is what we've been waiting for,' he said. 'Not since this bloody war began has the elgi king shown his pointy ears. Now, we have a chance to kill the bastard and send the rest of 'em running for their ships.'

Brugandar was nodding. 'I agree. This is a mistake, born out of elgi arrogance. We must seize upon it.'

Gotrek wasn't listening. He turned to Thurbad, who was waiting dutifully behind him.

'Did the runner say if my son had already left the keep?'

'Two days ago, my king. He marches with his cousin and most of the garrison.'

'So, we won't reach him before he gets to Angaz Baragdum.' Gotrek knew the answer before it was given, and didn't care that his face betrayed all of his concern for his errant son.

'No, my king. We will not.'

A horn blared in one of the lower deeps. Its doleful echo carried all the way to the Great Hall, signalling the miners to the rockface. To Gotrek, it sounded like a death knell.

HAD HE BELIEVED his cousin would listen, Morgrim would have told Snorri to wait. True, the rift with his father had scabbed and healed over the last few years but the young prince was still convinced the only way to achieve the great destiny he so craved was to seize it for himself.

Slay the drakk, become king.

He had spoken of little else since word had come to Black Fire Pass that the elf king was in the Old World and marshalling an army.

'I am surprised,' said Snorri, marching at the head of an army twenty thousand strong.

'Cousin?' asked Morgrim, from Snorri's left. Drogor, ever dutiful and silent, was on his right holding up the banner.

'That Elmendrin is not here to dissuade me.'

There was hope in the prince's voice, not that the priestess would convince him not to fight the elf king but that she would be there before he did to see it.

'She would not wish this for you,' Morgrim answered.

'Of course she would. Elmendrin understands legacy and its importance. I don't want to usurp my father, I just want to ease the burden of kingship from his shoulders. Ending this war will let me do that.'

'Twenty years ago we were going to end this war, cousin. Seems we only started it, though.'

'Aye,' Snorri sighed. The attack on Kor Vanaeth had been rash, but necessary. 'But it was right that we did. Kill or capture the elf king and the war ends, though, Morg. *That* I know.'

'Do you wish she was here, Elmendrin I mean?' Morgrim asked.

Most of the Valayans had returned to Everpeak after the third siege. A handful remained at the keep, but Elmendrin was needed back at the capital.

Snorri nodded. 'It would have been good to see her again, but her brother takes up much of her time these dark days.'

At this, Morgrim looked down. All who had returned from the ambassadorial mission to Ulthuan had come back with deep scars. None more so than Forek Grimbok, and even then not all had made it. Gilias Thunderbrow was dead, slain through elven treachery. Morgrim thought this must trouble Forek the most. Few dwarfs had seen him since he had come back. In fact only the High King and his closest advisors knew where the shamed dwarfs were now, and the priestess who ministered to them of course.

'I knew she was there, you know,' said Snorri.

'Where, cousin?'

'At the first siege. I saw you talking with her as she tended the wounded.'

Morgrim frowned. 'And you wait until now to mention it?'

Snorri shrugged. 'Seemed as good a time as ever. Besides, we have been busy.'

The war had thrust the cousins apart for the last few years. Ever since the end of the first siege and the retreat, both Snorri and Morgrim had returned to their clans to prepare further musters. The elves had surprised them with their discipline and the size of their armies. Not content to merely soak up the dwarfs' punishment, the elves had gone on the offensive. Several lesser holds had been attacked, particularly in the south. Most notably Karak Azul had sustained serious damage to its some of its upper deeps during one assault. King Hrallson was still refortifying his walls and sealing off the damaged areas, which had become infested with greenskins and giant rats, if the rumours were to be believed.

Morgrim had gone south to bring reinforcement, and turned back the elf army camped on Azul's doorstep so its clans could return to their forges and fashion the engines and armour the dwarf war effort so badly needed. Snorri had greeted him warmly upon his return, but couldn't entirely conceal his jealousy at his cousin's success.

Now, it seemed he was just glad to have him back at his side.

'What did she say to you in the field of the dead, Morg?' he asked.

Morgrim snorted with amusement. 'She asked me to try and keep you alive.'

Snorri clapped him on the back. 'Well, you've done your task well then.' He laughed. 'Do you ever wish we were back in the ruins of Karak Krum chasing talking rats, eh?'

Morgrim laughed too but stopped when he saw the seriousness in his cousin's eyes. 'Every day,' he muttered soberly.

Snorri slowly nodded.

'Lords,' Drogor interrupted. 'The Angaz Baragdum is over the next hill. We should be able to see the elgi throng arrayed.'

'And they us,' noted Snorri, signalling a halt. He turned to one of his rangers, who was outriding at the edge of the army. 'Any sign?' he called.

'The skies are clear, Prince Snorri.'

'No eagles, that's a good thing,' Snorri said to himself.

Morgrim drew close to him as the dwarf column ground to a halt with a clattering of armour. 'Are you certain of this plan?'

'Arrogance has brought the elgi king to this place. He must be made to realise the folly of that, and when he does he cannot be allowed to escape. For the same reason we strike now and do not wait, you must do what I've asked you to next.' Snorri smiled, gripping Morgrim's armoured shoulder with his gauntleted hand. 'Do not fear, cousin. Drogor is by my side. Neither I nor the banner will fall this day.'

Not entirely convinced, Morgrim summoned his warriors. He gave Drogor a parting glance but could find no clue as to the Karak Zorn dwarf's thoughts. His own were fraught with concern that he would not be there to temper the prince's eagerness. Certainly, Drogor would not do it.

Half the army would go with Morgrim. Sheltered by the foothills, they would take the wide and rugged path east, come around the back of the enemy and close off any route of escape. Dwarfs knew the mountains better than anyone; they could sneak up on elves easily enough. It would leave Snorri with only ten thousand to face whatever host the elf king had amassed. According to their scouts, it was considerable.

Before he left, he said to Snorri, 'Hold them until I get there, cousin. Hold them and only then engage the king.'

'Aye.' Snorri grinned. 'I'll cut off his pointy-eared little head.'

CHAPTER FORTY

The Spilling of Noble Blood

NO CEREMONY, NO celebration of any kind had greeted the army of Barak Varr when it had returned to the Sea Hold. Led by Brynnoth, a battered and brutalised king, the dwarfs were a returning tide, washing up on the borders of the great fastness with all the detritus that had survived the siege of the elven city.

No, as Heglan remembered that day, just as he had remembered it every day since, it was more like a funeral procession. All along the Merman Pass, trailing back down to the shipyards many miles behind, were dour-looking clanners shouldering biers of shields the colour of the ocean. Upon them were their fallen brothers. And there had been a great many. At first, Heglan had hoped some of the warriors had remained with the High King to garrison the lesser citadels but the mood was too sombre, too withdrawn and bereft of hope for that to be true. A defeated force had returned to Barak Varr, carrying its dead. But they clung to something else too, a very familiar emotion to Heglan now – vengeance.

That sight, the returning dwarfs, the warriors lain in silent repose upon their shields, had stayed with him for over twenty years. It was his waking thought, his last memory at night, at least when he managed sleep. During the dark hours, Heglan's workshop became his refuge. He laboured until exhaustion claimed him and sent his mind into an agonised hell of remembrance. Running down to the Merman Pass, barging the gathered crowds from his path, ignoring their curses. Watching the procession pass, listening to the weeping, the declarations of revenge, the wailing of the women. An impenetrable line of hearthguard prevented the crowd from approaching closer than the edge of the road. With every bier that passed by, Heglan's hope grew, until he saw the eighty-first shield and the dwarf dead upon it.

Unmarked by war, no wound to be seen, Nadri Lodrison was a cold corpse.

Heglan had lost his brother, and in that fateful moment of realisation became the last of his line. Few of the clan Copperfist returned, and though some spoke words of conciliation, Heglan heard not of it. Instead, a tiny fire grew into being inside his stomach. Quickly it became a fist of flame then a blaze, until the conflagration of his hate and desire for retribution was born.

Sheltered in his workshop, bent towards dreams of invention and prosperity, he had been untouched by the war. With Nadri's death, it had gouged him and left a gaping wound behind. From the sky and the sun, Heglan retreated downwards to the earth and the desolation of his brother's tomb.

Cold stone pressed against his forehead. Heglan opened his eyes, returning to the present. He could smell grave dust and dank, though whether this was real or a trick of his grief-stricken conscience he could no longer tell. Somewhere in the back of his mind, a doleful tolling announced the dead.

'Copperfist...' a gruff voice intruded on the funerary bell.

Heglan looked up to see sky and sun, not the hollow dark of a tomb.

'Yes, master.'

Burgrik Strombak was standing behind him, arms folded. 'I was wrong.'

* * *

DARK AGAINST THE sun, driving against the wind and rising, the skryzan-harbark flew. It was an airship in every sense, with a huge leather bladder of gas attached to masts with stout rope giving the vessel the necessary buoyancy. There were rudders and paddles, barrels of ballast to alter loft and direction. Great turning whirls, like windmills, provided impetus and power. It was the single most impressive piece of machinery any dwarf had ever constructed and it had launched from the Durazon like a soaring crag eagle. But the dream for Heglan was flawed, forever so, tainted by the fact that his brother would never get to see it.

He had found a captain too, and Nugdrinn Hammerfoot steered the airship like he was born to it. In another time, Heglan would have been expelled from the engineers' guild for such rampant diversion away from tradition but times were changing, and with them the attitudes of the dwarfs. The Sea Hold had ever been a bastion of invention and progress, looked down upon by some of the traditionalists of the Worlds Edge. No good could come of the new, of the untried, untested. Dwarfs were creatures of earth, grounded in stone and steel. They did not reach for sky and cloud, and yet…

'Is it ready?' asked another, and Heglan turned to address his king.

Brynnoth didn't meet his eye, he kept his gaze on the airship as it returned to the Durazon. It grew larger by the moment, transforming from a shadow silhouetted against the sun to a behemoth with a dragon-headed prow and armoured flanks of copper in the shape of scalloped wings. It was a beast in every aspect, powerful, intimidating, brutal, and seemed to almost growl at the dwarfs as it landed on claws of steel.

'I still need to arm it, my lord.'

'Bolt throwers?' suggested Strombak with an appraising eye. 'It wouldn't support a catapult.'

'Yes, and something else I've been working on.'

Strombak raised an eyebrow, but Heglan didn't elaborate. The weapon wasn't ready yet and he wouldn't reveal it until it was, even to his guildmaster.

Heglan was not a warmonger. It had never been his intention to create something with the purpose of killing. Exploration, technological achievement, the mapping of the skies had always been at the forefront of the engineer's mind, but unfortunately death had a way of making peaceful men warlike.

'It's a marvel,' Strombak conceded, in spite of all his reservations.

'No,' said King Brynnoth, a darkness in his eyes that had never lifted since Agrin Fireheart. 'It's a war machine.'

Strombak nodded, sucking on his pipe as he turned to its creator. 'And what will you call it, lad?'

Heglan's eyes mirrored the king's.

'*Nadri's Retribution.*'

SNORRI WAS NOT impressed. Ranks of spearmen hiding behind high shields that protected their scale-armoured bodies marched into formation before the dwarfs. On the opposite flank was a host of elven cavalry, the shining-helmed knights clasping lances and riding barded steeds. Archers occupied a slight rise, but there was little to distinguish the army save for a small retinue of warriors bearing long-hafted glaives and shimmering like fresh-forged gold in their heavy plate.

Estimating twenty thousand men, Snorri wondered what the king of the elves hoped to achieve with such a paltry show of strength. He had yet to see the great lord himself and suspected he was as craven as many dwarfs made him out to be.

Angaz Baradum was an iron mine long fallen out of use. Its old quarries and tunnels went deep into the earth, and its heath stretched into a vast plain of grassy tussocks far south of Black Fire Pass. The elf king had arrived in the Old World by sea, though not across the Sea of Claws like the bulk of his fleet. He had gone south, presumably along the Black Gulf to alight so far away from Karaz-a-Karak. Perhaps he wanted to oversee what remained of his forces still encamped at the edge of Karak Azul, or he might have been leading a spearhead to attack the dwarfs from their southern borders. It mattered not. Regardless of his ration-ale, the elf king had made a grievous error in coming here. Snorri was determined to ensure he realised that.

The young prince cast his gaze over the field where the elves and dwarfs had pitched. Little advantage would be gained from the sparse terrain, but it better suited the dwarfs who could make their battle line strong by keeping their clans together.

'Shoulder to shoulder,' Snorri muttered to Drogor, who lifted the banner.

A horn clarioned and then came drums as the dwarfs drew together, slowly locking their shields.

'Hold here!' yelled Khazagrim, the prince's chief hearthguard.

'You see him yet?' asked Snorri, scrutinising the sea of elven silver.

'Perhaps we should advance further, a show of aggression to goad the elfling out?' suggested Drogor.

Khazagrim looked for his prince's sanction. Snorri nod-ded, but said, 'Keep us out of their archer range for now. Don't want those pointy-eared bastards sticking us before I've seen their king. Until I'm sure the coward is even–' The words stuck in Snorri's throat as three elves mounted on horses broke off from the host and rode towards them. Flanked on either side by his standard bearer and knight protector was an elf who could be none other than the king, the one they called Caledor.

'What is he doing?' asked Snorri, reaching for his axe.

Drogor raised his hand for calm.

'I think the elgi wants to talk.'

'Talk?' Snorri was nonplussed. 'About what?'

'Surrender?' Drogor suggested, before looking the prince in the eye. 'What should we do?'

Snorri scowled at the sheer arrogance of the gesture, that the elf king thought parley was still on the table. He con-sidered having his quarrellers shoot the elves down but dismissed it at once as dishonourable.

'We meet them,' he replied, deciding he would not be out-done by an elf. If an elf could stride boldly into his enemy's midst and demand parley then so could a dwarf.

'Is that wise?'

'No, but I'll not have that pointy-ears show me up on dawi ground. Khazagrim, you're with me.' He turned to Drogor. 'Throng holds here, but be ready.'

'Tromm,' said Drogor, bowing.

Snorri stomped off with Khazagrim.

The elves had been waiting for several minutes by the time the dwarfs reached them.

King Caledor muttered something in elvish to his protector who smiled and nodded back.

'Something amuses you, elgi?' Snorri snapped, his half-hand resting on the haft of his rune axe. 'A joke to lighten the mood, is it?'

The banner bearer leaned forwards in his saddle to look down on the diminutive dwarf retinue.

'The Phoenix King remarks on your stature, and how it must take interminably long to get anywhere and do anything. He wonders if you are faster at digging than you are walking?'

Snorri bit his tongue. He could feel Khazagrim trembling with anger next to him, his leather gauntlets creaking into fists.

The elf king was sneering, but despite his levity his blue eyes were like chips of ice. He had the look of a hunter about him, and carried a long spear as well as sword and bow. Tendrils of golden hair slipped from beneath his helm and here Snorri paused. For the war helm sitting upon Caledor's brow was shaped to resemble a dragon. His entire armoured body was fashioned thusly, wrought in fire-red plate and silver scale akin to the hide of such a beast. Edged in gold, the king's armoured skirts carried further effigies firmly establishing the aspect he wanted to promote.

Words spoken what seemed like an age ago now returned to the young prince.

Snorri's lip curled into a snarl. '*Drakk…*' he breathed, and felt the touch of destiny upon him. It was no beast at all that Ranuld's prophecy spoke of, but an elf, *the* elf. All thoughts of negotiation evaporated.

The elf banner bearer looked confused at this declaration, turning to his liege-lord. His comment elicited another bout of sarcastic humour.

For his part, Snorri jabbed his finger in the elf king's direction.

'You,' he said, before turning to prod at his own chest, 'and me.'

Smiling, King Caledor trotted forwards on his steed.

'Are you challenging me, mud-dweller?' he asked in perfect Khazalid. 'Do you mean to say I have brought all these warriors and only you and I will get to fight? Seems a pity.'

Snorri was taken aback. 'You speak our tongue?'

'When I must.' He scoffed, apparently amused at the prince's boldness. 'I came to answer your plea for surrender, but it seems dwarf stupidity really *is* without limit.'

'Aye, and elgi arrogance is boundless too. By Grungni, you will meet me on the field of battle and we'll settle this honourably.'

Looking Snorri up and down, the elf king frowned. 'Are you certain you want to do this? I am the Phoenix King of Ulthuan, greatest warrior of this age.'

Now it was Snorri's turn to smile. 'We have many names for you, elgi, but king is not amongst them. The Coward, the Friendless, He Who is Frightened of Loud Noises. My favourite is the Goat Worrier, for you have the hunter's eye.' Jabbing a finger back at the elf king, Snorri bared his teeth in a mocking grin and bleated at him.

Caledor's expression hardened at once to chiselled stone.

'Have your shovels ready,' he told the prince, 'for they will soon be needed.' Turning his horse around, Caledor rode off to prepare for the duel and took his scowling retainers with them.

Snorri nodded as he watched them go.

'Well,' he said to Khazagrim. 'I thought that went well.'

As THEY RODE back to the army, King Caledor turned in the saddle towards his seneschal.

'Hulviar,' he said, 'as soon as I have cut that imp down signal the attack. Every dwarf on this field shall die today.'

'All of them, my king?'

'Every last one. They attack my cities with impunity, a message must be sent. It's why we are here and why I must miss the beginning of the hunting season. Soon as it's done, we return and these dwarfs will go back to their holes in the ground. See them dead, Hulviar.'

Hulviar nodded grimly and went to ready the Silver Helms.

RAIN BATTERED AT Morgrim's forces as they slogged through the foothills in an ever-thickening mire. The summer storm had come from nowhere, splitting the sky with dry lightning in the east and hammering them with a downpour in the west.

'Have you ever seen the like of this?' Morgrim remarked as rain teemed off the nose guard of his war helm, trickling down his face and beard.

Tarni, his banner bearer, shook his head, spitting out a mouthful of the sudden deluge.

Ahead in the road, Morgrim saw one of the rangers had returned and was beckoning them onwards. The dwarf pointed to a high cliff of rock that hung over the trail and would grant some respite from the storm.

Morgrim nodded, though he had no idea if the ranger had seen him or not. He waved his army on. 'Forward, to the crag,' he yelled, and horns blared down the ranks to relay his order. Their clarion was answered a moment later by a peal of thunder that shook the earth underfoot. From the sky there came a jag of pearlescent lightning. Bright as magnesium, Morgrim had to shield his eyes from it, and when he looked back the bolt had struck the cliff face, shearing off a chunk that had collapsed across the road and buried the poor ranger with it. There was no sign of the dwarf and no sign of the trail either. The way ahead was cut off.

'Should we go around?' asked Tarni, shouting to be heard.

Harsh sunlight was blazing through the sheeting rain, making it shimmer and flash. Morgrim nodded, and with little choice the dwarfs trudged back. All the while they were delayed Snorri fought alone.

* * *

SNORRI ROTATED HIS shoulder to loosen the muscles and hefted his rune axe one-handed, gauging the weight.

'Shield or hand axe?' asked Drogor, proffering both.

Snorri was sitting on a stout wooden throne as Khazagrim made sure his armour was secure. The hearthguard was tightening a vambrace when the prince answered, 'Shield.' His gaze was on the distant elf king who was undergoing similar preparation. Behind him, the elf army waited silently. 'Against that spear, I'll need a shield.'

Drogor nodded.

'Do not be nervous, my prince,' he whispered as he came close to strap on Snorri's shield.

'I am not,' Snorri snapped. 'I will end the war, claim my destiny. It is written.'

'Yes, but perhaps you should wait for your cousin. No one would think less of you if you did, my prince.'

Snorri narrowed his eyes. 'I've asked you before not to call me that,' he said.

Drogor smiled but there was no warmth to it, no feeling at all. 'But that is what you are, a prince.'

'I...' Something disturbing had just happened, a tiny seed of doubt had been planted that was already taking root.

Drogor was still smiling that deadened smile. It chilled Snorri like a winter's breeze, but there was no time left to question it. Horns were blowing on both sides, the call to arms. The duel was about to begin.

Snorri stood, his armour clanking as it came to rest. It felt heavy all of a sudden, his axe haft greasy in his armoured fist.

'My prince?' asked Khazagrim.

Snorri was still looking at Drogor.

'Go and meet your destiny, Snorri Halfhand,' he said.

'Come,' the prince said to Khazagrim, trying to banish the malaise that had settled over him like a shroud. The elf king was already striding to the middle of the battlefield. Silence reigned, interrupted only by the wind and a distant summer storm.

'Strange weather,' Snorri remarked. Even his own voice sounded distant to him.

'Aye,' he heard Drogor answer, in a way that suggested he did not find it strange at all.

Eyeing the horizon behind the elf army, Snorri looked for his cousin as if just the sight of Morgrim would steady his inexplicable nerves. But Morgrim wasn't there. Snorri was on his own.

The few hundred feet to the middle of the battlefield felt like leagues. Sweat lathered Snorri's face. It dripped off the end of his nose, and made him want to remove his winged helmet. His heart was racing, faster than it should be, and he had to suppress a tremor in his injured hand as phantom pain he hadn't experienced in years returned.

'I call you forth to face grudgement, elfling,' said Snorri, trying to bolster his fractured resolve. 'Let it be known on this day that Prince Snorri Lunngrin did meet Caledor of the elgi in honourable combat to settle the misdeeds of his race and exact recompense in blood.'

Caledor was sheathing his sword after making a few practice swings. He had decided on his spear to open with and made a quick thrust before turning to the prince.

'Were you speaking, little mud-dweller? I didn't hear you all the way down there, I'm afraid.' He settled into a ready stance, spear held in one hand. 'Shall we begin?'

Snorri was incensed, his momentary fear eclipsed by rage, and he roared, 'Elgi bast–'

The spear lashed out like quicksilver, ripping open a gash down Snorri's face and splitting his war helm apart. Dazed, the prince half spun then staggered, almost losing his footing. A second blow, a downstroke with the haft, put the dwarf on his back.

The elves cheered, whilst the dwarfs were stunned into silence at the abrupt turn.

Snorri raised his shield, fending off a flurry of jabbing thrusts. The last went straight through, pinning his shoulder before the spear was withdrawn in a welter of his blood.

Crying out, Snorri punched back with the remains of his shield, swinging his axe wildly so he could regain his feet. Laboured breaths that felt like knives sheared from his mouth. His armoured chest heaved and ached. The elf king hadn't even broken a sweat and stared coldly at his prey.

'I knew you dwarfs were weak,' he said. 'You are diggers and labourers, not warriors. You have erred here, and you will die for it.'

Snorri charged, with a cry of 'Grungni!', but found a spear in his thigh arresting his forward momentum. He jerked to a halt, and felt the ground rush up to meet him, smacking into his back like a battering ram and pushing the air from his lungs. Snorri reached for his axe, but it was no longer in his hand, nor was his shield. As the elf king glowered over him, he was defenceless.

'My father will–' The words died as Caledor left his spear pinning Snorri to the ground and opened the prince up with his sword.

'Sapherian steel,' he told the dwarf, showing Snorri the bloodied blade. 'Deadly.'

Numbing cold spread through the prince's body, a deepening chill that would freeze him unto death. He thought of his father, of the destiny that would not be his, of Morgrim and Elmendrin. Until the very end, he fought, spitting blood and mouthing curses at the slowly fading figure of the elf king. It would do no good because Gazul had Snorri now and would take him to his gate.

Snorri Halfhand was dead.

MORGRIM BARRELLED OVER the rise and saw Snorri fall.

'No!' Half rasp, half shout, the thane's agony echoed across Angaz Baragdum. It incited a riot in the dwarfs, who came forwards to protect the body of their prince. Too late, though, for the elf king had cut Snorri's arm from the elbow and brandished it like a trophy to his warriors.

Elven riders were already spurring their horses and beginning to charge. They had not yet seen Morgrim's army.

'Uzkul!' he bellowed, consumed by wrathful grief. 'Crush them!'

Led by Khazagrim, the hearthguard surged forwards to protect the prince. Several were cut down by Caledor before the elf king withdrew on a horse brought by his banner bearer.

Engaged by foes from behind, the knights' charge failed to materialise and they faltered.

Laughing, and only pausing to cast Snorri's severed arm into a deep, flooded quarry, the elf king signalled the retreat. In disarray from seeing their prince so savagely struck down, the dwarfs were unable to contain them. Morgrim had abandoned the plan and was forging towards his cousin with all haste, driving through the enemy and hacking down any elf that got in his way. His hammer was crimson by the time he reached Snorri's side.

A ring of armoured hearthguard parted to let him pass.

Battle din faded in the distance as the last few skirmishes between the fleeing elves and pursuing dwarfs subsided. Morgrim looked down on his cousin's broken, mutilated body and wept.

Snorri was already ashen. A grimace of defiance etched upon his face, he looked far from at peace. In pursuit of destiny, he had died an ugly, painful death.

'Dreng tromm...' uttered Morgrim, sinking to his knees.

'He would not listen,' said a voice beyond the hearthguard.

Morgrim looked up and through his tears fixed Drogor with a steely glare.

'Speak plainly,' he rasped.

'I told him to wait.'

'And is that what you did, Drogor? Did you wait? I saw the throng rooted to the spot whilst my cousin was cut apart. Why did you not aid him?'

'I was forbidden, and by Grungni's oath I couldn't believe what I was seeing. It happened so quickly, the elgi king striking our prince down like he was a beardling.'

'And heaping further ignominy on him by cleaving his arm! Gods, Drogor, he will wander Gazul's underworld a cripple because of this!'

'Perhaps with your army to reinforce us...'

Morgrim's face darkened further. 'We were delayed. By Valaya, the very elements turned on us.'

'They can be capricious.'

Morgrim glared but Drogor had already lowered his gaze.

'It is I that failed the prince, Morgrim, not you. I am sorry.'

Bustling through the throng, Khazagrim returned, preventing further recrimination.

'The elgi have fled, back to their ships,' he said. 'We won't catch them now.'

Morgrim shook his head in disbelief. 'And so we suffer further indignity. Gather the throng. We're going back to Karaz-a-Karak to bring the High King the body of his son.'

CHAPTER FORTY-ONE

Awaken my Wrath

GOTREK'S FACE WAS as cold as the marble slab upon which his son was lying.

The tomb was hewn by Everpeak's finest craftsmen, and the hoard of a lesser king would have been needed to fashion it. Opulent yet austere, it was a monument to dwarf grief and a reminder of a father's abject failure.

'It should be me,' he said to the dark.

Thurbad answered. 'You could not have known the elgi's intentions, my king.'

His granite features stained by tears, Gotrek looked up to a shaft of hazy yellow light breaching the ceiling. It peeled back some of the shadows that had settled like a veil upon this sombre place. Statues, great monolithic effigies of the ancestors, were revealed in it. They looked down sternly but benevolently on the High King, who still found it hard to meet their stony gaze. The rest of the vast chamber was lost to echoing darkness, a hollow tomb of broken vows and empty promises.

'He was to be my heir, Thurbad. I never wanted this for him. I strove to carve out a kingdom that he could rule in peace and prosperity.'

'Yours has always been a just rule, my king.'

Gotrek sagged. He was only wearing a furred cloak, simple tunic and breeches, but he felt the weight of Snorri's death like twenty suits of chainmail. Old hands gripped the edge of the marble tomb for support.

'Fathers should not bury sons, Thurbad. This is not the way of things. It should be me lying upon this slab in grim quietude. It should have been me that met the elgi king at Angaz Baragdum.' The High King let out a long breath that shuddered with the power of his grief. 'He baited us. Snorri went to meet him on the field and could not have known he was stepping into a trap. It reveals something to us, though,' Gotrek added, his back straightening as he found inner reserves of strength.

'What is that, my king?'

'This Caledor, son of kings, is arrogant. To believe he could set foot in our lands, slay my son and return without retribution… It will be his death when I meet him on the field. Throughout this sorry affair, I have held on to the belief that war could be averted. Even when the first battles were fought, when cities were burning, I clung to the hope that we could still find a way out of conflict and return to some measure of civility. That has ended with the death of my son.' His fist clenched like a ball of iron. 'I will level the full might of the Karaz Ankor against these interloping murderers. No elgi will be safe from my wrath, for it has been awakened by this perfidious deed! Every axe, every quarrel and bolt and hammer shall be bent towards the destruction of this enemy in our midst. Vengeance will be done. So swears Gotrek Starbreaker!'

THE GRONGAZ ECHOED like a tomb. Ranuld Silverthumb embraced the silence gratefully, hunched in deep contemplation before the statues of the gronti-duraz. Morek was gone, bound for Tor Alessi and the fourth siege. For his endeavours fashioning the axe and armour of Snorri Halfhand, Ranuld had granted his charge the use of an Anvil of Doom and bestowed upon him the title of 'master runesmith'.

Great had been the undertaking to forge the prince's rune weapons. After fashioning the axe, Morek had left the hold in search of what was needed to begin his labours on the armour. Scarred was the young runesmith now, and more furrowed than ever. For the blood and scale of monsters, jewels that could only be found in the dark, forgotten places of the world, were required to craft such an artefact. Rites were not enough; like all magic, rune forging needed ingredients. Since his return, he had not spoken of his journey nor would Ranuld ask him to. The runelord had his own dark travels to remind him of such endeavours.

Over two decades of toil had changed him, and Morek was apprentice no longer.

And though the death of Prince Snorri had grieved them both, Ranuld allowed himself a sigh of relief. Perhaps the old magic was not dead after all. Perhaps there were those that could still wield it when his like was gone forever from the world. The tremor in the old runelord's heart told him his thread was thinning, that soon it would become so frayed that the tendrils of his life would unravel and snap, and then Grungni would welcome him to his halls.

Soon... he prayed.

Elves were gathering. The death of the High King's only son had galvanised and emboldened them. Gotrek would retaliate. Death would be the only victor, and once again Ranuld was reminded of the darkness that infected the Old World. It came from the gate in the north and could not be gotten rid of now that it was closed. He had to endure, at least until the conclave was concluded and the stone giants roused from their millennia of slumber.

Ranuld opened his eyes, saw the axe and the armour, knew at once who would bear them into battle now.

'*Dawi barazen ek dreng drakk, un riknu...*' He spoke the ancient words of the prophecy aloud. 'He who will slay the dragon, and become king.'

Four other runelords, ancients all, nodded in agreement.

Feldhar Crageye, Negdrik Irontooth, Durgnun Goldbrow.

Last of all was Thorik Oakeneye, he who had taken the place of Agrin Fireheart in the Burudin. The runelord of

Barak Varr carried his own darkness from all he had seen on the island of the elves.

More were needed – the conclave was not yet complete. Around a circular table of stone, three empty places remained.

'We know his name,' uttered Feldhar Crageye of Karak Drazh, stroking the forks of his black beard and squinting through his good eye, the other shrouded by a stone patch.

'Aye,' said Negdrik Irontooth, grinning to reveal metal-plated bone. '*Elgidum*.'

The blond-maned Durgnun Goldbrow nodded. 'The elf doom.'

'The dawi known as Ironbeard,' concluded Thorik Oakeneye.

A vein of fire ran through the dragon-slaying axe lying on the table before them. Its master runes shone, eager to be ignited; so too the armour alongside it, which was impervious to flame. Fate not design had guided Morek's hand in their creation.

'Let it be known,' said Ranuld Silverthumb, folding his arms, determined not to make another mistake. 'Morgrim Bargrum will be the one to lift the doom of our race.'

◄ EPILOGUE ►

SEVEKAI AWOKE IN a feverish sweat. The nightmare was already fading, evaporating in the chill night like the heat from his cooling skin.

A darkling forest. A frantic flight into a barren glade filled with such a terrible gloaming. The trees alive, and the chittering, snapping refrain of their pursuit…

'Hush, my love…' soothed Drutheira. Her hands upon Sevekai's half-naked body were like pricks of fire against his icy skin.

'Did you see it again?'

Sevekai nodded weakly.

'It is always the same.'

'Visions always are.'

Sevekai turned to face her, lying naked next to him under their furs.

'You believe it is real? That the dreams are prophecy?'

Drutheira was playing with her hair, more coquettish and much less the viper than she had once been. Strange, Sevekai thought, that their alliance had brought them to this place in their relationship. 'Perhaps,' she conceded, but was unconcerned. 'It was a vision that brought us here, was it not?'

They had left Athel Maraya several months ago, bound for the mountains, when the dwarfs had begun to amass near its borders and their subterfuge as refugees of Kor Vanaeth had started to slip. For one, Sevekai was glad of it. By the nature of their work, spies and assassins needed to blend in to their surroundings, to escape notice, to become nothing more than backdrop. For twenty years, since the dragon rider had left them alone, he and the others had done just that. Asleep until their dark master chose to wake them again. If ever.

Escape was unconscionable. Malekith was silent and travel almost impossible without armed escort. Even for a warrior as gifted as Sevekai, the passage south would have been difficult. They would lie low until summoned again, and if not they would try to endure until the war ended or Malekith attacked and conquered Ulthuan.

The dark dreams had been recent. Drutheira believed they presaged the will of their lord and that he would make himself known to them again soon. She was right, at least about the latter. One night, as they were sleeping fitfully in their bed, Malekith had returned. Seemingly possessed, Drutheira had risen from slumber. She had gone off into the night and killed the innkeeper of their lodgings, slit his throat wide until it painted the wall in the dark lord's image.

Malchior and Ashniel had risen too to form the blood communion with their mistress.

Orders were given, and they had all left that night, meeting at the outskirts of Athel Maraya.

'There are times,' said Sevekai, as his breathing slowly returned to normal, 'that I wish we could have stayed.'

'Stayed where?' asked Drutheira, carving out a graven rune upon the floor of the cavern. She had left the warmth of their bed to do it and was crouched naked in the half-light.

'In Athel Maraya, or perhaps some other city.'

'After the ritual slaying of that slave, that would have been unwise,' hissed a voice from the shadows.

'Kaitar.' Sevekai didn't even try to hide his vitriol.

The other dark elf nodded. He looked to Drutheira.

'Are you close?'

The sorceress had finished her malediction and spoke words of power unto it.

'It is here, the creature we seek. Deeper in the bowels of the earth, it slumbers.'

Sevekai glanced around at the cavern, the endless rock surrounding them. He had forgotten how deep they had already penetrated in the mountain.

'We must go further into the dark?'

'Yes, but Bloodfang is near.'

Sevekai was on his feet, getting dressed. 'I'll rouse the others.' He looked over to Kaitar but the shade was already gone. In all the years they had been travelling together, he couldn't remember ever seeing him sleep.

'I have not forgotten our pact,' he said to Drutheira.

'Nor I, my love,' she purred, uncoiling to reveal the curves of her sinuous body.

'We will still kill him, and the dragon rider?'

'Why else do you think Lord Malekith has brought us to this place?'

'I honestly don't know.'

'Yes,' said Drutheira, slithering to her feet. She padded over to touch Sevekai's arm, sliding her hand behind his back and whispering in his ear. 'We shall kill them both. Soon, my love. Very soon.'

⫷ CHARACTERS ⫸

The Dwarfs

Karaz-a-Karak
Gotrek Starbreaker – High King
Snorri Lunngrin 'Halfhand' – Prince
Morgrim Bargrum – Thane and Snorri Lunngrin's cousin

Ranuld Silverthumb – Runelord and one of the *Burudin*
Morek Furrowbrow – Runesmith and Ranuld
Silverthumb's apprentice

Elmendrin Grimbok – High Priestess of Valaya
Forek Grimbok – Reckoner

Thurbad Shieldbearer – Captain of the Hearthguard
Furgil – Pathfinder and Chief of Rangers

Barak Varr
Brynnoth – King of Barak Varr
Nadri Gildtongue – Merchant Guildmaster
Burgrik Strombak – Engineer Guildmaster
Heglan Copperfist – Engineer
Nugdrinn Hammerfoot – Sea Captain of Barak Varr

Northern kings
Grundin – King of Karak Kadrin
Thagdor – King of Zhufbar
Luftvarr – King of Kraka Drak
Bagrik Boarbrow – King of Karak Ungor
Hrekki Ironhandson – King of Karak Varn

Southern kings
Varnuf – King of Karak Eight Peaks
Aflegard – King of Karak Izril
Brugandar – King of Karak Drazh
Hrallson – King of Karak Azul

Lesser dwarf lords
Valarik – King of Karak Hirn
Drong – King of Krag Bryn
Borri Silverfoot – Lord of Karaz Bryn
Drogor Zarrdum – Thane of the Lost Hold of Karak Zorn

Runelords
Feldhar Crageye – Runelord of the *Burudin*
Negdrik Irontooth – Runelord of the *Burudin*
Durgnun Goldbrow – Runelord of the *Burudin*
Agrin Fireheart – Runelord of Barak Varr and
one of the *Burudin*
Ungrinn Lighthand – Runelord of the *Burudin*
Jordrikk Forgefist – Runelord of the *Burudin*
Kruzkull Stormfinger – Runelord of the *Burudin*

Hill dwarfs
Skarnag Grum – 'High King' of Kazad Kro
Rundin Torbansonn – Champion of the Skarrenawi
Kruk – King of Kagaz Thar
Orrik – King of Kazad Mingol

The Elves

The Asur
Caledor II – Phoenix King
Imladrik – Prince of Caledor
Liandra – Princess of Caledor
Hulviar – King Caledor's seneschal

The Druchii
Sevekai – Shade
Kaitar – Shade
Verigoth – Shade
Numenos – Shade
Hreth – Shade
Latharek – Shade

Drutheira – High Sorceress
Malchior – Sorcerer
Ashniel – Sorceress

Dragons
Draukhain
Vranesh

⊰ KHAZALID ⊱

The Language of the Dwarfs

Az – Axe
Az un klad – Donning one's weapons and armour, readying for battle

Bar – A fortified gateway or door
Bozdok – Unhinged as a result of constantly banging one's head on low roofs and pit-props; 'cross eyed'
Brodag – A festival of worship to honour Grungni and the art of brew-making
Brodunk – A festival of worship to honour Grimnir and the art of battle
Brozan – A festival of worship to honour Valaya and the bonds of brotherhood between the clans
Bugrit – An invocation against ill-luck uttered by a dwarf who has banged his head, hit his thumb, stubbed his toe or some other minor misfortune; usually repeated three times for luck

Bruz – Gold that has a purplish tinge only visible by twilight

Bryn – Gold that shines strikingly in the sunlight; anything shiny or brilliant

Brynduraz – Rare mineral, a stone that glows in darkness

Burudin – The sacred order of runelords of the dwarfs

Chuf – Also 'chuff'; a very old piece of cheese a miner keeps under his hat for emergencies; a declaration of exasperation, usually in response to foolish, stupid or remarkable behaviour

Dammaz kron – The Great Book of Grudges

Dawi – Dwarfs

Dawi zharr – Fire dwarfs

Dokbar – Gate of 'seeing'; a runic artefact of the elder ages used to commune with dwarfs from distant kingdoms

Dongliz – Nethers; the parts of a dwarf's body impossible for him to scratch

Drakzharr – A potent dwarf beer, a special reserve

Drek – Wastrels or bandits; also far, a great distance; great ambition or enterprise

Dreng tromm – A lament, usually in response to some terrible act or misadventure; literally 'slay beard' in that it refers to the act of a dwarf pulling out the hairs of his own beard

Drengudrakk – Dragon slayer or honoured title bestowed of any dwarf who has killed a dragon

Dunkin – Annual bath traditionally taken whether needed or not

Elgi – Elves

Elgongi – Elf friend; a mild insult

Frorl – Dusty gold with a farinaceous layer obscuring its brilliance

Galaz – Gold of particular ornamental value

Geln – 'Get gold' that is borrowed from others but not returned

Ghazan-harbark – Paddle-driven dwarf sea vessel

Ghuzakk! – Imperative shouted to mules, goats or beardlings to get them to move faster

Gorl – Gold that is especially soft and yellow; the colour yellow

Gorlm – 'Green' gold, which has achieved a patina of age

Glam – Especially shiny or silver gold whose appearance belies its actual meagre worth

Gronti-duraz – The stone giants, runic golems of the dwarfs; literally meaning 'enduring stone'

Grunti's – Dwarf undergarments (usually soiled)

Grobi – Goblins

Grongaz – Runic forge

Gronti – Giant

Grubark – Oar-driven dwarf sea vessel

Hnon – 'Rainbow gold'; in certain subterranean light this gold captures a myriad of hues

Hruk – Breed of dwarf mountain goat

Kalans – Clans

Karadurak – Enduring stone through which the most potent of runes can be crafted

Karaz Ankor – Mountain Realm, the lands of the dwarfs

Karinunkarak – Gesture of protection and farewell, usually invoked when a dwarf is about to go to war

Klad – Armour

Klinkerhun – Common runes or 'chisel runes'

Khazuk! – War cry of the dwarfs, 'the dwarfs are going to war, the dwarfs are on the warpath'

Konk – Gold that is ruddy in colour; a large and bulbous nose

Krut – A discomforting disease contracted from mountain goats

Kruti flu – A discomforting disease contracted from mountain goats

Krutting – A 'practice' frowned upon by all dwarfs

Kurz – Pitted gold, very dark in colour

Ngardruk – A heinous beast of dwarf legend
Rhun – Rune, word of power
Renk – Gritty gold, often veined with lesser minerals
Ril – Gold ore that shines brightly in rock
Rinkkaz – Gathering of dwarf kings at the behest of the High King
Rinn – A lady dwarf or king's consort
Runk – A one-sided fight; a sound thrashing!

Skarrenawi – Hill dwarfs; literally dwarfs of the sky
Skaz – Thief
Skryzan-harbark – Dwarf airship or zeppelin

Thaggi – Treachery or murderous traitor; sometimes also spelled 'thagi'
Tromm – Beard, but also used in respectful greeting or as a way of showing respect to another dwarf
Trombaraki – The act of cutting another dwarf's beard during a duel of grudgement; a weakling gesture; a cowardly act

Ufdi – A dwarf overfond of preening and decorating hsi beard; a vain dwarf; a dwarf who cannot be trusted to fight
Unbaraki – An oathbreaker, the very worst insult a dwarf could level at another dwarf
Urk – Orc or enemy; also fear, to be afraid of, to retreat
Uzkul – Bones or death, usually to the enemies of the dwarfs
Uzkular – Undead.
Uzkuzharr – 'Dead fires', the unquiet spirits of slain dwarfs

Wanaz – A disreputable dwarf with an unkempt beard; an insult
Wattock – An unsuccessful dwarf prosector; a down at heel dwarf; an insult; a credulous dwarf
Werit – A dwarf who has forgotten where he has placed his ale; a state of befuddlement; a foolish dwarf
Wazzock – A dwarf who has exchanged gold or some other valuable item for something of little or no worth; a foolish or gullible dwarf; an insult

Wutroth – Wood from ancient mountain oak.
Zaki – A crazed dwarf who has lost his sanity and wanders above and below the mountains aimlessly
Zharr – Fire
Zonzharr – Potent dwarf incendiary; highly volatile, often used in sieges and blasting tunnels

ABOUT THE AUTHOR

Nick Kyme is an author and editor from Nottingham. After working for several years as a staff writer and journalist on the magazine *White Dwarf*, he moved to the Black Library as an editor. He has written several novels in the worlds of Warhammer and Warhammer 40,000 including the Tome of Fire trilogy featuring the Salamanders, the Space Marine Battles novel *Fall of Damnos* and the Time of Legends novel *The Great Betrayal*. He has also written a host of short stories and several novellas, including 'Feat of Iron' which was a *New York Times Bestseller* in the Horus Heresy collection *The Primarchs*.

You can read his blog at *www.nickkyme.com* and follow him on Twitter *@NickKyme*